The Balance of Guilt

The Balance of Guilt

Simon Hall

Published by Accent Press Ltd – 2010

ISBN 9781907016066

Copyright © Simon Hall 2010

About the author...

Simon Hall

Simon Hall is the BBC's Crime Correspondent in the south-west of England. He also regularly broadcasts on BBC Radio Devon and BBC Radio Cornwall.

Simon has also been nominated for the Crime Writers' Association *Dagger In The Library* Award.

For more information please visit Simon Hall's website

www.thetvdetective.com

To Mum.
As you once carried the thought of me,
now I bear your memory.

Acknowledgements

Sisters Angela and Clare, and all at St Joseph's for their wonderful care and compassion, and the NHS and its staff, for everything they've done for Mum and Dad.
Charlotte Rockey, for her excellent historical research and analysis.
Mr Lewis, Mr Warr, Mr Butterworth, and Ms Dams, former tutors of the tearaway Hall, who were such inspirations, and to all the teachers who've had the misfortune to handle me over the years – I hope these books are a little compensation that I may actually have listened and learned something!
Finally, Exeter, the beautiful city that's become my home, and all the fine friends I've found here who've made me so very welcome – sorry about the explosion…

Prologue

ON THE FIFTH FLOOR of one of Britain's biggest hospitals, in a stark and sterile room, lies an unconscious man.

He's suffering from concussion and has been unconscious for a day and a half. The doctors, if pushed, demur a little in that way so beloved of the medical profession, but estimate he'll probably come round in a day or two.

Which is just as well. Because the man has a great many questions to answer.

His name is Dan Groves and he's a television reporter. He specialises in covering crime, and has just been involved in the biggest and most extraordinary case he has ever known, one which is now drawing attention from around the world.

At his bedside sit two women, one on either side. The woman to the left is a little older than Dan, the woman to the right a little younger. They are both waiting for him to come round. They have sworn to stay here, day and night, hour to hour and minute by minute, for as long as it takes.

The woman on the left wants to thank Dan for what he's done and the courage he's shown, remarkable for a man who in the rare moments of real honesty acknowledges himself an inveterate coward. The other woman wants a great many things, but, in simple summary, if time were limited and were she given only three words, she wants to tell Dan she loves him.

There is a policeman keeping watch outside the door of the room, but after all that has happened over the past few days the women cannot trust him. He is a young man and appears kind and genuine, but he is a part of the establishment, a symbol of authority, and after what they have experienced the women will never again put their faith in the reassurances of the state.

The women are effectively on guard duty. Occasionally, one may leave to fetch a cup of coffee, buy a sandwich, or just stretch their legs and get some air, but never both together. They have agreed that one will always be alongside Dan until he wakes, however long that may take.

For both the women know there are some powerful and ruthless people who may want to harm Dan for what he has done.

On a table, by the side of the bed, is a photograph of an Alsatian dog, which the younger woman has brought from Dan's flat, and a pile of newspapers. There are broadsheets and tabloids and even a couple from other countries. The headlines are all of the same story and each speaks of shock and scandal, terrorism, murder, treason, conspiracy, spies, and a breathtaking cover-up.

Each also mentions Dan, carries his photograph – an awkward-looking official pose with the standard forced smile – and speculates about his role in bringing the scandal to light. And each raises the same question. How could he possibly have had any part in doing so when he was resolutely unconscious in a hospital bed when the news broke, and has remained that way as the story tumbled, flared, fired and flamed?

There is a television on the wall. The picture is on, but the sound is turned down. The chosen channel is dedicated to 24-hour news. The story is the same as that covered in all the papers. A reporter is standing outside the House of Commons, talking about the discussion taking place there. A caption below reads *Bombing Cover Up Emergency Debate*.

At the hospital's main entrance is gathered a press pack. Cameramen, photographers and reporters, some thirty in number. They're all waiting for Dan. Every few hours a doctor will walk out from the automatic doors, stride over and give a progress report. Of late, the doctor has joked that it's more like a lack of progress report. The patient is still stable, still doing well, but still steadfastly unconscious.

The moment turns. In the narrow, austere, bed Dan twitches, mutters, and shifts onto his side. Now, both the women stand. They bend over him and wait expectantly. The younger woman runs a hand over his head. His skin is flushed and hot and his hair is damp. He fidgets once more, but does not wake.

The women sit back down and exchange a brief half-smile. These small movements have happened several times before. He must be dreaming, they say. They talk a little more about how he is looking and agree there is sign of improvement, but their conversation is short. Over the past day and a half of vigil they have run out of things to talk about.

Dan sleeps on. He's a carefree passenger on the train of dreams, just as the women suspected. At least, he thinks he's dreaming. Because all that is going through his mind is surely too unbelievable to be anything approaching reality.

Chapter One

THE SUNSHINE COUNTY OF Devon had come to be Dan's home for a pleasant host of reasons. There were the wonderfully mundane that most would instantly identify; the beauty of the unspoilt countryside, the green hills, soft sand beaches, rugged moors and, of course, the cream teas.

In fact, it was sometimes difficult to convince outsiders that people in Devon and Cornwall ate anything much else.

There were other reasons too – the mild climate, lack of pollution, tranquillity, even the simple delight of being able to see the diamond spectacle of the night sky. But for Dan, suffering the inevitable ailment of slowly growing older, there was another resonant benefit. He had watched with horror the suicide bombings in America and London and so many other places; and the weekly procession of news stories as the police and security services broke up yet another ring of extremists dedicated to the twin charming aims of suicide and genocide.

For a man slipping into his forties, Devon felt a whole lot safer than almost anywhere else in the world.

So today's terrorist bombing, here in the beautiful backwater county, came as one of the greatest shocks of his life. And even then, the attack itself was to be only a small fraction of the tangled story he would be sucked into, and which would lead him to question so much of the society of which he was a part.

But all that was for later. The day, an ordinary Monday, began in an unusually entertaining way. Dan had never been inside a brothel before – honestly, he insisted to the police officers he was working with, he really hadn't – so it was certainly an interesting experience.

He sat with Nigel, his cameraman, in the half light of the back of the police van, as they listened to the briefing on the raid.

And in another quiet corner of peaceful Devon, the real story, the one which would dominate the country for the coming days, began to unfold.

The great western face of the historic building loomed ahead. Just a few more yards to go. Just a few more minutes until martyrdom and paradise.

But he couldn't stop thinking about Mum.

The rucksack shifted on his back and the glass bottles clinked together. The young man hesitated, angled his head and listened hard. There was no hissing or fizzing, none of the telltale sounds that said the explosion was imminent, the packed shrapnel of the hundreds of nails about to shriek towards their targets.

Not yet.

No one was watching. There was nothing to see. He was just another fellow human, taking a stroll, eating an ice cream, and enjoying the weather.

But he had a secret.

He walked carefully on. It wasn't worth checking the bottles again, as he had so many times now on this final journey, rearranging the football kit carefully wrapped around them. His favourite yellow goalkeeper's shirt which he'd brought for luck, the gloves, shorts and old socks too.

And luck had been with him. He was almost at the target.

The sun was in his eyes, making him squint. Across the green, a woman called to some children.

She was throwing a ball to two young boys. He followed its looping passage through the warm air, and remembered the instructions. Repeated them to himself.

He must try not to kill any children. It was good if one or two were injured, but it was better if none were killed.

Wounded children taught this foul society a finer lesson. See them scream. Feel their suffering. Dead parents, wounded children. That was the ideal. It was what the infidels deserved.

He walked on. The sun dipped behind the great towers of ancient stone.

A tolling bell chimed out its welcome.

The beckoning doors slid open.

He walked on.

*　　　　*　　　　*

'It's nice and simple,' grunted the wizened sergeant, who was evidently enjoying himself. 'We smash in the door and arrest anyone in the place. Good old-fashioned police work.'

The half dozen officers around them donned riot helmets and checked stab vests and body armour. Nigel glanced down at his own attire. He was wearing jeans and an old jumper, neither of which looked likely to deflect any kind of attack, let alone one with a knife.

'Feeling underdressed for the occasion?' Dan whispered. His friend nodded, tussling his dishevelled greying hair. 'Don't worry. We'll just follow them in. If there's trouble, pick the biggest cop you can find to hide behind.'

Nigel managed a tight smile. Despite all his years on the road, at least ten more than Dan, he still grew a little nervous before the action of a story.

It was a few minutes after noon on a sunny mid September day. They were parked on a tree-lined street in the Stonehouse area of Plymouth. Just around the corner was the brothel, apparently busily at work despite the hour. Dan couldn't stop himself wondering about the psyche of the kind of men who found themselves in need of sex while others were thinking more about sandwiches.

He found himself looking forward to meeting them.

Dan's years of experience of crime reporting had taught him that every English police force must carry out monthly crackdowns, as if this was one of the most important lessons drilled into senior officers at their training schools. Much of it was inspired by public relations, to create the impression of policing progress, even if the reality was that life returned to illicit normality usually only a few hours after the campaign ended. So far this year the targets had included underage drinking, driving while using a mobile phone, the carrying of knives, truancy, car-tax evasion, and quite a few others which had slipped into the dusty oblivion of undistinguished history.

September's chosen suspect for the might of local law enforcement was the sex industry. It promised to be the most media-friendly by far, so Dan had arranged to join a raid. And

6

here they were, amongst a group of Greater Wessex Police officers, about to give some unfortunates a sexual experience they would undoubtedly never forget.

The police team clambered out of the van. A couple of people stood on the pavement, watching. A dog started barking. The officers began jogging around the corner; Dan and Nigel following.

'Number 19,' one called, pointing. It was an ordinary, terraced house, carefully painted and maintained, even a bird feeder in the small, paved garden.

Two policemen stepped forward, grasping what looked like a miniature battering ram. Nigel lifted his camera onto his shoulder to film the action. The cops swung the bulky metal. The door thudded, buckled, splintered and cracked, but held. One reached out, kicked at it, then again. Now the lock gave, wrenched open, and they tumbled inside.

A hallway. Cream white, matching carpet. Nicely decorated. A fish tank, golden shapes flitting in opaque water. A pair of easy chairs. Impeccably clean and tidy. Dan vaguely thought how well-presented modern brothels were. Perhaps the plague of Health and Safety legislation reached even here. Illicit and illegal sex might abound, with all the hazards to health that entailed, but there must be no risk of the customers or staff tripping on a loose floorboard.

A couple of screams drifted down the stairs. The officers were running up, in a line. Nigel panned the camera to follow them. Heavy feet thudded on the floorboards, doors opened and closed amidst muffled shouting.

'Shall we follow them?' Nigel asked. Dan was tempted, but shook his head. 'Not much point. The pictures might be good for a porn film, but imagine the whinging letters if we showed them on the daytime news. A couple more shots of people being led out – when they're suitably clothed – will do us.'

He sat down on one of the soft chairs. Nigel stayed standing, camera trained on the stairs. At his side, Dan noticed a board detailing the services on offer and their respective prices. Some he had never heard of, but happily whoever ran the brothel had anticipated that and thoughtfully provided rough diagrams. Dan blinked hard. Far from enjoyable, several looked extremely painful.

A couple of men in dark suits stepped down the stairs, saw the camera and instantly covered their faces. Unfortunately, that had the effect of highlighting the wedding rings each wore. Both the men's shirts were mostly unbuttoned, revealing mats of dark hair, and one had the flies of his trousers still open. They shouted some abuse at Nigel.

'Good afternoon,' Dan chirped in reply, and received a tirade for his trouble before the men were led off to the police van. He couldn't blame them. The bashing down of the front door must have been one of the most savage forms of *coitus interruptus*. Combine that with being hauled from your expensive bed of lust by a police officer, and then finding a television camera downstairs, the day must surely be a contender for *The Worst of Life So Far* award.

The men would be watching the news tonight with trepidation bordering on hysteria. He wouldn't show their faces, but they didn't need to know that. Years of alleged evolution and civilization had in no way diminished the irresistible allure of schadenfreude.

Dan sat back down and grinned to himself. It was proving to be an unusually pleasant Monday.

The door swung open and the young man stepped inside, blinking hard to accustom his eyes to the long shadows of the half light.

It was cool and quiet here. Conversations were whispered and footsteps soft. Reverence filled the calm air. The faint smell of candle smoke lingered. His rucksack shifted. The bottles clicked and clinked once more.

It didn't matter now. There were just seconds left.

His body was shaking. He wiped the gathering sweat from his face with a sleeve.

The space was cavernous, even more so than he remembered. He passed under a fluted arch. Symmetric spans of dull white stone. Angels looking down from the heavenly host. Blossoming flowers hung in freshly shaped sprays. His feet shuffled over the smooth and worn flagstones. Some pitted with long forgotten names, dedications, much love and so many memories. Past the tower of the organ, dark carved wood with pyramids of pipes, shining dull in the twilight.

Standards hanging in regimented rows. Union jacks, the red and white of Saint George, the navy and yellow of the Royal British Legion.

An agonised Christ on his gleaming cross. And a dark oil painting, worshippers and adorers attending the new born Lord.

All with eyes watching the young man as he edged past.

An alcove and a black rack of fat red candles. A haze of winding air with every one aflame, careful notes inscribed beneath.

For Joyce, forever loved and missed. For Andrew, in my prayers always. To my darling Chrissie, please come back to me again. Bert, you were my faithful friend always – thank you. To the Simms, eternally in our thoughts.

A taper flickered, gathered, faltered and died.

A smiling saint in a wall of stained glass waved a welcome and proclaimed that God loved him. The beaming sun cast rainbows on the ground. Augustine and Ambrose, Peter and Paul, Gregory and Jerome, all reached out to him in their reds, greens and golds, offering help on this long journey to find salvation.

He hesitated and gulped hard.

There weren't as many people here as he had hoped. Most were outside, sitting on the green, enjoying the warmth of the weather.

But there were enough.

Find a corner. A confined space amplifies the explosion. Maximises the carnage. And the sacred message.

A corner with a group of people.

The young man started walking again.

His steps were slower now.

He kept thinking about his mum.

And that he would never play football again.

Never wear the precious lucky gloves, patched up and held together with tape. Never patrol the pitted and muddy goal. Never feel the hands upon his shoulders to congratulate him on another save. Never know that hour and a half of pure, heady acceptance.

Be a vital part of the happy team. And of this society. As he had so longed to be.

Until he was shown another way.

The pure way.

The right way.

As he told himself. Again and again.

But the young man's footfall faltered. Each step grew slow and heavy. And breathless.

He clutched at the hard wooden certainty of a pew. Studied the line of kneelers, embossed with birds and flowers. Nuthatch and yellowhammer, water lily and rose. Tapped at a Book of Common Prayer with an unsteady trainer. Harder now. Watched it slip from the pile and fall open on the stone.

And he waited.

Now a noise. Footsteps. He half turned. Ready for the uniforms. The shining buttons. The faces of authority. The commanding words. The handcuffs.

And wondered whether he'd welcome them.

His eyes focused through the creeping tears. A couple walked past, lost in their tunnel of love. They didn't waste a glance, cuddled together, moving onwards.

The woman was wearing a short skirt, light denim, riding with the easy rhythm of her stride, showing off the long lines of her tanned legs. A spray of freckles on her thigh.

Even here, even in this place they called sacred, their whores couldn't cover up their flesh.

It was a sign. They must pay for their sins.

They deserved it. He repeated the words, over and over again.

They deserved it.

Ahead was a corner. Some display boards. This great holy edifice throughout the long ages. The foundation and rise. Its thousand years standing. The struggle through the Reformation. The fears and raids and bomb damage of the Second World War.

And a group of people.

A young girl with a blonde rope of pony tail, clutching a shoulder bag in the shape of a puppy. Wearing a T-shirt of the Eiffel Tower, pulling up knee socks, now texting.

A knot of men and women with cameras at their faces. They're exchanging quiet words with Midlands accents. A fiftieth birthday party tonight. For Uncle Frank, in a local hotel. A slide show of photographs of his childhood. A woman is looking forward to remembering how they all used to be. A man prefers the idea of the buffet and free bar. He gets a dig in the ribs for his thoughts, but also a ripple of laughter.

An older woman, leaning on a stick, studies a guide book of Devon. She pulls her cardigan a little tighter around her chest. From her bag edges a theatre ticket. It's packed amongst a lipstick, a compact, an embroidered handkerchief and a bag of cat treats.

There's a thin man, eyes wide, face a little flushed. He keeps checking his watch and picking at a thread on the sleeve of his jacket. He's smartly dressed, with an impeccably ironed shirt and trousers and smells of a little too much cologne. He's carrying a bunch of flowers, half a dozen red roses. On a small white card, in an unsteady hand, is written, *Be mine, always*.

A middle-aged man holds the hand of a woman. Flares of light flash from the diamond on her finger. He slips a kiss onto her cheek and whispers about the beauty of this place.

And of his bride-to-be.

At the back of the group are a couple of children, wearing matching rugby tops. Two boys. One pushes the other. He pushes back. A woman doesn't look round, but tells them to stop. She's intent on a polished bronze plaque, commemorating the men from the Royal Lancers who fell in India in the 19th century. She's writing in a notebook. The page is headed *Family tree – Exeter end*.

The young man lets his cloudy eyes run over them. And gathers his will.

"Loud" Jim Stone, the engineer, was in his usual fine form. Where some people brought a shining light to life, he radiated a beam of darkness.

'I'm not happy. I've got a bleeding toothache.' Loud's thicket of a beard twitched as he chewed at his lip. 'It hurts. A lot. And I bet it costs me hundreds to get it sorted out. Bleeding dentists.'

Dan handed him the tape and climbed up into the van, picking his way around the engineer's bulk. Today's shirt was subdued by Loud's trademark standards, navy blue with forks of yellow lightning. He must have chosen it to parade his suffering. The engineer was never one to do anything quietly. Dan had sometimes wondered if even after Loud died he would still be complaining about how much his last moments had hurt. He could be the first person to require a sound-proof coffin.

'Quick edit, if you will,' Dan ventured. It was coming up to half past twelve. The lunchtime news was on air in an hour. They could get the story cut by around one, leaving plenty of time for the live broadcast.

Loud grimaced and grunted, but began spooling through the tape, checking the pictures, while Dan sketched out a script. Television worked best with short, sharp sentences, written to complement and explain the pictures. So, to begin, perhaps just one line of commentary – "A coordinated series of raids on houses identified by intelligence as being used as brothels."

Loud edited the pictures of the cops running towards the house. Dan kept quiet as they used the sound of the door being broken in. Sometimes the images needed no words of embroidery. Next came a few lines about the raids, five in all, across Devon, and they dropped in an interview clip of a Chief Superintendent which they'd filmed earlier, the man talking about the links between brothels and organised crime.

To end the report, Dan detailed the number of people arrested and they used the shots of the businessmen being led down the stairs. Loud began a guttural giggling at the sight.

Five to one. Ideal. Nigel had positioned the camera looking

back on the house. A police officer stood sentry duty outside. It would make a good backdrop. They were ready in time aplenty, for once.

With just a minor alteration to update the number of arrests, the report would do for tonight's programme. An enjoyably quiet afternoon was in prospect. Dan mulled over how to spend it. Perhaps some shopping? It was a chore, but a necessary one. The fridge in the flat was in its usual state of bareness, and, more importantly, the beer cupboard was almost empty.

It had been running dry worryingly fast of late, he knew, but sometimes, sitting alone in the flat at night, it was the only way to obliterate the memory of five months ago.

Dan flinched. Yes, some shopping while the high street was quiet, then home and a long run with Rutherford. Perhaps if he got back early enough they could even go out onto Dartmoor. September was the King of the Devon months. The weather was still kind, the evening light beautiful in its mellowness, and most of the tourists had left for the year.

It was a plan. A good walk on the moor with his beloved dog. Dan felt himself starting to relax at the thought.

And that was the fatal error.

Only later did he come to realise it must have been just about that moment, 12.57 exactly, that the bomb went off.

Chapter Two

THE HILLS WERE LOSING their summer lustre, starting instead to colour with hints of rust as the land sensed the colder days to come. The drive from Plymouth to Exeter was pure Devon, a guide to the county's contrasts. Salt and sugar; two dissimilar beauties for contrasting tastes.

To the north was the bleak glowering expanse of Dartmoor, rising from the road and topped with the dark scatterings of its jagged granite rocks, the famous tors. To the south, the gentler, classical countryside of the long slide away to the sea. The oblongs and angles of fields of crops; all greens, yellows and browns, the lines of hedgerows and woodland and the odd nestling village.

Today though, there was no beauty to the drive, hardly even a passing notice, no interest except in getting it done and as fast as possible. It was 45 miles, and Dan had followed the dual carriageway so many times, but never had the journey felt so laboured.

Today was different.

Most radio stations had begun rolling coverage of the bombing. For the first ten miles, an eyewitness spoke of a flash and shattering boom within the nave. Of a silence, sheer with shock. And then people screaming. Piercing and hysterical. And running, blind and blinkered, in all directions, to anywhere and everywhere, just away. And of blood and injuries and body parts littering the ancient stone floor.

Dan noticed the car's speedometer creeping up.

They had dropped the lunchtime outside broadcast, thrown all the kit into the back of the satellite van, run to their cars and gone. There were no thanks and friendly goodbyes to the police officers they had been working with, no apologies to the group of people who had gathered to watch the spectacle of live television in action, no hint of hesitation or delay.

This was no time for niceties.

They passed the twin towns of Buckfastleigh and

Ashburton, cut into the edge of the moorland. A pair of steeples rose from the slate rooftops, along with the tower of the Benedictine Abbey. The journey was half done. A herd of Friesian cows crossed an overpass spanning the road, moving slowly, tended by a young man on a quad bike.

Now the car's radio shrieked with the hysterical voice of a woman. She was breathless and babbling, about the scores of police, fire crews and paramedics converging on the greens around the great historic building. About the hoses trained on the magnificence of its gothic stone columns and statues. About the crying and sobbing. And the stretchers, covered in blankets and carrying lifeless forms that were once the shape of people.

Dan checked his mirror. Nigel was right behind. The look on the cameraman's face said he was listening to the radio too.

They crossed the River Teign, shallow and fast, churning white waters, and the levels of its flood plain. A ramshackle flock of sheep drank at a cutting in the bank, the order of a camp site on the opposite side, the rows of colour of its hardy tents fewer now as another tourist season faded.

The voice on the radio changed. An Inspector Humphries was saying the region's emergency plan had been put into action. The police's investigation was at a very early stage. He could confirm only that a bomb had exploded and it was a suspected suicide attack. There were unconfirmed reports of several deaths and scores of injuries.

The Inspector concluded by quietly saying that yes, these outrages were often carried out by teams of attackers. And no, he could not rule out the possibility that other bombers might be in the area. Armed police were at the scene. The public were being asked to look out for any suspicious activity, particularly involving people carrying rucksacks.

Dan found his mouth felt very dry.

The road climbed the long ascent to Haldon Hill. A pair of horses grazed in a clearing. The darkness of the gathering forest closed in around the traffic, only the white tower of the Belvedere breaking through the tree line.

They slowed to round a chugging tractor and topped the

hill. Below stretched the panorama of the Exe Valley, lit bright by the sunshine, miles of plain, and the city of Exeter. The brick and glass towers and halls of the university one boundary, the grey lines of the airport and motorway the other.

A tail of black smoke was rising from the city's centre, first winding, then dissipating, a dark smear on the blue sky.

The road shifted steeply downwards. The car radio hissed and crackled. A man was repeating the words, "I just can't believe it", over and again. The presenter was adding his agreement. Dan's mobile rang, but he ignored it.

They turned off the A38 and reached the outskirts of Exeter. The main road in to the city was conspicuously clear. But outbound it was gridlocked. The faces in the windscreens were pale, taut and drawn.

Dan turned up the volume. A reporter was at the scene of the attack. She was describing the crowds of people milling around. The relentless ringing of mobile phones as panicked people called those they knew were in the city. The frightened families looking for mothers and fathers, sisters and brothers, sons and daughters. They were wailing, shouting and screaming, calling out the names, pushing and pulling at people in the crowd, checking faces.

The hugs of relief as some were reunited, too emotional even for tears. The continuing anguish of the many still searching.

The roar of the police helicopter hovering in the air. The impending arrival of the security service, FX5, and SO15, the Counter-Terrorism Branch of the Metropolitan Police.

Always these things happen to someone else, a woman was saying. Always.

But not today. Today, it happens to us.

One more road. One last turning.

The air was full of sirens. Streams of people were walking, jogging, stumbling away. Some were sitting, smoking, propped against walls and buildings. Others sat on benches and car bonnets with heads bowed or just staring. Eyes wide, filled with fear.

Terrorism had come to Devon.

They parked just inside the remains of the medieval wall, on double yellow lines, but it wasn't the kind of day to worry about that. Nigel scrambled the camera, tripod and microphone from the boot of his car, Dan helping. Police cars kept rushing past, their blue lights washing from the glass of the shop fronts. They jogged across the road and into the green.

Professionalism dictated they started filming at once. But not today, not on this story.

Dan and Nigel stopped, stood still, and joined the crowd around them in simply staring.

The famous view which had graced tens of thousands of newspapers, magazines and postcards, websites and billboards, and recreations from artists' canvases to schoolchildren's notepads, the very symbolic heart of Exeter, had been defiled.

The magnificent stained glass window of the façade had been destroyed by the force of the explosion. The cobbles were strewn with jagged fragments of rainbow glass, many shining in their spectrum of soft colours as they caught the afternoon sun. Some of the pieces were larger, one depicting a green valley and running river, cut in half by the blast. Another, the body of a shepherd, the words *find redemption* beneath. Others were shards and splinters, angled edges of blue and red.

Wessex Minster had been blinded.

'Shit,' Nigel hissed. 'Just – well – shit.'

From the peak of the open arch, a trail of smoke wound up towards the sky. The once bright stone had been blackened with charcoal stains. A few lonely fragments of sharp glass around the base of the window had survived the blast. Dan, squinting, could make out the remnants of a disciple's robes and half a cross.

He breathed out heavily. Around him, in the crowd, people were pointing, some shaking their heads, others just staring, but for such a mass of people there was a remarkable silence.

They could sense the violation. No words were needed. All understood the hatred unleashed here today. The desire to anger, rage and outrage. To spit bile into the face of society.

Dan reached out a hand and gently held Nigel's shoulder.

'Sorry,' his friend whispered, slotting the camera onto the tripod. 'I just – well ...'

Dan stood behind him, watching Nigel's back as he captured the scene. As they filmed, another slice of the window slowly peeled from the stone frame and clattered onto the cobbles.

A low moan echoed through the crowd.

A couple of paramedics emerged from the side door of the Minster, supporting an elderly man. Bandages covered his head. They walked slowly towards a waiting ambulance. A couple more emerged, carrying a stretcher. A child was lying upon it, her blonde hair trailing. They could hear her crying.

Dan shuddered. He suddenly felt a lonely stranger in a hostile land.

And recording, writing and reporting this the most futile gesture of an ephemeral life.

He was vaguely aware of some noise. Words. Close to his ear.

'Are you OK?' Nigel was asking.

'Err, yeah. A bit – shocked, but mostly yeah. Why?'

'You were muttering to yourself.'

'Was I? Oh, right. Sorry, I was just, err – thinking. OK, you keep getting the pictures, I'll start finding us some interviews.'

Dan pushed his way through the throng, to one of the benches surrounding the green. He held up his press pass as a symbol of unquestionable authority, gathered his breath and called, 'Was anyone inside the Minster when it happened?'

Faces turned. A few shaking heads. He tried again, but still no luck. Dan hopped down, picked his way to another bench and tried once more. This time a young woman raised a slow hand.

'I was. I'd just come in the door to have a look round. All I saw was ...'

'Hang on,' Dan interrupted. Nigel had spotted her and was pushing his way over, holding out the microphone.

She could only have been in her early twenties, had short dark hair and a cute, freckled face. 'I'm not sure I want to be on telly,' she said, her voice shaking. 'Not after ... this.'

Dan smiled, reassuring, but firm. 'This story needs to be told. And you're the one to do it. What's your name?'

'Rosie.'

'What a beautiful name. It suits you.'

She gave Dan a look that suggested his charm had proved as effective as firing custard pies at the walls of a castle. Perhaps another angle of approach, then. Experience had equipped him abundantly.

'Rosie, it's easy enough. I just want you to tell me what happened. All the words I come out with can never let the viewers know what it was really like in there. Only you can do that.'

She still didn't look convinced.

'You do realise it's nothing short of your duty? You'll be helping to set down history.'

Dan thought he heard Nigel groan. But now she looked more impressed.

'Well, since you put it like that. I'd just walked into the door – I was going to join one of their guided tours – and I was looking at the ceiling when there was this noise ...'

'What was it like?' Dan prompted. 'Describe it to me.'

'It was like a crack to start with, then a really loud boom. It echoed all around the Minster. It was deafening. Then there was a crashing noise, like glass shattering. That must have been the windows blowing out.' Her expression darkened and her voice fell. 'Those beautiful windows. There was this hot wind, it felt like a hurricane battering me. Everyone stopped. Then people started screaming and shouting. But some weren't screaming ... they were lying on the floor – just lying there, still. And there was blood. Seeping onto the ground. There was smoke coming from over by the big window. Everyone was running, trying to escape. Then I just got out.'

The time was approaching three o'clock. They were well on the way with compiling the report. Time for one quick call, to a trusted source of information and friend.

'I'm a little busy,' replied Adam, in a strained voice.

'I guessed you would be. But I could do with a word. I take it you're at the Minster?'

'Me and every other detective we've got.'

'Can you spare me a minute later on?'

'Maybe. We might well need your help on this one – again.'

Dan kept working his way through the crowd and found another eye-witness. The man was a little closer and had seen a bright flash of light as the bomb exploded. He'd also spoken in faltering, but eloquent terms about the injuries. People staggering out of the Minster, holding their heads, pouring with blood.

It was brutally graphic for a daytime news programme. But with a story like this there was no way to soften the sense of shock.

A police media liaison officer bumbled through the crowd and informed the hacks that a press conference would be held shortly. The Deputy Chief Constable, he hinted, had important information, but the man would tell them no more.

Dan called the newsroom as he waited. They were sending Craig, *Wessex Tonight's* main anchor to present tonight's programme live from the Minster. It was a standard news technique to mark the importance of a story.

Loud had arrived, and somehow managed to talk his way through security and drive into the Minster grounds.

'They could only see the front of the van on their monitors,' he explained. 'I told 'em I was the police canteen wagon. That always works.'

He'd changed his shirt to a plain, navy model, which he kept in the van for serious stories, but was still holding his jaw. 'Bloody inconvenient time for a big story,' he grumbled. 'I was hoping to get off to the dentist later.'

More satellite trucks were arriving, and journalists too. There was now a crowd of about fifty hacks, and half a dozen camera crews. In the dishonourable tradition of the disreputable media, the first thing many wanted to know was where to get a decent coffee.

A café at the end of the run of shops facing the Minster was doing good trade. Its owners had placed a chalkboard outside reading, "Still open, two fingers to the terrorists!" Other shopkeepers were doing the same, cameramen filming them.

Armed police were patrolling the green. They walked past in their pairs, eyes continually scanning the crowd, hands ready on semi-automatic rifles. Rumours had been spreading of more suicide bombers. Knots of people were leaving now, most hand in hand or with arms wrapped around each other. Strangers shook hands and patted shoulders. It was a day for the comfort of companionship.

A distant clock struck three. The media liaison officer called the pack around and introduced the Deputy Chief Constable, Brian Flood. A portly man, he stood up on a bench with some difficulty and surveyed the cameras and microphones clustered before him. Dan followed Nigel as he shoved his way to the front, ignoring the irritated looks and attempts at retaliation.

'I have a brief statement for you,' Flood intoned, checking a piece of paper. 'I will not be taking any questions.'

He glanced at the notes again and drew himself up. 'At just before one o'clock today, an improvised bomb was detonated in Wessex Minster. One person was killed, another one badly hurt. Around twenty people suffered more minor injuries. The man we believe carried the bomb into the Minster was not killed and will be taken for medical treatment under police guard.'

Flood paused and looked around the pack. A breeze flicked at his hair and the sun blazed from the polished buttons of his tunic.

He shifted position a little and continued. 'We are not currently naming the man we believe to be the bomber, but I can tell you this. The explosive device was contained in his rucksack. It seems that he lost his nerve at the last moment, took the rucksack off and attempted to flee. It was then that it detonated.'

Another pause. The pack was silent, entranced. Flood checked his paper again.

'The final thing I have to tell you is this, and it is perhaps the most shocking. The bomber is a young man, a schoolboy in fact, and only sixteen years of age. We believe he has been indoctrinated and put up to this attack by Islamic extremists

21

who wish our society harm, but who are too cowardly to take such dreadful actions themselves.'

Flood clambered down and pushed his way through the crowd. He ignored the questions shouted at him, but they were few. Reporters were too busy calling their newsrooms to file this latest copy. The story was moving fast.

Next to Dan, a newspaper reporter began sketching out a headline on the top of his notepad. In black ink, and underlined, it read *The Schoolboy Terrorist*.

Chapter Three

IT SHOULD HAVE BEEN a straightforward, if dull, day, a rare nine to five. A decent buffet laid on by the grateful "partner agencies", as the modern, caring, all and everyone-inclusive terminology had it. *A multi platform tomorrow angled interface*, the chairman had said, with a welcoming smile, but without a hint of self-consciousness.

A day discussing the public perceptions of crime and the need to *realign erroneous outlooks with empirical statistical realities.*

So read the briefing document, which had inexplicably and unfortunately found itself the soaking victim of a spilt coffee, and thus had to be consigned to end its brief life in the recycling bin.

Instead, just before the feast of the buffet was about to be unveiled, had come the call. And now Detective Chief Inspector Adam Breen was sitting in the passenger seat of a patrol car, sirens wailing, speeding towards the centre of Exeter, with a phone clamped hard to his ear.

'How long before you're here?' Flood was shouting.

'About ten minutes, sir.'

'Well, hurry up, man,' snapped the Deputy Chief, with his usual expectation of the impossible. 'What if there are more of the bastards? What do you think the chances are?'

'Difficult to say, but in cases like this – well, they don't tend to work alone.'

Flood swore, then added, 'Hang on, I'm getting an update.' There was some muffled conversation, then, 'The medics are taking the bomber to hospital.'

'Right now?'

'Yes.'

'Is he conscious?'

A pause for another consultation, then, 'Yes, just about.'

Adam hung up and leaned across to talk to the dark-haired woman with the calmly focused expression.

'The hospital?' asked Claire, before he had a chance to speak.

'Yep.'

She turned the car off the main road, sped through a red light and swung past a line of stationary cars. They rounded a bus, then a couple more cars. Ahead, a sign read "Ambulances only". She took the turning, tyres squealing their protest, and pulled up outside the entrance to Accident and Emergency.

'What the hell do you think you're doing?' a young man in a white coat asked. 'We're expecting a …'

A between the eyes close-up of Adam's warrant card stopped him. 'Is he here yet?'

'Who?'

'You know who.'

'No. He's due in a few seconds.'

'I need a word with him before you do anything.'

The doctor shook his head hard. He was young, perhaps not yet thirty, thin, pale and with a rash of raw acne on his neck.

'He's seriously ill. We need to get working on him straight away.'

'Just thirty seconds.'

'No way. I can't allow it. You can see him after we've treated him.'

From over the hedge came the sound of a siren blaring. An ambulance bumped around the corner and headed towards them.

Claire reached out an arm and laid it on the doctor's shoulder. 'We appreciate you need to take care of your patient, but – there may be other bombers out there. Right at this moment. Looking for targets. In the city centre. I take it you live in Exeter?'

The doctor nodded.

'You've got friends here? Family?'

Another nod.

'Then just give us a minute or two. That's all we need.'

The doctor was shaking his head. 'Look, I understand, I really do. But there's the oath. And the British Medical Association has all sorts of rules. If I don't …'

24

The ambulance juddered to a stop, the paramedics hopping down from the doors. Claire gave the doctor a warm smile.

'We do appreciate your problem. That's why ...' she nodded to the police car, 'we have special procedures at times like this. I take it you know the Zero Option Protocol?'

'The what?'

'I've got the forms in the car. Just come over here and I'll make sure there's no comeback for you.'

The doctor hesitated, then followed her guiding arm. Adam slipped past the paramedics and stepped up into the ambulance.

The flowers had begun to arrive. The modern day reflex of grieving, first a small bunch of daffodils, laid by a child as she held her mother's hand, then some chrysanthemums, now larger bouquets as a stream of people came to express their sorrow. The tributes formed a growing stream of colour by the edge of the cordon, next to the white stone cross of the war memorial.

Dan watched as Nigel and the other camera crews filmed from a respectful distance. All the reporters would want to interview the people laying the flowers, but this was a time for sensitivity, rare though it might be amongst the media. He had a brief chat with his peers, agreed that he would approach people as they walked away from the Minster, and if they were happy to talk he would call the rest of the pack over.

Dan wasn't surprised to find most people did want to be interviewed. It felt good, perhaps even cathartic, to speak out against the unseen attackers and make clear the defiance.

It was almost four o'clock, just over two hours until they were on air. Time to think about editing the report. It could be done in an hour, but with a story of such magnitude he wanted plenty of time to get it right. Weigh the words and measure the meaning.

Nigel suddenly swung the camera, Dan hopping out of the way. The flag of St George flying above the Minster, the proud red cross, was being slowly lowered to half mast. Around them in the crowd more people noticed and fell quiet at the simple gesture of mourning.

Sometimes silence was the only thing to say.

Craig arrived, then disappeared again. He was going into town to buy a black tie. They'd had a quick discussion, and he was happy to work out most of what he was going to say himself. Craig was unusual amongst presenters in being a low-maintenance model. Many might look good on the television, but weren't the brightest and tended to flap when sent out of the studio, away from the safety of the autocue. They were often as fragile as crystal glass.

A final call to the newsroom to check on any further developments and it was time to begin editing. Another *Wessex Tonight* crew was filming a police search at a house in the Stonehouse area of Plymouth. It was believed to be where the bomber lived. Armed cops were crawling over the neighbourhood.

That would be a separate report. Lizzie, the programme's editor, was in full flight, and had also arranged for a live interview with a terrorism expert from London. The bombing would take up almost the entire bulletin, as it should.

It was one of those rare stories of such significance that it dominated the day. Usually in news terms, Dan would be given a duration of about one minute forty seconds for his report. For bigger stories, that might reach two minutes, or even two and a half. Today, he was asked simply for as much as he could provide. He hopped up into the outside broadcast van, handed the tape to Loud and began writing.

The words came easily. They usually did with the biggest stories. They told themselves.

The better reporters and producers learnt early that the basis of a successful outside broadcast is a sound structure. As they hadn't yet been allowed inside the Minster to film, the golden shot, the one which told the story in a second, was the ruined stained glass window. So Craig would want to talk about that in his live opening link, which meant Dan had to start his report with a more detailed, close up image.

The fragment of glass peeling away and falling would be perfect. It was pure pathos. Loud laid the shot, Dan writing to complement it.

'It was a poignant symbol of the damage inflicted on this sacred and historic building in the terrorist outrage.'

Not a bad start, if he did say so himself. Even Loud was nodding, the nearest he came to appreciation. Next, they used some close-ups of the shattered glass littering the cobbles. Dan wrote what they knew of the attack, that it was a suicide bomber who appeared to have lost his nerve and run at the last moment.

He wouldn't include the details of deaths and injuries. There was always confusion about the exact numbers after such an attack, and they could easily change right up to the moment they were on air. By leaving them out of the report, it gave Craig maximum flexibility to include the information in his live links. It also removed the prospect of panicked, last minute, re-edits, a stressful experience which was well worth avoiding.

Now they put in the eyewitnesses. It was powerful television, following the simple rule of using your best pictures and interviews first.

'What next?' Loud grunted, rubbing at his jaw. 'Me bleeding tooth's getting worse, if you're interested.'

Dan very much wasn't, but made some understanding noises. They'd seen plenty of the Minster and heard about the bombing, so now it was time for a change of angle. Loud edited some pictures of the flowers being laid, followed by a couple of clips of interview. It was more raw and powerful emotion.

Then came the Deputy Chief Constable's statement and a little of the local council, expressing shock, but saying Exeter would never be cowed by terrorists. Dan ended the report with the Minster flag being drawn down. Semiotics, the unspoken language of film; it simply felt the right way to conclude.

Craig returned, and together they watched the report and worked through a plan for the broadcast. He was a tall man with a permanent and enviable tan, but had put on weight since the last time they met. Dan noticed he kept drawing in his stomach self-consciously. Perhaps it was the familiar story of the over-indulgence during a long summer holiday, a classic

September phenomenon.

The time ticked on to a quarter past five. Dan sat down on a bench while Nigel got them a couple of coffees. They could do with taking it easy for a few minutes. It had been quite a day. The memory of that earlier raid on the brothel felt very distant. How quickly life could change.

'Well, who'd have thought it?' Nigel said quietly. 'Who could have imagined we'd ever see such a thing here?'

They watched as a couple walked past, holding the hand of their young son. He stepped hesitantly forwards to lay some flowers on the growing pile. They stood in silence, then turned slowly away.

'What are you going to tell your sons?' Dan asked Nigel.

The cameraman ran a hand through his hair. 'The truth. That the world they're growing into can be a dangerous one. But that there are still lots of good people out there, many more than bad.'

Dan smiled. 'That's very you. I wish I were more like that. It's at times like this I'm glad I don't have a family.'

And, as if responding to a cue, a thought of Claire formed, grew, and ran dominant through Dan's mind.

He swallowed hard. 'Well, we'd better start getting ready for this broadcast. I reckon ...'

'Hey!' Nigel interrupted. 'Look!'

A couple of armed police officers were running past, sweating hard. Two more followed. Nigel grabbed the camera and they set off in pursuit.

A young lad, just a trainee, jumpy with nerves at being pitched into his first big emergency, but good police work. He'd kept a distance and whispered into his radio for orders.

'What's your name, son?' Adam replied.

'Danny, sir.'

'What's he doing?'

'Just standing in the crowd, sir. Watching the Minster.'

'How did you notice him?'

'He took off his baseball cap to scratch his head. That's when I thought he looked like the guy in the description. Plus there was …'

'What?'

'You'll think this is silly, sir.'

'Try me.'

'Well, there was this look on his face. It wasn't like everyone else's. Not – you know, sorrowful. It was more satisfaction.'

If the day hadn't been so grave, Adam would have smiled. 'You've just passed the first test of being a cop, Danny. Keep your eyes open and follow your instincts.'

'Have I? Thank you, sir. So far I've only been filling out forms in the station. I really want to be on the beat. I want to get into CID, like you. Do you think …'

'We can talk about that later,' Adam interrupted firmly. 'Just keep watching him, but make it look like you're not. The firearms teams will be with you in seconds.'

Those two minutes in the back of the ambulance had been precious. They now knew exactly who the bomber was and where he was from. He was lying face down on the treatment table, an oxygen mask over his face, but muffled groans were still clearly audible. He'd been badly injured, suffering extensive burns and shrapnel wounds, and was in severe pain, despite the morphine.

It was clear he was in no way whatsoever fit to be interviewed.

'I want a word with you,' Adam said, pulling off the mask. 'If you can spare a moment before you die.'

'I'm not saying nothing.'

'There'll be no treatment until you do. No hope for you.'

'No way.'

'Give me your name.'

'No.'

'They won't make you feel better until I hear your name.' Adam knelt down so they were eye to eye. 'Come on, I need to call you something.'

He was no more than a boy, and one who now had a halved face. He may have run at the last minute, but the bomb caught up with him. He couldn't resist looking around at the detonation. And the shrapnel had cut through cheek, nose and brow.

The other side of his face was curiously untouched. There was still a speckling of stubble around his chin and a couple of patches of spots, raw against the pallor of his skin. He was breathing hard, gasping and moaning with the pain, trickles of blood flecking the white of his teeth.

'No feeling better until you talk to me. Come on. What's the matter with telling me who you are? If you don't, we'll just use dental records. But that'll have to wait until you're dead. Mind, that shouldn't take long, the state you're in.'

The boy tried to cry out but didn't have the strength to project the sound. The ragged remains of his lips began to form whispers of words. Adam had to put his ear to the fluttering mouth, so quiet was his voice. And then came the name, and the address.

'Right, time to get you some treatment. I'm a man of my word. But just one more thing first – who are you working with?'

'Piss off,' he muttered.

'OK, fine.'

Adam took a step towards the ambulance doors, then another. The flickering eyes shifted with him.

'If I leave now, I'll make sure no one gets to come in here. Not for ages. Not until it's way too late for you.'

'I'm not saying anything else. You have to help me.'

Adam paced around to behind the table and flicked at the drip running into the boy's arm. He tried to follow the movement, but couldn't twist his head. His T-shirt was ripped in patches and melted in others, the soft material melded into the raw, weeping wounds of the flesh.

The doctor had said some of the burns were third degree. Oddly enough, they wouldn't be hurting as all the nerve endings were gone. But the others would.

'Burns – a really nasty way to die,' the detective said softly. 'Painful – agonising in fact. And that's only talking about now. Do you know one of the biggest dangers of burns?'

The boy swallowed hard. 'Leave me alone.'

'It's infection. It sets in so fast – frighteningly quickly – if you're not treated properly. And if you think it hurts now ... wait until the infection starts creeping through you. Eating away at your body ...'

Someone was pulling at the ambulance's doors. 'Just a sec,' Adam called. 'We're almost done.'

The boy looked up. Glimpsed the white coat of the doctor. 'Help me,' he groaned.

Adam eased the doors shut. He tapped a foot against a couple of oxygen cylinders. They clanked dully. The gloom of the cramped space closed in.

'Last chance. Who were you working with?'

'Leave me alone. The doctor's here now. He'll look after me.'

'OK. If that's how you want it.'

Adam lifted his notebook to write some words and carelessly let it slip through his fingers.

It landed in the small of the boy's back. He screamed. And gasped, and moaned, and began sobbing to himself.

But started talking.

A team of detectives was at his home within minutes. And straight away they had more information. On a suspected accomplice.

And a tip. An ominous one. A word that he too was in Exeter.

Every cop they could gather was on the beat in the city, plus special constables, police community support officers, even traffic and parks wardens. Bouncers, shop, store and security guards, bus and taxi drivers were also looking out for him.

And they had been fortunate. Got their break. Danny had found him. And was watching him, just as he had been told.

But then came the bad luck. One of the press photographers decided to start taking some shots of the crowd. Their man had seen him coming, turned away, and noticed the young cop, looking at him.

And he'd begun walking, fast, away from the Minster. Towards the High Street. Where hundreds of people were still gathered. Some carrying on with the everyday business of life,

31

despite the attack; shopping, walking and talking, looking in windows, eating sandwiches, drinking coffees, waiting for buses. Others trying to compose themselves, ready for a journey to the safety of home.

So many people. An invitation for more carnage, if the man had another bomb.

The armed cops were almost there, but still a few seconds behind. Too far to stop him.

Danny was following. Providing his reports. Breathlessly.

And now the man was jogging. Continually looking behind him.

And now running.

Towards the busiest part of Exeter, the heart of the city, and its men and women, office workers and shoppers, strollers and passers-by, children and their mothers and fathers.

And Danny was running fast too. Sprinting now. And the armed teams, and Adam. As fast as they could.

But the man was in the High Street. Amongst the crowd.

And he was carrying a rucksack.

Chapter Four

ADAM CAREERED AROUND THE corner of Minster Green, saw the man ahead. He'd run out into the middle of the High Street and was looking quickly back and forth. Lines of shops, banks, building societies. A queue of people at a coffee stand. Children and parents watching a clown, tottering on stilts. Buses packed with shoppers. A crowd milling around the stalls of a farmers market. Hundreds of people. Hundreds of targets.

Each shopfront shone with thick plate glass. If that rucksack contained a bomb – if he exploded it here – thousands of splinters of screaming shrapnel would fire through the air, a lethal complement to the nails they already knew had been used in the Minster bomb.

The man ran forwards, into the Exehall Shopping Centre. Modern, low ceiling, narrow walkways, also packed with people. A perfect terrorist target. Adam swore to himself. If a bomb went off there, in the confined space, the destruction would be horribly magnified.

The two firearms teams caught up. The young probationer too. Five cops and himself, that was all he had.

No time to debate. Just to decide. His best bet. With terrifying stakes.

'Get after him,' Adam snapped. 'Armed teams first. He calls himself Ahmed, if you need a name. But you're cleared to shoot if he so much as hints at posing a threat.'

They lurched into the Exehall. Fleeting faces twisted with alarm. Children pointed. Adults stared. A woman started screaming. It found an echo, then another. The shopping centre was fast filling with fear.

They ran past a jeweller's, feet pounding on the tiled floor, then a sports shop, a book store, came to an intersection, scanned back and forth. People were walking past quickly, some stumbling, others running from the arcade. More screams and cries resounded from the shopfronts.

'Danny, get as many people out as you can,' Adam panted.

'Shout, long and loud, shove them even, just get them clear. Where is he? Where the hell is he?'

The four armed officers spread out, their guns trained ahead. People were still running past, some sobbing, others breathing fast and ragged. Danny was ushering the crowds away. He was scared, but he'd pulled off the sacred trick of looking calm.

Good lad. He was going to do just fine as a cop.

Adam would tell him so later. If they got out of this alive.

If.

More police officers were arriving now, joining the effort to clear the shopping centre.

There was no sign of Ahmed. The armed cops formed a line, walked forward, pace by careful pace, their guns sweeping back and forth.

There were too many hiding places. In a shop. In a doorway. Behind the large tubs filled with trees and plants.

If he had a bomb in that rucksack he could set it off in a second. There'd be no chance to stop him.

Adam braced himself for the blast. He noticed he was treading softly, silently. At any instant the arcade could explode in blinding light and shattering sound.

He thought of Annie, at work, totting up rows of figures, that picture of him and Tom on her desk. And his son too, probably in an after-school sports club. What was Monday's? Football, wasn't it? Tom's favourite. They were planning to go to the Plymouth Argyle match on Saturday.

Adam patted a hand on his wallet where the picture of his family lay.

'Sir,' hissed one of the armed officers. 'There's no sign of him. What do we do?'

'He's here somewhere. There are more cops blocking the other entrances. He can't have got out. Keep going. Keep searching.'

They stepped slowly on. A pigeon fluttered past. Adam could have sworn one of the marksmen tracked its path with his gun.

An elderly woman blinked up at them from a bench. 'I'm

too old for this running around,' she rasped. 'And why should I run for a damned terrorist anyway? I never did for the Nazis.' Danny helped her up and walked her outside. 'I think he went that way,' she added over her shoulder, pointing straight down the arcade.

It was mostly clear now, just the odd person emerging from the shops, seeing the police officers and scuttling past. None resembled Ahmed. The arcade was quiet, the only sound their measured footfall.

They passed a grocer's and its colourful display of fruit and veg, an optician's, then a second-hand shop, the window full of cameras and mobile phones. Ahead was a small supermarket, outside a couple of fake trees, some benches, and a corner.

Adam held up a hand and they paused. A strip light buzzed and clicked. But there was nothing else.

No noise. No movement.

Nothing.

They paced on.

Dan and Nigel got to the shopping centre just in time to see Adam and the armed officers run inside. Nigel lifted the camera to his shoulder and began filming. People were stumbling out, some screaming. One man dropped a bag of groceries. A couple of oranges rolled across the pavement. Dan stood beside Nigel and took the brief opportunity to think.

Ah, the angst of an instant dilemma. And he was faced with two, and both absolute award-winners.

They could be on the track of a fantastic story; film exclusive pictures of the arrest of another terrorist. And equally, they could get themselves killed as the man set off his bomb, or shot it out with the police.

If it was him alone, Dan thought he wouldn't have hesitated. He wasn't the bravest of men, but the bitter fact was that, of late, he'd spent many a night lying awake wondering what he had to live for.

But standing next to him was this kind, thoughtful, optimist of a friend and cameraman who also happened to have two young sons. And who was bringing them up alone since the death of his wife. But who Dan knew would go in there and film if he was asked to.

Dilemma one resolved.

Which happily also helped with Dilemma Two. Because if they both went in there, and got caught in a siege, or worse, then one of the biggest live broadcasts *Wessex Tonight* had produced for many years would be missing an indispensable element – a cameraman.

Dan hastily explained his thoughts, and wasn't in the least surprised by the reaction.

'But we could get a world exclusive. It'd be the scoop of our careers. And anyway ...'

'Yes?'

'I want to be a part of it.'

'I know.'

'And you need me there. What if something happens? Say you're hurt? You could get blown to bits.'

'Yeah, I know. But that's it. Decision made. There's no time to argue. Get back to the satellite van.'

The cops were moving on into the shopping centre. But Nigel wasn't giving up.

'Surely we can't risk missing the pictures.'

'We won't.' Dan held up his mobile phone. 'I'll use the camera on this. Nothing like as good as yours I know, but plenty to get us a decent sense of what's going on.'

Dan gently shoved Nigel away, and before his friend could argue further, turned and jogged into the arcade. He had to dodge, left and right, weave his way through the people streaming out. The marksmen were just ahead, the tall outline of Adam in the centre of their line. Even in this panic and confusion, his navy blue suit and dark hair looked impeccable.

How very like his friend. Even when facing a terrorist, a dishevelled state just wouldn't do.

A young policeman stood in Dan's way, his arms outstretched. He was sweating hard and looked flushed, but determined.

'Turn around, sir, please. We need you to get out of here.'

Dan prayed the constable wasn't a *Wessex Tonight* fan and

au fait with its on air team. He slipped his finger over the part of his press pass which said "Reporter", held it out and barked, 'Security service, sonny. Out of the way please.'

They held a stare. The policeman faded away. Dan breathed out his relief and ran on.

It had been a mantra since the golden discovery in the early days of his career; the secret of a successful bluff is to make it big.

The marksmen had paused, were just about to round a corner in the arcade. Dan turned on the phone's camera and held it up. It was an effort to stop his hand from shaking.

He wondered how it felt to be close to an exploding bomb. Nothing like in the films when the hero gets knocked over, lies there for a few seconds, hums a little tune, then hops backs up, dusts himself off and carries on.

Dan suffered a strange image of working through one of the tedious Hazard Assessment forms that *Wessex Tonight* reporters were given for any assignments containing an element of danger. Explosives, firearms, violence, unpredictable situation, noise, bright light, there were few boxes he wouldn't tick. To save time, he could just write – 'Insane risk, but doing it anyway. So there.'

It felt good to tweak the nose of the modern behemoth of health and safety.

Or perhaps it was just the momentary distraction from the suffocating threat of imminent death.

He edged forwards, following the marksmen. They were inching around the corner, step by tentative step, guns trained unerringly ahead.

Dan noticed his breathing was fast and shallow. His back prickled with sweat.

They were passing a travel agent's, its windows filled with the delights of cruises and winter sunshine in the Mediterranean and Canary Islands. The beat of summer, disco sounds slipped through the doors.

Now a charity shop, one that helps animals who need vets. Dan wondered what would happen to Rutherford if he were killed. He hoped the dog was lucky enough to find a new owner who loved him. He thought about whether Rutherford would remember the oddball master who kept strange hours and suffered vertiginous mood swings, but who always meant well, took him for good walks and runs and who sometimes cuddled him and confided his myriad demons.

They were almost around the corner. Dan gulped hard. He steadied his hand on the phone and held it as far forwards as his arm could stretch. The imaged flared and blurred, then steadied.

A packet of half-eaten fish and chips was lying open on a low wall. The smell of salt and vinegar tingled through the arcade.

A shout pierced the silence.

'Armed police! Put your hands where I can see them! Do it now! Do it and you won't be harmed!'

Dan forced himself to take another step, then one more. He shuffled past a bin, filled with cans and paper wrappings and rounded the corner.

Ahead, silhouetted in the streaming sunlight, Adam was standing still, his hands raised in a calming manner. All the marksmen had their guns at their shoulders. No one was moving.

Another command, loud in the quiet. 'Stay still! Keep your hands where I can see them!'

Still no one shifted. A breath of breeze made the plastic plants twitch. The long black barrels of the guns gleamed in the light.

The phone was trembling badly, the image dancing. Dan gripped it tighter, forced himself to keep still.

Sitting on a bench, his legs crossed, but his arms held up in the air, was a slight man with dark hair and olive skin. He wasn't moving, didn't look frightened, or angry, just sat and watched.

The marksmen converged on him, pace by wary pace, their guns trained on his chest the whole while. Red dots on the white cotton of his shirt. Each hovering over his heart.

An old and tatty rucksack lay on the ground next to the man's feet. It was black and silver, frayed in patches, marked with a "Surf Time" motif, and zipped back and wide open.

Dan craned his neck. He strained his eyes to see the trigger, the wires and batteries, the canisters of chemicals and scores of shining nails.

He blinked hard, frowned.

The rucksack contained a newspaper, a baseball cap and some sandwiches and crisps.

Chapter Five

MINSTER GREEN WAS QUIETER now, the light shifting to the amber hues of the sunset as the day slipped away. Pools of darkness lay in the undulations of the grass. Crows hopped and pecked at the pickings of litter. The iron streetlamps that marked the green's boundary blinked on as Dan approached.

Nigel was pacing back and forth, continually looking over towards the shopping centre. Even Loud was glancing out of the door of the satellite truck. The cameraman squinted, then came jogging over, held out a hand, and Dan shook it.

'Bloody glad to see you,' he muttered. 'Was it worth the risk?'

Dan briefly explained what had happened. 'The cops reckon this guy radicalised the bomber. They've taken him away for questioning. We're the only media with the shots.'

'But I'd appreciate it if you didn't do that sort of thing very often – despite what you might think about no one missing you if you're not around any more.'

They held a look, Dan nodded and handed his mobile to Loud. The truck was equipped with a machine which could take the video and turn it into a broadcast format. Few were the stories they came across nowadays where someone hadn't recorded the action on their phone.

He stood with Craig and went through the plan for the broadcast. They would begin with Dan's report. Following that would come a live interview with the Principal of the Minster. Then Craig would voice over the mobile phone pictures of the arrest. After that, they would cross to Plymouth for an update on the search of the bomber's house, followed by the interview with the terrorism expert in London.

Another presenter back in the studio would read a brief round-up of the rest of the day's news, then it would be back to the Minster for Craig to sum up the day's events. Dan left him rehearsing his lines, walking back and forth and talking to an imaginary audience complete with the odd histrionic gesture, just as an actor might.

A gang of young lads turned up on their bikes and asked what was going on. Dan groaned to himself. The last thing you needed on a story of this magnitude was kids in the background, waving at the camera and shouting. They seemed fairly well behaved, but you could never tell. Dan had known one lad bare his backside while he was live on air. He used his standard trick, sent them over to the van to watch the broadcast from there. It had the dual advantage of keeping them out of the way, while also annoying Loud.

Armed police were still patrolling the green and the streets of the city. Adam had said they didn't think anyone else was involved, and were almost certain there were no more bombers, but they weren't taking any chances. Besides, it was good for public reassurance to see cops on the beat. It would be a familiar sight in the frightened region in the days to come.

The September sun was sinking faster in the sky, casting long shadows across the green. But the Minster's façade faced west and was evenly lit by the yellowing light. It toyed with the colours of the remnants of the stained glass in the great shattered window. A steady procession of people were still laying flowers by the war memorial, watched by a couple of police officers who were standing sentry duty on the cordon. Some of the visitors had come from miles away.

One older man summed up what Dan suspected many had been thinking. 'We're in another war, aren't we?' he said quietly. 'Well, we've won them before and we'll win them again.'

Dan wrote the words down and passed them to Craig, who nodded. They would be ideal for the summing up at the end of the programme.

The countdown to the broadcast came fast, as ever. For Craig's opening link, he talked about the attack and the death, injuries and damage it had caused. Nigel panned the camera to find the ruined window. As he did, the sun slipped behind a cloud. Sometimes nature's symbolism defied words.

The interview with the Principal, a Dr Edward Parfitt, was powerful. A scholarly man with a classic pair of teacher's

41

glasses, he talked movingly of the pain of seeing the damage to this wonderful Minster, and also about forgiveness.

'It is the duty of a Christian to forgive,' he said, in a measured voice. 'But sometimes, it can be difficult. This is the hardest case I have ever known. I think it will take some considerable time for myself, and my fellows, to find forgiveness for this appalling act. It strikes at the heart of our nation.'

Craig narrated flawlessly over the pictures of the arrest of Ahmed. The section from Plymouth was also impressive, the area around the house filled with marksmen. The investigation was concentrating on a computer which was kept in the bomber's bedroom. He still had not been officially identified, but the police expected to announce his name later.

Finally came the summing up from the Minster. Craig quoted the man's words about war, and Nigel panned the camera off to end the programme with a shot of the flag flying at half mast.

Lizzie rang and fizzed her delight. Well, almost, Dan thought. That was just his translation. She described the programme as "pretty good", which was stratospheric praise for her. There was always a barb though, and this time it was that he had to stay there to present a live update for the 10.30 bulletin.

That was fine. He'd expected it, always kept an overnight bag in the car ready for stories like this. Plus Dan would have his little revenge. One of Exeter's finest – and most expensive – hotels was on Minster Green. It was of the ilk which had tables laid with glasses and cutlery sufficient for three meals, let alone one, and attendants on hand for every task, bar breathing. But it was the obvious place to stay if they were to make sure they were at the heart of the story.

Dan wondered what they would make of the caveman curmudgeon that was Loud. He would be as incongruous as a tramp at a black-tie dinner.

He called his downstairs neighbour to ask him to look after Rutherford for the night and was about to make for the hotel when the Press Liaison officer called the media around. The forensic search of part of the Minster had been completed. In a quarter of an hour they would be taken inside to film and photograph where the bomb had exploded. There would also be a news conference to update them on the investigation.

Dan caught Nigel's look. A long night was in prospect.

The smell was everywhere. Of the explosion and of death. The acrid tang lingered in the still air of the wounded Minster.

There had been the usual banter as the media pack was led towards the main door. But it quietened as they walked inside. Their footsteps echoed in the cavernous space. As one, their eyes were drawn to the shattered window. The last remnants of the evening light were fading outside, casting a jagged silhouette of the surviving shards of glass.

'Half an hour,' the press officer announced. 'And that's it. We'll do the news conference outside afterwards. Just there, that's where the explosion happened.'

He pointed to a corner at the back of the Minster, by the end of the rows of pews. A flare of photographers' flashes blazed in the dim light. The camera crews began setting up their tripods, filming the spot. All that marked it was a slight shading of the smooth flagstones.

The real story surrounded it. The dark oak of the nearest pews was further blackened by the blast, and pitted and chipped by flying shrapnel. Dan knelt down and studied the surface. A spray of pock marks had been scored from it, scars of lightness in the smooth wood.

The nails had been removed by the police forensics team, but there might still be something worth filming here. Dan squinted hard, ran his hand along the ragged edge and found what he was looking for. A fragment of green glass, a tiny icicle protruding from the bench.

Nigel bent down and filmed a close up. Television always worked best with detail. Dan would write about the shrapnel of broken glass from the bottles, the containers for the chemicals which made up the bomb. If it could cause such damage to the hardy, antique wood, the viewers would be left with no doubt about what it would do to a person.

None of the rest of the pack had noticed it. Some of the other TV reporters were intent on recording addresses to camera, talking about the exact spot where the bomb exploded. It was a classic error of vanity, so common in a trade filled with bloated egos.

If there was still shrapnel damage to the pews, the clean up was by no means complete. There would probably be another legacy of the bomb here too. But it wouldn't be easy to spot in the half light. Dan left Nigel filming the shattered window and paced slowly back and forth. Where else would most visitors congregate?

To his side was a display, some boards bearing the story of the Minster. Dan pretended to tie his shoelace, bent down, checked the flagstones and quickly found what he was looking for. Nigel followed him over, got down on his knees and began filming the dark, misshapen stains.

A side door opened and a tall man walked in carrying a broom. He started sweeping up fragments of glass under the remains of the great window. All the cameras followed him. It was Dr Parfitt.

'How are you feeling?' one of the reporters ventured with the classical clichéd question of the thoughtless hack.

'I'd rather not say,' came the reply. 'Not here, not in this place of God. But what I will tell you is this.'

The Principal waited until he was sure all the cameramen and radio reporters were recording, and the other journalists taking notes. 'We will be cleaning up the Minster as best we can tonight. And we shall be opening to visitors, as usual, at ten o'clock tomorrow morning. We will never be cowed or intimidated. And we will never submit.'

He went on with his sweeping, but refused to answer any more questions. 'That sounded rehearsed to me,' Nigel whispered.

'No kidding,' Dan replied. 'I don't imagine he's the one who usually cleans the Minster, either. But it'll be all over every media outlet going and I bet you that tomorrow the place is the busiest it's ever been. The fund for the repair project will be doing nicely.'

Nigel filmed some more shots of the interior, while Dan did a final check that they had all the pictures they needed. Other journalists were starting to look around to see what else there was to mention in their reports. Some were coming dangerously close to the bloodstains and fragment of glass in the pew.

Dan laid his hand on one of the great fluted pillars. He ran a finger along the cold stone and let out a loud whistle.

'What?' one of the other reporters asked.

Dan pointed to a dark stain on the white surface. 'Look. The force of the blast even reached here.'

The press posse gathered around it and started photographing and filming, the newspaper reporters writing descriptions. They were all intent on what looked to Dan like nothing more than a perfectly natural and very long-standing flaw in the historic stone.

As they filed out of the Minster, Dan started to feel guilty at his flippancy on such a sombre day. He worked his way to the front of the pack, paused at the door and made a very public show of placing ten pounds in the contributions chest. The other hacks had little choice but to follow.

For the half past ten bulletin, Dan re-cut his report, starting with the new pictures inside the Minster and including the blood and fragment of shrapnel. Combined with the damage to the window, and the interviews with the eyewitnesses, it gave the viewers a stark sense of what had happened.

They'd even managed to get something to eat. Nigel had found a kind landlord in a pub along the green who'd agreed to allow his staff to bring them food and drinks in the satellite van. It was the first time Dan had enjoyed waiter service as he worked. Even Loud was impressed, until he bit too hard at a bread roll and hurt his damaged tooth.

The Deputy Chief Constable had held another short media briefing to give an update on the case. The person killed in the bombing was a woman and from the local area, but the police were not yet naming her as all her family had not been told. One other person was seriously hurt, as was the bomber himself. Another 22 had more minor injuries.

The first reports of many people being killed were inaccurate, as was often the case. Exaggeration was one of the dangers of a disaster. Dreadful as the attack was, it could have been much worse.

Aside from the bomber, another man had been arrested in connection with the attack and was now in custody. As Flood spoke, a couple of the other hacks cast irritated glances at Dan. He just about managed to keep a straight face. Word went around fast when you had a scoop, particularly one as impressive as an arrest by armed police, and journalists were jealous creatures.

Once again, Flood saved until last the most dramatic part of the statement.

'I am now in a position to reveal the bomber's name to you. He is John Tanton, a schoolboy from the Stonehouse area of Plymouth. He will be formally questioned when doctors tell us he is well enough. His house is currently being searched.'

The press conference ended and the reporters picked up their mobiles, began filing the information to their newsrooms. But Dan just stood there.

Nigel reached out a hand and placed it on his shoulder. 'You OK?'

'Yeah. It's just – John Tanton. I think I've met him. I reckon he was at some prize-giving ceremony I did a year or so ago. I'm pretty sure I met his Mum. Alison was her name. She's a businesswoman. We got on well. She even gave me her phone number and said if ever I needed help on a business story to call her.'

Nigel whistled to himself. 'That could be useful.'

'Yeah, to say the least.'

After the broadcast they walked wearily along to the hotel. Dan sat with Nigel and Loud for a beer, to calm down after a chaotic day. It tasted good. He drank one, then another, was about to have a third when he saw Nigel's look.

Dan made an excuse about feeling tired and went up to bed, quietly ordering a double whisky from room service on the way. The suite was more luxurious than any he'd ever slept in before. It even had a choice of pillows, boasting the feathers of an impressive range of birds.

Some good sleeping was required and the white duck pillows and whisky would help. That was all it was, just medicinal, nothing more. Dan sipped at the amber liquid and enjoyed its smooth burn. He found himself staring at the empty glass. That was the problem with spirits. They disappeared too quickly.

He thought about ordering another, but decided against it. Tomorrow would be filled with reporting a follow-up to the bombing and promised to be just as busy as today. He might even be able to get an exclusive interview with Alison Tanton.

Or then again, maybe another little dram wouldn't be so bad. He deserved it, after that day.

The porter must have misheard the order. He brought a double by mistake. Ah well, it would be churlish to complain.

Funnily enough, the same happened with the next measure Dan called for. Perhaps it was the hotel's way, to make sure the guests were comfortable.

It too vanished quickly. It must be the heat of the room, making the liquid evaporate.

Dan debated having one more for the road, or for the bed, but he was already feeling light-headed. He plumped up the luxurious softness of the pillow and was about to turn off his mobile when it rang. Adam.

'Just a quick call to let you know about tomorrow,' he said. 'I take it you're staying in Exeter?'

'Yep.'

'Me too. Can you come to Heavitree Road Police Station at nine for a briefing?'

'Yep. Any news on the investigation?'

'Yeah. Some good and bad.'

'In what way?'

'The spooks are here. FX5, that lot. They've been here all afternoon, in fact.'

'That was quick.'

'A couple of their officers were at some liaison meeting near Bristol. They came straight down.'

'They'll be a help, surely?'

Adam sounded far from convinced. 'Maybe.'

'Meaning?'

'I've had dealings with them before. In any terrorist case it's supposed to be handled by the local force, with them in an "advisory" role.'

'But?'

'But, I've never known spooks manage to limit themselves to advice in their shady little lives. They're not exactly good at taking a back seat.'

'Turf wars?'

'Oh yes. And they're already well underway.'

'What about the rest of the case?'

'We tried to question Ahmed, but he wants a specialist solicitor and we can't get one until the morning. That's OK. We're sure now there are no more bombers out there. I've found him the coldest, most uncomfortable cell I can. He is a strange one.'

'In what way?'

'Terrorist suspects almost always stay silent. It's drilled into them by their handlers that it's the best way to frustrate interrogation. But not Ahmed. He's already been railing against the police. "A despicable tool of a disgusting state", he called me. And when he saw Claire ...'

The world stopped. Claire.

She was part of the case. Of course she was. She always worked with Adam. And Greater Wessex Police needed all the detectives it had on this one. But still, somehow the news was an ambush of emotion.

Claire.

He hadn't seen her for five months. Since that last, vitriolic night.

Flaming words in the darkness.

When he'd finally found the resolution to call her, and their midnight meeting.

And the things they'd said. And then shouted, and screamed. The toxic, searing words.

And now he was about to see her again. In the midst of a

48

high-profile and intense investigation.

Claire.

Dan was vaguely aware that Adam was still speaking. 'Well, Ahmed certainly didn't like Claire. He practically hissed at her, called her a harlot, a slut, and a whore, just for having the cheek to be wearing a short-sleeved shirt. So, that's the sort of thing we're up against. See you in the morning.'

It took a few seconds before Dan realised his friend had hung up. He turned off the phone and lay back on the bed. Tomorrow, for the first time in months he would see Claire, and he would be working closely with her in the days ahead.

Claire.

And he would be facing an extremist suspected of radicalising a schoolboy and turning him into a terrorist, one who attempted mass murder by bombing a sacred building. It was the biggest case he had ever worked on, not to mention a huge story.

Dan closed his eyes and tried to sleep. But he knew there was little chance of that. He was too aware of a sense of the extraordinary events to come.

Chapter Six

LYING AWAKE, KNOWING YOU'RE tired, but being unable to sleep is one of the meanest sufferings life can inflict. The harder you try to reach the elusive paradise of blissful unconsciousness, the more determined it seems to be to evade you.

Dan found himself tracing the dark patterns of the wallpaper, and studying the details of the plasterwork on the ceiling. Several times he got up, sipped at some water, shifted the thick drape of the curtain and stared out at the Minster, lit only now by a slice of the moon. A solitary policeman paced a bored guard beside the shattered window.

The stairs creaked with the night sounds of the porter, or the occasional late or restless guest. The odd footfall passed by outside, but otherwise all was quiet.

The thick pile of the carpet reminded Dan of the options to help him rest, and he finally opted for some swan-feather pillows. But despite their comfort, and the softness of the hotel bed, the warmth of the room and the mellowness of the décor, Dan only managed to secure a few hours sleep before dawn.

He finally did so by concentrating on how many laps of the hotel pool he would swim come the morning, and what a pyramid of a plate he would pile up from the breakfast buffet as a reward.

But both delights were to be denied Dan. It clearly wasn't his week.

He was woken just after half past six by the phone ringing. It was the early producer. There had been a violent assault overnight on an innocent Muslim in Plymouth, and a graffiti attack on the city's biggest mosque. The police believed both were connected to yesterday's bombing of the Minster. Lizzie required him to cover the stories, along with any other follow-ups that might surface during the day.

Dan would have argued, but knew there was no point. Disputing with Lizzie was like trying to take on a frigate in a rowing boat. He would have to miss Adam's briefing, but with luck he could get back to Exeter later to join the investigation. Being in Plymouth would also give him a chance to get in touch with Alison Tanton.

There was another advantage in that seeing Claire again would be delayed. She had stalked almost all his sleepless night-time thoughts.

He'd even got up at one point and debated whether his feelings meant it would be possible for him to join the investigation. All his instincts were to do so; it was only the fear of seeing Claire which held him back. Dan found a piece of paper on the bedside table, divided it roughly in half and made a list of pros and cons.

The positives filled the left side of the sheet.

> *You love helping the police, it's been a new life for you, you think of yourself as an amateur detective, you're good at it, you've helped to solve cases before, Adam wants – perhaps even needs – you, you could do some real good, help to find the people who radicalised a young man – led him to kill – bring them to justice, get great insights and exclusives for your reports,* and finally – *IT'S THE RIGHT THING TO DO, STUPID!*

On the cons side was simply, *Claire.*

How one small word could carry such weight. Dan sighed to himself and got back into bed.

The early morning did bring one gift of luck. He'd missed it last night, but on the window was a small schooner of sherry, a present to welcome guests to the room. That was four-star treatment, all right. Dan poured it out into a glass. It would do nicely in lieu of breakfast. It was a one-off, a little tipple to fortify himself for the day, that was all.

The phone rang again. The producer had forgotten to mention Lizzie's explicit command that he wasn't to wait around in Exeter and enjoy a leisurely breakfast, but was to head straight back to Plymouth. A wash was acceptable, but that was the limit of the luxuries in which Dan was permitted to indulge himself.

He interlaced some forthright comments into a long yawn, got up and knocked on Nigel's and Loud's doors. The awakening engineer looked even more disconcerting than usual, with his hair and beard so dishevelled they resembled an aura. He was holding his jaw and still muttering about the malevolent tooth. Nigel was already up and reading a newspaper. Being a father of two young lads made a lie-in bed a long forgotten pleasure, he explained.

The paper's headline was "The Sickest Outrage", a picture of the shattered window of the Minster underneath it.

It wasn't the most eloquent piece of graffiti, but the writer had obviously been dedicated to making the point. And for emphasis that point had been made repeatedly, perhaps even obsessively.

Dan was reminded of one of Adam's favourite little musings. Ignorance isn't as common amongst criminals as most people think, the detective would often say, particularly when they were confronted by an investigation where the felon had selfishly left little in the way of clues.

It's certainly the case that many people who commit crimes are amongst the more intellectually challenged, their acts often opportunist or just simply thuggish. The courts are filled daily with their wretched procession. But, the man Dan had come to think of – quietly – as the philosopher detective, would say, take the example of the much-vaunted chip and pin technology, which was supposed to put an end to credit- and debit-card fraud. Nothing like it. It merely opened a new field of criminality. The system, which the great ranks of the gullible public was assured was nigh on foolproof, was cracked by thieves almost as soon as it was unveiled.

And so it has been with cashpoints and internet banking and just about any innovation, the security standards of which were promised to be mighty and impassable. Criminals apparently see them as challenges, and ones to which they never fail to rise.

The pickings in the shadowlands are too lucrative. Crime doesn't pay is a comforting mantra for the law-abiding majority. But it is lamentably far from the truth.

There is though one area of lawlessness where ignorance always prevails, Adam's argument ran, and that is with hate crime. Be it homophobic, racist or vented against people with disabilities or religious faith, it is invariably the product of not just misunderstanding, but having no desire whatsoever to even try to understand.

These thoughts slid across Dan's mind as he stood behind Nigel, watching his friend's back as he filmed the graffiti on the mosque. The message was straightforward, and gave the police an obvious clue that on this occasion they weren't looking for a master criminal.

BASTERD TERORISTS

The words had been sprayed in red, in letters several feet high, and had been repeated on as many spaces of wall as the vandal could find. The final attempt had either been interrupted, or the offender had run short of paint.

BASTERD TERORI

It was the sort of attack which would usually have been ignored by the media. But after yesterday's bombing, and the assault on a Muslim last night, it encapsulated a fear that the police, local authorities and minority communities themselves had all felt, but none voiced, in case it precipitated that which they had now witnessed. An upsurge in hate crime.

It was just after nine o'clock on another fine September day. The morning light was shining from the red brick of the Islamic Centre. It was a long, squat building, looked like a standard 1960s masterpiece, which had been converted as a focal point for Plymouth's growing Muslim community.

As they parked outside, Dan called Adam to apologise for being unable to make the briefing. He'd received a strange response.

'That might be a blessing. I'll talk to you later.'

Dan couldn't stop himself asking the question. 'Is it about Claire? Doesn't she want me there? Is that it?'

'No. It's nothing to do with Claire. It's far more murky. I can't talk to you now. I'll call you later.'

'Any news on the case?'

'I think we've found the vital clue. It's just a question of making it stick to our suspect.'

'What clue?'

'I reckon our radicaliser was in Exeter at the time of the bombing.'

'Ahmed, you mean? But you know he was there. You arrested him.'

'Possibly it was Ahmed, but we've got a problem with that theory. We could be looking for someone else. Someone who couldn't resist coming along to see their little protégé carrying out his deadly work.'

'Like who?'

'Well, it would have to be someone who knew John Tanton – and knew him well.'

'Who? Adam, what are you talking about?'

'Later! I've got to go.'

Dan was left staring at his phone and wondering what was going on. He'd have to get back to Exeter later. The investigation was moving fast.

A caretaker emerged from the doors of the mosque. He was carrying a bucket and brush and began scrubbing at the graffiti. Nigel swung the camera and started filming. A few photographers were also taking snaps, Dirty El amongst them. His chubby and freckled face was usually set in a sleazy grin, particularly at the scent of a big story and the prospect of good money to be made, but today El was looking oddly glum.

'What's up with you?' Dan asked. 'I'd have thought you'd be wallowing in this one.'

El nodded over his shoulder in a furtive manner, lumbered along the road, and Dan followed. It was only when they were well away from the other media the photographer said, 'That attack on the Minster. It …'

'Yes?'

'It, well …'

'Yes?'

El looked genuinely at a loss, a state which was almost a story in itself. 'Well, it's got to me.'

'Got to you?'

'Yeah.'

Dan couldn't keep the bafflement from his voice. 'You mean, as in you're suffering an emotion?'

'Yeah.'

'Even – an empathy? For the people who suffered, and the damage to the Minster?'

El's glumness intensified. 'Don't take the mick. That's exactly what I mean.'

He fiddled distractedly with his camera and lowered his voice to the most confidential of whispers. 'Did I ever tell you I was religious as a kid? Me parents sent me to Sunday school and all that. I grew out of it, but I've always had this thing for the church. I reckon that's what's done me in. That, or I'm losing me edge. It's got me well worried.'

Dan was too surprised to reply. The revelation that the infamous Dirty El, acknowledged master of sleaze and low tricks, might have some small and shrivelled corner of his mind which nonetheless hosted the shrunken remains of what was once a conscience was almost too much to take in.

He was about to try to find some words of reassurance when the wooden doors opened again and a tall, heavily built man wearing a black suit stepped outside.

'The Imam will see you,' he announced.

Dan and Nigel took off their shoes and were led up a staircase to a large office. The Imam was working at a desk. He was wearing a stark white robe. The man in black stood beside him and folded his arms, but didn't speak.

He'd obviously chosen the suit to emphasise his physique, which was impressive to the point of being over-inflated. The jacket was struggling hard to contain his muscles. As for other issues of fashion, his taste in colour was noticeably limited. To match the black suit, he wore a black shirt and black tie. His shoes were also black. On the walk up the stairs, Dan had noted that even his socks were black.

He was tempted to ask if the man also wore black Y-fronts, but suspected the joke wouldn't be appreciated.

They waited. The Imam's pen scratched at some paper. The occasional deep breath emerged from the block of humanity as the air completed its long and wearying passage around his lungs. Still they waited, static and silent. It was almost comical. Finally, the man at the desk looked up and gave them a warm smile.

'Imam Tahir Aziz,' announced the man in black loudly. He stood up and they shook hands. He was small and slight, his white robe giving him a ghostlike presence.

'And my assistant is Abdul Omah,' the Imam replied, in a gentle voice. There was another round of hand-shaking, the man's grip making Dan wince.

'It is not our way to speak out,' the Imam began. 'We try to live a quiet and modest life. But given the events of yesterday, I believe we have no choice. I am prepared to go on your television station and answer the questions you wish to put to me.'

Nigel began setting up the camera, watched carefully by Abdul.

'Thank you,' Dan replied, taking out his notebook. 'What is it you wanted to say?'

'I need to tell you that Islam is a peaceful religion. We utterly denounce terrorism. Those who choose that path, and claim the backing of our faith for it, are entirely incorrect and utterly misguided. The Koran preaches the greatest respect for life.'

'And yet some do choose that path?'

Dan was aware the man in black had taken a step towards him and was now uncomfortably close. He shifted on his chair.

The Imam's smile didn't falter. 'What is your religion?'

'I'm afraid I don't have one.'

'Then were you born into a faith?'

'Catholicism.'

'And you would say it's a peaceful religion?'

'Yes.'

'Yet it was responsible for dreadful persecutions in the Inquisition.'

'Which was hundreds of years ago.'

'And not so long ago, did not many in Northern Ireland claim the faith as the basis for their terrorism?'

'I think there was a little more to it than that.'

The Imam spread his arms. 'My point precisely. There is always more to it. Any person may take any belief, twist it in their minds and use it as justification for their actions. It is the nature of the weakness of man. But it does not change the fact that Islam is a religion of peace and tolerance. We may have different ways to many in the western world, but we can disagree, yet still live side by side.'

The large man in black emitted a low grunt. The Imam gave him a fond look. 'Abdul is a little less accommodating than me. He finds many western habits difficult to take. But he is still a man of peace too.'

Another grunt from the dark rectangle.

The sunlight was beaming through the windows, straight into Dan's face. He blinked hard and shifted on his chair again. Abdul moved too, so that he remained just a little too close. He had a dense presence like the air before a storm.

'I'm ready and rolling,' said Nigel, cheerfully. The man in black took a couple of paces back until he was by Tahir's side and folded his arms once more. They made an odd pair, everything about them a contrast, from their clothes to their build.

Dan was about to phrase a question, but the Imam spoke first. 'This is what I am willing to tell you. All true Muslims condemn yesterday's bombing as strongly as anyone else. We believe terrorism is an evil which must be eradicated and we will do all we can to help the police in that. We ask for no more attacks on our mosque, or our followers. We simply wish to live in peace together.'

Dan nodded. 'Did you know the bomber, John Tanton?'

'I am not prepared to discuss that.'

'Did he ever come here to the mosque?'

'I am not prepared to discuss that.'

'Another man has been arrested on suspicion of radicalising him, a man called Ahmed Nazri. Did you know him, or did he come here?'

'I am not prepared to discuss that.'

'Did you know the man who was attacked last night?'

'That too I am not prepared to discuss.'

Dan nudged Nigel and he stopped recording. It was hopeless. The Imam had adopted the old politician's trick. He had one message he wanted to spread, so that was the only thing he was going to say. He might not be a fan of western culture, but he wasn't above adopting one of its tactics.

They packed up the equipment and prepared to leave. Dan remembered the earlier conversation with Adam. The words had stayed in his mind – to find the radicaliser they were looking for someone who knew John Tanton, and who was in Exeter at the time of the bombing.

Questions, as ever it was down to questions. The arts of both detective and journalist were all based on asking the right questions. But the Imam was far too sophisticated for a direct approach.

'What did you think when you heard about the bomb attack?' Dan said conversationally as they made for the stairs, closely escorted by the looming black mass.

The Imam's smile faded. 'I was deeply shocked.'

'And what did you do at a time like that? Did you gather everyone here around to talk about it?'

Tahir studied him impassively. Dan was almost sure he understood the point of the question. He wondered if he would be getting an answer.

'I was not here at the time,' the Imam said finally. He paused and laced his hands together, then added, 'By sheer coincidence – quite remarkable chance – both myself and Abdul were in Exeter for a meeting with the trustees of the mosque there. It was indeed an extraordinary coincidence.'

Dan reached for the door, but hesitated. The word *coincidence* danced up and down the stairs in the narrow corridor.

The mosque was Plymouth's biggest and busiest. It was likely, to say the least, that Tanton worshipped here. Which meant Tahir and Abdul could both know him. And both were in Exeter yesterday.

Dan found his thoughts interrupted by the door being pushed open, and a less than gentle hand from Abdul ushering him out.

Chapter Seven

NIGEL AND DAN WALKED blinking in the sunlight to find an already difficult morning had decided to bless them with a new set of problems. On the pavement, opposite the Islamic Centre, was a small demonstration by the British People's Party.

A dozen people, mostly older, but a couple of younger men and women too, stood, staring from behind a wall of placards. They were all alike, stamped with the party's logo, and each read, *Britain for the British*.

It was a strangely quiet and static protest. None of the banners waved and there was no chanting, but the expressions of the people were intent with implacable hostility. All glared at the mosque, as if its temerity to even dare to exist was an affront to the very principles of civilisation, and the power of their resentment would be sufficient to see it turn to dust before them.

From the passing cars came the odd supportive hoot of a horn, but there were many more obscene gestures as fingers waved angrily out of windows.

One of the men walked over to Dan and held out a hand. He hesitated, then shook it.

'Norman Kindle, BPP Regional Organiser,' came a deep and confident voice. 'As I recall, the law says you broadcasters have to cover stories fairly. Every significant strand of opinion must be aired. We got ten per cent and more in some wards around here in the last local elections.'

He pointed over to the Islamic Centre. 'They got to do their bit. I'd like to do mine.'

The man was looking at him expectantly. Dan gave Nigel a nod, and he slowly walked over and began filming the demonstration. The cameraman would normally play a crowd, chat to them, jokingly ask them to show their best side or say that Hollywood would be on the phone the moment the story went out, but this time he went about his work without saying a word.

Kindle watched, then smiled, checked his appearance in a car window and rejoined the demonstration. Across the road, Abdul stood watching from the doors of the centre, his arms folded across his chest. A couple of the protesters whispered to each other, pointed and shook their heads.

A police car drew up, two officers climbing quickly out and donning their hats. One stood by the demonstration, the other outside the Islamic Centre.

'To keep our little foreign friends nice and safe,' came a mocking voice from the crowd. 'Where are you when old ladies are getting mugged, eh? You should be ashamed of your bloody selves.'

One of the police officers fixed the woman with a long look, but didn't reply.

Nigel stood up from the camera. 'I've got enough pictures. The cops on guard, wide shots of the demo, close ups of the placards. You should have heard what some of them were saying about …'

Dan held up a hand. 'No thanks. I can guess.'

'Are we really going to interview them?'

'What choice do we have? They got enough votes in the last election to have a party political broadcast. And our job's about free speech. There's no asterisk by the side of that marked *only so long as we agree with what's being said.*

Kindle walked over. 'My turn then, I think. Where do you want me?'

Nigel positioned him so the demonstration was in the background. He was a tall man, probably in his late thirties, well-dressed and so clean-shaven that there wasn't a hint of a nascent hair trying to colour the surface of his skin. His suit and overcoat looked expensive, and the rich scent of a fine cologne drifted in the air around him.

'What's your first question then?' he asked.

'It'll be something about – why the demo?' Dan replied.

'Something about? Come on, what is it really?'

'It'll be along those lines. I can't say exactly how I'll phrase it.'

Kindle nodded slowly, took one more check on how he was

looking, smoothed his hair and turned to the camera.

'This demonstration is irresponsibly provocative at a time of considerable tension, isn't it?' Dan began.

'We in the BPP believe in fighting to keep the traditional character of Britain. We also believe in fairness,' Kindle replied smoothly. 'We think there are too many immigrants, and they're being given benefits, housing, health treatment and education ahead of the people who have inhabited this proud island for thousands of years. That is simply unfair and wrong.'

'An interesting coincidence you should be here after the graffiti attack on the Mosque, some may think?' Dan countered.

'A coincidence is all it is. We in the BPP would never advocate breaking the law. However, we do say this. We can understand the frustrations of many of the people of this country boiling up as immigrants take over. They see their beloved nation changing around them, without anyone having the care to ask what they think. We can understand how that may spill over into making a statement like this.'

'You agree with equating Muslims with terrorists then?'

'We say only that the facts speak for themselves. A young man walked into one of our most beautiful and sacred buildings yesterday and killed and injured innocent people in the name of Islam after being radicalised by Muslims. I don't feel I need to comment any further.'

'And what would you say to all the Muslims who pride themselves on being peaceful, count themselves as British as you do, and are shocked by the attack?'

'I doubt they could ever count themselves as British as me, or the vast majority of the population of these islands. We have a proud Anglo-Saxon and Christian heritage, a tradition of tolerance, and we in the BPP believe in keeping the country that way – the way it should be.'

Dan tried a couple more questions but got exactly the same responses. He gestured to Nigel to end the interview. One of the police officers began walking along the line of protesters. He tried asking a couple how long the group planned to stay, but got only monosyllabic answers.

'Enjoy the media training course, did you?' Dan asked, as Nigel switched off the camera.

Kindle shrugged. 'I don't know what you mean.'

'Come off it. The BPP aren't going to allow just anyone on air. And your clothes could have come out of the TV-friendly catalogue. It's hammered into you that the most important factor in how the audience perceives you is appearance.'

Another shrug.

'And as for your answers – short, sharp, and resolutely "on message",' Dan went on. 'Designed to appeal to your supporters and any others who may have a sympathetic ear. And for future reference – asking what the first question is, that's a dead giveaway.'

Kindle didn't look flustered at all. 'I'll take that little rant as your way of saying I did pretty well in the interview, then. And anyway, what's the matter with wanting to do your best? When it's something you believe in? Well, whatever, no hard feelings.'

He stretched out his hand. Dan hesitated once more.

'Come on, I bet you shook hands with that lot in the mosque.'

Dan reached out slowly and made a brief contact. Nigel turned away and busied himself polishing the camera's lens. A car roared past, the man in the passenger seat screaming abuse at the demonstration. Several banners waved in reply.

Kindle waited for Nigel to take the camera off the tripod and put the lens cap on, then said quietly, 'I knew John Tanton, you know.'

Dan was about to head for his car, but stopped. 'Really?'

The BPP man leaned back on a wall. Now the business of the interview was done, he had become chatty, almost friendly.

'I didn't want to say in the interview, too much danger of mixed messages, but I help run the local kids' football clubs. John used to come along and play. He was a good goalkeeper. A nice lad too. But he was always a bit of a loner, never had too many friends or that much confidence. I reckon if someone came along and pretended to be his mate, indoctrinated him, gave him a mission, he would have been vulnerable to being

63

radicalised.'

'Any chance of saying that on camera?'

Kindle shook his head knowingly. 'No thanks. I've done my bit.'

Dan thanked Kindle and picked up his mobile to call Adam when he remembered another question he should ask. But as with the Imam, it would have to be done surreptitiously.

'I guess this is one of those stories we'll all remember where we were when we heard the news of the bombing,' Dan said in as relaxed a way as he could manage. 'Where were you?'

Kindle didn't show any hint of suspicion. 'I was on a day off. Funnily enough, I was over in Exeter, doing some shopping.'

Dan watched thoughtfully as he walked back to the demonstration. Kindle was a long shot. Why would someone from the BPP be interested in radicalising a young man to commit a bombing outrage in the name of Islam? Surely only in an attempt to spread racial disharmony and stir anger and resentment.

It was far-fetched, but not impossible. In the years working with Adam, he'd seen stranger.

It wasn't bad for an hour's journalism and unofficial police work. They now had film and interviews sufficient for a story, and three more suspects ripe for investigation.

Dan drove back to the studios, Nigel following. It was only a quarter past ten. He could sit down for quarter of an hour, read a newspaper and have a cup of coffee and some toast before editing the report. He would also call Alison Tanton. That would be the interview to get.

Dan yawned hard and rubbed at his aching eyes. The car mirror suggested they were sporting an unattractive hint of bloodshot and were supported by dark crescents. A break would be very welcome.

He should have known better. Empathy and sympathy were a delightful couple who not only had Lizzie never entertained, she had erected notices around her personality stating they'd be most unwelcome visitors. Dan only just had time to park when he heard the ominous clicking of fast stilettos striding across the tarmac. Nigel heard it too and ducked back into his car, but Dan was caught in the killing ground of his editor's machine gun list of demands.

This was an unpleasant first. Lizzie often sprung her ambushes when a reporter walked into the newsroom, but never before had she been known to come down to the car park to pounce.

'What the hell are you doing back here?' was her welcoming opening gambit.

Dan opened his mouth to find some justification, but the growing words were swept away in the breaking storm. Any attempts at defence were as effective as whispering at thunder.

'One of the biggest stories we've ever had and you're slinking back here! Get out there and cover it. I want everything you can give us. I want interviews. I want the injured blubbing at the horror of what happened. I want the cops telling us how they're getting on with the hunt for the radicaliser. I want it all and I want it good.'

'We've just done the Islamic Centre …'

'Bravo. Whoopee.' A sharpened fingernail began a rhythmic jabbing, her dark hair flying in time. 'That's a start. But all the action's at the Minster. Get back there. Get going. I want a live broadcast for lunch. I want a report. I want tears and shock and outrage.'

A small group of people had gathered outside the canteen to watch the verbal mugging. Lizzie in full flow was a celebrated spectacle, on the proviso the hapless victim wasn't yourself. It was pure schadenfreude, a modern day equivalent of going to watch Christians being thrown to the lions.

He didn't argue. It was pointless. Dan got resignedly back into his car and drove off.

As he passed under the trees that surrounded the exit, an unseen bird let loose a dropping, right onto the centre of the windscreen.

How quickly can news pass into history.

The Minster was open and as busy as Dan had expected, but around it people came and went, just as they had before yesterday's bombing and probably would for the next thousand years or more. Some cast glances over at the ruined window, a few stopped to stare, but most just got on with their lives.

Loud's sullen face warmed into a rare smile at the sight of Dan and Nigel. 'You got lumbered with coming back too then,' he clucked. 'Me tooth's still hurting, if you're interested enough to care.'

Dan handed him the tape, sat down on the step of the Outside Broadcast van, steeled himself and found Alison Tanton's name in his contacts book. Like most good journalists, he rarely discarded a number. You never knew when it would be useful again. Early in Dan's career he'd got into the habit of noting down the names and numbers of all the people he'd spoken to that day in a large, and now very tattered old book. It was filled with memories.

The phone rang and rang until the answer machine kicked in. Dan briefly debated whether to leave a message, then did so. He wondered if she would call back, given all she must be going through. The chances had to be against it, but it was worth a try. Every hack in the country would be trying to contact her.

Partly to spite Lizzie, but mostly for himself, on the way over to Exeter Dan had stopped off at his flat to give Rutherford a quick cuddle. It was odd how much he missed the dog when he was forced to spend nights away. Rutherford did his whirling and yelping dance of delight at the appearance of his errant master.

'Promise you I'll be home tonight,' Dan told him. 'And we'll go out for a walk, no matter how late it is.'

He closed the door, convinced that Rutherford had put on his smiling face and couldn't help grinning too. What a fine companion the dog was, always there for him, always delighted to see him, never a hint of reproach nor ever liable to make a sudden decision that their relationship was over. Not like …

Dan stopped the thought before it grew. He would see her soon enough, when he rejoined the investigation.

You going to write this report then?' came the sullen voice of Loud. 'Or just stand there daydreaming?'

'I was thinking about how to put it together,' Dan replied, not altogether convincingly.

They started the edit. As he was tired and struggling to concentrate it would be best to keep the broadcast simple. In the live scene set, Dan would stand in front of the Minster's façade and talk about the aftermath of the attack, the great building reopening in a show of defiance. Then the studio would cut to his report. Finally he would sum up by talking about the police continuing to question a man in connection with radicalising John Tanton, but also that they were following other lines of investigation.

He began the report with the graffiti on the Mosque, wrote about how the bombing had heightened racial tensions, and also mentioned the attack on the Muslim man. He had been fortunate and escaped with only cuts and bruises. They used the clip of the Imam, talking about Islam being a religion of peace and denouncing the attack.

After that Dan used the pictures of the BPP demonstration and some of Kindle's interview, when he spoke of disagreeing with people breaking the law, but understanding their frustrations. He'd gone through it with Lizzie who agreed the party had to be given their say. *Wessex Tonight* would get complaints, but that was the nature of being a news broadcaster in a democracy.

The Minster's bells struck one. Dan sat on a bench in the easy autumn sunshine and gave himself a few minutes to unwind. It had been a busy but relatively smooth morning. He wondered what the afternoon would bring. Life inevitably moved fast on a big story.

His mobile rang. Alison Tanton's number was flashing on the display.

'Hello, Dan.' A gulp, then another. 'This will have to be a quick call. I'm at the hospital, hoping to see John. They haven't let me yet. He's been badly injured and there are lots of police here, guarding him.'

'I'm sorry, Alison. For you, and all that's gone on.'

A quick rush of breath, then a tumble of words. 'I knew he was interested in Islam and talking about becoming a Muslim, but I thought it was just a phase. He didn't show any signs of ... well ...'

Her voice broke. 'Look, you were very kind, coming along to the Prize Day and giving out the awards. John went on about it for weeks afterwards. I would like to talk to you about what's happened, but can it wait a few days? I hardly know what I'm doing with myself at the moment.'

'Yes, of course. Alison, one more thing – all the other reporters will be wanting to talk to you, and ...'

'Don't worry,' she interrupted. 'I won't be talking to them. I'll give you a ring, or call me within a day or two.'

Dan thanked her and hung up. He sat, staring at the Minster. Her voice sounded so fragile. He remembered the Prize Day, how she was wearing what was obviously a new suit, and her pride at John being given an award for the efforts he had made that year. He was a quiet lad, a little overweight, with a trusting face, painfully nervous as he walked on to the old wooden stage. His school tie was an inch askew and his hand trembling and sweaty to shake.

Dan shook his head, got up and walked back to the satellite truck. It was time to get ready for the live broadcast. His mobile rang again. Adam.

The detective's voice was sharp and urgent. The familiar sound of trouble.

'You back in Exeter?'

'Yes.'

'Good. I need to see you this afternoon. As soon as possible. We've got real problems.'

Chapter Eight

ADAM'S TERSE INSISTENCE WAS sufficient to override the need for a decent lunch. Dan grabbed an unappetising-looking roll from a café, along with a piece of cake to bridge the taste deficit, and walked across Minster Green towards Heavitree Road police station.

It was warm enough for the lawns to be filled with people enjoying their lunch hours in the sunshine of the early days of autumn. Students sat in a group, some juggling balls and clubs with a conspicuous lack of success. But, being students, they still had the cheek to pass a hat around, and being the kind folk of Devon, plenty of people donated some change. Dan tipped in a few fragments of silver. At least it would stop that annoying jingling as he marched.

He noticed he no longer felt tired, but wasn't surprised. He was rejoining Adam on another extraordinary case. Again he would attempt to straddle the twin worlds of reporting on a crime and secretly helping with the investigation. It was a heady mix.

As Dan had expected, he had to field a call from the newsroom. Lizzie professed herself "satisfied" with lunchtime's broadcast, but quickly launched into a series of demands for tonight. She wanted another report, plus a live interview to follow. Dan popped into the Minster office and had a word with Reverend Parfitt's secretary. Yes, the Principal was available later and would be happy to grace the airwaves again.

That was predictable. The Minster was busier today than Dan had ever known it. Another plug of publicity would do no harm at all. It was fair enough. In the modern money-obsessed world, even men of God had to have an eye for the finances.

A couple of crows hopped and stalked across the green, pecking at the remnants of a picnic which had spilled from a bin. A young child balanced carefully on the low wall that divided the lawns from the cobbled old street. Streams of shoppers slipped past, proudly holding bags boasting of a legion of designers.

Life went on. Come what may, it always did.

As it would for him. He should be able to get home for about half past seven, ready to take Rutherford for a run around the park. He had promised, and it would happen. Dan grinned at the thought of his dog lolloping across Hartley Park, sniffing around the trees.

There was just the one nagging itch in his easing mind. The usual one, the standard one, the ever-present one. It was quite likely Claire would be at the police station. Perhaps working on a computer in the incident room, or on the phone, talking to potential witnesses. No doubt wearing one of her familiar black trouser suits, the dark ruffle of her bob as attractive as ever.

Dan crossed a main road, patted his hair into place and tried not to notice the patches where it was thinning. He was almost at the police station. He began rehearsing what he would say when the inevitable finally happened and they met again.

Heavitree Road police station is a slug of a building. Long and low, it bends around the thoroughfare from which it gets its name. Only a perfunctory patch of downtrodden grass outside the entrance softens its austerity, and even then not by a great deal. It has much the same soothing effect as trying to make someone comfortable as they're tied to a post, waiting for the firing squad.

The reception is just as unwelcoming, a less than fetching mix of concrete and plate glass. Adam was waiting there, pacing back and forth. He quickly took Dan's arm and led him back out of the door.

'We can't talk here,' he muttered. 'The place is probably bugged.'

They found a café, just down the road, towards the bus station. The chipped plastic tables were stained with the rings of scores of tea and coffee mugs. It would once have been filled with more smoke than an 80s pop concert, but now instead the doorway was circled with a throng of social lepers, all puffing away.

70

Dan nodded to himself. For years, he had railed against the injustice of smoking being permitted in public places, his hair and clothes, eyes and lungs continually tormented by the foul fumes. The sight of the outcasts of the smoking ban never failed to cheer him. It was a spectacle best enjoyed in the cold months of howling wind and driving rain, but that time would come around soon enough. It was one of the few benefits of the winter.

He bought a couple of cups of tea and carried them to a table at the back of the café where Adam had positioned himself. 'Counter surveillance,' the detective said meaningfully. 'I want to be able to keep an eye on who's coming and going.'

Dan didn't know what to say, so sat down and took out his notebook. A dusty rubber plant had been positioned on the windowsill, the place's sole attempt at contriving a relaxed atmosphere.

Adam was scanning around, his eyes constantly shifting from the door to the window. There was only one other customer inside the café, an elderly woman who was hunched over a newspaper, coughing gently to herself, oblivious of the world. The detective studied her carefully, then relaxed.

'OK, I reckon we're safe.'

Dan also took a look around. 'Err, yeah,' he said. 'I can't spot any immediate deadly perils. That old woman looks a bad one, but if both of us stick together we can probably handle her.'

Adam gave him a reproachful look. 'Don't joke. Things have changed. No one knows what's going on, or who to believe any more. The case has become a smoke and shadows world.'

It could only have been more melodramatic if an unseen orchestra had provided a sudden musical sting. Dan folded his arms. 'Perhaps you'd better explain.'

'Yeah.' Adam took another quick look around, leaned forwards and lowered his voice to an almost imperceptible whisper. 'The spooks have taken over.'

'What?'

'The spooks. The spies. FX5. They've come in and taken everything over.'

'But I thought you told me this was going to be a Greater Wessex Police investigation?'

'Yeah, it was. And on the surface it still is. But that's just for pride's sake. The High Honchos have been overridden by the Home Office. The spooks are running the game now.'

Dan braced himself and sipped at the tea. It was surprisingly good.

'You don't sound too happy about it,' he said.

Adam loosened his tie. He looked unusually dishevelled today, his dark hair spraying up in patches and the shadow of his beard pronounced. There was even a whisper of fluff on the shoulder of his suit, a rare sight indeed for a man so scrupulously proud of his appearance.

Dan pointed to the offending material and the detective petulantly brushed it off.

'Bloody right I'm not happy,' he replied. 'They dish out their orders, but don't tell us anything. They get together in their little clusters for conflabs, but don't ask any of us to join them. They've taken over everything. They've got their own people with John Tanton, their own interrogators with Ahmed and their own scientists looking at all the forensics stuff. We're barely even the supporting cast. I wouldn't be surprised if they try to get me making the damned tea.'

The door opened, a couple of men walked in and made for the counter. Both were wearing overalls splattered with paint. Adam watched them carefully.

'Country bumpkins, that's what the bloody spooks think of us,' he continued. 'They reckon we're too backwards to run a proper investigation.' He added a couple of choice obscenities, making Dan blink hard. Adam rarely swore.

'Look,' Dan said, to distract his friend. 'Why don't you tell me how the investigation is – or, at least, was – going. You must have got somewhere before the spooks came in.'

'We were doing fine without them,' came the haughty response.

'So?'

Adam sipped at his tea and took out his notebook.

'Is this for me to broadcast, or just to know?' Dan asked quickly.

'The way I feel at the moment, for whatever you like.'

'OK. Go ahead.'

'Right. This is where we've got to so far. I reckoned we had the radicaliser in Ahmed, but now I'm not so sure.'

'Why?'

'Well, first of all I was surprised at how fast we got him. Alison Tanton told us all about him, how John had been hanging around with him. How he'd seemed to change under Ahmed's influence, started spouting some worrying things.'

'Like what?'

'Going on about western society. How depraved and despicable it was. How it needed to be punished. Just the sort of stuff that Ahmed believes. She gave us a description. We got his mobile number and traced it to Exeter. A cop spotted him and you know the rest.'

Dan looked up from his writing. 'Job done then, isn't it? That sounds like it makes perfect sense. Ahmed radicalised Tanton, set him off to attack the Minster, then couldn't resist coming along to see the results of his handiwork.'

'Yeah, that's what I thought – initially. But here are the problems. One, John Tanton himself. In what little he's been able to say so far, he's insistent it was all down to him. He says he made his own decisions about wanting to become a martyr, and that he found out how to make a bomb on the internet and built it himself.'

'You don't believe that though, surely? He's too young, nothing like sophisticated enough. He's been brainwashed.'

'I think so, but let me give you our other problems. You know how Tanton seemed to lose his nerve at the last minute, dumped the rucksack and tried to get away before it exploded?'

'Yes.'

'Well, here's the bit we're keeping nice and quiet. Just a few minutes before the blast, Tanton made a call on his mobile. It was a reasonably long one – it lasted for several minutes.'

'Who to?'

'Who indeed? The answer is we don't know. But I reckon that call is the key to finding out who radicalised him.'

'But surely you've got the number he called?'

'Yep. We seized Tanton's mobile. But the number is a pay as you go phone. There are no records of who bought it. They're untraceable. All we know from the analysis is that whoever was using it was in the centre of Exeter when he took the call.'

'So that's why you're looking for someone who was in the city at the time of the explosion?'

'Spot on.'

Dan debated whether to tell Adam what he'd learned earlier, about Kindle, the Imam and his minder all being in Exeter yesterday, but decided against it. He was learning too much interesting information. Far better to let the detective talk while he was in the mood. He could chip in with his own thoughts later.

He took another sip of tea. 'Regarding this call Tanton made. Any guesses what it was about?'

'He won't say. So – have you got any ideas?'

Dan tapped on the table with his pen. 'If he thinks he's about to die … to his mum, to explain and say goodbye?'

'No. We checked that.'

'Any other close family?'

'No.'

'Any friends or girlfriends?'

'No. We've checked all those. We've gone through all the numbers stored on his phone, and all his family and friends. It was none of those. The call was made to the mystery owner of this pay as you go mobile which was in central Exeter.'

Adam looked at him expectantly. Dan felt a nudge of irritation. His friend was a great lover of the dubious art of delayed gratification, and it could be annoying.

'I give up,' he said finally.

Adam's face warmed into smugness. 'Well, as there are no records of the conversation, and as Tanton won't tell us, I can't say for sure, obviously. But I can tell you the theory I'm working on.'

'Which is?'

'I reckon he was ringing his radicaliser. I think he was having second thoughts and needed a pep talk. Hence the length of the call. It can't just have been – "Hello, I'm here and about to do it." It must have been to fortify his courage.'

Dan breathed out heavily. 'Wow. That would have been some call. But fair enough, if he's about to kill himself and others he might well need some comforting words. OK, your theory makes sense, but surely it points to Ahmed. He was here in Exeter. There's good evidence from Alison Tanton that he indoctrinated John. And he ran when you lot descended on him.'

'Plenty of people run when the cops come calling,' Adam replied. 'That doesn't mean a thing. The other evidence is better. But there's just the one problem. We seized Ahmed's mobiles and neither was the number Tanton rang in that final call.'

Dan was writing fast, struggling to keep up. 'Sorry, you've lost me there. You said Ahmed's mobiles? He had more than one?'

Adam nodded. 'Yep. When we arrested him, he was carrying a mobile in his jacket. But being the suspicious chap I am, something occurred to me about when we chased him into the shopping centre.'

'What?'

'Think about it.'

Again Adam waited, his face expectant. Dan just about managed to stop himself from growling.

'I think it might be better if you just tell me,' he said levelly.

'His disappearing time.'

'His what?'

'When he ran into the shopping centre we were watching him on CCTV, or a cop had sight of him for almost all of the chase. There's just one part when no one can see him. It lasts for about 40 seconds or so. Apart from that time he was always in view.'

'So what was he doing for those 40 seconds?'

'Exactly the question I asked myself.'

'And?'

'What do you think?'

Dan sighed heavily. 'Well – would he have disappeared deliberately? Could he have been sure he wasn't being watched?'

Adam nodded. 'I think so. The CCTV cameras in the arcade are old-fashioned and very obvious. He'd have known when he was in sight of one. And he could see us chasing him. We weren't exactly being subtle. He'd have known when he wasn't being watched.'

Dan swirled the remains of his tea and thought for a few seconds.

'The only reason he could have needed to disappear was that he was doing something he didn't want you to see.'

'Precisely.'

'Which would be – hiding, or getting rid of something. Something important.'

'Exactly.'

'Like what?'

'What do you think?'

Dan sat forcibly back on his seat. Sometimes the temptation to throttle his friend could grow overwhelming.

'Give me a clue?'

'I don't need to. I told you only a few seconds ago.'

'Of course. His other phone.'

'Exactly. I had the shopping centre sealed off and searched. The teams looked everywhere. In the gutters, the drains, the bins, the plant pots, the shops, the doorways, even the ceiling lights. The whole lot. Anywhere he could possibly have hidden something.'

'And they found this other mobile.'

'Bingo.'

'Except it's not the number Tanton rang?'

'No. We've checked it. There are no records of any calls from Tanton's mobile to it, either stored on the phone itself or with the phone company. It can't have been that mobile which Tanton rang.'

There was a silence. Then Dan said softly, 'Quite a puzzle then.'

'Yes. Very much so.'

Dan massaged his temples, to see if it might persuade his brain to find inspiration.

'And there was nothing else Ahmed could have hidden?' he said. 'Not another phone, or some notes, or a diary, or, well – anything?'

'I had the place taken apart. There was nothing else.'

'And what was on these phones of Ahmed's?'

'On the one we found in his pocket, only the names and numbers of a couple of family, sports clubs, taxi companies, restaurants, that kind of thing. We've checked them all. There's nothing suspicious.'

'So there must be something on the one he tried to hide.'

'Yep.'

'And what's on that one?'

'Now that's more interesting. There are eleven numbers stored on it, along with names. They're all mobile numbers, no landlines.'

'And you've tried calling them?'

Adam rolled his eyes. 'The thought had occurred to me.'

'Sorry. I was just thinking aloud. So, who did the numbers belong to?'

The woman from behind the counter ambled over and gathered up their empty mugs. Adam waited until she was back at the till, then said, 'That's the real puzzle. Four are genuine numbers. But the names in the phone don't match the owners. And they claim to never have heard of Ahmed. We've checked them out. They all seem entirely innocent. There's a businessman from Hull, a housewife in Aberdeen, a student in London and a hairdresser in Bath.'

'And the other seven numbers?'

'Unobtainable. We've checked with the phone companies. They're not working numbers. They haven't even been assigned to any mobiles in the past.'

Dan wrote all that down and let out a low whistle. 'So what do you make of that then?'

Adam shrugged. 'No idea. That's partly why I wanted to talk to you. You've got a weird brain for all this cryptic stuff. You solved the riddles in those other cases.'

The thought of the two most recent investigations they'd worked on together made Dan shudder. He didn't want to go back there. Neither had exactly been enjoyable, nor anything approaching a triumph. Far from it.

'He's hidden something,' Dan said slowly, wondering where the words were coming from. 'Ahmed's hidden something in the names or the numbers, or maybe both, and it's something very important. That's why some are real numbers and others aren't, and why none of the people know him. There's some kind of message or code in there, disguised in all the letters and numbers.'

Adam stood up. 'I thought that's what you might say. So let's go have a look at it.'

Dan got up too, hesitated, left a tip, then made for the door. The woman behind the counter gave a nod of appreciation.

'Is he clever, this Ahmed?' Dan asked.

'I think so. Does that bother you?'

Dan tried to hide his smile. 'What do you think?'

'I think you prefer it that way. Your vanity wouldn't be satisfied with a nice easy case to crack.'

Dan didn't bother arguing. They knew each other well enough by now. As they walked back towards the police station, a memory intruded.

'Partly?' Dan said.

'What?' Adam replied.

'Just a few minutes ago. You said the business about Ahmed's phone was partly what you wanted to talk to me about. So – what was the other part?'

'Ah, that. I was going to mention it.'

Dan felt his pace slow. 'It's Claire, isn't it? Is she in the station? Is that it?'

'No, it's not Claire. Nothing to do with her.' The detective sounded puzzled. 'I think she's out on inquiries.'

Dan wondered if he managed to disguise his relief. 'What then?'

78

They were only a hundred yards from the police station. Adam stopped and put a hand on his friend's shoulder.

'It's the spooks,' he said. 'I've mentioned to them about you coming to help out on the case.'

'What was the reaction?'

'I have no idea. It's impossible to tell. They don't really show reactions. It's like working with robots. They're impossible to read.'

'What did they say then?'

'They said they wanted to see you. So, come and meet them.' He hesitated, then added, 'But do me a favour, will you?'

'What?'

'Just remember this. I've seen it before, and I don't want it to happen to you.'

'What?'

Adam gave him a knowing look. 'Don't get too excited, just because you're dealing with spies and it feels all mysterious and sexy. Keep your cool.'

Dan just managed to stop himself chuckling. 'Come on Adam, I'm on the TV most days. I've interviewed celebrities and government ministers. I've been at the centre of some of the biggest police investigations the country has ever seen. There's not much I haven't taken on and come through. I think I can handle a couple of spies without too much trouble.'

'It's just a warning, that's all.'

'Well, thanks for the thought, but don't you worry yourself. I'll be absolutely fine.'

Chapter Nine

DAN FOLLOWED ADAM ALONG a couple of long, dim and narrow corridors. Heavitree Road police station was cursed with that artificial smell of pine which comes from the disinfectant of choice of the great majority of cleaners of public buildings. The only break in the scent came when they passed the cell block and it was not a welcome one; waves of the reek of stale vomit assailed them.

It was ever the way in police stations. Drunks were the most common guests of the no-star hotel of law enforcement.

A woman rounded the corner ahead and walked towards them. The lights were behind her, casting a silhouette and disguising her features in a fluorescent haze. Dan stopped, felt his heartbeat pick up in a second.

Claire was out on enquiries. But she could have finished early. Something might have come up. Perhaps an urgent call. She might have been forced to return to the station. Be waiting around every turning, inside each room, or poised to skip down a flight of stairs, straight into him.

Dan felt his hands press together, his fingers interlace and tighten.

The woman walked on. Closer now. The colour of her hair, the shape of her face, her figure slowly resolved into clarity.

She was young, probably in her early twenties, perhaps only a probationer.

'Hello, sir,' she chirped at Adam as she passed.

Dan began walking again.

One of the carpet tiles was missing. A patch of lightness in the dark floor. A small yellow triangle warned of a trip hazard.

The grey ceiling was stained with patches of brown, the faded memory of a burst pipe.

A metal rubbish bin overflowed with sandwich wrappers.

A voice rose in an office. A woman's.

Dan stopped again. He was right by the door.

Now the words had become a laugh. A story was being

shared. About a fuss at a supermarket after a driver reversed over someone's shopping trolley.

The chuckling was high-pitched. Far too shrill for Claire.

Dan swallowed hard and walked on once more. They were almost at the end of the corridor. A woman eased past, pushing a tea trolley. Mugs and plates rattled.

'You've gone quiet. You OK back there?' Adam said, over his shoulder.

'Fine,' Dan managed, in that traditional English way of meaning absolutely anything but.

To distract himself, Dan checked his watch and thought his way through the demands of the day job. Half past two it said, so the time was probably around a quarter to three. One day he must get a new watch, to replace the stylish but hopelessly inaccurate Rolex.

There shouldn't be too much else to do this afternoon, provided there were no significant developments in the story. He could use the lunchtime news report, a similar live opening to set the scene, and then interview Reverend Parfitt.

From ahead, a woman called Adam's name. The voice sounded familiar. Dan stopped dead. He was directly below a light. It felt as though it was illuminating him mercilessly, stripping his defences and exposing his emotions for all the world to see. Slowly, hesitantly he craned his neck to see around his friend.

Dan noticed a poster on the wall. It offered relationship support and guidance. Above a picture of a happily intertwined couple the headline was – *It's never too late to make up*.

His eyes slipped to the woman standing in the corridor. She was wearing black boots and black trousers. Classical Claire. Her legs were slim, but strong. Elegant Claire. She was carrying a couple of thick files. Diligent Claire.

An odd thought struck him. Her hands were remarkably soft for a detective. He never knew why, but Dan always expected a woman who worked in CID to have roughened skin and gnarled fingers. Not Claire. She also kept her nails trimmed, with just the slightest of an edge, not sufficient to be an encumbrance if she had to grapple with a suspect, but enough to be subtly feminine. How many times he had felt those gentle hands in his.

Dan allowed his eyes to travel upwards, ready to find the face of the woman he had once loved. Who had sat with him as they enjoyed the tingle of anticipation in looking through the property pages of the local paper, searching for their first home together. Who had slept with him and woken with him on countless mornings and nights, and hiked with him across Dartmoor in the snow, and walked beside him along Devon beaches and over cliff tops.

Claire.

The woman whom he hadn't seen for five months, since that last acidic night. Whom he was about to meet again in the narrow, half-lit corridor of a police station which smelt of artificial pine.

He was ready. He was calm.

Those together days were done. Over, gone, dead, buried, finished and through.

There were no feelings left for her. Just a void. An impassive indifference. An easy disregard.

Hardly even a shrug to her existence.

Dan steadied himself to say the words he had been rehearsing. How they had an important job to do. How this was such a big investigation that personal feelings could not be allowed to interfere. How he could work with her if she could with him.

The time for talking would come. But it would not be yet.

The words sounded jumbled in his head. In this tiny fragment of the world, this small stretch of dim corridor, time had begun moving remarkably slowly.

Dan steadied himself to meet Claire's look. He stared, coughed, then began spluttering, blinked hard and screwed up his eyes to make sure.

It wasn't Claire.

The woman was a little older, probably around forty, and she was talking to Adam about checking the background of some of Ahmed's friends. Dan watched for a moment, then leaned back against the wall. A couple of uniformed cops walked past and cast a curious look.

Adam finished his discussion and beckoned Dan on. 'You sure you're OK?' he asked.

'I'm – fine.'

They pushed their way through a couple more pairs of swing doors. Now they were nearing the end of the police station. The air was noticeably colder. At the top of the corridor a door was open, a rumble of chatter spilling out. Inside Dan could see a group of people, some on phones, others working at desks.

'The Bomb Room,' Adam explained. 'I'm not calling it the Major Incident Room, or the Incident Room, or any of that usual police talk. Who the hell would just call the attack an *incident*?

It was the size of a large classroom, a raft of desks set together in the centre, all with computers and phones. Around the outside was a series of whiteboards bearing a time-line of the inquiry, along with notes on witnesses. The windows looked out on to the main road, a stream of traffic waiting at the lights.

'Remember what I said about playing it cool,' Adam whispered.

'Yeah, yeah. Look, stop worrying. I'll be absolutely fine.'

The room quietened as they walked in, the detectives all looking around to see the new arrivals.

Adam paused in the doorway and folded his arms. And there he stood and waited. One by one, the faces which had turned to him and Dan now shifted expectantly to a man and woman standing in the corner.

For a few seconds, no one spoke. Finally, the woman said, 'Would you all mind leaving us for a few minutes? We need to have a little chat with our guest.'

The detectives filed out of the door. When the last one had left, the man walked over and checked the corridor outside. A couple of uniformed cops were standing there talking. He gave them a look and they sauntered away. The door was closed, locked, checked twice, and he walked back over to the woman.

Both stared at Dan. Their expressions were impassive, but their looks were clinical and analytical, shorn of emotion, but intent with observation. It felt as if they were scrutinising everything from the size of the shoes Dan wore to his haircut, mentally noting down each detail. He shifted his weight a little, but held their stares.

Outside, a lorry rumbled past. Still the pair didn't speak. A computer hummed. Footsteps echoed along the corridor. Eventually, Adam stepped forwards and said, 'Well, I'll do the introductions then. Dan, this is …'

The woman coughed pointedly and held up a hand. 'I am … Sierra,' she said. 'And this is …' She glanced at the man. 'Oscar.'

The silence returned. Dan itched at his ear. 'Sierra and Oscar?'

'Yes,' she replied.

'Sierra and Oscar?'

'Yes.'

A fly buzzed against the window, beat itself on the pane, then stilled.

Dan forced his face into an awkward smile and said lightly, 'Forgive me for saying this, and don't think me extraordinarily perceptive, but I reckon those aren't your real names.'

He tried to keep his voice warm and friendly, but there was no response. The spooks just stood, looking. Adam let out a long breath.

'Dan is here at my request because he's been helpful to us in the past and I believe he could be useful again.'

The woman who called herself Sierra was still looking at him. Dan noticed she wore no make-up and no jewellery. Her hair was mousy, her figure average, her appearance ordinary. She was as nondescript as anyone he had met. Perhaps in the twilight world of spies it was an axiom that the less which distinguished you, so much the better.

Oscar stood slightly behind her, perhaps a mark of their respective ranks in the secret hierarchy. He had an athletic figure, neither full nor slight, but powerful. On the floor beside him was a black briefcase, at which he would occasionally glance. The man kept his foot against the case the whole while.

'We welcome any help, Chief Inspector,' she said finally. 'Dan, please don't think us hostile, but you'll appreciate we exist in a world of suspicion. We are fighting a ruthless enemy who can often seem so elusive as to be near invisible. Many in our organisation believe we are in the midst of another war, the quietest and most insidious we have ever known, but no less lethal for that. As the attack on your Minster has shown us, that quiet can instantly be shattered with the sudden force of hatred.'

Another pause, and then she reached out and shook Dan's hand. Oscar did so too. As the man leaned forwards, Dan heard a metallic clink from his jacket. The tight material was shaped with the unmistakable outline of a gun.

Sierra saw his look. 'I would appreciate it if you would not mention our presence here, what you have seen and what we have discussed, even though it may go against your instincts as a journalist. I would ask you to remember this – there is a greater purpose to consider.'

Dan nodded. 'I understand.'

'We have only limited time,' she continued, 'so perhaps you could help by telling us about your visit to the mosque this morning. We're particularly interested in your discussions inside – those details which you did not include in your television report this lunchtime.'

Dan couldn't hide his surprise. 'How did you know about that?'

'The mosque is – of interest to us,' she replied.

'Because Tanton went there?'

'It's probably better if you just answer our questions.'

Dan related what had happened in the mosque, his discussions with the Imam and Abdul's looming presence.

'Did anything strike you as suspicious?' Oscar asked. He had a sharp voice with a hint of a cockney accent.

'That they wouldn't answer my questions about Tanton, or anything else that I wanted to know in fact. And that ...'

'Yes?'

Dan found himself unable to resist telling them. 'That Tahir and Abdul were both in Exeter at the time of the bombing. Which struck me as very interesting, if not just plain suspicious.'

No reaction from the spooks. Not even an exchange of looks.

Dan noticed he was still talking. 'They could easily have had something to do with the attack, those two. The Imam talks about being a peaceful man, but you never know. And as for his minder – he just has an air about him, something ominous. Call it a hunch, but sometimes hunches can be important. Wouldn't you agree?'

Oscar's eyes were fixed on him. Sierra was nodding, just a little.

'And I reckon that BPP man, Kindle, he's worth looking at too,' Dan heard himself adding. 'He was in Exeter when the bomb exploded, as well. And he knew John Tanton. I've no idea why, but I just found him suspicious. Who knows what that BPP lot could do to advance their cause?'

More nodding from Sierra. 'And what do you intend to do now?'

'I'm going back to the Minster to do a live broadcast. You can even come over and watch, if you like. But I'm free later, if you need my help. I've worked on investigations before. I can find out things without the people I'm talking to realising the information's going to get back to you. That could be useful.'

Dan thought he heard Adam draw in a breath.

'I can use my position to help you in handling the media too. I've done it before on cases I've worked on. And I can broadcast stuff which might influence some of the people you're interested in, get them to do things which could give themselves away. That's worked before too. I really enjoy investigation work. I'd love to help you.'

Adam had closed his eyes and half turned away. But the two spies were still watching. Oscar's face had shifted a little. His expression looked like the beginnings of a smirk. His foot tapped softly at the briefcase.

'Well, whatever,' Dan added lamely. 'If there's anything I can do … I'd be very happy to help. Really happy.'

Another silence settled on the room. The air felt warm and close. Flecks of dust drifted past the window. Dan noticed Oscar had a long scar on his neck, like a thin worm creeping over the soft flesh.

Now Sierra spoke, but her voice had changed. It was sharper, more businesslike. More final.

'Thank you for your information. But I have to say – we are not sure what you could bring to this inquiry. Apart from being ...' she hesitated, then added, 'a dangerous complication.'

Dan had a sudden sensation that he was standing at the bottom of a pit, looking up at the two spies. He'd rushed headlong towards them, seeing only their open arms, but not noticing the great hole they had dug and covered with only the flimsiest layer of sticks and leaves.

'I ... I can be relied on to be discreet, you know,' he stammered. 'Despite being a journalist. I can keep a secret. And that's what you do, isn't it? What we could do.'

He tried a smile, but it was as effective as casting a pebble onto permafrost.

'Look, I appreciate how sensitive and important all this is. I was just a little nervous, meeting you. That's all. That's why I went on a bit. Well, it's understandable, isn't it? Surely?'

Even to Dan it sounded like he was babbling. But he didn't seem to be able to stop.

'I can help. Really I can. You can trust me. Honestly.'

Still no reaction.

'I mean ... I'm up to speed with investigation procedures. I have worked on lots of other cases, you know. I helped to crack ...'

'We know.'

Oscar interrupted, the words as effective as a gag. He glanced at Sierra, who gave another slight nod. He produced a file and started reading from it.

'Daniel Groves, TV reporter, specialising in crime. Lives in Plymouth. Became involved with the police when shadowing the Edward Bray murder inquiry. Has been part of several more inquiries since, of which the outcome of the latest two were most unpleasant.'

Dan gaped. 'Hey, now look,' he stammered. 'Look, that wasn't my fault. I did my best. Do you realise ...'

But Oscar interjected again, turned over a sheet of paper. 'Lives on his own, apart from an Alsatian dog, named Rutherford. Has difficulty sustaining relationships – with people, at least. Reputation as a maverick. Does not respond well to discipline or authority. Has been drinking heavily in recent months – following the disintegration of yet another relationship – sufficient to prompt him to ring Alcoholics Anonymous. His call began with the classic words, 'I'm not an alcoholic, but ...'

Dan felt Adam's eyes on him. 'How the hell did you ...' he stuttered. 'I mean, what gives you the right to ...'

'No criminal record, but has been arrested three times now for breaching a police cordon, and has six points on his driving licence, all for speeding. When approached by the security services at university to see if he might be interested in joining, he asked facetiously – *Do I get to dress up in a dinner jacket and act like James Bond*? When told not, he said he would prefer a *more glamorous career*.'

Dan just stared.

'Analysed as having above average intelligence, but those assessing him conclude he is by no means as clever as he thinks. Also believes himself to be something of an amateur detective, as he has in fact boasted to his few friends, usually when the worse for drink – a common occurrence. Psychological profile concludes him to be vain and arrogant, entirely unable to work as part of a team, and almost incapable of appreciating when he is wrong. In summary, a highly flawed man who is a danger both to himself and others.'

And now a silence, as thick and choking as any Dan had ever known.

Oscar's smirk grew. He closed the file and slipped it back into the briefcase. Before he did so, Dan saw there were scores of sheets of paper in there, all covered in thick lines of black type. Attached to one was a series of pictures of him.

Getting out of his car. Walking down the street. Holding a

mobile phone. Jogging with Rutherford. Drinking a pint in a bar. Standing on a beach, gazing out to sea. Checking a list while looking in a shop window. Talking to a camera.

Each was also marked with a date and time.

'So,' Sierra said levelly. 'We thank you for your offer of assistance. But it is respectfully declined. We suggest you limit your involvement in this case to reporting on it – from the outside.'

The two spies turned away and began a hushed discussion. Neither looked back.

Dan felt a hand on his arm. It was Adam, leading him out of the Bomb Room.

The walk back to the Minster felt a long one. Dan hardly noticed the yellow autumn sun shining into his eyes or the people he passed, busy going about the daily trade of living. A car hooted. Dan started in surprise. He'd walked out into a road without seeing the traffic. He waved an apology to the driver and got a scowl in return.

There wasn't sufficient a supply of spirit even to return the look.

He plodded on, through the shopping precinct, as busy as an ants' nest. His mind kept wanting to go back over what had happened in the police station, but Dan didn't dare let it.

That image of languishing in a pit, looking up helplessly at the two spies returned. Time and again. Burned itself into his brain.

A man was shaking a bucket, collecting money for the restoration of the Minster. He nodded appreciatively. 'Good reports you did on it. Who'd have thought it, eh?'

Dan managed an unconvincing smile. A bus rumbled past, greying the air with a cloud of diesel fumes. A pigeon landed on a bench and pecked contentedly at the remnants of some discarded sandwiches. Dan could taste the exhaust smoke in his throat. He started coughing. A clock in a shop window said it was coming up to four.

Two hours until he needed to get ready for tonight's broadcast. And there was a pub on Minster Green.

The trudge turned to a stride.

The first pint helped him realise. He should have seen it coming. Sierra and Oscar indeed. The phonetic alphabet.

S O. Or, in more common parlance, sod off.

They'd told him what they really thought from the start and he'd missed it. They wanted whatever information he could provide, and he'd fallen for it. And then they'd discarded him, just like that.

He'd been as easy as a light switch. Click on or off, with only the twitch of a finger.

The dark liquid suddenly tasted sour. Dan pushed the glass away, leaned back on the wooden chair and tried to stretch his aching back.

And where the hell did they get all that information on him?

Adam called just as Dan was about to walk into the pub and did his best to soothe his friend.

'You'd be amazed who they've got files on,' the detective said. 'They've no doubt got one on me, and all the other senior cops in the force. Loads of people come to their attention in some way. It was probably what you said to that recruiter at university that started them off at you. They don't forget easily. Did you really say that?'

'Yeah. But I was younger then. Cockier.'

'Well, younger, certainly. Listen, don't worry too much about it. They're bound to have been watching the mosque. As for the rest of the stuff, it wouldn't take much research to find out your involvement in the other cases. The remainder of it they've probably just made up. A bluff, that's all. To put you off your stride.'

'Well it's bloody worked.'

Dan realised he kept looking over his shoulder. There were a handful of other committed drinkers in the pub. Any one of them could be watching him. None looked remotely like a spy. But then, that was how a spy should look.

He shook himself. There was enough going on in his life without paranoia joining the already impressive procession of concerns.

'Listen, I've got to back to the investigation,' Adam said.

'But what they did in there – just be aware that I was no part of it and I didn't care for it. In fact, we had words about it afterwards.'

'What did they say?'

'They said wars mean people getting hurt.'

'Nice.'

'Yeah.'

The phone line clicked, then Adam said, 'Just because you're not officially involved in the case doesn't mean I won't be in touch. I still think you could help us.'

'Thanks,' Dan managed weakly.

Workmen had already erected scaffolding on the Minster's façade and were carefully checking the stonework around the shattered window. Dan watched as he sipped at his pint. It had depleted remarkably quickly. Perhaps it was the sunshine, making it evaporate. Still, there was time for another before the broadcast.

The woman behind the bar had earrings just like Claire's. Silver studs embedded with tiny diamonds. Dan's gaze fixed upon the flashing darts of shooting light as she pulled the pint.

He felt his eyes starting to sting, blinked hard and took a long swig of beer. When the broadcast was over, he would drive straight back to the flat, give Rutherford a big cuddle, then take him out for a good walk. Afterwards, Dan would lie out on his great blue sofa, listen to some music and try to unwind. He deserved it after this day.

A phone call from the newsroom interrupted his thoughts. It was Lizzie with her usual list of demands, but Dan hardly noticed. He heard himself reassuring her that yes, lunchtime's report would be fine to use tonight, yes, the live interview would be good, no there had been no significant developments, and yes, of course he would find a follow-up on the story for tomorrow.

He hung up, laid down the phone, finished his pint and walked slowly outside.

There were always positives in any situation if you looked hard enough. It was just a question of finding them.

Dan lay back on the sofa, lifted a glass to the spooks and giggled to himself. Whisky was such a wonderful invention. It didn't fill you up, or require such effort to drink in the way beer did, and it spread its soothing warmth through your mind so much more efficiently.

So – he was off the case. Well, so what? Who cared? It would give him more time to enjoy the lovely whisky. Instead of careering around with Adam and putting himself in danger, trying to catch terrorists, he could lay here in safety and drink.

It was a winner if ever he'd heard one.

Dan giggled again, reached down and ran a hand over Rutherford's head. The dog let out a low whine of appreciation. He would lie here with his only true friend and his whisky, and Claire and bombing investigations and spooks could go chase each other in a pathetic little merry-go-round. What did it all matter in the end? Here it was safe and warm and no one bothered him with irritating talk of the need to find the people behind terrorist murders and outrages, and to get some justice for victims and their families, and to cover endless stories on it, and all of that junk.

Bollocks to the lot of it. Yeah!

Who needed it? You did your job as well as you could, and all you got was your editor on the phone demanding more. You volunteered to help the police on a big investigation, do your bit for society, so far above and beyond the call of duty that it was around the corner and out of sight, and you got it thrown back in your face. You gave a woman your fragile heart and she held it in her hand, promised to care for it always, then cast it down and ground it into the dirt with the heel of her boot.

Sod them. Sod them all. The whole bloody lot of them.

Today hadn't been so bad after all. That broadcast at the Minster went well. Parfitt was a good interviewee, eloquently voicing sorrow for the attack and a determination the damage would be put right as soon as possible. But it was what he'd said when the camera was turned off that was by far the most interesting. He was no fan of Islam, that was clear.

'A dangerous religion. Despite what they say, it is dedicated to taking over the world, you know,' he had confided, quietly.

'Whether it's the fanatics who want to do it with the bomb or the gun, or the moderates relentlessly spreading their teachings, the ultimate aim is the same. To make the world a caliphate, an Islamic state. We have a proud history of Christianity in this country and we should defend it robustly. Britain needs a wake-up call. We are sleepwalking towards becoming a Muslim state otherwise.'

Dan couldn't help his instincts activating.

'I meant to ask,' he said, as casually as he could. 'Where were you when the bomb went off? Did you see it?'

'No,' Parfitt replied sombrely. 'I suppose I was lucky. It was hard enough to bear, seeing the aftermath. I was over in the shopping centre, buying a gift for a long-serving volunteer who's retiring next week. A tedious chore, but someone has to do it.'

So, Reverend Parfitt was in Exeter city centre when the bomb exploded, and he was a strong critic of Islam. And Adam said earlier that he had detectives checking the Minster's CCTV and visitor register, to see if Tanton had carried out any reconnaissance of his target before the attack, and if he had been seen with, or spoken to anyone.

Perhaps Parfitt and Tanton had met. And talked ... and not for the first time.

Parfitt was a long shot for the radicaliser, surely. But, Dan thought, he would have to tell Adam about the man's views. Experience of the cases he'd worked on had taught him early that the smallest of insights could take on the greatest of significance.

Or would he tell Adam? Hadn't he just decided that all he would be doing was lying here on the sofa, with his beloved dog, drinking the bottled nectar that stood on the battered old coffee table? He was better off out of the world of investigations and spooks, terrorists and danger.

Yeah, bollocks to it.

At least Rutherford was happy. They'd been for a run around Hartley Park, twenty laps no less, the maximum Dan ever managed. He suspected he'd only achieved the target because of the promise of a whisky or two if he did.

It was important to set yourself meaningful goals in life.

The dog careered back and forth across the dewy grass, in an agony of dilemma about which of the scores of fascinating scents to sniff at first. The oak and lime trees of the park's boundary, the wall around the underground reservoir, the fence guarding the children's play area. Rutherford was a black blur of chaotic delight in the creeping twilight, leaving his zig-zag tracks on the moist grass.

For what felt like the first time in days, Dan burst out laughing.

They ran together, enjoying the stillness of the clear air and the emboldened silver stars emerging from their inky hide. Halfway through the run Dan stopped, found a stick and hurled it until his arm ached. The dog sprinted back and forth in heady pursuit.

Back at the flat, as a special treat for his loyal and wonderful friend, Dan gave Rutherford a good brush. The dog started emitting that strange low whine of delight as the ghosts of his discarded fur floated and flew.

And now it was coming up to twelve o'clock. The midnight clouds were streaming past the bay window and the glass on the table had emptied itself again. One more, just one, then it was time for bed. To sleep, and to forget.

So, it was decided. He was better off out of that realm of smoke and shadows. Dan wondered why he had ever found it so fascinating.

He picked up the whisky bottle and went to pour a sizable goodnight measure when his mobile rang.

He recognised the number, but could hardly make out the words on the line. They were too stifled by the sobs and gulps and whimpers.

Dan waited. Discerned a word or two. Then a few more.

It was Alison Tanton. And she seemed to be saying that her son was dead.

Chapter Ten

THE INTERVIEW ROOM WAS too comfortable. It was the antithesis of his favourite; Number Two in his home police station, Charles Cross in Plymouth – a low ceiling, a tiny, grimy and barred window, and dimly lit and permanently cold, even in the summer months. It was nigh guaranteed to make a suspect talk with the unspoken promise of escaping its oppressive presence. That was how an interview room should be.

This model had doubtless been designed by someone with the qualification PC after their name. The irritating influence of political correctness was shamelessly evident. It was new and modern, a clean and tiled floor, smart white walls, and even the chairs were annoyingly padded and comfortable. The windows were large, bright and clean, the early morning sunshine streaming in cheerfully.

The only thing missing was some nice floral prints on the wall. Perhaps one day it would come, Adam reflected, but hopefully not before he had been blessed with retirement. He turned the thermostat on the radiator up to maximum, stalked out of the room and returned carrying an old and battered wooden chair, a portable heater and bearing an expression of satisfaction.

Adam exchanged the comfortable chair on the opposite side of the table for the wooden version, closed the blinds, plugged in the heater and turned it too up to maximum.

Detective Sergeant Claire Reynolds raised an eyebrow.

'It's similar to your "Zero Option Protocol", Adam explained. 'What did you get that doctor to sign, by the way?'

'One of those fascinating and indispensable Home Office *Sexual Orientation and Racial Origins when subject to Stop and Search* surveys. I folded it so he could only see the dotted line – told him the rest was national security stuff, too sensitive for him to see. So, what's this interior decoration thing about?'

'The spooks will be here in a minute with Ahmed. If they're

setting the rules of the game now, we might as well have some influence over the battleground.'

'And what are the rules now, sir?'

'We get to do the questioning, they sit back, observe, and chip in if they feel they need to.'

'Politics?'

'The best compromise we could manage. This is still a Greater Wessex police inquiry, on the face of it at least. Just carry on as you would normally.'

'Interrogation by committee?'

'No. They observe. We interrogate. When I bring up our little surprise I'll hammer away at him for a bit, then you take over. But first, have a look at this.'

The sheet of paper was headed simply, "Ahmed Nazri," and contained a briefing. He was in his late twenties, parents from Pakistan, but Ahmed himself was born and grew up in Birmingham. He went to a state school before going to university in London to read computer science. He'd graduated with an upper second class degree, had taken a job as a computer engineer back in Birmingham and lived a life of no interest whatsoever to the police until a couple of years ago.

Ahmed had disappeared; the only clue to his whereabouts was that immigration records showed he had taken a flight to Pakistan. The briefing suggested Ahmed may have studied at a madrassah, one of the more fundamentalist religious schools where he could have been indoctrinated in Islamic extremism.

He reappeared in Britain just under a year ago, in Plymouth, where he carried out consultant computer work. He had been tagged by Special Branch as mixing with a group of young Muslim men suspected of having radical views. They had been put under surveillance, but nothing was found to justify any arrests.

The men seemed content to rage about oppression, and discuss vague notions of making a statement against Britain and her western allies, but there was, the briefing said, "No substance to their talk". They had been dismissed as classic angry young men, more hot air than action, and the attention of the security services had turned to the alarmingly large number of others deemed a sharper and more immediate threat.

'All clear?' Adam asked.

'Yes, sir. Just one further question.'

'Yes?'

Claire paused. 'Is – err ...' she hesitated, before adding quickly, 'Is Dan coming to join the questioning?'

'No. The spooks don't want him involved.'

Adam pushed the door closed. 'Claire, it's none of my business I know, but what's happened between you? You both seemed so happy only a few months ago. And now ...'

'Has he said anything to you?'

The emotion in her voice made Adam hesitate. 'No. It's only that – when he came in to the station earlier he seemed more concerned about whether you'd be here than anything else.'

Claire swallowed hard. 'I'd rather not talk about it, sir, if you don't mind.'

Footsteps echoed along the corridor. Adam held her look, then leaned back against the wall. The door swung open and Oscar pushed Ahmed over to the wooden chair. He looked around and sat down. Sierra walked quickly in, shut the door, joined Oscar at the back of the room and nodded to Adam.

Ahmed glared at Claire. 'I'm not talking to that whore again.'

'Shut your mouth,' Adam snapped. 'We decide who interrogates you. If I want it done by a stripper it will be. Got that?'

'Fuck you.'

A pointed cough cracked from the back of the room. Adam ignored it, said. 'Right, now we've all got to know each other, let's get down to talking about what happened in the Minster.'

Ahmed's face warmed into a mocking grin. 'The bombing? Nice one, eh?'

'The killing of innocent people?'

'They weren't innocent. They pay their taxes for your government to spend on its little crusades.'

'Is that what this is about? Revenge for Iraq and Afghanistan?'

Ahmed sat back on the chair, crossed his legs and ran a finger over a white trainer. 'Dunno, mate. I was nothing to do with it. You'd have to ask whoever was. But that'd be my guess.'

'You were nothing to do with it?'

'Nothing.'

'You know John Tanton.'

'I know a lot of people.'

'His mum said you were good friends.'

'He was one of my mates.'

'You went round to his house.'

'I go round a lot of people's houses.'

'You spent time on his computer. Surfing the internet with him.'

Ahmed folded his arms. 'Welcome to the 21st century, mate. It ain't exactly radical to surf the net.'

'What sites were you looking at?'

'I dunno. It's a while ago. Games. Bit of social networking. That kind of stuff.'

'Jihadist websites? Holy war?'

'Not that I can remember.'

'We've checked John's computer. He was looking at sites dedicated to Islamic extremism; bombing, terrorism and war on western society.'

'Not with me. We just looked at fun things.'

'Really?'

'Really.'

There was a silence. Then Adam said quietly, 'Do you know he's dead?'

'Who's dead?'

'Who do you think? Adolf Hitler? John Tanton.'

Ahmed shrugged. 'Hardly surprising, is it? If you carry a bomb on your back and set it off it don't tend to do you the world of good.'

'Don't you care?'

The man chewed at his lip and considered the question. 'I'm a bit sad, I suppose.'

'He was supposed to be your friend.'

'We weren't that matey. He was a good lad, but a bit of a kid. I didn't mind hanging around with him sometimes, but that was it.'

'There was quite an age gap between you.'

'He was interested in Islam. I helped him find out about it.'

'Indoctrinated him?'

Ahmed rolled his eyes. 'Yeah, you would see it that way. I just taught him, that was all, answered his questions.'

'His mum said he looked up to you. He started talking like you. Echoing your opinions.'

'Yeah? Well, they're pretty good opinions.'

'What – on murder? Holy war?'

'We've already done that bit, haven't we? If we're gonna keep going over the same thing this is gonna take a long time.'

'I'm in no rush. 28 days the law gives me. I'm sure you'll enjoy the inside of a cell for a month.'

Ahmed shrugged, shifted his slight figure on the wooden chair, unzipped his top and adjusted its hood. The room was growing uncomfortably warm.

Claire took off her jacket, leaned forwards and said gently, 'What are your views, Ahmed? About British society for example?'

He gave her a glare which overflowed with loathing. 'I don't wanna talk to you.' He pointed distastefully to Claire's chest. 'You make me feel dirty with your tarty clothes and your disgusting flesh everywhere. Cover yourself up, woman.'

Adam slapped a hand on the table. There was another pointed cough from the back of the room.

'Answer her questions,' the detective said.

Ahmed grinned. 'You her boyfriend then?'

'Just answer the questions.'

'Well, since you ask, I'm no fan of not very great Britain. The place is decadent, immoral and full of shit – if you want my view.'

'In what way?'

His face contorted into a sneer. 'Are you blind, mate? Haven't you looked around you? Like at a Saturday night in Plymouth? Gangs of women going out almost naked. Throwing drink down their throats. Staggering around, being sick everywhere. Men getting drunk senseless and fighting in bars. People having sex in the streets. You call that a society, do you?'

'Then why,' said Adam forcefully, 'do you live in such a disgusting place? Why not go somewhere else?'

'I might. Someday. But for now I'm trying to do me best to change it.'

'By murdering people?'

Ahmed gave Adam a pitying look. 'I told you all that. I ain't nothing to do with any bombing. I've got me views, but I air them peacefully and that ain't against the law, is it?'

'What were you doing in Exeter on Monday?'

'I was shopping. Looking for some new clothes.'

Adam leaned forwards. 'Yeah?'

'Yeah.'

'Bit of a coincidence you happened to be here when your mate's letting a bomb off, isn't it?'

'Maybe. But it happened. It's a bit of a coincidence you're ugly as well as stupid, ain't it?'

Adam didn't respond, instead let the silence run. The second hand of the clock turned. Then he said quietly, 'We have found it, you know.'

Now there was a reaction. It was only slight, just a widening of the man's eyes, but it was definitely there. 'Found what?'

'Your mobile. The one you tried to hide.'

'You're bluffing me. Trying it on.'

'No. We found it.'

'You're bullshitting. Trying to get me to talk.'

'No. I knew you were trying to hide something with your little disappearing act. So I had the arcade searched. And we found it.'

Ahmed was leaning forwards, his arms folded tight across his chest. 'Bollocks.'

'No, we've got it.'

'Bollocks! You're trying it on, you bastards.'

'No. We found it, right where you tried to hide it, in that drain.'

Ahmed sat back on his seat. 'So? So you've found the phone. So what?'

Claire said quickly, 'Why have two mobile phones, Ahmed?'

'Dunno. I think I just forgot to cancel one when I got a new one.'

'And two different sets of numbers on them?'

'I couldn't be bothered to transfer them all over together.'

'So why try to hide that second phone in the arcade?'

'Dunno. Suppose I just didn't want any trouble for my mates. It's got some of their numbers on. I knew you'd go through it and hassle them.'

Adam snorted. 'But if it's all innocent, why worry?'

''coz I know what you're like. Anyone with a different-coloured skin, anyone who believes in Islam – they're all terrorists to you.'

'And your mates, the numbers on the phone – a hairdresser in Bath, a businessman in Hull amongst others, none of whom have even heard of you, and lots more numbers which don't belong to anyone? Which aren't even in use? Care to explain that?'

'Guess my friends must have changed their numbers then.'

'You're lying.'

'Am I?'

'I think so. I think you radicalised John Tanton, set him off to bomb the Minster and came to Exeter to watch the show. I think you're a coward. You wanted to hit out at Britain, but you didn't have the guts to do it yourself. So instead you found a patsy.'

Ahmed grinned and smoothed his jeans with a calm hand.

'Nice fantasy,' he said, then nodded towards Claire. 'Are you getting all uptight with me 'coz you're not getting any from her?'

Adam ignored the jibe. 'There's something hidden in that phone of yours, isn't there? Some number, some code, something which will give you away.'

The smile grew. 'If you say so, mate. Good luck in finding it then.' Again he nodded to Claire. 'And with Miss Frosty there.'

Adam stared at him. Ahmed's expression was easy, his face glowing with smugness in the closeness of the room. The detective reached out and slapped the young man's hands from behind his head.

A body was by his side in a second, a firm grip on his shoulder. Oscar.

'Naughty naughty,' Ahmed clucked as he was led grinning from the interview room.

The Bomb Room was almost empty, just a couple of detectives making calls and another tapping away at a computer. It was pleasantly cool after the heat of the interview room. A woman was making coffees and teas from a kettle at the far end. She brought over a tray and they helped themselves.

Sierra positioned herself beside Adam and said quietly, 'No more of that. However much we might think they deserve it we don't do things that way. It's also counterproductive. It just makes them more sure of their righteousness and helps them recruit. I understand your feelings, but please control them.'

Adam didn't reply. They formed a semi-circle around one of the boards. It was dominated by a series of numbers and names, in three groups.

    07987 122311 Jim
    07109 570285 Achmel
    07463 098261 Stan
    07310 645367 Erin

'Those four are the numbers which are actually in use,' Sierra said. 'I've had background checks done on their owners, and there is absolutely nothing suspicious about any of them. As for the names, they do not in any way correspond to the owners.'

She pointed to the next list.

    07104 772097 Libby
    07263 585712 Steve

07991 340654 Susan
07711 439071 Prit
07232 401301 Ed
07809 317563 Jazzy
07074 119463 Leanne

'And those seven are the unobtainable numbers,' she added. 'We've put them through our computers and the code-breakers have been working on them, but they've come up with nothing. So, any ideas?'

Their eyes wandered up and down, left and right over the list, worked through the names and numbers. A telephone rang, but went unanswered.

Claire tapped at her teeth with a pen and ventured. 'Grid references?'

'For where? Not to mention what and why?' Sierra replied.

'Something hidden. Something incriminating.'

'But grid references contain six numbers. And we're dealing with a set of eleven, in which each actual number itself has eleven digits. Which means just about any grid reference you care to name could be found in them.'

'Are there any patterns in there?' Adam asked. 'You know, like the third digit of each number, or the penultimate one, or some sequence like that?'

Sierra shook her head. 'Acrostics, you mean. No, the code-breakers have been working on all that. No go. No sign of any pattern.'

Claire said, 'Might another phone number be hidden within the eleven?'

'Yes, but there's a similar problem with that theory. Given the eleven numbers, if you took one, or maybe more digits from any of them, you could make just about any phone number on the planet.'

Sierra ran a finger down the list and came to one number, set apart, at the bottom.

07754 983064 ???????

'The mystery number,' she said. 'The one that John Tanton rang just before he went into the Minster to explode his bomb. The pay as you go mobile, whose owner was in Exeter city centre. Answer those question marks, fill in the name and …'

'The key to the case,' Claire said quietly. 'Summed up in one line.'

There was a silence while they all gazed at the number.

Finally Adam said, 'Going back to those other entries in the phone then – what about the names? Libby and Steve and Susan and all that lot. Is there any hint of anything in there?'

Sierra sat down on the corner of a desk. 'Not a thing. Again the cryptographers have been all over them. They've looked for any kind of patterns or codes, they've checked all the names against our databases of suspects or people associated with terrorism or extremism and they have come up with precisely nothing.'

'But there must be something in the names and numbers,' Claire said. 'Something important. Otherwise why would they be there, and why would Ahmed have made such an effort to hide the phone?'

'That,' Sierra replied, 'is the question.'

Adam swirled his tea. 'You know what's bothering me? It's how confident Ahmed was when we talked to him. He didn't seem ruffled at all that we'd found the phone. There was one moment when I was sure he was worried, but then he relaxed again. And when I went on about the code that was hidden in there, he didn't even flinch.'

They sipped at their drinks, then Oscar spoke. 'Don't let that influence you too much. He thinks he's clever. And one of the first things you notice when dealing with these people is how sure of themselves they are. They're zealots and fanatics. That's what makes them so dangerous.'

'Any news of Ahmed's associates?' Adam asked.

'We've checked them out. None were in Exeter when the bombing happened. And there's no indication any were friendly with John Tanton, or involved in the plot. I think we can rule them out. We've searched Ahmed's flat and gone through his computer. He's been looking at plenty of Islamic websites, but none dedicated to terrorism or even extremism. There's no hint of any bomb-making research or activity.'

'So, what next?' Sierra concluded.

Adam ran a hand over his chin. Even this early in the morning the stubble was starting to grow.

'Ahmed has to remain our prime suspect. He knew Tanton well. He could have radicalised the boy without leaving a trail. Whispers in his ear, encouragement to look at the right websites, a bit of advice on bomb-making, all done with no trace of his involvement. Then a nice little trip to Exeter to watch the results of his handiwork. And he walks away from the carnage, unharmed and untouchable.'

'I agree,' Sierra said. 'But to convict him, we have to have something to link him to Tanton and the bombing. And at the moment we don't. It all comes down to that phone call Tanton made just before he went into the Minster. OK, it appears most likely it was to Ahmed, but how? And how do we prove it?'

'We can't just work on that theory though,' Claire added. 'It could have been someone else. We do have other suspects. The Imam and his minder, and that BPP man, Kindle. They all knew Tanton. They might have motives. And they were all in Exeter at the time of the bombing.'

'We've checked their mobiles of course, along with those of all known associates of Ahmed and Tanton,' Sierra said. 'And it's not any of those numbers that Tanton called before the explosion. But that's not to say they couldn't have got themselves a pay as you go mobile for the day and given him the number to ring if he needed help, or had doubts. As it seems likely he did.'

Adam said, 'We'd better start looking at those other suspects. We'll let Ahmed sit in the cells for a while. It might put a bit of pressure on him. In the meantime we can get on with going through all the others. Kindle, and that Imam at the mosque to start with.'

The two spies exchanged a quick glance.

'What?' Claire asked, then again, 'What?'

Adam folded his arms. 'Is there by any chance something you think you should be telling us?'

Oscar looked to Sierra, who gave another of her little nods of authorisation. 'The mosque,' he said. 'We've got an issue with you going in there.'

Chapter Eleven

DAN OPENED THE FLAT door and the morning sunshine streamed into the darkness of the hallway. It felt like a laser beaming into the stem of his brain. He grimaced, blinked hard, and went back inside to find his sunglasses. They were somewhere in the lounge, but he couldn't quite remember where. Rutherford watched as his master fumbled his way through shelves filled with piles of papers, his eyes screwed up against the painful light.

Dan switched his attention to the mantelpiece, then another jumble of newspapers and notes from old stories. He shifted a file and found himself staring at Claire's smiling face.

It was a photograph from a night out they'd had to celebrate the successful end of a case she was working on, the conviction of a thoroughly unpleasant man for domestic abuse. Claire was wearing a black, shoulderless dress, and looked stunning. Dan groaned to himself, went to throw the photo into the bin, then stopped, clicked his tongue, and slowly put it back in the pile.

He took some deep breaths and tried to clear his thoughts. The plan had been to get up early and go for a good run with Rutherford to wake himself up, but he had overslept. And now he had to get in to the newsroom to prepare for the interview with Ali Tanton. In between her tears of last night she'd said she wanted to speak out. It was a big story and he needed to be sharp for it. Or, at least, a lot sharper than he felt at the moment.

A persistent drummer was playing an enthusiastic bass beat in the back of his mind. Dan caught a glimpse of himself in the mirror and wished he hadn't. He found the sunglasses – in a place where he had already looked, naturally – with an afterthought swallowed a couple more headache tablets and made for the car. He said goodbye to Rutherford, closed the door, yawned hard, fished the car key from his pocket and stopped, stunned.

Dan was no fan of cars, could never understand people who

raved about them, their sleek lines, their power and performance, and endlessly fantasised about the purchase of the latest model. He was quite content with the company-issue Peugeot, a passably comfortable, anonymous diesel model. It transported him to and from stories and on to Dartmoor to walk Rutherford, it was reliable, economical, reasonably green, and that was sufficient. It was a background factor in his life, one Dan was hardly aware of.

But today he very much noticed it.

The car had been vandalised. Or perhaps, Dan thought as he gaped, that was a masterpiece of euphemism. It might be more accurate to say it had been the subject of a frenzied attack. Where once the Peugeot was a standard dark blue, now it had been sprayed with paint in a range of colours. On the bonnet it was red, the roof white, the sides green and the back orange.

And each carried the same message.

KEEP YOUR NOSE OUT

Dan drove into work, thankful it was only a five-minute journey. Almost every face he passed was staring. At a set of traffic lights a couple of students even took photos with their mobile phones. Dan tried to slink lower in his seat, but that just made his head pound anew, kindly accompanied by a wave of nausea.

He got to the studios car park just before nine, was going to park right at the back, out of the way, but with an afterthought manoeuvred the car into a space by the main reception.

There are few places gossip travels faster than a newsroom, and within a couple of minutes the car was surrounded by journalists, picture editors, cameramen, engineers, producers, even the kitchen staff, all gawping and asking questions about what had happened. He found his head starting to clear with the potent medicine of being the centre of attention. The familiar clip-clop of fast-moving stiletto heels duly followed, just as Dan had expected it would, and Lizzie arrived, her hair flying.

'What the hell have you done to valuable company property?' she barked.

And good morning to you, Dan thought, before saying, 'I just found it like this when I came out this morning.'

'Any ideas why?'

'It can only be the bombing story. I think someone's taken exception to the questions I've been asking.'

'Who?'

'Well, Islamic extremists have to be a good bet. But I wouldn't rule out the BPP, or someone associated with them. It's a bit of a coincidence that the mosque was covered in graffiti yesterday and now my car's suffered likewise.'

'How the hell do they know where you live?'

Dan hesitated. As ever, Lizzie had cut right to the core of the story. Whoever attacked the car clearly knew more than a little about him. Just as the spooks had yesterday. And equally clearly they weren't members of the Dan Groves fan club.

'Don't know,' he muttered uneasily.

Lizzie ground a heel into the tarmac, and then said something which took Dan by surprise. 'Well, you be careful. You're dealing in a dangerous world at the moment, with these terrorists, murderers, fanatics and spies. Just watch yourself.'

Dan felt his mouth falling open. He was about to thank his editor for her unexpected pastoral care and unprecedented concern when she added, 'It's a huge story and I don't want anything messing up our coverage. Now, what have you got for me today? I want a follow-up, I want it on the lunchtime news, I want it exclusive and I want it good.'

The rest of the crowd began drifting away. The show was over, normal service resumed. Dan explained about his interview with Ali Tanton, received a brusque 'acceptable' by way of approval, and the news-seeking missile that was Lizzie was away, heading back upstairs.

'And you'd better report the damage to the police,' she flung over her shoulder. 'Make sure you get a crime number so we can claim it on the insurance.'

Dan walked slowly to the canteen to find Nigel. He sent his friend outside to film the car, just in case it became part of the bombing story, then got himself a coffee and phoned the police. An officer would be dispatched within half an hour to take a statement.

Dan sat down, focused on his notes about the Minster bombing, and started working through what he needed to ask Ali Tanton.

The Stonehouse area of Plymouth, where Ali lived, was an up and coming residential district, bounded by the docks and city centre. It was once the focus of the red light industry and filled with pubs that served as much in the way of measures of drugs as beer, but many of the houses are beautiful Georgian buildings and ripe for gentrification.

As Plymouth grew in wealth, so the efforts to rejuvenate Stonehouse followed and were advancing towards success. Dan suspected Ali's choice of home indicated her business was doing OK, enough to comfortably live on, without being in danger of propelling her into the ranks of the rich.

It was the same area where they'd joined the brothel raid, only three days ago. They passed the street, the house still looking just as ordinary. But how much had happened in those days. It felt as though the world had changed, and by no means for the better; the arrival of terrorism in gentle Devon, along with murder, spies and intrigue too.

Nigel drove them, sticking carefully to the speed limits, as ever, and taking advantage of the time together to administer one of his fatherly lectures. The twin themes were warning Dan to be careful, as he could be dealing with some ruthless people on this story, and also a few words about his drinking.

'What drinking?' Dan asked in surprise.

'Come on. I can smell it on you. Whisky.'

'Can you?'

'Yes.'

Dan felt his face flush. 'OK, I had a couple of glasses last night. But it was just to make me sleep. I couldn't get off, and it sometimes helps to have something like that to make you relax and ...'

He caught his friend's look. 'OK, I'll try to take it easy on the drinking.'

To escape the subject Dan called Adam. The detective could

only speak briefly, but did say he had been interviewing Ahmed.

'Get anywhere?' Dan asked.

'On balance, I would say not.'

'Got any updates for me?'

'Not really.'

'Any chance of me coming to join the investigation after all?'

'Don't think so.'

'Come on, Adam, I've helped out before. I could be useful.'

'You mean you're dying to play detectives again.'

'I mean I'm trying to help.'

'There's no chance of you getting in at the moment. The spooks are in charge and they're going to do things their way.'

Dan snorted. 'OK then, are you getting anywhere with the mobile numbers and names in Ahmed's phone?'

'No.'

'Any hope of me having a look?'

Now Adam paused, and Dan could sense his friend deliberating. Finally he said, 'Look, I'd love you to see them. But if you had them, the spooks would know they could only have come from me and they wouldn't hesitate to have me thrown off the inquiry and probably suspended too.'

'I'm not going to give up, you know. I will get back in somehow.'

'Why doesn't that surprise me? Look, just be patient for now. Let's see how things go.'

Dan was about to hang up when he remembered what had happened to his car. He related the story.

'Blimey,' Adam replied. 'Looks like someone's got it in for you.'

'Thanks for that. The suspicion had occurred to me.'

'Well, just make sure you watch your back,' the detective added, and hung up.

It was the third personal safety warning Dan had received in an hour and none were serving to make him feel any more comfortable. He turned on the radio to distract himself and tried to tap along with the beat of some modern hit he had no hope of recognising. It barely sounded like music, an indiscernible melody accompanied by indecipherable lyrics. He must be getting old.

Nigel stopped at a petrol station and Dan bought a packet of mints. It would scarcely be ideal for Ali to smell the drink on him. As he queued at the till, he was aware of a woman to his side, watching him. She was striking without being obviously attractive; tall, thin and flame-haired. He looked over and she smiled.

'Can I have a word with you in a minute? Outside,' she added, in a way that sounded meaningful.

Dan nodded. 'Sure.' He paid for the sweets, waited outside the kiosk, then remembered Nigel's comments about his breath. He quickly opened the packet and chewed on a couple, being careful to run them all around his mouth.

'Sarah Jones,' she said, holding out her hand as she emerged. 'I think you drink in my local sometimes. The Castle, on Mutley Plain.'

Dan shook the hand. It was cool and smooth, the nails long and painted emerald green. 'Yes, I do. They serve good beers.'

She chuckled. 'I prefer the wine, but I like the atmosphere. I've tried to catch your eye a couple of times, but you've always seemed engrossed in what you're thinking about.'

'Have you? Hell, the things I miss.'

Sarah laughed again, took a step forward so their faces were close together and whispered, 'I've got something I need to talk to you about. I think you'll find it interesting.'

'Really?'

'Yes.'

Her eyes were so distractingly green that Dan was struggling to find any words to say. 'Err, what's it about?' he managed.

'I can't tell you here. We'd have to have a proper chat. If I give you my number will you call me?'

Dan hesitated. 'Err, yeah, of course …'

Sarah gave him a look. 'Then I think I'd better take yours.'

She held out her hand. Dan found himself placing his mobile in it. She typed in her number, then rang it. In her bag a phone trilled. 'There,' Sarah said. 'That's you logged on my mobile. Now there's no getting away. I'll look forward to seeing you.'

She got into her car, a low-slung, gleaming black sports model. Dan walked automatically over to Nigel, who was grinning broadly. As she pulled out of the petrol station Sarah wound down a window and blew a lingering kiss.

'I think she likes you,' Nigel observed.

They climbed into the car and set off for Ali's house. It was just a couple of minutes away.

Dan checked his phone. The name the vision of emerald and flame had typed in was "Sexy Sarah".

Outside Ali Tanton's house a sizeable press pack was gathered, all moaning about the lack of any pictures or interviews. The news of John's death had been released to the media and it was the story of the day. Ali was the interview everyone wanted, and no one had got it.

At least not yet.

Dan found himself smiling, a rare and unexpected experience of late. It was an expression which was only enhanced by a lingering hint of the perfume Sarah Jones had been wearing rising from his shirt. He helped Nigel to get the camera kit from the car and they made for the house.

Dirty El slunk through the pack and materialised beside them in that spectral way of his.

'You got an in with her?' he whispered. 'Care to share it with your old pal? A snap'll be worth thousands to poor El. It'll help tide him through the lean winter months.' He patted his far from emaciated stomach, then looked down and stopped with the realisation he was unlikely to convince anyone of his poverty. The only six pack El would ever boast would be made up of tubs of lard.

'Anyway, beers on me if you can grease me way in, and maybe a little rhyme too,' he added, and produced a sleazy grin.

'You're feeling better,' Dan noted. 'We haven't had the privilege of one of your dreadful bursts of improvised poetry

113

since the bombing, and oh how we've missed them. Sunday school hangover lifted, has it?'

'You can't keep a good man down for long. Or a bad one.'

'I'll see what I can do. I can't promise, not even for you. It depends how she is.'

El's chubby face slipped into a conspiratorial wink. Dan picked his way through the disgruntled mass.

'Don't bother, mate,' grumbled a reporter from The National News. 'She's not answering.'

'Yeah, it's pointless,' added another, who Dan recognised as working for one of Britain's most disreputable tabloids. 'She won't even come out to pose for a piccie, the selfish bleeding woman.'

The feeling of enjoyment grew. Dan put on his best smile, led Nigel through the last of the photographers and reporters and knocked gently. A curtain twitched and the door opened.

In the hallway Dan reached out a hand, but Ali ignored it, stepped forwards and gave him a squeezing hug. She had been crying, her eyes angry and rimmed in red.

'They won't even let me see him,' she said, her voice thin and trembling. 'They say there are more tests they've got to carry out and they can't release his body for burial.'

Ali led them to a lounge at the back of the house. It was small, but impeccably neat, as was often the way with people who had suffered a bereavement. Tidying was a common palliative, a distraction, for a few minutes at least. Through the window they could see a photographer sitting on top of the garden wall.

'It feels like I'm under siege,' she whimpered. 'When will they go away?'

'They won't, I'm afraid, not until they get something. I might be able to help, but we'll sort that out in a while,' Dan replied. 'How are you coping?'

She managed a forlorn smile. 'Not very well. I've had a couple of friends come and look in on me, but I'd rather be alone most of the time.' She pointed to a photo of John on the wall, wearing his football strip, covered in mud but smiling broadly. 'I still can't believe what's happened ... and he died without me even getting to see him again,' she burst out, and began crying once more.

Dan sat her down in an armchair and sent Nigel to the kitchen to make a cup of tea. The last time they'd met, at some conference, Ali had looked strong and full of life. Now she'd crumpled. Her face was lined and gaunt, her green top clashing with her blue trousers, her dark hair lank and unwashed, and she was visibly trembling.

'Are you sure you want to go through with this interview?' Dan asked.

She nodded forcefully. 'Yes. I've got to tell people what John was really like. And what they've done to him. It wasn't his fault, they made him do it …'

She reached out for another hug. Dan could feel the dampness of her tears spreading through his shirt. Nigel brought in a tray of tea and began setting up the camera. Ali watched him warily.

'How's business been going?' Dan asked. 'It's publishing you do, isn't it? Have you put out anything good recently?'

Another sad smile. 'It's all good. We haven't produced any blockbusters, but a book on the hidden history of Devon has sold well. We're going to do another one on Plymouth soon. And something on the best walks in the South-west.'

'That sounds like my sort of book. I could do with some new ideas. I think my dog's getting fed up with the same old ones all the time.'

They talked on; about the merits of walking Dartmoor compared with the coast, safe subjects, a world and more away from bombings and death, until Nigel gave Dan's foot a subtle tap.

'Well, I suppose we'd better get on. Are you ready, Ali?' he asked and received a tense nod in reply. 'First of all then, we've heard a lot about John and what he did, but tell me about him. What kind of a boy was he?'

She bit at her lip. 'He was a great son. It's always been just him and me, and even from when he was young he tried to take care of me. I remember when he was only ten, for my birthday present he paid for his own babysitter so I could go out for the night with my friends. She wouldn't take his money, said she'd do it as a favour, so he insisted on giving me ten pounds to buy myself a bottle of wine. That's the kind of boy he was.'

Dan adopted an encouraging smile. 'And what was he like as he grew up?'

'To be honest, he wasn't great at school. He didn't have that many pals. He seemed to find it difficult to make friends. Some of the kids picked on him because he was quite big for his age and wouldn't have a go back. But he did all right. He had a few mates. He did well at woodwork and he was thinking of becoming a carpenter. He made a couple of things for me.'

She pointed to the mantelpiece where a small wooden model of a dolphin stood. It was well-worked, the lines sleek and smooth. After they'd finished talking, Nigel would film it. Cutaway shots were always useful to help illustrate an interview.

'It was when he started playing football that he really became happier,' Ali continued. 'The school second team was short of a goalkeeper one day and he was the only one available. I remember him telling me some of the kids went out on the pitch saying they'd lost already because John was in goal. But he played really well, saved all the other team's shots, and his team won two nil. He came home so happy because the lads said he'd done great. For the first time he felt accepted.'

Dan nodded, paused before asking his next question, to give himself a chance to compose it and to allow Ali to dab at her eyes. They were approaching the difficult ground.

'He sounds like a very normal boy, but how did he change? And what do you believe changed him?'

She swallowed hard. 'It was some of the people he fell in with. One person in particular, that Ahmed. John started going on about Islam and wanting to be a Muslim. The things he was saying – they worried me.'

'What sort of things?'

'He started saying that Britain was rotten. That it needed to be taught a lesson. That it was full of loose women and immoral men. Other things about how much better Islamic

116

countries were.'

'And what did you do about that?'

'I talked to him. But I thought it was just a phase. He's had infatuations before. That's his character. He got totally hooked up in the Young Christian Fellowship for a few months once. Another time it was a cycling club. He's easily led. If people made him feel a part of something, made him feel wanted, he'd go along with it.'

'And that's what you believe happened with the bombing? What led him to it?'

She was crying again now, the tears sliding down her pale face. Dan heard the hum of the camera's motor as Nigel zoomed in the shot for the powerful close-up, revealing every twitch of emotion.

'Yes,' Ali replied. 'It must have been. He couldn't have done it himself. He would never have thought like that on his own. He wouldn't have been able to ...'

Her voice cracked. Dan kept quiet and let her find the thoughts. Silence, the secret art of interviewing.

Ali let out a shuddering breath, twined her fingers together, and then the words came again and fast, a rush of feeling.

'He wouldn't have been able to make bombs. Not John. Not my boy. He would never have been able to make them and would never have wanted to blow himself up, and other people too. He would never have gone into the Minster to explode a bomb if he hadn't been indoctrinated and radicalised. They used him. And now ... now ... he's dead. And they've got what they wanted and they're safe and free and they're laughing. The bastards, the evil, vicious bastards.'

Again Dan let the silence run. They had almost all they needed, just time for the last question. It had to be asked.

'Finally then, I have to put this to you. You've defended your son, of course. But – he took a bomb into a sacred building, detonated it and killed and injured innocent people, and no one made him do that.'

Ali Tanton stared at him, and Dan wondered what reaction he was going to get. She dropped her head and stared down at the floor. Long seconds edged past. But when she finally spoke, her voice was the calmest it had been.

'I understand what people must be thinking of John. But I'd ask them to remember this. John was young and he was vulnerable. He was no more than a boy. He was preyed on. My heart goes out to the families of the people killed and injured in the explosion. But my son died too. He wasted his young life. That was the price he paid for nothing more than being vulnerable and trusting. I believe he was as much a victim in this as anyone else.'

It was one of those rare stories that stops a newsroom. Dan made a point of sitting next to Lizzie as the lunchtime bulletin was broadcast. All the other hacks gathered around the TV monitors, quietened by the drama of Ali Tanton's words.

It had been an easy report for Dan to cut. He used most of her interview, interspersed with a brief recap on the story, some of the pictures of the damage to the Minster, a photograph of John and a couple of shots in his bedroom. After the interview, Ali had said that her son spent many hours in there on the computer, often with Ahmed for company.

Dan explained that to the viewers, but didn't use Ahmed's name. It was also bleeped out of the section of interview where Ali mentioned it. Lizzie had consulted with the legal department, who feared he could sue for libel if he was named. As far as the law was concerned there might be suspicion, but there was, as yet, no proof, and that meant he was officially innocent – for the moment, at least. It was the same reason they had obscured the picture of his face and not used his name when Ahmed had been arrested in the shopping arcade.

When the report ended, Lizzie announced it was, 'Not bad.'

'Not bad?' Dan queried.

'Not bad at all.'

He sighed, but didn't say anything. His editor sometimes failed even to reach the heights of damning with faint praise.

'I'll have more of the same for tonight,' she continued. 'And no resting on your laurels either, just because you've got a minor scoop to your name. I want each twist and turn and every update going on this story. I want it first, I want it on

118

every bulletin, and I want it good.'

Dan walked downstairs to the canteen to get a sandwich. He took satisfaction from the continual ringing of phones as journalists from across the country called to ask for permission to report some of Ali's quotes. They would be used to complement the photos El had taken. Before they left, Dan suggested that a way of getting rid of the press pack would be to let just one photographer in to take some snaps. She had agreed, and Dan called his scurrilous friend.

The paparazzo gushed with a geyser of thanks, promised Dan "the mother of all nights out", and also produced the threatened rhyme. El's trademark eccentricity – or at least, the most notable of the many – was back.

The bomb, it shocked,
Even El was rocked.
But then normality returns,
Heals society's burns,
And with a piccie, El's cashflow's unlocked!

Aside from the usual score of dreadful on the poetic meter, the little doggerel ran with a hint of being subdued. 'I reckon I'm still feeling a bit bumped by what's happened,' the paparazzo explained.

As he queued at the sandwich bar, Dan's thoughts kept slipping to the investigation. There could be no other conclusion than that Ahmed must remain the prime suspect for radicalising John Tanton. Those hours spent together in John's bedroom could easily have been used to lead him to websites which provided instructions on how to build a bomb. Keep whispering the propaganda into his ear, drip by poisonous drip, and a terrorist had slowly built the ideal machine to carry out an attack without any harm to himself. There would always be suspicion about who was ultimately behind the bombing, but never proof.

The theory, though, did have complications. Ali mentioned that John had indeed been coached by Kindle at football training and looked up to the man. She didn't think they'd spent a great deal of time together, but Kindle would undoubtedly have had occasions when he was alone with John, and perhaps enough to influence his thoughts.

She confirmed that John had visited the Islamic centre regularly, usually on a Friday for prayers, and had talked about speaking to both the Imam and his minder. He seemed in awe of them. They too would both have had the chance to talk to John alone.

Ali said John had also visited Exeter a couple of times in recent weeks. To shop, so he claimed, but he could have been to the Minster, perhaps even met Parfitt. And who knows what might have been discussed in a quiet corner of the magnificent old building?

Dan shook his head. His ideas were getting too far-fetched. What possible motive could the Principal have for helping a young Islamic convert blow up the Minster? OK, so he clearly had a dislike of Islam, but that was scarcely reason enough.

As for Kindle, what could be his motive? Increasing racial tensions, perhaps. That would certainly benefit the BPP, make its message resonate with some. And what of the Imam? He had appeared a peaceful and gentle man. His minder perhaps less so, but there was no evidence that he could be violent, only that little hunch Dan had felt.

Still, Adam had always told him never to ignore a hunch. Where was his friend when they needed to talk all this over?

A polite cough interrupted his thoughts. It was Doreen, the lady behind the sandwich bar. Dan apologised and hastily chose a ham and cheese baguette. Another lick of Sarah Jones' perfume floated by. He wondered if she would call him. Dan doubted he would ring her. It would be just another complication in a life which was already quite sufficiently full of them, replete even. If the cares of the world were a banquet, Dan felt he had dined on his share.

Ali had said something else which set Dan's mind at work. She too had been in Exeter on the day of the bombing, to look around the shops and get a feeling for potential books which might find a gap in the market. She also wanted to do some hunting for new clothes – or so she said.

Her reasons for being in the city sounded innocent and plausible enough, but neither required any corroboration. How convenient. Or perhaps, Dan thought, he had been working with the police too long and become overly suspicious. Surely Ali couldn't possibly have had anything to do with a bomb attack by her own son, one which had cost him his life.

Such plots were the stuff of fiction. But he had seen some very strange things in his time working with Adam.

Not that he was doing so any more.

Dan took his sandwich to the quiet room and started eating. He was alone and glad of it. He hardly noticed the taste of the food, just chewed mechanically. He tried to read a paper, but the thought wouldn't leave his mind. He should be with Adam, working through his ideas, helping on the inquiry. Not here, just sitting around.

The phone call. This case came down to the phone call John Tanton had made, most probably to the radicaliser, the dark silhouette of the unidentified person who was using an untraceable mobile phone in Exeter city centre. And now they knew that person could be Ahmed, Tahir, the Imam, Abdul, his minder, Kindle, Parfitt or even Alison Tanton.

No one else had appeared on the radar. No one else had the necessary connections to John, or the ability and opportunity to guide him to murder. There was no one else for him to call to be offered a warped justification for the atrocity he was about to commit.

The images of the blood stains in the Minster, the shrapnel scoring of the pews, the stretchers carrying away the wounded returned to Dan's thoughts. And the silent horror of the onlookers.

A hiss escaped his mouth. He should be sitting with Adam, going through all this, discussing a way to trap the person they were hunting. Between them they could do it. Solve another notorious case. Find some justice for the families of the dead and all those who had been injured in the attack.

He should be working on it, right now, not wasting precious time.

Dan tried to think of Rutherford and taking him for a good walk at the weekend, Sarah Jones and her green eyes, perhaps seeing her in the Castle for a drink, even Claire and what he would say to her when finally they had to meet.

Nothing distracted him. Dan walked outside and called Adam.

'Not a good moment. I'm busy.'

'I know, but I've got news. I've found things out. I've got ideas. New suspects, new possibilities.'

'Who? What suspects? What possibilities?'

Dan hesitated. It sounded so stupidly childish, utterly pathetic, but he said it anyway.

'I'm not telling you until I get back in on the case.'

'You know I can't do that.'

'I'm not telling you then. And it could be important.'

'Look, you're being stupid.'

'I want back in!'

'I can't.'

'But it's the way we've always worked. It makes sense. It gets results.'

Adam was sounding increasingly irritated. 'Dan, it's not my case. It's not my decision to make. Can't you understand that?'

'Then put me onto the bloody spooks. I'll tell them.'

'Look ...'

'Just put them on!'

Dan could hear a brief and muffled exchange of words in the background, then Sierra's calm voice came on the line.

'How can we help you?'

'I've got some new information.'

'What is it?'

'Do I get to come back in on the case?'

'I can't say that until I hear what it is you've got to tell us.'

'I'd like to come back in.'

'I can't decide until I hear what you've got to say.'

Again Dan hesitated.

'Can I?' Sierra prompted, her voice rhythmic, reasonable and relaxed. 'How can I judge until I know what you've got to tell me?'

Dan ground a foot in the dust. He closed his eyes, took a couple of paces, kicked out at a bush, then told her what he'd found.

The phone line hummed. The doors opened and a couple of engineers walked out, chatting animatedly, made for a van. Dan edged away, behind a tree. In the distance, a pneumatic drill began hammering. He noticed his chest felt oddly tight.

'Thank you,' Sierra said at last. 'We will have a look at what you've told us. You've done your duty as a good citizen. But I'm afraid we can't have you inside the inquiry. Now, please excuse me, I have work to get on with. Goodbye.'

'But ...'

The whine of the disconnection hit Dan like a flying fist. He physically recoiled, stared at the phone and tried to call back. It rang, but clicked in to Adam's answer machine. He tried again with the same result.

Dan raised his face to the sky, swore loudly, let out a yell of frustration, drew back his arm and hurled the mobile down onto the grass.

Chapter Twelve

COME THE MORNING AFTER the night before, some things still seem like a good idea, others less so.

The first business of the day was to clear his head – again. It wasn't becoming a habit, Dan reassured himself. It was simply that these were extraordinary times. But at least the task was straightforward, and even relatively pleasurable. He fished the lead from the back of the hallway cupboard, Rutherford prancing circles of yelping joy. They walked over the road to Hartley Park, Dan did a quick stretch – perfunctory might have been a better description – and they started running.

It was another beautiful autumn morning, the weather stuck in a benevolent groove. A couple of children were making their way to school and tried to call Rutherford over, but the dog ignored them with his usual lofty disdain. There was a whip of chill in the air, not quite enough to make a fog of their breath, but the world was turning inevitably onwards towards winter.

Rutherford's coat was growing thicker. The flat would soon be full of his floating hair, and Dan made a mental note to buy more vacuum bags. That, or get a cleaner, something he had been promising he would do for years now and no doubt would for many more years hence. Some chores simply grew old with you.

Dan found himself wondering how Sarah would react to an aerial ambush of dog hair. He hadn't asked if she suffered with any form of reaction to it, and it was a common ailment. A woman who dressed as well as she did certainly wouldn't welcome its irritating adherence to every form of known fabric in the human wardrobe.

Dan spluttered at himself. One night didn't make a relationship. Anyway, he had something far more important to consider. His instincts were being vocal in warning him of the danger he might be about to get into, but, as usual, that only served more as a temptation than a deterrent.

They ran under the line of oak trees at the southern edge of the park, the yellow morning light strobing through the gaps in the branches and leaves. A twig fell, then another, just missing them. In retaliation Rutherford left his traditional calling card on one of the trunks, then ran on wearing his tongue-out, smiling face.

'Such behaviour is nothing to be proud of,' Dan panted at him.

Running was hard work today. Dan winced as his head pounded anew, but he kept going. There was plenty he had to do, and he would get through it. He waved two fingers in the air to an imaginary audience of Sierra and Oscar. 'I'm on the inquiry, whether you like it or not,' he panted to himself. 'This is my patch.'

Last night had certainly been interesting. After the lunchtime news, the rest of the day was quiet. His report had again led *Wessex Tonight*, quite rightly too, with just a couple of added lines that the police still had one man in custody being questioned in connection with the bombing and that inquiries continued elsewhere.

Dan got away early, pleading the extra hours he'd worked of late, and after the usual sceptical hearing the merciless Judge Lizzie had allowed him to go home. She'd inserted the proviso, naturally, that he kept his mobile phone on and would reappear back in the newsroom within an instant, if not sooner, if there were any developments on the story and would work on them until he dropped.

He would have been surprised by anything less.

Rutherford had been walked and fed, and Dan even managed to feed himself with some beans and out of date cheese on a couple of pieces of flaky bread, well toasted to hide their staleness. He was in the Old Bank pub on Mutley Plain by seven with a notepad, a pen and a couple of pints on the table. There was thinking to be done.

Dan Groves had great cause to be in the rich debt of two teachers from his schooldays. A lad from a working-class background, his family had no history of higher education. Dan had managed to stay at school to take A levels, then was set on getting out to work and earning some money.

But Mr Lewis, his maths teacher, and Mr Warr, his chemistry master, had persuaded the recalcitrant youngster that university was really little more than one big party, which he would enjoy a grant for, that there were girls aplenty, and the odd bit of work for a degree was merely a passing inconvenience, an almost unnoticeable distraction from the glorious business of having fun.

The sound of this he liked. Off he went, got involved with the university radio station and duly found a career in broadcasting. Without the intervention of the two kindly teachers Dan didn't like to think what he would have ended up doing.

He had one further big thank you for Mr Lewis. The man had a memorable mantra. It was simple and clever, and it was this; turn your weaknesses into strengths. Every disadvantage can become an advantage – if you think cleverly enough.

Many times before Dan had remembered the words and used them. Tonight, he did so again. Sitting at the back of a pub, avoiding the curious gazes and the odd outbreak of unsubtle pointing from those other patrons who had recognised him from the television, he worked through the plan. And he was amazed at how easily it came.

The piece of paper was satisfyingly full, just as the third pint slipped threateningly close to exhaustion. The timing was perfect.

It could only be a sign.

The clock on the wall said it was a quarter to nine. Dan sat back on his chair. The world was looking a much happier place, and there was still another couple of hours drinking to be done, maybe even more.

And perhaps some naughtiness beckoned too.

He took his phone, sent the text message, got up and headed outside, towards the next pub.

The Castle.

Adam was back in the bus station café, but this time with Claire for company.

'Is there any particular reason you chose here?' she asked,

looking quizzically around at the sticky tables, grizzled patrons, and the customary semi-circle of fumigators gathered outside the door. 'It doesn't immediately strike me as your kind of coffee shop.'

Adam nodded. 'That's exactly why. It's out of the police station and it's not where they'd expect us to be.'

'The spooks?'

'Yep.'

'You take me to all the nicest places.'

Adam managed a smile, but it was brief. 'I thought we needed to talk. There's something bothering me.'

On the road outside, the rush hour queues were at their height, the car windscreens filled with a line of resigned faces. It was just after half past eight. Adam had again chosen a table in the corner of the café, where he could see the door and the pavement outside.

He checked around and leaned forwards. 'What did you make of what they had to tell us yesterday?'

'About the mole?'

'I think the modern spook parlance is *asset*, but yes.'

In the Bomb Room, Sierra had explained the spies "issue" with the investigation turning to the mosque. Someone from a high level there was a security services' informer. Or, at least, that was what Adam inferred from what little he'd managed to glean.

'So, who is it?' he asked Sierra.

'You know I can't tell you that.'

'What's his position then?'

'An important one.'

'What?'

'A useful one.'

Adam sighed heavily. 'What exactly?'

'I can't tell you that.'

'I thought we were sharing information.'

'We are.'

'Well, that's a new definition of sharing to me. Maybe I'd call it the only-child syndrome. Or one-way sharing. We share, you don't.'

127

Standing at the side of the room, Oscar was watching and smirking. The light fell along the scar on his neck, a living weal in the thin flesh. He was straddling the briefcase, as though protecting it.

'I mean,' Sierra said heavily, 'That if you knew, it might compromise the asset and that could seriously endanger him.'

'So you want me to leave the mosque alone?'

'No. That in itself could raise suspicions.'

With a strained calm, Adam asked, 'So – you want me to go in half-heartedly?'

'No. That would be suspicious too.'

'So what the hell do you want me to do?'

Oscar had interrupted, 'All right, let's keep our tempers. We're all supposed to be on the same side here.'

'Really?' Adam retorted sarcastically.

'We are merely saying,' Oscar continued, 'that we expect you to question the Imam, and his minder, and anyone else you wish at the mosque. But please bear in mind that they were not in any way responsible for radicalising John Tanton, and nor was anyone else there.'

'And you're sure about that?'

'Quite sure.'

'Has it ever occurred to you that your "asset" might be – what is it you call them? A double agent? Feeding you duff information to put you off the track?'

The spies exchanged a condescending look. 'Funnily enough, Chief Inspector,' Sierra said levelly, 'yes it has. We are more than familiar with assessing the reliability of sources, and I would ask you to respect our conclusions.'

And there, the conversation, as such it was, had ended.

Claire tapped a hand on the table, found it sticking to the surface, gave it a distasteful look and stopped. 'I know what you mean, sir. If they want us to behave normally in the inquiry, then why tell us about this informer at all? Maybe they are trying to help us, but are bound up by the way they work.'

Adam snorted unpleasantly. 'Maybe. I just think it's odd. Something doesn't quite add up.'

'When you put it like that, I think you're right. It really

annoys me, the way they stand in the corner, whispering to each other. Not to mention that smirk Oscar always wears. So what do we do?'

'We keep investigating. Bear in mind what they've said, but …'

'But?'

'I think we just handle the case our way, regardless. Shall we get back to the station? It's time to see our spook friends for the morning briefing.'

They got up from the table, Claire leaving her cup of coffee untouched. It wasn't what she'd wanted anyway, but the request for a herbal tea had been met with incomprehension.

'Just one more thing,' Adam added, as they made for the door. 'As we work through this case, don't feel obliged to tell Sierra and Oscar everything. I'm not convinced there aren't some details we might just be better off keeping to ourselves.'

The text came back within five minutes, just as he expected it would.

I'll be there in half an hour. Got to glam up for you! x

Dan got himself another pint and found a table for two at the back of the pub. Perfect. It gave him just enough time to go through the plan again.

The title he finally chose, Dan wasn't sure about. It seemed a little personal, perhaps unprofessional, but it also felt good and so he had written it anyway. Beneath it came the individual headings.

1. The unlikely angel.
2. Computer geeks – chase the hunch.
3. News library etc for suspects.
4. Secret filming?
5. Ali Tanton – anything more?
6. Adam – keep pushing.

Below each heading, Dan had scribbled the outline of his ideas. And it would all start tomorrow. He raised a glass and toasted his reflection in a mirror, ignoring the puzzled expression of a couple at a nearby table. He sent a text to El, to confirm their arrangement and received one back saying fine, it'd be a pleasure.

The little mission was not just right up the photographer's street, it was parked firmly on his driveway.

The door opened and Sarah Jones walked in. Relaxed and confident, escorted by every admiring male eye in the bar, and each jealous female one.

She had enhanced her already impressive stature by wearing heels of which even Lizzie would have been proud. They must have taken her to well over six feet, and she moved with none of the self-consciousness of a woman unused to dynamite dressing. The black trousers rippled with the length of her legs, the green top was just as effective at emphasising her body, and her copper hair was tied up in a way which enhanced the angles of her face and greenness of her eyes.

'Buy a girl a drink?' she asked, coyly. Dan got up and went to the bar. With an afterthought he returned and kissed her cheek, then went back to the bar. With another afterthought he came back again to find out what drink it was that she wanted.

He had, he reflected ruefully, never quite got the hang of a date.

'Wine. Red wine.' She puckered her lips. 'And a bottle, please. It's been quite a day.'

Already flitting in the rarefied atmosphere of Dan's upper esteem, Sarah now managed to rise even higher. He brought the drinks over, trying hard to ignore the knowing looks from the barman and a couple of other customers. One man even gave him a thumbs-up.

'So, err – busy day then?' was Dan's inspired opening gambit.

Sarah frowned. 'Yes. Very busy. OK, let's get the small talk over. I work for a marketing company, I live in my own flat just around the corner from here, no I don't have a cat, I'm 38 years old, I like doing my own thing, but I also like clever men. I don't like beating about the bush, children and beards. I'm single because I want to be, because horribly few men trump my own company and I certainly haven't met anyone like that lately.' She paused, then added meaningfully, 'Though I'm hoping that might change in the near future. You?'

Dan was struggling to think about anything apart from those eyes. The other five and a half feet of pure body beneath was making an impact too, he had to admit, but the eyes were mesmeric. They were like swimming in an emerald sea.

'I'm 40 years old, live in my own flat at the top of the hill, a fantastic mid-Victorian place, with my Alsatian Rutherford. I've got my own teeth, or at least I had the last time I checked, and most of my own hair, although it does seem to be thinking about migrating south for the winter.'

A giggle at the fantastic triumph of witticism reassured Dan it was safe to proceed.

'I like walking, particularly on Dartmoor. I like pubs and beer, I like my job because it's a brain-bending challenge some days and I can guarantee I'll never get bored. And I also like my own company, but I too wouldn't be above sharing time with someone who's worth it.'

Dan thought he would gloss over why he was single. He could almost see Claire out of the corner of his eye. She was sitting at a table, silently watching him, her face impassive. Her ghost never knew when to take a hint and have a few hours off from its haunting duties.

'Good,' Sarah replied slowly, and Dan thought he felt a touch of leg against his. 'Then shall we see if we're both worth it?'

She lifted the glass to her lips and took a long drink of the claret liquid. A kiss of lipstick held to the rim, dark patterns on the shiny surface.

'So, what was it you wanted to tell me?' Dan asked.

'You want to know the truth?'

'Is it pleasant?'

'I think so.'

'Go on then.'

'I've got nothing to tell you at all. I just recognised you from the television, I noticed you were on your own and I wondered what you were thinking about. You looked – interesting.'

Now Dan chuckled, couldn't help himself. 'Like the way a gorilla in the zoo is interesting? Because it looks weird and does bizarre things? Or a road accident – the sort of interesting where people want to slow down to have a good look, but no one wants to get involved?'

She raised an eyebrow, but didn't react, instead she asked, 'What are you thinking about? When you're on your own?'

'Well, it could be a range of things. Maybe something as mundane as it's about time I did some food shopping, but when will I find the time? Or perhaps that I could do with some new socks with the winter coming on.' He paused, let a couple of seconds slip by, then added, 'Or sometimes it's trying to work out who a murderer is from a range of suspects.'

Her mouth turned into an alluring O. 'Really?'

And now, as the laws of life dictate it must be with men who are faced by beautiful women, the sensible side of Dan's brain, the one which had warned him to be discreet and modest and self-effacing and all those other noble traits melted away into the evening. He told Sarah about the extraordinary cases he had worked on with Adam and his role in solving them.

The pint glass was empty, but Dan didn't notice. The time ticked on, but he was totally unaware. The pub could have been demolished around him, the swing of a wrecking ball taking out each and every brick, and he would only have stood a remote chance of realising.

'And what about this current case?' she asked. 'I bet you're working on the Wessex Minster bombing, aren't you?'

Again the warnings which whispered in Dan's mind were as effective a barrier as air. He told Sarah all about the story, laced with plenty of his inside knowledge and never hesitating to play up the attack on his car and the threat to his personal safety.

Dan concluded the tale with another pinnacle of first-date humour. 'In fact, it's such a dangerous assignment that you're darned brave to risk sitting next to me.'

Another chuckle, but then Sarah's face changed. She leaned forwards and whispered, 'I think you're right. It could be too much of a risk. Perhaps we should go somewhere safer. Shall we head back to my flat for a nightcap?'

And so they had, and Dan had lain there in bed afterwards, wide awake, waiting for the icy downpour of guilt to fall. And it had failed miserably so to do. But what had instead intruded was the thought of tomorrow and his plan. So Dan got up, made the familiar excuses about work, oozed some unconvincing platitudes about seeing her again soon, kissed Sarah on the cheek, let himself out of her flat and walked home.

The cackle of a magpie brought him back to the park. Dan realised he had no idea how long he had been running, or how many laps he'd completed. But his head was clear, so it was enough. He put the reluctant Rutherford on the lead and they walked back to the flat. He still wasn't sure what to make of last night. It was as if his mind was in shock, not yet ready to venture its conclusion.

That was enough recapping. What was done was done. In time he could regret or enjoy the memory, but for now there were other matters to attend to.

It was time to put into action the first part of the plan that Dan had entitled, *Screwing the Spooks*.

Chapter Thirteen

THERE IS A CHANGE in the atmosphere of an investigation when news of a possible breakthrough comes. You can see it in the eyes of the officers, the purposefulness of their movements, their eagerness. Tiredness is banished and drooping heads lift. It spreads an invisible energy, an imperceptible expectation. And it's magnified many times over when it is an inquiry into a major or shocking crime, one in which the detectives feel a personal involvement, and where they have struggled in the search for justice.

Adam always thought of it as a primeval instinct, little different from the excitement of a hunters' pack at the scent of a quarry.

And they had picked up a trail.

The call came to Oscar, on his mobile, just as they were about to start the morning briefing. The source was not disclosed, naturally, but the man's smirk had, for once, disappeared, as he told the Bomb Room, 'Ahmed's got a cousin. He's kept it quiet, but we've got ... some new intelligence. The man's name is Tariq. He's from Plymouth. And get this – he lives in Stonehouse.'

The unspoken thought engaged each detective's mind. The lightning forks of shared insight and experience. This man could have known John Tanton through Ahmed. He lived in the same area of the city, plenty close enough to have been in contact. Enough to influence the boy, perhaps to radicalise him.

Oscar was still listening to the secret voice on the line. He hung up and added, 'And here's another thing. The mobile phone registered to this Tariq isn't the number Tanton called just before he set off the bomb, but it was in Exeter that day.'

And as one, that thought also spread. Tariq could have been using a pay as you go mobile to talk to Tanton. He believed he was smart, that he had covered his tracks and wouldn't be traced. But he was wrong.

It was too much to hope for, that he still had the phone, the one elusive piece of evidence which would solve the case, but they had to try.

'Get the firearms teams scrambled,' was all Adam needed to say in reply. 'Let's go.'

Dan was sitting in the News Library when the text message came through. It made him knock over his coffee and prompted a well-deserved scolding from Petra, the librarian. She quickly fussed around with a cloth, chiding him with every sweeping stroke. Drinks were not supposed to be brought in here, there was too much precious material which could be damaged. He apologised vaguely as he gawped at the message.

The morning had been going so smoothly. The firing squad that was interrogation by Lizzie had, for once, been successfully faced down. She wanted another follow-up story on the bombing, and, like a child who had been told about a unicorn, she wasn't remotely prepared to be convinced that such a beautiful and desirable creature existed only in her imagination. Dan had managed to get away by promising he would make some calls and see what he could find.

In reality, he wanted to get to the library to make a start on the research for his plan.

He'd expected the message to be from Sarah, wondered what he would read. Thanks for a fun night, but I don't think it'll work? Let's do it all again tonight? He wasn't surprised to find himself hoping it wasn't the latter. He was no longer nineteen years old and pumping with hormonal vigour.

Dan wondered if he should have texted Sarah first. It felt more gentlemanly, the modern equivalent of sending a handwritten note, or his calling card. But he still wasn't quite sure what to make of their night together. Perhaps it was cathartic, maybe just sleazy, perhaps it would be repeated, maybe not.

Claire was sitting in the corner of the library, watching him. She had changed her clothes from last night and was no longer in jeans, but had put on one of her black trouser suits. Her face was still impassive, perhaps a little sad or disappointed, but not obviously so.

Dan clicked his tongue. He'd just about finished the research he needed to do and was planning to slink quietly down to the canteen for a relaxing coffee and half an hour reading the paper. He hadn't got as much sleep last night as he would have liked. But the text message meant that delightful prospect had just been banished.

Lizzie would be getting her follow-up story.

Dan gathered up his notes and put them carefully into his satchel. The library had turned up two revelations of considerable interest. The first concerned Parfitt. He was an even more trenchant critic of Islam than Dan had thought.

The Principal had written a book entitled *The Clash of Civilisations*. In it, he had expounded the view that Christianity and Islam were fundamentally incompatible, and could not coexist.

He went on to argue that the modern day "threat" posed by Islam was not one of guns and swords and war, but instead a creeping and insidious change inflicted upon any society in which the faith took hold; a corrosion from within, stealthy and secretive, day by day, unnoticed until the mighty edifice fell. It was a view which generated considerable controversy, but Parfitt had stood by his opinions.

Intriguingly, one of the newspaper articles on the book contained a quote from Kindle. It argued the Principal had got his conclusions exactly right, and should be congratulated for being brave enough to speak out in the face of the prevailing gale of political correctness.

The other gem of information the library yielded concerned Kindle himself. He had been arrested following a BPP demonstration outside a church on Easter Sunday. Some of the worshippers complained it was intimidating and offensive on the most important day of the Anglican calendar. The police had been called, there was a minor altercation and Kindle was taken to the cells, all the while protesting his right to free speech was being infringed.

The Crown Prosecution Service must have come to the same conclusion. Kindle was released without charge and even received the apology he had demanded.

The protest was designed to draw attention to what the BPP claimed was the Church of England's lamentable vacuum of resistance to its waning influence in the country and unwillingness to exert its supremacy over other faiths, in particular Islam.

Dan nodded to himself. It had been a productive morning. He needed time to think through what he had learned. But for now, thinking space was to be a scarce commodity.

Petra asked if he was OK and had to ask again before he responded with a vague, 'Yeah, fine thanks.'

Dan looked at the message once more. It was from Adam. He rarely texted, thought of it as the preserve of the young, and hadn't quite got the hang of it. But what he wanted to communicate was clear enough.

Can't speak. Do NOT call. Got lead. Armed raid in Plym in 1 hour. Dock Street, Stonehouse. DON'T break cover until u see cops. My neck on block if u do. We need 2 talk LATER.

*   *   *

They'd learned the lessons of the past. Plainclothes armed cops no longer wore tight T-shirts to emphasise their muscles. Now it was old jackets to hide them. Short haircuts were also discouraged. A couple in the hurried briefing looked more like hippies than police officers, and one even had a thick beard reminiscent of a 1970s Open University lecturer.

The pistols and automatic rifles in their hands, dark and menacing in the gloom of the back of the police van, quickly dispelled that illusion.

They were parked around the corner from Dock Street. The drive from Exeter had taken a little over half an hour, sirens screaming the whole way, bullying the daily traffic from their path.

'Standard procedure,' the Tactical Firearms Adviser said quietly. 'A pincer movement. Surprise is the advantage. Use it ruthlessly. We go in the front, another team is going round the back. Mr Breen, I take it you want our target taken alive and mostly undamaged?'

'Yes please.'

'Tazer your preferred weapon then?'

'Yes.'

'How dangerous is he?'

Adam considered the question. 'We've got evidence he may be associated with Tanton and could even have played a part in radicalising him. So we can't rule out the possibility he may have firearms, or explosives, and could be willing to die to detonate them.'

One of the marksmen let out a low whistle.

'Then it's simple,' the Firearms Adviser said calmly. 'If there's any show of resistance whatsoever, stun him with the tazer. But if it looks like he's got a rucksack, or anything that might contain a bomb, then it's your sidearms. We can't risk the electricity setting it off. All clear?'

There were some mutters of yes, a few nods. Each man looked focused, their eyes bright in the half light. They started checking their weapons.

'Two minutes,' the Firearms Adviser murmured.

All was silent. One officer shifted his weight, making the van creak. Another itched at his nose.

A man at the back checked his Tazer. The red dot of its laser sight played on the metal roof.

A radio crackled. The driver reached out and turned it down.

Someone cracked their knuckles, the noise loud in the quiet of the van. Another officer took off his glasses and polished them on a sleeve. A motorbike buzzed past.

'One minute. Standby.'

A young man took out his wallet and kissed a picture of a woman and girl. The marksman to his side smiled and patted his shoulder.

'Your first big one?'

'Yeah.'

'It'll be all right, don't worry. These terrorists are bloody cowards. When they're blowing up women and children they're real hard men. But faced with us they shit themselves and can't surrender fast enough.'

A car drove past. The silence returned. At the back of the van a man coughed and cleared his throat.

'Thirty seconds.'

A couple of loud breaths. The windows of the van were fogging, make it even darker.

The Firearms Adviser held up his watch. 'Ten seconds. Good luck to us all.'

Dan and Nigel were sitting in the cameraman's car at the end of the street, watching a van. Nigel was wearing his baseball cap, pulled low down over his eyes. Dan had donned a pair of oversized shades he'd picked up from a garage on the drive down and a moustache he'd grabbed from a fancy dress shop. He was too well known not to make a reasonable attempt at disguise, but wondered if all he'd achieved was to draw attention to himself by resembling an ersatz porn star at a stag party.

'This tash keeps itching,' he complained.

'You shouldn't have to wear it much longer.'

'Good. I think it's giving me a rash. Any sign of action?'

'For the twentieth time – still no.'

They'd been waiting for almost half an hour. Dan had started to grow convinced they'd got the wrong place and had to forcibly stop himself calling Adam. Then the large white van had trundled slowly up the street and carefully parked. It looked absolutely ordinary, could have been any tradesman, but it was low on its axles as if heavily loaded, had manoeuvred with rare precision, and the man in the front was a little too watchful.

Since the van's arrival there had been nothing. The driver sat there, turning the pages of a newspaper, continually glancing up the street, but there had been no other movement.

Dan poked the moustache back up his lip. 'Bloody thing,' he muttered.

'You only have to wear it to make sure no one clocks us.'

'I wish they'd get on with it. I hate all this hanging about.'

'You sure about this?' Nigel asked.

'Yeah, I think so. It'll be a hell of an exclusive if something does happen.'

'Any idea what we're expecting?'

'No. I just got a tip off it was some kind of a raid connected with the bombing case.'

Nigel had the camera on his lap, primed and ready to go. 'Well, we're all set for when something happens. I don't think ...'

He stopped suddenly. The doors of the van had swung open. Men were jumping out. And they were carrying guns.

Adam was running, fast, up the street behind the pack of marksmen, his leather shoes pounding hard on the pavement. Panting breaths filled the air. He dodged around a lamp post, kept running. A couple of curtains twitched, a woman pushing a pram stopping to stare. All the passengers on a passing bus turned to watch too.

They ran on, focused only ahead. Along the street he was aware of a familiar figure getting out of a car, a camera being pointed towards them.

Adam felt himself starting to sweat, reached up, unbuttoned his collar and pulled down his tie. It was just like playing football with his son. The lad was getting faster and fitter as he grew into his teens, leaving his old dad behind with the wonder of the new stamina and strength.

At the front of the pack one of the cops had stopped, was pointing his arms towards a house.

An end terrace, painted white with blue windowsills. A For Sale sign in the front garden, a paved path, small rockery, a couple of well tended bushes. It was absolutely ordinary. A Neighbourhood Watch sticker in the window.

If this was the home of a terrorist, the man had an unexpected sense of humour.

A shove and the low metal gate flew open, swinging on its hinges, clanging into a fence. A door, painted blue. No hesitation. A swing of the battering ram, a cracking crunch of splintering wood. They tumbled inside.

Two marksmen clambered up the stairs, two more along a hallway. Adam stopped, watched, eyes wide, breathing hard. This was their time. A second to decide how to react to what they found here. To pull a trigger or not. To kill, or let live.

Panting and gasping. Thudding and shouting. 'Clear! Clear!'

Adam's mind spun to his own firearms training. A morning on the shooting range, an afternoon of role-playing. The deafening noise, the pumping adrenaline. It had taken less than a day to decide it wasn't for him.

The agonising pressure of an instant's decision.

A door ahead, plain white and wooden, a poster of some vaguely familiar painting, pastel spring colours. A foot, kicking out, flinging it open. A kitchen, fridge freezer, work surfaces, cupboards, one half-open, some packets of cereal. A toaster, silver and shining. A bread bin. A plant on the windowsill.

Nothing else. No one here.

Another door, closed. A foot, reaching out, ready to kick. Then halting, suddenly, in a second.

A muffled thud from the unseen room, another shout and then a sound no one could mistake.

A sound that stopped everything, everyone.

A sound that echoed in the sudden silence.

A whipping crack.

A pistol shot.

Chapter Fourteen

THE HEADQUARTERS OF GREATER Wessex rose from a green field site a decade or so ago, and was created akin to the principle of a medieval castle. There are layers upon layers to traverse, a Russian Doll of departments to work through in order to reach the sanctum of the Keep.

At the fringes of the building are the administration offices, then comes Community Relations, Traffic and Neighbourhood Policing, before finally moving on to the Major Crime Team, Intelligence, Special Branch and Serious and Organised Crime. The transition is easily spotted – doors of anterooms, which once were open at the start of the journey are now all firmly closed and there are no signs upon them to proclaim the business of their inhabitants.

At the very centre of the building is the Command Suite, and a surprise. Visitors here usually expect to find the Chief Constable's office as the nexus, but of that notion they are disabused. It is situated close to the building's reception, along a corridor which is refitted with a new and comfortable carpet every couple of years, and boasts watercolour prints of classical Wessex scenes by a variety of local artists.

The office itself is large and light, with sizeable windows, soft furnishings, and yet more cheerful paintings. It's a room designed for taking tea, shaking hands, smiling, presenting awards and being photographed.

The brutal business of the reality of the guts and gore of policing goes on in the Deputy Chief Constable's office. The daily running of the force is carried out here, disciplinary matters, and the most sensitive of meetings and decision-making. The room is inexpensively furnished and functional, with just the one, relatively small, window, and the walls are plain. It is no place for an invitation to receive warm and hearty congratulations on how jolly well your career is going.

And if the office itself is austere, the waiting area is so nondescript as to be nigh unnoticeable. It is effectively an extension of the corridor, merely a begrudging widening to accommodate a row of plastic chairs and the desk of a secretary. The sole decoration is a water fountain, which has dripped for almost three years now, and still not been repaired.

Upon one of the uncomfortable chairs this sunny morning, trying to ignore the incessant dripping, which was just a little out of time with the rhythm of a burgeoning headache, sat Adam Breen.

Katie, the Deputy Chief's Secretary, had already offered tea, which he had declined. She smiled understandingly and slid back behind her desk. Once, at a leaving do, after a couple of glasses of wine, she had confided to a colleague how remarkably few people who were summoned here fancied a cup of tea. A small box of tea bags could last for many months. It was a story which spread around the force within a day, and almost as quickly became a saying applied to the less conscientious staff.

He's as hard working as the Deputy Chief's tea bags ...

Adam was the last to be called, which could be good news or bad. It meant either the breaking storm had dissipated some of its power, or instead that it had worked itself up nicely to something more approaching hurricane force.

It had been a busy couple of hours here. Katie, an elegant lady in her early fifties, used to work with CID, and had been kind enough to offer Adam a brief précis of what had passed before his arrival.

The Home Office were on the phone almost incessantly, demanding increasingly detailed explanations about the Plymouth raid, in tones of escalating hysteria. The press office had matched the level and ferocity of the calls with their requests for an official statement to throw to the frothing jaws of the media pack.

The Deputy Chief Constable expounded "formal words" upon the FX5 officer who had fired the fatal shot, a young and worried looking man known only as Delta, according to Katie. It was all Flood had it in his power to do, she whispered. He was not the officer's boss, but he was determined to make very clear his censure. And so he did. There would be an inquiry into what happened, and it would be added to the agent's service record, along with the recommendation he be suspended from firearms work and retrained.

The words had boomed easily through the closed door; Flood was not one to allow the niceties of departmental divisions to neuter his ire.

'As far as I am concerned, your sloppiness was unforgivable. It was only by sheer luck that the outcome of your actions was not far worse. You have brought my force into disrepute and you will not be welcome here again. Now get out.'

Flood, like many in the police, was once a military man. His nickname, due in part to his build and part his manner, was The Tank. And that this may have been inappropriate given that he served as a Royal Marine made no difference whatsoever. It fitted and it stuck.

The phone on Katie's desk warbled. She gave Adam another sympathetic smile, a look she had perfected within a very short time of becoming Flood's secretary, and directed him in.

'This investigation is a shambles, isn't it?' the Deputy Chief barked, in his usual forthright manner, before Adam had even a chance to consider whether to sit down.

'I wouldn't say it's a triumph, sir, certainly.'

'It is one of the biggest cases we have ever handled, and to be frank we're getting nowhere.'

'Well, we do have a prime suspect and some leads, but …'

'Spare me the platitudes, Adam,' Flood interrupted. He looked and sounded tired. 'I'm not blaming you for what happened. But it's not good. The Home Office are going mad and I'm running out of things to tell them. This debacle has made all the national media.' He pointed to one of the chairs. 'Sit down. Now tell me straight. What the hell is going wrong?'

Adam sat, ran a hand over his stubble. 'Honestly, sir?'

'Damn right.'

'It's a bloody mess. We're nominally in charge of the inquiry, but the spooks tell us what to do. They feed us what information they choose and we have to act on it. I don't have access to everything I need to know. I can't judge what's reliable and what's not and who to trust. It's worse than an investigation by committee.'

Flood nodded. 'Just as I suspected. Right, get back to the inquiry. But first, let me be clear. The information on this Tariq came entirely from the spies?'

'Yes sir,' Adam replied, emphatically.

The spooks were waiting in the Bomb Room, at the back, whispering to each other. When Adam walked in, they ushered the other detectives out. Claire pointedly didn't move from her desk.

'We'd like to talk to Mr Breen alone,' Oscar said sharply, pointing to the door.

'I'm his deputy on this case,' she replied. 'I'm staying.'

Sierra added softly. 'It might be in your interests to leave.'

Claire stood up to face her. 'What are you going to do? Shoot me too?'

Adam held up his hands. 'OK, that's enough. Claire's staying, so get on with what you want to say.'

Sierra stared at him, then sat down on the edge of a desk. Oscar leaned back against a wall, hooked out a foot to shift the briefcase alongside and folded his arms in front of his chest.

'What the hell were you doing, tipping off your little mate about the raid?' she hissed.

Adam too folded his arms. 'What makes you think I did?'

'He was there. With his cameraman. That's why the story's all over the country now.'

Adam snorted. 'The story's all over the country because of your crap so-called "intelligence", and your trigger-happy bloody officer. So don't try that shifting the blame stuff on me. Funnily enough, when a hack spots a mob of armed cops running around, he does tend to follow to see what happens.'

Sierra said, 'You're denying you tipped him off?'

'I'm saying the problem was your screw-up, not mine.'

'Stick it, arsehole,' Oscar snapped.

Adam turned to him. 'Ah, the attack dog's turn to talk

bollocks, is it? Or to do your best to muddy the waters around your own inadequacies?'

The spy was shaking his head, the scar on his neck throbbing. 'You know nothing. You're a countryside cop. You might as well ride around on a bike. You've never been out there, facing terrorists, putting your life at risk for your country. This case is too big for you. You can't handle it.'

'Yeah, if by that you mean I can't raid innocent people's homes and go shooting my little gun everywhere, then you might be right.'

'Fuck you.'

'Beautifully put. How impressive. My, the things they teach you in spy school.'

There was a glowering silence. Then Sierra said, 'Look, maybe we'd all better just calm down. Why don't we go get a cup of tea?'

Adam nodded. 'Good idea. Come on Claire, I could do with a walk.'

He made for the door and closed it pointedly behind them to stop the spies from following.

It was coming up for lunchtime and the bus station café was busy. Adam studied it, said, 'We can't talk here,' got a couple of take away teas and they crossed the road into Southernhay. He made for a park bench in a circle of shade cast by an aged beech tree. Other people were sitting out on the grass and low walls, enjoying their sandwiches in the sunshine.

The area was a favourite amongst Exeter shop and office workers, a Georgian parade, full of solicitors and estate agents, facing onto well-trimmed lawns and colourful flower beds. Tame and tubby sparrows hopped beneath the groups of people, begging crumbs and crusts.

Some of the birds were so fat that flight would present a Herculean challenge. The epidemic of obesity was not, apparently, confined to the human world.

A display offered an insight into the area. Southernhay was the most fashionable part of the city in Victorian times, boasting a spaciousness denied the major part of Exeter, confined as it was within the old Roman walls. There was even a public baths. The sense of space still lingered here, as the greens and gracious buildings managed to resist the merciless attack of the aggressive and destructive alien race known with some irony as Town Planners.

Today Southernhay has been made a cul de sac, sparing it the relentless noise, pollution and ugliness of the obsession with the motor car, a green breath of tranquillity at the heart of the city.

Adam rolled his neck, took off his jacket, loosened his tie and sipped at his tea. 'How would you say we're doing?' he asked Claire.

'Not well, sir. We've got a prime suspect in Ahmed, but we've got nothing on him. Or nothing that would stand up in court, anyway.'

'And still nothing from the interviews?'

'Oh, plenty, just nothing of any use. When he saw me this morning he called me a prostitute because I had the cheek to wear boots with a one inch heel. I got fed up with his ranting and sent a couple of the others in, hoping they might get on better. One got a broadside for having a tattoo on his arm – despoiling his sacred flesh, Ahmed called it. The other he just lectured on Anglo-American foreign policy and the historic repression of Muslims. He even came out with a little history lesson about the crusades. The two lads say it was highly informative, but not in any way helpful in building a case.'

Adam sighed. 'And nothing from the numbers and names on his phone?'

'No, sir. I got our own techno crime department to have a look at them without telling the spies, but they came up with nothing. No ideas, no leads.'

Adam watched the patterns of the shadows, flickering under the prompting of a gentle breeze. 'There must be something in there though, mustn't there? Otherwise, why do that disappearing act in the arcade when we're following him, all in order to try to hide the phone? And I'm sure that was the only point in any of the interviews when he was worried.'

Claire nodded. 'I agree. But we can't find a thing.'

'We're missing something,' Adam replied impatiently. 'I can't shake off the feeling there's something wrong in this case, or that we're missing something.'

'So what do we do?'

'Keep at it, as ever. Keep hoping for a break. We'll have to see the other potential suspects too, Kindle, the Imam and that lot.'

Claire sipped at her tea and flinched. It was more stewed than a hot pot. She poured it onto the grass.

'We're sure this Tariq can't in any way be implicated in the bombing?' she asked.

'I don't think so. The evidence from others in the family is that him and Ahmed didn't get on. By all accounts, Tariq is entirely law-abiding and finds Ahmed's views abhorrent. And he couldn't have been the one John Tanton rang just before the bombing. He was in Exeter city centre, but in a business meeting with his bank. We've got two bankers and an accountant giving him a cast-iron alibi. It's a total no-go.'

'So we went in all guns blazing on an innocent man.'

'Not just innocent, but a well-respected pillar of the community type.'

'That's not going to go down well.'

Adam nodded and managed a tight smile. 'No, indeed it isn't.'

Dan sat in the edit suite with Jenny, his favourite picture editor, and put the report together. He noticed he was humming to himself as he worked. With pictures and a story like this, it was a pleasure.

The one oddity had been that earlier call from Adam. Dan answered with some trepidation, expected pleas and then perhaps even threats not to broadcast the story. But the detective's attitude was very different.

'You got the lot?'

'Yep. All the cops running in and bashing the door down. We even got the sound of the fatal shot on tape.'

'So you're going to put it out at lunchtime?'

'Yes.'

There was a strange pause at the end of the line. 'It hardly looks good.'

'No,' Dan agreed hesitantly. 'But I've got to report it. It's too important a story not to. It'll be on all the other media too. I know you probably tipped me off because you wanted the public to see the police taking action to fight terrorism, but I'm sorry, I have to report this.'

Another pause, then Adam said quietly, 'Yes. Of course. I understand. You're just doing your job.'

'Are you OK?' Dan asked, puzzled. 'I mean, I expected – well, you to be angry, or upset, or ask me to tone the report down, or something like that anyway.'

Still no reaction from Adam.

'Are you there?' Dan asked.

'Yeah, I'm still here,' the detective replied. 'I was just thinking.'

A long breath on the line. Eventually Adam said, 'I understand you've got to report the story. I appreciate all the media will want to. I've just got one question for you – I guess as you were the only journalist there, all the other outlets, radio, TV, newspapers, the works, they'll all use the information you've got.'

'Yeah. That's standard. If one hack gets something no one else has, everyone reports it afterwards.'

'OK, well, I'd better leave you to it. You've got all the info you need, I take it?'

Adam's tone was distant, thoughtful. 'I think so,' Dan replied. 'Unless there's anything else you want to tell me.'

'No, not really. Only, I suppose, one important point. Just for accuracy's sake.'

Dan picked up his pen. 'Which is?'

'Just that this was an FX5 operation. They uncovered the intelligence which initiated it. They led it. It was their officer who fired the fatal shot. Greater Wessex police came along to provide back up, but it was an FX5 operation. I think it's important that's made clear.'

Dan nodded to himself and began writing the script. Adam was right. That was indeed an important detail which needed emphasising.

He started the report with the armed officers running up the road and bursting into the house, just one line of commentary to explain what the viewers were seeing.

'This was a security services operation designed to follow up a lead in the Wessex Minster bombing case – but it turned into a fiasco.'

Dan paused for the sound of the commotion and the door being broken down, the combination conveying the drama to the viewers.

'The FX5 officers were looking for a suspected terrorist,' Dan continued, 'but found only a well-respected and entirely innocent local businessman.'

Jenny edited in a couple of shots of the house, while Dan wrote the next line. It was the killer, the one which would take the story around the country and so effectively ignite the flames of public anger.

It always had been, and probably always would be a quirk of the British people, one Dan had often commented on, and rarely in a positive way, but which could now be very useful. The masses might tut at genocide in Africa, be a little upset by an earthquake in China, or sigh at a tsunami in India, all with the attendant loss of tens of thousands of human lives, but the slightest of injury to an innocent animal would instantly provoke gibbering, incandescent outrage.

Dan finished his script and read it into the microphone. 'As we were filming,' he intoned in his best sombre broadcast voice, 'from within the house came a gunshot.'

Again he paused, to let the viewers hear the unmistakeable sound. And now Dan delivered the sting of the story. 'An FX5 officer, apparently startled by the sudden movement, had fired his pistol – at the owner's cat, killing her instantly.'

Jenny let out a hiss. 'The bastard,' she spat. 'How could he? The poor cat.'

Behind her, Dan couldn't help smiling. The old adage about revenge being best served cold came to mind. It was true to an extent, but no doubt conceived in the times before television news. These days revenge was at its best by far when

150

broadcast.

He concluded the report with a couple more pictures of the house, and a final piece of commentary. 'The man who lives here, local businessman Tariq Nazri, was too upset to be interviewed. But he has released a statement saying he is shocked and appalled by what happened, and intends to sue the people responsible – FX5.'

Dan sat back, sketched a couple of contented doodles on his notepad and watched Jenny edit the final pictures.

The lunchtime battle with Lizzie beat a little of the lustre from Dan's mood, but not too much. It was a rite of passage for any *Wessex Tonight* reporter, one which had to be accepted and faced.

Her verdict on the world exclusive, cat-killing FX5 terrorist raid story was "acceptable to reasonably good". More of the same was required for tonight, along with any updates, new angles or interviews.

'I've got an idea I'd like to think about trying,' Dan ventured when the list of demands had eased.

A stiletto grated into the newsroom carpet. 'What?'

'The police think the Islamic Centre may have had a part in the bombing. I'd like to try some secret filming there. You never know what we might find. They could be preaching hatred and holy war.'

'Have you got any evidence of anything like that?'

'Not exactly.'

'Exactly?'

'Alright then, at all.'

'So it'd be a fishing expedition for what you can find?'

'Or an investigation.'

She pointed a sharpened fingernail at a copy of the Editorial Guidelines on the newsroom shelf. 'Volume one, Chapter one, page one – no secret filming without first having evidence of wrongdoing. Haven't you read it?'

A large and newly updated copy arrived on Dan's desk every year, and always proved most useful. Three had been used as kindling for a fire. One was propping open the kitchen door in the flat. Two more were elevating the screen of his computer, their giveaway spines turned from public view, naturally.

'I guess that's a no then,' he said.

'Well spotted.'

'OK, what about this? The cops think there might be a computer element to the case. I'd like to have a word with some people I know about how the internet can be used for radicalising, that kind of thing.'

An eyebrow raised. 'Acceptable. So long as you keep on top of the raid story and don't go disappearing into the police investigation like you have before.'

Dan nodded his way to the newsroom door. A score draw, not a bad result when taking on the might of Lizzie's forces. He made the call and drove down to Devonport, the historic naval district of Plymouth, home of warships, a vast military dockyard, and also the favoured haunt of some strange, underworld creatures.

The flat was even more full of monitors, keyboards, hard drives, speakers and circuit boards than the last time he had been here. There was scarcely room to move without upsetting a ramshackle pile of technical equipment. It smelt of an unpleasant mix of solder and damp and all the curtains were closed, the presence of a pattern of intricate spiders' webs suggesting they hadn't been opened for some considerable time.

'Have you got something against daylight?' Dan asked the two young men sitting together at the console.

'You never know when they're watching you,' the one with the longest hair replied, without turning around. 'You can't take any chances in this life.'

They started giggling. Dan shrugged and looked around for somewhere to sit. The sofa was covered with computer magazines. He moved one, found a third of a congealed pizza in a box underneath and put the magazines back.

'Hey, I'd forgotten that,' said the man with the slightly less long hair and reached over and took a slice. He offered the box to Dan. 'Want one?'

It was an easy offer to refuse. Dan had never tried greening pepperoni, and now didn't feel like the time. Copper might be encouraged to turn green to make an elegant architectural statement, but meat verdigris was a far less appetising prospect.

The two men at the terminal chomped away happily on the newly discovered food detritus. They called themselves Flash and Gordon, and refused to answer to any other names. Dan reflected ruefully that his last few days had been spent in a world where the name given by the person you were speaking to was the least likely to be anything approaching the one with which they had been born.

There was no point arguing. He'd tried that the last time they met and was greeted with hysterical giggles. It was a year ago, when he was covering a story about a hacker breaking into the computer systems of the dockyard. They'd emailed him, invited him to the flat and given Dan an insight into how easy it could be, all anonymously of course.

And all punctuated by incessant giggles.

The place was as dirty now as it was then, perhaps more so, but a couple of new posters had been added to the walls. They advertised the merits of computer operating systems Dan had never heard of, and seemed to be based more on the Greek alphabet than English.

Both Flash and Gordon were young, probably in their mid twenties, and both had very long hair and the kind of unhealthy, pasty complexions which befitted the nocturnal. They both wore jeans, trainers and glasses.

They might as well have also worn T-shirts emblazoned with the word *Geek*. The casting section of the drama department could scarcely have provided better examples.

'So, how can we help you, Dan, Dan, the TV man?' Flash asked, still without looking around from the monitor.

Dan swallowed his annoyance. 'I've got a case to work on and there's a suggestion computers might be a part of it.'

'Is it this terrorism one?'

'Yes.'

As one, they span on their swivel chairs and chorused,

'Cool!'

Dan sighed. He felt like a children's TV presenter giving a personal show. He explained about the list of numbers and names in Ahmed's phone.

'And they don't correspond to real people?' Gordon asked.

'No.'

'So there must be some code, or message, or something important hidden in there?'

'That's the theory.'

Another chair spin, another chorus of 'cool!' When the latest burst of giggling had subsided, Flash said, 'But you haven't got the list?'

'No. I just needed to get an idea of what kind of thing could be hidden in there.'

The computer emitted a beep. Flash turned back to it and beat out a furious rhythm on the keyboard.

'Hexadecimal,' Gordon announced.

Dan blinked hard. 'What? What the hell is that?'

More giggles.

'It's a number base system computers use,' Gordon said, when the hilarity had subsided. 'It means you don't just have to stop when you get to ten, like we're taught at scabby old school. You can count up to 16. I sometimes use it to get myself to sleep at night.'

Dan didn't want to think about that. 'So why do you reckon it might be the key to the list?'

Flash giggled. 'That's cute. Real banana head. You're so dim for a TV man.'

Dan hid a groan. 'No, I'm just normal. Something you two clearly don't suffer from. If you wouldn't mind explaining?'

'Letters and numbers!' Gordon chirped, holding up his hand for a high-five from his oddball friend. 'If you want to count past nine, you have to start using letters. So hexadecimal uses A for 10, B for 11, C for 12 and so on. Letters and numbers all together. That's your code cracked, Dan, Dan, the TV man.'

They performed another spin on their chairs and once more chorused. 'Cool!'

Dan quickly let himself out of the flat, accompanied by the

sound of giggling.

The evening was going to be a quiet one. Dan needed to be fresh for the coming morning. He was rejoining the investigation. Adam was back in charge and had called earlier.

'Can you come over to Exeter for ten? I'd like to go through a briefing and then we'll talk to Ahmed. I want to see what you make of him. Your strange interviewing skills could even give us a way into him.'

Dan didn't bother trying to hide his delight. 'Sure. The spooks are off the case then?'

'They're still around, but only in an "advisory" capacity. After the debacle of that raid, the powers that be had no choice, really. But don't start thinking we've won yet. This is a hell of a case, high-profile and very sensitive and we're being carefully watched. There's real pressure on for results.'

Dan added what he'd discovered about Parfitt and Kindle, then hung up and sat on the sofa, staring out at the evening sky. His mouth felt parched. He got up, headed for the kitchen, opened the beer cupboard and gazed at the multicoloured array of comforting cans.

Tonight was going to be dry, but sometimes a man needed a drink. It was fair enough. It had been a good day. That exclusive on the raid had even forced Lizzie to profess herself "quite pleased" at tonight's programme review meeting. He was back on the inquiry and the spooks were banished, for now at least.

A good day deserved a good drink to celebrate. Or maybe two or three.

Rutherford padded into the kitchen and sat down. Dan was almost sure the dog gave him a meaningful look. Slowly, he closed the cupboard.

'Are you trying to tell me something?' Dan said. 'OK then, let's go have a quick run, shall we?'

They jogged over to Hartley Park and ran a few laps. It was a beautiful evening, but Dan noticed he couldn't think about anything apart from the case. He wondered if the hexadecimal idea could come to anything, whether he would see Sierra and

Oscar tomorrow and what their reaction to him might be.

Night was stretching across the city, the countless lights of the thousands of streets and homes shining in the darkness. The evening air was gentle and warm. It was Claire's favourite time of the day. When they were together, she would love to take Rutherford for a walk around now. Sometimes Dan would have to insist she waited for him to get home so he could join them.

Claire. And he would be seeing her tomorrow.

Dan speeded up the run, began sprinting. He could feel his heart pounding and lungs burning with the effort. Rutherford ran effortlessly alongside, his mouth hanging open. Dan tried to think of Sarah Jones and last night, but the memory wouldn't take hold.

He slowed to a walk. It was time to go home, read a book and have an early night. Tomorrow was a big day.

Chapter Fifteen

IT MIGHT HAVE BEEN a man thing, it might just have been a part of their friendship, or perhaps it was dictated by the pressure of this case, but the handshake Adam gave Dan lasted longer than usual. They stood in the front office of Heavitree Road Police Station, watched by a couple of bemused officers and members of the public.

'Good to have you back on the case,' Adam said.

'Good to be here,' Dan replied, with feeling.

They walked through the long corridors to the Bomb Room, Adam leading and moving at speed. 'We've got a lot to get through today,' he said over his shoulder. 'I want to see all our suspects. We've got to start making some serious progress.'

The police station was busy, people continually emerging from offices and side doors. Dan expected every one to be Claire. He had his speech prepared, had worked on it last night and again this morning while he took Rutherford for a run.

He would look her in the eye and tell Claire – *I know this is difficult for you. It is for me too, don't doubt that. But we're working on a big case. It's too important to allow personal feelings to get in the way. We can't afford to be distracted. I know you're professional enough to do that. I will be too.*

Adam pushed his way through a couple of swing doors. 'We'll do Ahmed first,' he said. 'He's still our prime suspect. Then we'll go see Parfitt. I've got a little surprise for him, which should make for an interesting reaction.'

'What?'

'Wait and see.'

Dan swallowed a snarl. 'I do find your love of delayed gratification irritating.'

'As do I your tendency to melodrama,' Adam replied smoothly. 'So, as I was saying. After Parfitt – and his surprise – we'll head back over to Plymouth to do the Islamic Centre and Kindle. We'll brainstorm the case in the car on the way.'

'With me driving, I suppose?'

'Yep.'

Adam strode into the Bomb Room. Dan found his eyes flicking around it. A man at a desk on a phone. An older woman at the back going through some files. A couple of uniformed police officers looking at a clipboard. Another man working at a computer. Traffic rumbling past.

He checked again.

Even looked behind.

Twice.

No Claire.

Dan heard himself let out a long breath.

'Right,' Adam was saying. 'Before anything else, I've got that puzzle for you.' He pointed to the board with the list of names and numbers from Ahmed's phone. 'Any ideas?'

Dan studied it. He wondered for how long he should pause. Sufficient to make it apparent he was thinking hard, but also a short enough interval to be impressive.

Vanity was one of his oldest and most loyal friends.

'Hexadecimal,' he announced finally, and was rewarded by Adam's blank stare.

'What?'

'It's a number base used in computing. Ahmed's a computer scientist. I reckon that might be the key.'

Adam's hand went to his already impeccable tie and straightened it. 'Blimey, the things you know. And you might have something, too.' He briefed Dan about Ahmed's nervous reaction in the interview, when told his phone had been found.

'OK, keep thinking about that "hexa-base" thing,' the detective added. 'I'll have a copy of the list made for you. But first, let's go see Ahmed. Bear your idea in mind when you're talking to him. You ready?'

'Yep.'

Adam collected his papers. Dan used the moment to pop out into the corridor to find the loo. It had been a long drive from Plymouth, the traffic coming in to Exeter sticky with the remnants of the rush hour. He walked straight into Claire.

'Ah, err ...' he managed.

'Oh, umm ...' she replied.

They stared at each other, just stared. She hadn't changed at all, had perhaps lost a little weight, but that was it. The wonderful figure was still just as fine, the dark hair, the sharp cheekbones.

Claire. Standing here, not a couple of feet from him.

Claire. The first time they had met for months.

Claire.

Dan stood, wondering what to do. Vaguely, unable to believe it was happening, he reached out a hand.

Hesitantly, she shook it.

Dan could smell her perfume. She was wearing the silver necklace he'd bought.

It was a sign. She hadn't forgotten him. She was wearing it to tell him so. She wanted him to know she still loved him, still treasured the times they had together, still wanted to believe there was some hope for their future.

Or perhaps she just liked the necklace.

He'd kept everything she ever gave him. It was all in a box, under his bed. Several times Dan had tried to throw it away, cast it into a skip, once even dump it in the sea. But he had never quite been able to do so.

Five months on and more from that night they had shouted and screamed at each other, now they stood in the corridor of a police station, staring in silence.

A man coughed loudly, slid his way around them and cast back a curious look. Neither noticed.

Dan remembered he had something to say. His little speech. The fragile, frail, thin and pitifully inadequate words which might at least allow them the grace to work together for a few days.

He took a deep breath and was about to begin, but Claire spoke first.

'Look,' she said softly. 'I know this is difficult for you. It is for me too, don't doubt that. But we're working on a big case. It's too important to allow personal feelings to get in the way. We can't afford to be distracted. I know you're professional enough to do that. I will be too.'

The words sounded oddly familiar. All Dan could manage

was an open-mouthed nod. Claire held the look for a second, then turned and walked into the Bomb Room.

Dan found a toilet, shut himself in a cubicle and sat there for a few minutes, doing his very best to recover some elusive composure.

Adam had been silent all the way to the interview room. As he was about to push open the door, he stopped, but said only, 'Don't let him wind you up. He loves to try.'

Ahmed was sitting at the table. The room was uncomfortably warm again and in half light, shadows lingering and lurking around the walls and across the floor.

Ahmed looked up. 'New pig, eh?' he said to Dan. 'I hope you're better than the old ones. They're crap, no fun at all.'

Adam sat at the table, opposite Ahmed. Dan took his customary position, by the wall at the back of the room. He was never quite sure why, perhaps because he seldom felt a truly legitimate part of an investigation and so the physical separation seemed appropriate.

Then again, it might just have been more to do with the police dramas he'd watched on the TV, where one cop always stood. And it was usually the nasty, yet talented, intuitive, handsome and charismatic one.

'What do you want this time then?' Ahmed asked.

'The truth,' Adam replied levelly.

'Yeah, yeah. Hey, you know what I worked out?'

'What?'

'It's why you cops are so dumb.'

Ahmed waited, but Adam didn't bite. 'When I was at university,' he continued, 'what did people wanna do? They wanted to go into the city, to make some money, or the government, or the press or whatever. But no one wanted to be a cop. So all the clever people go and do the cool and interesting jobs, while all the idiots join the cops. What do ya reckon?'

Again, no reply from Adam. But the detective's neck had turned a dull red and one hand bunched into a tight fist.

'So who's you then?' Ahmed asked Dan. 'You FX5, or

CID, or CIA, or FBI, or just a …' He spelt out the word, 'a D-I-C-K?'

He chuckled to himself and squinted at Dan. 'Hey, hang on. I recognise you. Ain't you that geezer off the telly? The one who does all the crime stuff? You gonna interview me for the TV then?'

Dan stepped forward and joined Adam at the table.

'That'd be well cool, eh?' Ahmed went on. He held up an imaginary microphone and proffered it to Dan. 'Why don't you interview me, so I can tell everyone what clueless idiots these cops are? How they arrest innocent people just 'coz they're mates with some guy who blows himself up?'

'I'm just here to ask you some questions about what happened,' Dan replied, neutrally. 'But you're right, I am hoping to get you on the TV – when I report that you've been charged with conspiracy to murder by radicalising John Tanton.'

Ahmed sat back and rolled his eyes. 'I reckon I've heard all this stuff before. And as far as I can tell, I ain't been charged with nothing yet. I should've known better. You journalists are as bad as the rest of 'em. Peddling your lies and porn.'

He began tapping a tune on the table, his head moving in time. The tinny, arrhythmic drumbeat reverberated in the quiet of the room.

Dan studied the man and tried to think. But Claire kept intruding into his mind. He couldn't believe he had shaken her hand. Ahmed's jibe about him being a dick might just be well founded.

The tempo of the drum beat increased. Ahmed looked at Dan and produced a grin.

His breath smelt a little stale and his hair looked greasy, shining in the dim light. There were a couple of pockmarks under his left eye and a rash of whiskers around his cheeks. The rhythm was rising to a crescendo.

'Stop that bloody noise!' Adam shouted.

Ahmed gradually slowed the beat and finally hit out at an imaginary cymbal. 'Crash!' he chuckled. 'Don't you like my drumming then?'

He sat back on his chair and picked at a fingernail, then lifted his hand and chewed it.

'You're a computer expert, aren't you Ahmed?' Dan said.

The chewing stopped. 'What?'

'A computer expert?'

'I dunno about expert.'

'Come on. You've got a degree in computer science. You know the things inside out. That's smart. I can barely make email work.'

He sounded suspicious. 'Yeah, whatever, mate.'

'You know what I think is amazing about computers?'

'What?'

'How fast they've progressed. I mean, I read somewhere – isn't it the case that modern watches and mobile phones have more computer power than the spacecraft that took men to the moon?'

'Yeah, that's about right.'

'And the way they operate now. Compared to how it was when I was a kid, it's all so simple. Back then, when you turned on a computer you just got a flashing dot. Now they ask you what it is you want to do.'

'Yeah, suppose so.'

'Things have changed, eh? Computers, mobile phones. And there's so much information you can store in them.'

'Yeah. But so what man? You trying to butter me up, to get me talking? Playing the Mr Nice Cop? 'Coz it ain't gonna work.'

Dan allowed himself to smile. 'Ah, you've seen through me. You are as smart as I was told. In that case, I might as well stop wasting my time.'

He got up from the chair and made for the door. Dan saw a fleeting expression of puzzlement on Adam's face.

'Is that it then, man?' Ahmed asked. 'You just wanted to talk about computers and phones?'

'Yeah,' Dan replied. He paused in the doorway and turned on the lights. Ahmed screwed up his eyes in the sudden brightness and blinked hard.

'That's better,' Dan said. 'Yep, that was all it was. Just a little chat to get to know each other. All about computers and phones.'

He paused, stared right into Ahmed's eyes. 'Well, that and – hexadecimal codes.'

Parking space around the Minster is as rare as a moral banker, so they walked. It was another fine day and worthy of the exercise.

'So then?' Adam asked, in that detective's way of his. It could have been a lure to a range of topics; about Claire, life in general, even Sarah Jones, but Dan assumed his friend was talking about Ahmed.

'Well, he's certainly a man with an attitude.'

'Yes, I'd noticed that. I meant the hexadecimal thing.'

Dan thought for a moment. 'I'm not sure. I think he reacted, which could tell us we're on the right track. But then again, it could just have been surprise at me throwing a word like that at him.'

'Yes,' Adam mused. 'But it's our best shot at the moment. So keep working on it. By the way, that trick with turning the lights on at the end …'

'Clever eh? Good notion to throw him off balance.'

'I thought it was melodramatic. Very you.'

'Thanks.'

They dodged across the main road, the traffic light and willing to wait for once. Drivers always tended to be in a better mood in the sunshine.

'I don't know how much longer we've got with Ahmed,' Adam said. 'The law gives me another three weeks at least to hold him, but I'll never be able to do that. His solicitor's been on the phone twice a day, demanding we either produce some decent evidence or let him go.'

'And what you've got isn't good enough? His association with John, his being in Exeter at the time?'

'It's purely circumstantial. The lawyers reckon if I don't get something more substantial in the next couple of days, we'll have to release him.'

'But he's our prime suspect.'

'Yep. Don't let anyone ever tell you the law's not on the side of the criminals.'

Dan clicked his tongue. 'No pressure then. Well, we'd better get on with it.'

They walked on, along Southernhay. A gardener was watering the flower beds, talking to the plants as he did. Dan checked his watch. Half past ten it said, so probably a quarter to eleven. They weren't due to see Parfitt until the hour.

'Do you mind if we go via the arcade where you arrested Ahmed?' Dan asked.

Adam gave him a look. 'I know I should be used to your whims by now, but any particular reason?'

'On this occasion, nothing concrete that I can think of. Just – well, a feeling. I got the impression from Ahmed that ...'

'What?'

Dan hesitated. 'You won't like this, but – an instinct, I suppose. That we were on the right lines with him, but not quite in the target area. When I talked about phones it definitely bothered him, but it didn't shock him. It was just – well, like that kid's game, when you're looking for something that's been hidden. He was giving us a kind of you're warm vibe, without being hot, right on the nose.'

Adam changed direction, towards the shopping centre. 'Come on then. We've got a few minutes, we might as well use them. But remember, we don't have time to mess about.'

They walked across Minster Green, groups of people sitting on the grass, chatting. A ring of young children chased each other around an oak tree. Pigeons bobbed up and down along the cobbles by the ruined stained glass window.

'Walk me through it,' Dan said, at the entrance to the arcade. 'Don't leave anything out.'

'He comes in here, through the main entrance. He's running and there are cops on his tail, but a bit behind.'

They waited for a bus to pass, then walked on into the arcade and came to an intersection of shops. There was a greengrocer's, a pile of fruit and vegetables on display, an optician's, and a second-hand shop, the window full of cameras and mobile phones. Ahead was a small supermarket, trolleys lined up outside. A couple of stalls were selling a colourful selection of scarves and hats for the coming winter.

Adam stopped. 'Now we lose him. For forty seconds exactly. The cops behind can't see him. There's no CCTV on him.'

The detective pointed along the intersection. 'Now we pick him up again, sitting on that bench. We close in and arrest him, as you saw.'

'And when he came along here, could he have been absolutely sure he wasn't on CCTV?'

'It's a fair bet. The cameras are old and pretty obvious. He'd have seen there wasn't one here.'

'So, what was he doing in that forty seconds?'

'Hiding the mobile.'

'Where?'

Adam took a couple of strides forwards and bent over, pointed to a drain. 'In there.'

Dan sat down on a low wall and looked around. 'Was it well hidden?'

'Not particularly. It didn't take too long to find.'

'How long would it have taken to hide?'

'A few seconds.'

'Not forty?'

'No.'

'How many?'

Adam shrugged. 'Forgive me asking,' he said heavily, 'but is this relevant?'

'I don't know yet. Let's try it. Walk round that corner, look around you, spot the drain, open it, then close it again and walk on. Do it all fast.'

Adam shook his head, but did so. 'Ten seconds,' said Dan, looking up from his watch.

'So?'

'So – what was he doing with the other thirty?'

'I don't know. Maybe nothing. He must have been panicking. Perhaps it took that long to spot somewhere to hide the phone. Maybe he couldn't get the drain open.'

'Maybe.'

Adam sat down beside Dan. 'I know that look. What are you thinking?'

'That he was doing something else in our thirty missing seconds.'

'Like what?'

'That is the question. What if he was trying to hide something apart from the phone?'

Adam shook his head. 'No go. I had this entire area searched. The teams looked everywhere. Roof, floor, ceiling, bins, drains, shops, you name it. They took it apart. We found nothing.'

Now it was Dan's turn to frown. 'Hmm,' was all he said.

'Look,' Adam replied, standing up. 'I know you love your bit of drama and complicated cases, with riddles and puzzles and whistles and bells, but take a tip from me. This one is straightforward. We need to find who Tanton rang before he exploded the bomb. Get that person and we have our radicaliser. I'm not saying Ahmed wasn't involved. In fact, I'm sure he is – somehow – but that call is the key to the case. And we've got some possible suspects, so let's go work on it.'

They called at Parfitt's office, to the side of the Minster, and were made to wait. Dan and Adam exchanged glances. They had agreed on the way over that a man as important as the Principal would always be too busy with pressing work matters to see them immediately.

As they waited, Dan made one final attempt to get Adam to tell him. 'What's this surprise then?'

'Wait and see. But let me take the lead on this one.'

Dan contented himself with thinking his way back through the shopping arcade. But it wasn't easy to concentrate. Claire kept stalking the fringes of his mind, her expression still impassive. Dan wondered if she was thinking about him, or just getting on with her inquiries. He wondered too what he hoped she was thinking.

Dan tried a memory of Sarah Jones and their night together, but that prompted no reaction either. He sighed. Curiously, even after all the days and weeks of raging about what had happened with Claire, the numbness was not a welcome sensation. It felt unpleasantly inhuman.

A door opened and Parfitt appeared. They shook hands. He was wearing a suit today, a trendy three-button jacket and clearly bespoke.

'Non-clerical day,' he explained. 'Meetings with money men. In these days even Minsters must endlessly seek sponsorship, like some tawdry football club. A suit seems to go down better than the frock. Look, as it's a fine day, why don't we make the most of it and talk outside?'

He led them back to the green and found a bench in a secluded corner, beneath a large oak tree. A crisp packet fluttered on the ground. Parfitt stooped down and picked it up.

'I don't know what society's coming to, some days,' he complained. 'You'd think people would behave better, here in the Minster grounds. But there's little respect. We have a constant problem with litter and dog mess, even vandalism.'

Adam nodded sympathetically and asked a couple of questions about how the Minster was coping in the aftermath of the bombing. Visitor numbers were up considerably. Money had already been received from an anonymous donor to replace the stained glass window. It was being recreated, exactly as it had been, but the work would take months. For now, it was boarded up, the same fate as would befall a broken window in any ordinary shop or house. Across the green, a succession of people were still stopping to photograph the memory of the attack.

Dan watched a jackdaw hop across the grass and pick at some discarded food. He'd have to see Flash and Gordon later, to show them the list of names and numbers from Ahmed's phone. He winced at the thought of the two oddballs, spinning around on their chairs, gleefully dissecting the evidence. Some of the things he had to do for his job were ridiculous.

A flock of white clouds was gathering above one of the Minster's towers. The sun shone from the glass of the shopfronts, casting silhouettes of the people passing by. A woman ran after a young boy who was trying to climb a wall. Couples walked, hand in hand, easy and relaxed. A man in a red coat lectured a group of visitors about the city's history. There was a sense of making the most of the last days of the benevolent weather, before the darkness and cold of the English winter set in, obstinate and omnipotent in its long months of dominance of daily life.

Adam was guiding the conversation to where he wanted it to go. 'Do you mind me asking if you know any of these people – firstly, John Tanton's mother, Alison?'

'No,' Parfitt replied.

'The Imam, Tahir Aziz, and his assistant, Abdul Omah?'

'Yes. I know the Imam from our inter-faith meetings. We have them twice a year, to promote religious harmony. His assistant is the big man who always dresses in black?'

'Yes.'

'Then I've met him, but not spoken to him. He doesn't talk much, as I recall.'

'How well do you know the Imam?' Adam asked.

'Not terribly well. We exchange the odd letter about religious matters, or working groups, that kind of thing.'

'A professional relationship?'

'Yes, I suppose so. Why?'

'And the last time you saw him was …?'

'I couldn't say for sure. Probably a couple of months ago. Why?'

'We're just establishing who knows whom amongst all the people that might be connected with this case.'

The Principal studied him carefully. Adam found another page in his notes. 'And what of Norman Kindle?'

'The BPP man?'

'Yes.'

Now the Principal shook his head. 'I've never met him.'

'You're sure about that?'

'Yes.'

Adam held his look and said, 'It's just – he was quoted as supporting your book, wasn't he? The one about the clash between Christianity and Islam.'

'Was he?'

'Yes, he was.'

'Well, I still don't know him. He's hardly the sort of person I would want to associate with, is he?'

'I don't know. You tell me.'

Parfitt looked down his nose and said sniffily, 'No. He is not. Look, what is all this about? Am I supposed to have done something wrong?'

'No, sir, just a few questions, that's all,' Adam continued. 'On the subject of which, you're no fan of Islam, are you?'

The Principal exhaled heavily. 'Ah, now I see. You think I might have a connection with the bombing from some speculative motive to damage the cause of Islam. Is that it?'

Adam smiled, but it was humourless and without warmth, the sunshine above the ice cap.

'That's very good, sir. I might just write it down. No, it wasn't that. It was another issue which was bothering me.'

'Yes? Well, what is it?'

Parfitt was sounding peeved. Dan leaned forwards on the bench to make sure he caught every word. Adam was flicking through his notes again, ostensibly to find a page, but Dan had seen the technique many times before. Unsettle the suspect with an ominous build-up, like a fast bowler pounding down the wicket, about to unleash not a small red ball but a hand grenade.

'Well, it was just this,' Adam said slowly. 'You told us you'd never met John Tanton before – never even heard of him, prior to the bombing.'

'That's correct, yes.'

Another pause as Adam thoughtfully watched two young women wheel pushchairs past the Minster.

'Well, given that, how would you explain this? It was taken in the Minster itself, just four days before the bombing.'

Adam opened his file to reveal a picture. A little grainy and marked with an electronic date and time in the top corner, it was clearly taken from a CCTV image. The picture was dark and not perfectly focused, but it was nevertheless instantly recognisable.

It showed Parfitt talking to John Tanton as they stood together in the knave of the Minster.

Chapter Sixteen

KINDLE ALSO CITED THE good weather and asked to meet them outside, on Plymouth Hoe. He worked in the centre of the city, something to do with local government, but was shady about the exact nature of his job. Dan wasn't surprised. Being a BPP spokesman could make you impressively unpopular. *Wessex Tonight* had covered stories about companies and organisations being the target of protests for employing the party's supporters. Kindle wouldn't want to draw extra attention with the police turning up to talk to him.

Dan wondered if being interviewed in the open gave suspects an advantage. Perhaps it felt less intimidating than a small and close room and offered the opportunity of extra precious seconds to think about their responses to difficult questions. The scenery was an ideal pretext for gazing rather than talking. It also meant the interviewee could avoid eye-contact, something which was often a telltale and impossible with your interrogators facing you across a desk.

To help pass the time, Dan raised his ideas about open-air interviews with Adam. His friend rolled his eyes and said, 'More melodrama. Shall we just stick with the boring old facts and see if we can solve the case that way, before we launch the comet of your imagination?'

They were on the A38, just coming up to the Newton Abbot turning, a third of the way towards Plymouth. To the north, Dartmoor lurked, sulked, and brooded, as only the moor can. Even on a sunshine day, the greyness of the ancient granite and brown of the creeping bracken could dull the blessing of the weather. Thickening clouds lingered atop the highest tors. A line of pylons followed the road, made invisible by their ubiquity, but still painful to the clear-eyed lover of the countryside.

Dan was driving, as usual. Adam always insisted it gave him an opportunity to think, but there was more than a suspicion that the detective just liked being chauffeured.

Dan had protested that he didn't want to suffer the chore of having to drive back to Exeter later to get his car, but Adam summoned a traffic officer, handed over the keys and said the Peugeot would be delivered to Dan's flat by late afternoon. That was one of the great advantages of working with the police. They gave and took orders without hesitation and knew how to get things done.

The car had been resprayed, but Dan thought he could still see hints of the scrawled graffiti in shades of the blue paint.

KEEP YOUR NOSE OUT

He wondered again who had done it, who could know so much about him and not want him working on the Tanton case. But at least now he had a little plan to protect himself.

'What did you reckon to Parfitt then?' grunted Adam, emerging from his reverie.

'I thought he was certainly surprised.'

'Yeah, he was that.'

The Principal had stared at the photograph of himself talking to John Tanton in silence. It was several seconds before he spoke.

'I simply don't remember that,' he said finally. 'You're sure this is a genuine picture?'

'Yes, sir,' Adam replied heavily. 'I haven't quite got to the stage in the case where I'm ready to invent evidence.'

'Well, then I suppose I must have spoken to him. But I don't remember it. All I would say, Inspector, is this. We are sometimes not well off for staff in the Minster and I have to undertake various duties, such as walking the floor and talking to the visitors. It must have been during one of those times I met Tanton. I have no memory at all of it. But to be frank ...'

'Yes, sir?'

'Well, I'm not surprised by that. I talk to many people and I'm often rather on autopilot when I do. They all ask the same questions, about the roof, the bombing from World War Two, the architecture, that kind of thing. You end up answering by rote.'

Adam held the man's look, then thanked him and they walked back to Heavitree Road.

'I think the reason he gave was plausible,' Dan observed, pulling down the sun visor to shade his eyes. 'And there was no sign of panic, nothing that suggested he was guilty and knew he'd been caught. What are you thinking?'

'I'm thinking you're right. That was why I didn't arrest him. That CCTV is no evidence for anything really. It could have been an entirely innocent encounter with Tanton. The lad might have been on one of his reconnaissance missions for the bombing. But it's certainly interesting, both that it happened at all, and the timing – just days before Tanton carried out his attack.'

Dan struggled to keep the scepticism from his voice. 'You're suggesting the Principal could have radicalised Tanton and led him to attack his own Minster?'

'Well, Parfitt was in Exeter, so it could have been him that Tanton rang. We know the number Tanton called isn't Parfitt's personal mobile – just as it isn't with any of our potential suspects – but he might have had another mobile which he subsequently got rid of.'

'And a motive?'

'He's no fan of Islam. Perhaps he wanted to stir up anger against Muslims. Maybe it was even something far more mundane.'

'Like what?'

'Money. One of the oldest motives going. He's always moaning about how much it costs to keep the Minster open. If you want to be mercenary about it, look at the publicity and sympathy the attack has brought. The place has never been busier.'

Dan guided the car around a couple of lorries. 'Blimey,' he said. 'And you think some of my ideas are far-fetched. I got no sense of anything much from Parfitt, apart from him being a rather harassed and bad-tempered administrator.'

'Well, it's all worth keeping in mind. As far as I can see, he's got the potential means, motive and opportunity.'

'But a long shot for our radicaliser, surely?'

'Perhaps.'

The reached the outskirts of Plymouth. Dan turned the car off the main dual carriageway, on to the embankment. It was lunchtime and the traffic was light. They cruised along the River Plym, the low tide exposing acres of mudflats, wading birds pecking at the rich pickings. Dan felt his own stomach rumble. One of the problems of working with Adam was that he could become so engrossed in an inquiry he would forget to eat.

'Any chance of picking up a sandwich?' Dan ventured.

'So long as it doesn't take ages.'

Dan stopped at a deli and got them a couple of baguettes. He paid; it hadn't even occurred to Adam to offer any money. The detective only muttered a vague thanks when Dan handed over his lunch.

They parked on the road alongside the Hoe and walked across the great promontory, icon of Plymouth. The Beatles had sat here on their Magical Mystery Tour, the photographs of the four gazing out over the sea adorning many of the city's shops and homes.

The headland was quiet today, just a few people walking their dogs, couples taking the view, the odd parent pushing a pram. Seagulls wheeled in the sky, their keen eyes forever looking out for a discarded titbit. The sharp grey lines of a frigate slipped from the Tamar, heading for the open waters of the Western Approaches.

By the great memorial to the Navy's war dead, a line of flags of the world hung apathetically, awaiting the stimulus of a breeze. It wouldn't take long. To the west, a line of silver cloud hung in the sky. A front was approaching. The weather was turning.

Kindle was waiting on a bench beside Smeaton's Tower, the old lighthouse which used to guard the Eddystone Reef, its red and white hoops stretching into the sky. He stood up and they shook hands. As he sat down, Kindle glanced at his watch.

'Are we keeping you?' Adam said frostily.

'Sorry, it's just that we only get an hour for lunch.'

'This won't take long, sir,' the detective replied.

He began by asking whether Kindle knew any of the other possible suspects. Only Ali Tanton, came the reply, and just in passing. He'd met her a couple of times when she'd picked up John from football practice and they'd exchanged pleasantries and a few words about how the boy was doing.

Kindle sat back on the bench, his legs crossed, occasionally looking out at the view. He was as well dressed as before, another sharp suit and tie, and appeared relaxed, no obvious signs of evasions or tension. A couple of motorboats were zipping across the natural harbour of Plymouth Sound, the occasional growl of their engines floating over the Hoe.

'Now, about John himself,' Adam said. 'How well did you know him?'

Kindle shrugged. 'Reasonably well. I saw him most weeks. I tried to help him with his goalkeeping. I used to be a goalie myself and …'

'About John,' Adam interrupted. 'Aside from football practice, did you ever see him anywhere else?'

'Not really. I bumped into him a couple of times in town, but that was about it.'

'Did you spend any time with him, apart from the football?'

'No.'

'Did you ever see any signs that he might do something extreme, like the bombing?'

Kindle considered the question. 'No,' he said finally. 'He had started going on a bit about Britain and what a horrible place it could be. He seemed to think some Arab countries were better.'

Now a bitterness had edged into the man's words. 'We did talk about it. I said to him – what do you think is better about them? The beheadings? The repression of women? The desire for some kind of holy war against us? He just said it was better than this place, where all anyone did was get drunk, have sex and invade other people's countries. I told him what a fine place Britain was, how its character needed to be preserved, a little bit about the BPP and what we were trying to do, but he was – well, difficult to reach, to say the least.'

'What did you think of what he was saying?'

Kindle snorted. 'Funnily enough, I thought it was rubbish. It's bad enough, having all the bloody immigrants here, without them filling people's minds with their ideas. But you have to remember John was a young lad and not particularly advanced for his age. I thought it was just a fad he was going through. Basically, I reckon he was a decent lad who was …'

His words tailed off and he gazed out to sea, before adding angrily. 'He was got to, if you want it straight. Brainwashed, indoctrinated. By the damn Muslims. The bloody immigrants. And you've seen the result.'

Adam nodded understandingly. 'And so what would you do to get back at the "bloody immigrants", Mr Kindle?'

'What?'

'Would you indoctrinate a young lad with your own propaganda? Tell him to explode a home-made bomb in the Minster, a crime so heinous it was guaranteed to stir up real outrage against the people who put him up to it. The people who could only be extremist Muslims?'

Kindle seemed genuinely baffled. 'What?'

'I'm saying, Mr Kindle, that in my experience of the BPP, I wouldn't put anything past you. You had access to John. He looked up to you. He started to get interested in Islam. You fuelled his radical ideas, suggested the Minster might just be a good place for an attack – the symbolic heart of despicable old British society – and off he went. And you ride the wave of anti-immigrant feeling.'

Kindle gaped at Adam. 'You're seriously suggesting I …'

'You had the means, the motive and the opportunity. And if you want me to be straight – I think you could do it.'

A sudden gust of wind rattled the flagpoles. Kindle's face had turned a dull red.

With an effort, he got to his feet. 'I am ending this conversation before I say something I'll regret,' he snapped. 'But I suppose I shouldn't be surprised. It's the same old story, isn't it? If something happens to us mere white people, the police aren't interested. But if there's a problem for one of our beloved immigrants – and even worse, for a sacred Muslim – the cops are falling over themselves to do everything they can.

You're typical of all that's wrong with this country. If you want to talk to me again you'll have to get in touch with the party's solicitors. They know just how to deal with people like you.'

The wind was gathering strength and pulled at their jackets as Dan and Adam walked back to the car. The sky had turned a uniform grey, the front moving in fast. To the west, a softening of the view foretold of the rain to come. Adam was moving fast, striding with his anger.

'Do I get the feeling you don't care for Mr Kindle?' Dan ventured mildly.

'It's his bloody politics that get me,' the detective grunted. 'You know what really narks me about that BPP lot?'

'I get a feeling I'm about to find out.'

'Yeah, you are. They go on about the native population as if they're some race of supermen and women. And as for any immigrants, they're automatically evil. It's like they live in some weird world inhabited only by stereotypes and caricatures. In my experience, many of the "bloody immigrants" Kindle rants on about work a damned sight harder and give far more to the country than the so-called natives who are happy to lounge at home all day.'

They reached the car just as the first drops of rain started to fall. Dan fumbled for the wipers. 'The Islamic Centre next, to see the Imam?' he said.

'Yeah. Look, sorry. It's just people like Kindle get to me sometimes. Give me a straightforward murderer to deal with over a racist any day. At least I've got a chance of understanding a killer.'

Adam reached out and turned off the engine. 'Let's just take a minute to think,' he said. 'What did you make of Kindle? Give me a calm analysis. Could he be the radicaliser?'

Dan drummed a finger on the steering wheel. 'Apart from being a bigot, I didn't see any particular reason to suspect him. It is quite a leap, to believe he could be so driven by his views that he would set up a young lad to kill himself and others with a suicide bombing in the Minster.'

'Mmm,' Adam mused. 'Perhaps.'

The rain was pounding harder on the car now, a continual booming beat. Adam reached into his file, found a sheet of paper and handed it over. 'Have a quick look at that, then reconsider.'

It was a report from the Greater Wessex Police criminal psychologist, Dr "Sledgehammer" Stephens, entitled *The Radicaliser*. As ever, the good doctor had erred on the side of extreme caution in ensuring his findings would not be misunderstood, and typed all the major points in capitals.

"This is a FASCINATING psychological question," the report read. "The use by a motivated, clever and resourceful criminal of another person to achieve his or her ends. In many ways, it is the HOLY GRAIL of intelligent criminality – the committing of an act by REMOTE means; the goal achieved without the presence of the mastermind. Naturally, it makes bringing them to justice FAR MORE DIFFICULT.

"In the search for your so called 'radicaliser', you should look for someone sufficiently committed to his cause to appropriately be termed a ZEALOT. He will be CUNNING AND MANIPULATIVE, and quite probably CALM AND CONTROLLED, able to withstand considerable pressure during interrogation. The person you seek will be HIGHLY ADEPT at disguising his views. That is not to say they will be ENTIRELY HIDDEN, but often instead cloaked in MODERATE and seemingly REASONABLE terms. It is the classic case of the iceberg – what you see is only a SMALL FRACTION of the MASS of feeling which truly exists – and it is that mass which is BY FAR THE MOST DESTRUCTIVE."

Dan turned the page. "In conclusion, you should expect to have CONSIDERABLE DIFFICULTIES in identifying and bringing the perpetrator to justice. It is likely he will leave behind NO PHYSICAL EVIDENCE, meaning you will possess only the option of ensnaring him with questioning. I suspect this will prove EXTREMELY PROBLEMATIC with such a focused, calm and intelligent person.

"I can offer one element which may be of assistance. The perpetrator's weakness will perhaps be his own HIGH SELF-

REGARD. The circumstances of this case suggest your radicaliser had a burning desire to witness the act you are investigating, but the fact he did not carry it out himself indicates a powerful instinct of SELF-PRESERVATION.

"I wish you GOOD LUCK."

Adam waited for Dan to finish the report, before saying quietly, 'He's never wished me luck before.'

Dan nodded. 'He's saying it's a tough one.'

'And I would say, in that at least, he's certainly right.'

'But he's given us quite a bit to go on too.'

'Yeah, but that profile of the radicaliser could fit all our suspects – Ahmed, Parfitt, Kindle, the Imam and his minder.'

'But not Alison Tanton.' Dan observed.

'Did we ever really think she might have sent her own son to carry out a suicide bombing?'

'I suppose not.'

'Then at least that's some progress, however slight. But Stephens is right, isn't he? That's the problem with the case. We have no physical evidence. So we're left with our own wits to try to trap the radicaliser. Plus it looks like we'll have to free Ahmed soon, so time's running out.'

The rain beat harder on the windscreen, the running rivulets warping the view of the outside world. The car's clock said it was coming up to one.

'So, to the Islamic Centre?' Dan asked.

'Yep. Let's go see if we get any further there. Later we'll go back to Charles Cross to have a brainstorming session.'

Dan was about to start the car when his mobile rang. It was Lizzie, and the tirade was even more impressive than usual, and roughly a third full of obscenities.

'What is it?' Adam asked, when Dan had hung up.

'Can you spare me an hour, and a story?'

'What?'

Dan quickly explained. Six months ago, *Wessex Tonight* had joined the future of television news. Instead of recording all the programme's reports onto video tape, a computer server had been installed. It was promoted as offering a whole gamut of dazzling advantages; in brief, it was simply wonderful, incredibly advanced and utterly and comprehensively infallible.

And now, naturally, it had gone wrong.

In fact, that was something of an understatement. It was news Armageddon.

The server had managed to atomise every single one of the reports for the lunchtime bulletin in a whim of a computing mindstorm. Lizzie had fourteen minutes of airtime to fill and nothing to put in it. All the reporters were being frantically called and asked if they could come up with any kind of story about which they might simply sit in the studio and talk.

The bulletin was on air at half past one. They had just over 30 minutes.

'Do you know what?' Adam said slowly. 'There might just be a story you could put out which could help us. I think it's time to put a bit of pressure on our suspects.'

Chapter Seventeen

IT HAD LONG BEEN a belief of Dan's that on some days life is a supportive friend who'll uncomplainingly run with you, but on others it can grow mischievous and contrary, and decide to have a little jape or two at your expense. He didn't have much of a religious faith, despite being born a Catholic, just some nebulous sense of there being far greater powers at work in this inscrutable universe than mere humans could ever hope to understand.

On the days when life wasn't favouring him, Dan would often conclude the best way was to tread water. The forces he was facing were far too powerful to thrash out against; that would only lead to ever increasing frustration and exhaustion. Instead just waiting calmly until the tide turned was the better choice.

But sometimes that wasn't an option. Sometimes the issue had to be forced.

He turned the key in the ignition, the car emitted a couple of forlorn coughs and entirely failed to start. Dan tried again, this time without even the encouragement of any mechanical grindings or grumblings.

The rain beat in harder.

'There's something wrong with the car,' the master journalist and observer of life noted.

'Brilliant deduction,' Adam replied. 'Yet again you've reminded me why I like having you along.'

'I guess that's the lunchtime news idea scuppered then.'

'Never. Come on.'

Adam was out of the car, a hand raised as an ineffectual shield against the downpour. The road was quiet, with few cars parked and only the odd vehicle passing by, their wheels cutting through the weight of water. Dan and Adam ran along the pavement, splashing through the growing pools, the stinging raindrops firing into their faces. The cars by the side of the road were all empty.

A church bell chimed one.

Adam swore and turned along another street. Ahead was a car, two people vaguely visible in the front seats. He ran towards it, pulled the back door open and tumbled inside, spraying rain with him.

The couple in the front put their hands up in a gesture of surrender.

'Don't kill us,' the woman pleaded. 'We're only pensioners. We don't have any money or drugs. And we fought for you in the war.'

Dan blinked away the rain which was blurring his vision. At a generous estimate, the woman might just have been conceived around the time the Second World War ended.

'Don't be alarmed,' Adam replied, in the voice that always made Dan think being alarmed was exactly the right course of action. 'I'm a police officer.' He thrust his warrant card forward. 'This is an emergency. I'm commandeering your car.'

'You're what?' the man asked slowly.

'I need your car. It's an emergency. Swap seats so I can drive. Quickly please.'

The man tugged at an impressive thicket of silver hair which was growing, carrot-like, from an ear.

'My insurance doesn't cover anyone driving but me,' he replied at last.

'That doesn't matter right now. This is an emergency.'

'I don't know if that makes any difference. What do you think Ethel?'

'I don't know either Frank. You're always the one who does the insurance. Those forms are far too complex for me. I can't read that tiny print either. They do it deliberately, you know, to stop you from claiming half the time.'

The clock on the dashboard said the time was almost five past one. Adam emitted a low noise which sounded like a jet preparing to take off. 'Look, I don't have time to argue. Would you mind driving us then, please?'

'Driving you?'

'Yes.'

'Where?'

'Up to Mannamead. To the *Wessex Tonight* studios.'

Ethel turned around and stared at Dan through thick-lensed glasses. 'Oooh,' she exclaimed. 'I thought I recognised you. You're that man off the telly.'

Dan put on a forced smile, but thought it best not to comment.

'Will you please,' Adam said forcibly, 'Start the car and drive.'

And so began what was surely one of the strangest emergency responses in the history of law enforcement.

Frank was the antithesis of a police driver. Every single junction, roundabout and set of traffic lights was treated with a respect bordering upon reverence. He would begin slowing several hundred yards before reaching them, and even if the way was obviously, entirely and utterly clear would crawl the car across the potential obstacle, looking left and right the whole time.

Such was Frank's conscientiousness that Dan wouldn't have been surprised if he'd also started looking skywards, just in case some hazard might be approaching from that direction too.

Adam's urgings succeeded in increasing the rate of progress not at all.

'I've never had an accident in my life,' Frank said proudly, poking at the brim of his trilby with a finger. 'And I don't intend to start now.'

'Quite right, dear,' Ethel piped up, adjusting her own hat, one of the crocheted bobble variety. 'I don't know, these young people, always in a rush.'

Adam forced himself back on the uncomfortable plastic seats and closed his eyes.

Rounding one corner, heading towards a parade of shops, Dan received confirmation of what he had suspected. The rain had been a little too hard, the run along the street too chaotic to initially be absolutely sure of the vehicle they had piled into. But now, captured in the reflection from a newsagent, was an image of the offending automobile.

It was a toad of a car and an anachronistic one at that; a

brown Austin Allegro, with an S registration plate.

The time was a quarter past one. They were almost at the studios. Adam kept knotting his fists, then unclenching them again. To distract the detective, and to save time, Dan outlined his idea.

'Look, I think you should do the broadcast. Because – one, it'll sound more dramatic coming from you. Two, you know exactly what you want to say. If you have to brief me it'll take more time, and we don't have much. Three, this'll ensure it's the lead story and that it's picked up on all the radio stations and websites, which is exactly what we need. And four, it should bank me some credit with Lizzie which will mean I'm pretty much free to keep working on the case with you.'

It wasn't the hardest argument to win. Not only did Adam stop tightening his fists, he slipped into his familiar mannerism and began straightening his already pristine tie. The detective was even shameless enough to glance in the car window and check his reflection.

'You look lovely,' Dan sighed.

'I'll need some face powder.'

'There's plenty in the studio.'

'A hair drier.'

'We've got one of those too.'

The detective ran a hand over his beard line. 'And a quick shave.'

'There's a razor in the dressing room.'

Adam flicked some fluff from his sleeve and added ruefully, 'And this is one of my oldest suits.'

It was far more stylish, fashionable and expensive than Dan's best. 'It'll look fine,' he said patiently.

'I'll need to make one quick call then, to set up the operation.'

'When you've finished adjusting your ensemble, obviously,' Dan muttered.

They reached the *Wessex Tonight* building at twenty past one and quickly thanked Frank and Ethel.

'Anytime you need my help again, just call,' Frank said, with no trace of irony. 'Hard driving like that was really rather exciting.'

The low speed scramble would no doubt become the talk of a hundred bingo nights and whist drives. Dan pulled Adam away before he could comment. He ushered the detective into the studio and strode next door to the gallery to explain his thoughts to Lizzie.

'Done,' she said instantly. 'But – but …'

There was always a but with Lizzie, and usually more than one. Dan sometimes wondered if But was her maiden name. It would suit her.

'Yes?' he asked warily.

'How come you were with him when I called? You're not trying to be a detective again, are you?'

'No, no,' Dan soothed. 'I was just doing my job. Meeting up to check the latest on the case, to see if it could make a story for us.'

The glare of suspicion would have made a nun uncomfortable. 'Right then. But don't go vanishing like you have before. You're a hack, remember, and I want stories.'

Not a word of thanks for saving the bulletin, Dan noted. He wandered upstairs to the newsroom to watch Adam's performance.

The opening titles played and Craig came in. 'We can bring you exclusive revelations in the Wessex Minster bombing case,' he intoned. 'The police have made what they believe to be a major breakthrough. The man in charge of the investigation, Detective Chief Inspector Adam Breen joins me. What is it that you've found?'

Adam looked calm, smart and authoritative, not at all flustered by the unexpected live interview.

'We have discovered that John Tanton made a phone call, just minutes before he exploded his bomb. We believe that may have been to the person who radicalised him.'

'Saying what?' Craig interrupted.

'It's my view he was calling for support, or to be reassured he was doing the right thing in his bombing mission. He wanted to be told his plan for murder and suicide was justified.' Adam's voice fell. 'And difficult to believe though it may be, I can come to no other conclusion than that he was given that reassurance. That, in itself, tells you much about the person we are hunting.'

Dan noticed the newsroom had stilled, journalists stopping to watch the monitors. Craig paused to let the drama of the detective's words linger.

'And how much does this development help you?'

'We are currently in the process of tracing the phone which Tanton called and who was using it. I believe that will allow us to bring to justice the person who took advantage of a vulnerable young man and turned him into a killer.'

'And are you confident you will be able to get this person?'

Now it was Adam's turn to pause. The camera crept in on him, emphasising the calm determination in his face. It was a look he did well.

Finally, he said simply, 'We will get him.'

The rain was continuing to pound down as they drove to the Islamic Centre. Dan borrowed a car from the *Wessex Tonight* pool, a modern, energy-efficient and scrupulously green model. It looked pretty and boasted outstanding environmental credentials, but drove like a lawnmower.

They stopped at some traffic lights. Out to sea, a couple of forks of lighting split the glowering sky. Dan checked his mobile again. He was still struggling to believe it. How much entertainment the great game of life could have at the expense of the hapless human race. Just as he and Adam had been about to leave the studios two text messages came through simultaneously.

The first was from Claire.

Sorry if I was a bit off earlier. Didn't mean to be. It was just the shock of seeing you again. Hope we get the chance to talk more – if you want to, of course? x

Dan stared at the screen. She'd sent a kiss. Some people, when texting, littered their messages with kisses so that the screen resembled a *Spot the Ball* coupon. Dan often thought of it as the mark of the superficial. But not Claire. She was precise. Kisses were special and reserved for people she would give them to physically.

Her presence was so powerful she could have been sitting in the car, her breath teasing the hairs on the back of his neck.

The second text was from Sarah Jones.

OK, I give in, you can see me again. The tiger is hungry! Grrr ... xxx

Dan shook his head. Some days, it was an effort not to shake your fist at the sky. Suddenly, he felt the need to sit in a bar, have a beer or two, and do some thinking.

'How did it go?' asked Adam, for the third time.

'What?' Dan replied distractedly.

'Come on, concentrate. How did it go?'

'Your TV appearance?'

'What else?'

'Well, it was still great, just the same as the last time you asked. Still very dramatic and still effective.'

'Do you reckon it'll work?'

Dan slowed for a zebra crossing, a party of young schoolchildren winding their way across the road. Some kicked at the puddles in the gutter. They all looked happy, despite the rain. It was always sunny in the land of childhood.

'That's what's bothering me,' he said. 'Surely our radicaliser will have suspected you knew about the call Tanton made to him?'

'Probably, but not necessarily. He might have thought Tanton's phone had been destroyed in the blast. And he'd know Tanton hadn't said anything to us about who'd been manipulating him, or we'd have arrested him by now.'

'And so you give him a little poke and see what it does.'

'I did turn the screw a bit, with that talk about the kind of person we're hunting. And it's worked in other cases. Look at some of the crimes that using your little television advantage has helped us crack.'

'We haven't come up against terrorists before though.'

'They're still criminals,' Adam said forcefully. 'There's nothing special about them whatsoever.'

Dan put the car into gear and drove on. They were almost at the mosque.

'And your phone call, before you went on air. Is it all in place?'

Adam nodded. 'Yep. It was a bit of a rush, but we're used to these things. Everything's in hand.'

Dan found a parking space at the rear of the Islamic Centre. The rain had abated a little, a small and forlorn patch of blue sky lingering above them. As they walked up to the building Adam announced he would take the lead in questioning the Imam and his minder.

'Because of what the spooks said, about there being an informer in the mosque,' he explained. 'We'd better be a little cautious.'

Dan found himself relieved at the suggestion. His mind was full of Claire and Sarah. That list of names and numbers from Ahmed's phone was also flitting through his thoughts. There must be something in there, some clue, perhaps even the solution to the case. He would take it to the Geeks later, to see what they might make of it.

The pavement was soaking, streams of rain water cascading along gutters and driveways. Leaves were starting to fall from the trees, dislodged by the force of the storm. Shoppers hurried past, making the most of the gap in the downpour to head for their cars. The sudden change in the weather had brought a chill to the air, a reminder of the coming autumn.

Abdul was waiting for them in the doorway, dressed all in black, as ever. They were both regarded in silence and led up the stairs.

The Imam was in his office. Adam and Dan shook hands and were offered chairs opposite his desk. He nodded to Dan, as if to acknowledge seeing him again, but made no comment on his presence.

'So, how can I help you?' Tahir asked.

'It was just a couple of quick questions,' Adam replied.

'Firstly, to find out how well you knew John Tanton.'

The Imam studied Adam. Dan had a sense he was debating how much to reveal. Adam saw it too and added, 'Out of fairness, I should mention we already know he came here regularly.'

Tahir nodded slowly and straightened one of the sleeves of his robe. 'Yes. He would come in for Friday prayers and occasionally to seek advice about ...' he hesitated. 'Matters of faith.'

'What kind of matters?'

'He would sometimes have difficulty in understanding the more subtle points of Islam.'

'Such as?'

'In essence, the differences between cultural and religious influences.'

Adam's look made it plain that further explanation was required. The Imam stood up and pointed to a series of posters on the wall. One showed a pair of women, dressed in burquas, only their eyes visible. Next to it was a line of women wearing swimming costumes, standing beside a pool.

'The role of women for example. This poster depicts an Islamic beauty contest,' he said, pointing to the semi-naked women. 'Contrary to many people's belief, Islam is not repressive of women. In fact, it gives them a great many rights, sometimes more so than men.'

The words came easily, clearly an oft-repeated lecture.

'Yet some countries bar women from everyday things like driving and force them to cover up their entire bodies,' Adam noted.

'That is a cultural matter. It comes not from the religion, but the traditions of the country or the inclinations of those in power.'

The Imam pointed to another poster. It showed a kneeling man with a gun placed to his head.

'There is also the issue of capital punishment and other legal penalties, such as the amputation of limbs. That too is a cultural matter.'

He took a couple of steps and pointed to a final poster. It

captured the horror of the day the world changed, one of those rare moments everyone remembers; the Twin Towers, smoke billowing from the wounds inflicted by the airliners.

'And, of course, terrorism,' Tahir continued, more quietly now. 'The concept of Jihad, or holy war. It is a fact that the Koran teaches us the killing of just one person is as morally reprehensible as the killing of millions. Those who preach holy war are distorting Islam for their own ends, usually the pursuit of power and self-aggrandisement.'

'So,' Adam replied, 'John Tanton was asking about these kind of issues?'

'Yes.'

'Then it's fair to think he must have been under the influence of radicals and was trying to understand what Islam really did dictate he should be doing?'

The Imam smiled, the expression tinged with sadness. 'In my experience of young men, what he was going through was common. There are always voices filled with hate and they are loud indeed. And if they are not shouting at the man in person, they can do so on the internet, or via the media. Every time there is some kind of terrorist outrage, the papers are filled with discussions of Islamic extremism. It is well intended, to expose how wrong it is. But it can also have the effect of raising interest in the fanatics and their message, particularly amongst the more impressionable.'

Adam noted that down. 'Did you have any sense whatsoever of what John was planning to do?'

Now the Imam looked surprised. 'Of course not, or I should have spoken to you immediately. Chief Inspector, myself and all the people here were as shocked as anyone by the attack on the Minster. We may differ in our beliefs, but it is a place of God. For the avoidance of any doubt whatsoever, we utterly condemn the bombing.'

Abdul had taken a step towards Adam and was looming over him. The detective glanced up. The two men held a stare as hard as a midwinter freeze and Abdul returned to the Imam's side.

'There's one final question – for now,' Adam said

deliberately. 'How well did you know Ahmed Nazri? I understand he came here to pray too.'

Tahir interlaced his fingers and studied them. Finally, he said, 'Of all the people who came here, Ahmed was the one I worried about the most. He was bubbling with resentment and in possession of – some of the more radical views.'

'He was thinking about violence?'

The Imam sighed. 'I would not have put it past him.'

'Then why didn't you tell us?'

Another pause, and then, 'We believed we could deal with it amongst ourselves. It is our preferred way.'

'Is it?' Adam grunted. 'It doesn't seem to have been working so well.'

Tahir frowned. 'I understand your concerns, but that was our judgement. You may not agree with this, but we felt your intervention would only make matters worse. We tried to calm Ahmed, I can assure you of that, but it can be difficult to reach such a closed mind.'

'And he knew John well?'

Tahir nodded. 'Yes. They would often come here together. I did try to talk to Ahmed on several occasions, but my efforts were rebuffed. He was a young man filled with far more emotion than understanding.'

The towering black edifice folded his arms and emitted a low grunt. Adam looked at him. 'Yes?' he said, but the wall didn't reply.

'Go ahead, Abdul,' the Imam added gently. 'You have something you wanted to say?'

Finally, in a deep and gruff voice, Abdul said, 'Ahmed went on a bit, but it was all talk. We had a guy in here once and he was preaching holy war, going to Iraq and Afghanistan to fight the invaders, all that. We got rid of him fast when we knew what he was up to. But before we did, he tried it with Ahmed.' Abdul nodded hard and added scornfully, 'He didn't want to know. Ahmed could talk a lot, but he didn't have the guts to get involved in anything serious.'

A surprise was awaiting when they got back to Charles Cross,

190

and it was by no means the Christmas morning kind. The spooks were standing at the end of the Major Incident Room, whispering to each other. Oscar was smirking and had the briefcase by his side.

'It's the man from the telly,' he sneered.

Dan just shook his head, but Oscar pointed to Adam. 'I meant him.' He put a hand over his heart. 'Lovely interview at lunchtime. So emotional. And just so impressively discreet, giving out details of the investigation.'

'It was for a reason,' Adam replied levelly.

'Oh, really? I'd never have known. Let me try a wild guess – perhaps something like trying to prompt a reaction from your suspects? When the hell will you get this into your head? You're not dealing with sheep rustlers now. The people you're after will know exactly what you're up to. The only reaction you're likely to get from them is laughter.'

Adam gave Oscar a glare. 'Thank you for your input to the inquiry. It's been as helpful as ever. Now, if you've nothing else to add, I'd like to get on with *my* investigation.'

He opened the door of the MIR and added, 'You'll find the exit …'

Sierra interrupted, her voice softer but still forceful. 'What the hell did you think you were doing?'

'What are you …'

'The mosque. We warned you to take it easy. And you go blundering in there, stirring the place up.'

'I was doing my job. There were potential leads. I was following them up. Funnily enough, it's what detectives do. Why don't you go do your James Bond stuff, I'll get on with my investigation and we'll see who gets the results.'

Oscar appeared about to retaliate, but Sierra coughed meaningfully. He looked over, grabbed the briefcase and followed her from the MIR.

When the door closed, Adam uttered a couple of words that Dan had last heard when a builder who was doing some work on the flat dropped a toolbox on his foot. He gave his friend a few seconds to calm down, then asked, 'How did they know we were at the mosque?'

Adam shrugged. 'Their "asset" probably. More to the point, what are they doing here in Plymouth?'

'Investigating the case?'

'Or maybe keeping an eye on us. They're up to something, I can sense it. Anyway, forget them for a moment. What did you make of the Imam and Abdul?'

'Well, the Imam comes across as committed to peace.'

'Yeah, but maybe too much so? He just seemed – I don't know, perhaps too polished. He had all the answers, didn't he?'

Dan nodded. 'Maybe. But I didn't get any feeling he was trying to put us off the track.'

'And Abdul?'

'All he really came out with was that little speech about Ahmed. And that made it sound like he wasn't the type to get involved in anything dodgy, let alone a bombing plot.'

'Or perhaps he's exactly the type but doesn't have the guts to do it himself so he sets up John Tanton. Remember what Stephens's report said? That could fit Ahmed. Do we suspect either the Imam or his minder?'

'Well, they were there in Exeter, so we can't rule them out. But I didn't get the sense they might have been involved.'

'So Ahmed remains our prime suspect?'

'I think so.'

'I think I agree, and we're running short of time to get him. His lawyers have been on the phone to the legal department again, talking about raising a writ of habeas corpus. I reckon I'll probably have to release him tomorrow unless we can come up with some evidence.'

'So, where do we go from here?' Dan asked.

'See if my little TV trick has any effect on our suspects. They'll be under surveillance all day. I take it you can arrange for the story to be aired again tonight?'

'Yep.'

'Then you look after that. We'll talk later when we see if the surveillance teams come up with anything interesting.'

Dan drove back to the studios, noting the car struggled so badly with one hill that he wondered whether he should open the door, stretch out a leg and start scooting. The mercurial weather had turned dry again. It was only mid afternoon. There was no need to go into the newsroom yet, so he took a walk around the block. It was time for some thinking.

He took out the piece of paper with the list of names and numbers from Ahmed's phone and gazed at it as he walked. An old lady tutted loudly as he almost collided with her, and Dan muttered an apology. Despite spending most of the circuit thinking, he came up with no ideas about what the list could mean.

The last few minutes of the walk Dan reserved for answering the text messages from Sarah and Claire. Even the decision about who to reply to first took some agonising. Surely it was a statement about which was more important to him? Dan found he couldn't make up his mind, so he left it up to fate. If the registration plate of the next red car was an odd number it would be Sarah, if even, then Claire.

He looked up. A red van was approaching. Dan groaned. He hadn't thought about whether to include vans and lorries. He decided he should, screwed up his eyes and picked out the plate.

971.

Issue One resolved. Now, the far trickier matter of what to text. Dan realised he still hadn't discovered any feelings for Sarah, whether he wanted to see her again or not, so it would have to be a holding reply.

Hi tiger. Sorry no speak, been busy with work. Just on a story at the mo. Will give you a ring as soon as I free up some time, fear not. x

Dan studied the words. Texts were so unsatisfactory when it came to communicating. Just a few short words to get it right and so easy to misunderstand. Yet the younger generation seemed to survive on little but. Some even appeared to have evolved with a mobile phone permanently stuck in their hands, their fingers blurring across the keypad.

Maybe he should rewrite it. But then again, he was almost

back at the studios and wanted time to write a better text to Claire. Dan sighed, but sent the message.

Claire's text was even more problematic. Five times he typed out a message and five times deleted it. A drizzle of rain began floating from the sky, but Dan didn't notice. The studios were just ahead.

Finally, he wrote,

No worries, it was a bit of a shock for me too – but a nice one. Yep, would love to have a chat. Perhaps meet for a drink in Plymouth one evening? x

More fusillades of doubt. Too keen? Too formal? Or informal?

And that word "nice". So bland and meaningless, one he detested and always tried to avoid, but on this occasion his uninspired mind could come up with no other options.

Dan swore at himself and sent the message, dried his hair in the toilets and trooped upstairs to face Lizzie.

He spent all afternoon waiting for a reply to his texts. And all afternoon he was disappointed.

Some days, no matter how much you prodded, cajoled and implored it, life obstinately refused to respond.

Come the evening Dan found he wasn't sure what to make of the day, so he did as he often would when he needed to unwind. He put Rutherford on his lead, they crossed the road and began running around Hartley Park. The dog wore his tongue-out smiling face, and Dan found his mood improving too. How many times now had he been so glad the awkward, ungainly Alsatian puppy he spotted at the back of the litter had been the one he chose. The dog was that rarest of wonders, an unconditional friend.

Night was falling, the air clear and fresh after the earlier rain. The boundary of the park was patterned with fallen leaves, a tapestry of shapes and colour.

Dan tried to work through the day in his mind. First, and most straightforwardly, his job. For that evening's report, he had used some of Adam's interview from the lunchtime news and packaged it around pictures of the attack on the Minster. It was a simple task. Adam had been besieged by inquiries from other media about doing an interview, but – after a call to Dan, who had gently suggested it – cited pressure of work and declined. The exclusive was theirs.

Lizzie professed the report "reasonable", and naturally demanded another follow-up for tomorrow. Dan adopted a patient expression and said he would see what he could do.

He didn't let on that another story had already fallen into his grateful arms. Ali Tanton had rung. She was upset, crying down the phone, and it took a few minutes to calm her. The spies were still refusing to let her see John's body, or to release it for burial and she wanted to speak out about the way she was being treated. The thought of another exclusive, and one which included criticism of the spooks, was far too enjoyable to resist.

It would give him something to do at least, because it didn't look like he would be needed on the investigation. Adam had called a little earlier. The surveillance on the suspects had revealed nothing. All were behaving absolutely normally.

'Surely that means Ahmed still has to be the prime suspect?' Dan asked. 'By a process of elimination.'

'Yep,' Adam replied. 'But the problem remains I don't have anything like enough evidence to think about charging him and it's looking more and more likely that tomorrow I'll have to let him go. Unless you've got any ideas?'

'Nope. I've been thinking about it all day and I haven't got a thing. I keep going back to the arcade and what he was doing in those seconds when he disappeared. I'm sure there's something we've missed.'

'Like what?'

Dan sighed. 'Don't know,' he said resignedly. 'I've been going through the list of names and numbers on Ahmed's phone too, but I haven't come up with anything there either.'

With a supreme effort at tolerance and self-sacrifice, Dan had paid a quick visit to the Geeks. It was like babysitting two particularly annoying children, but without the reward of pay.

'Dan, Dan the TV man's back!' was the cackled greeting. There were a couple of spins around on their chairs and a high-five, but in terms of substance Flash and Gordon could make nothing of the list. Their conclusion was that there was too much information. The names and numbers could hide just about anything. Yes, there may be a hexadecimal code, but if so it was lost in the mass of letters and digits. To find anything, they would need a better idea of what they were looking for.

Wasting time was bad enough, Dan reflected. But having the empty moments filled with irritants was worse by far.

Adam's tired voice on the phone said, 'I guess we've hit a dead end, haven't we?'

'I fear you're right. So, what next?'

'I'll keep working on it. You keep thinking about it. But for now, I'm going home. I need to see Tom and Annie. I could do with a hug.'

Dan slowed to a jog and called to Rutherford. The dog was sniffing at the Children's Play Area, a forbidden zone. He came sprinting over and Dan grabbed him and gave him a cuddle.

There had still been no reply to the texts to Claire and Sarah. Maybe he'd got the messages entirely wrong and both women had taken offence. He wouldn't put it past himself. Dan wondered whether to send them another text when he got back to the flat. Maybe, but knowing him it would just compound whatever sin he had committed. It was an important, but hard learned lesson in life; how often silence was by far the best policy.

Still, at least he hadn't needed a beer today. He would go home, have a bath and an early night. The run was making him feel pleasantly tired. It had been a hell of a few days.

Rutherford was sniffing at some bushes on the edge of the park. Dan whistled, but the dog didn't move so he started walking over. It was time for the reassurance of home.

'Come on idiot,' he called, peering through the gloom. 'What are you up to?'

The dog was eating something, chewing hard. 'Hey!' Dan called. 'What have I told you about not touching the things you find? You don't know what they might be.'

Rutherford ignored him and kept munching. Dan jogged over, still calling. The dog turned, his eyes flashing in the half light. Dan was sure he saw fear in them.

'What is it?' he called. 'What's the matter boy?'

Rutherford stood absolutely still. Not even his tail moved. Saliva was frothing at his mouth. He let out a little yelp, took a faltering step forwards, then another, staggered, and dropped onto his side.

The hollow thud was a sickening sound.

Dan fell beside him. The dog's breathing was fast and ragged. Dan ran a hand over his head, then placed it onto his chest. Rutherford's heart was racing.

'Shit, shit, shit!' Dan heard himself yell. 'No, please no.'

In the grass, by the bushes, were a couple of pieces of raw steak. They were covered in pellets. They looked like the kind his neighbour used to kill slugs. Irresistible, but potentially lethal to dogs, Dan always took great care to make sure Rutherford went nowhere near them.

Slug pellets. A renowned dog poison.

Rutherford let out another little yelp. His breathing was growing more shallow. His mouth was frothing, the foam of bubbles gathering across his cheek. Dan heard himself moan.

He tapped at the dog's face, then again, harder this time. No reaction. He tried again.

Still no response.

From the canopy of a tree, a hidden crow cawed.

Rutherford blinked, his eyes flickered and slipped slowly closed.

Chapter Eighteen

IT WAS THE LONGEST night Dan could remember.

The lingering sicknesses of childhood, the slow minutes waiting for the deaths of close relatives, even those five months ago, that evening with Claire, so filled with bitterness and bile, even that didn't compare. Then, it was adults, able to understand what they were going through, to accept each had some part in the pain they shared. Then, he had the comfort of beer, the great blue sofa in the flat and his beloved dog. Now he sat alone, in a vet's surgery, staring at an innocent animal as he lay stricken on the operating table.

Rutherford was alive. But Cara, the young vet, had gently tried to prepare Dan for what might yet come to pass.

'He's holding in there. But it's touch and go.'

The question was almost impossible to ask. 'Be honest with me – please. Just how touch and go?'

She fiddled with a lock of her blonde hair. 'He ate quite a few of the pellets. That's the problem with them. They're irresistible to dogs and they're very toxic. Slug pellet poisoning is something vets see a lot of. We've often tried to talk to the manufacturers about changing the mix of chemicals, but ...'

'How damned touch and go?' Dan heard himself shout.

She put a hand on his shoulder and looked into his eyes. 'In his favour, he's a big dog, he's fit and we treated him quickly. Against him – he's not as young as he was and his system's taken quite a battering. I'd have to say it's about, well ... fifty-fifty.'

Fifty-fifty. The toss of a coin. Red or black on a roulette wheel. The turn of a card. To determine the fate of his wonderful dog.

Fifty-fifty.

And for a pessimist such as Dan, that sounded like a death sentence. He gathered his breath, thanked Cara and sat hunched over, gazing at Rutherford.

He had at least had one stroke of luck. On the off chance

that Claire or Sarah should text while he was out running, Dan had taken his mobile. Over the past couple of years Cara had treated Rutherford for a series of minor ailments, usually the dog managing to injure himself while out walking. Once he'd poked himself in the eye with a stick, then, just days later, cut himself on some rusty barbed wire. On another occasion he'd somehow contrived to get a piece of wood stuck in his throat.

One of her best customers was how Cara described the clown of a canine, as she fussed over him. Dan had got her on television a couple of times, when *Wessex Tonight* needed animal experts to interview, they'd become half-friends and she had given Dan her mobile number in case of need.

That night he had so very much needed. When she'd managed to decipher what he wanted through the tears and breathless, stuttering sentences, she had responded and fast, getting to the stricken dog within minutes. She'd had to slap Dan to make him realise she was there and to force some rationality into him.

Together they carried Rutherford to her van and she drove to the surgery. Dan sat with him, in the back, stroking the dog's head the whole way. He was barely conscious, occasionally opening a flickering eye, then closing it again, the bubbles of froth still forming around his mouth. Cara braked hard at some traffic lights, making Dan hit his head hard on a shelf, but he hadn't noticed. He could perceive nothing but his dog, hovering in the twilight hinterland between life and death.

When they got back to the surgery Rutherford started twitching, his legs and head shifting spasmodically. Even his beautiful tail was jerking back and forth. All Dan could do was hold his paws and stroke them.

'He's fitting,' Cara said. 'Come on, quick, help me get him inside. We don't have much time.'

They carried the dog's dense weight into the surgery and placed him gently on the operating table. Dan had to focus on each step, so badly was he shaking. Rutherford was anaesthetised and put on a drip, and that was about all Dan understood of what was going on.

Cara explained she was trying to make him rest while the

treatment flushed the pellets from his system. There was something about chemistry, and canine biology too, but none of this registered. All Dan could see was his unconscious dog, lying on a metal slab, a drip pumping chemicals into his body.

He had no idea of time. He was wearing his running kit, just shorts and a T-shirt, could sense the prickly sweat drying on him, but didn't feel cold. All he could see was Rutherford, prone, on the operating table, his breathing so shallow it was near to imperceptible.

'There's nothing you can do,' Cara said, her face a sympathetic smile. 'It's just a question of waiting now.'

'Uh huh.'

'That's all we can do. Just wait.'

'Uh huh.'

'It's OK to go home if you want to.'

'Uh huh.'

'I've put him deep under. He doesn't know you're here. He doesn't know anything and he's not suffering. There's nothing you can do for him at the moment.'

'Uh huh.'

'You might as well go home, really.'

'Uh huh.'

'You're going to stay, aren't you?'

'Uh huh.'

Cara had left Dan a spare set of keys to the surgery.

'I'm going to go home and get some sleep. I'll be back first thing in the morning. I'll keep my mobile by my bed. Just call if you need anything.'

'Uh huh.'

'It might be best if you go home and get some rest. You've had a terrible shock.'

'Uh huh.'

'Look, if you do decide to go home, just lock up the doors and give me the keys back in the morning.'

'Uh huh.'

She'd left, locking the surgery behind her. And Dan had sat and watched Rutherford, counting each one of the dog's shallow breaths.

The half-light of the surgery picked out the sleek beauty of his fur. There were so many colours in his coat. Dan wondered why he had never properly noticed them before. Black and white, brown and buff, tan and grey. He was an autumn dog.

On the subject of which, Christmas wouldn't be long in coming. Dan would have to do a proper shop and make sure he bought a big turkey. It was Rutherford's favourite and he deserved it. Unlike humans, he never grew fed up with the endless seasonal leftovers. Dan suspected Christmas was the dog's happiest time of year. There was the fresh poultry to look forward to, and his master could usually be guaranteed at least a few days free from Lizzie's tyrannical reign for plenty of walks.

Perhaps that was what he was dreaming of, as he lay on this slab of a table. Turkey and winter walks.

Dan blinked back the blurring in his eyes and focused on his dog. Rutherford's claws needed cutting. The curves of nail were growing just a little too long, made that sharp scrabbling noise when he turned on a pavement or the kitchen floor. Dan would have to get that sorted out. He couldn't have his beloved dog looking anything less than his best.

How he had changed since those puppy days. Then, the young Rutherford had been a shy and meek creature, sniffing hesitantly around the flat on his first homecoming, always with an eye to his new master, anticipating disapproval. But he had soon grown into a confident and fine dog, athletic and strong.

Until tonight.

Dan wiped away another wave of tears. His brain registered a thirst. There was no beer, here in a vet's surgery in the middle of the night. And how he could have done with one, and another, and another. He found the sink and slurped some water from the tap.

He circled the metal table. Rutherford's colourings were almost perfectly symmetrical, just a couple of sprays of his tan coat spoiling the balance. A puff of black fur floated from his tail. Dan reached out and caught it, was going to put it in the bin, but hesitated and instead placed it in the pocket of his shorts.

He noticed he was shivering. The T-shirt he wore was damp and clammy. Dan stripped it off, found a towel, dried his body, then wrapped it around his shoulders. He took a white coat from the wall, put that on too and laid another over his legs.

Rutherford twitched, just the slight motion of a paw. Dan was on his feet in an instant. The dog's eyes were still closed, his breathing slight, but it was a hint of life, an expression of his fighting spirit, a good sign.

It had to be.

Dan ran a gentle finger over the dog's flank. 'Come on old friend,' he whispered. 'Keep fighting. Pull through for me. Please. I don't know what I'd do without you.'

He turned away and walked around the white and sterile room. Posters for worm treatments. Lists of symptoms to look for with a variety of dog ailments. Cabinets of wipes and instruments, packets and bottles of pills and tablets.

Car headlights flared through the surgery, spinning shadows. Dan sat back down, rested his head in his hands, then got up again, walked to the sink and splashed water onto his face.

He looked back at the table. Rutherford's nose was oddly dry, more so than Dan had ever seen before. A memory surfaced of one of the dog's most annoying habits. If his master had the cheek to oversleep, a damp and insistent nuzzle was the standard alarm call. Dan almost smiled, but the expression wouldn't come.

He took out his phone. Its display said the time was just after midnight. Still no messages from Claire or Sarah.

It was late, very late to call, but how he could do with a hug. He found Claire's number, hesitated, then rang. Her answer machine clicked straight in. She was in bed, asleep, no doubt. Dan didn't leave a message.

He found Sarah's number. It rang and she answered quickly. Somehow, he knew she wouldn't be asleep.

'Hello tiger,' she chirped. 'I was wondering when I'd hear from you. It's a bit late, but it's always a pleasure.'

'Sarah, I could do with your help.'

She heard his pain and her voice changed. 'What's the

matter?'

Dan found a constriction had formed in his throat. He gulped it away and explained.

'Do you want to come round?' she asked. 'You're very welcome. I'll look after you.'

'I can't leave. I need to stay here with him. I was hoping – I was wondering …'

'I'll be there in ten minutes.'

Dan stood up again and rested his head on Rutherford's side. He could hear a heartbeat, but it was faint, so horribly tenuous, such a faltering link to life. He felt the tears forming again, wiped them away and sat back down. A shiver sparked through his body.

Headlights at the windows. A car door opened. Dan got up, let Sarah in and led her to the operating room. He had no thought about how he must look, dressed in trainers, shorts, a towel and a white coat. She was wearing boots, tight jeans and an even tighter black top.

Together, they stood looking at Rutherford. 'It's not exactly the way I wanted you to meet him,' Dan managed, before his voice broke. She reached out and hugged him hard. He closed his eyes and let her, felt her warmth encompassing him.

'You poor, poor thing,' Sarah soothed. 'You must be feeling dreadful. Let me look after you.'

She cuddled him more, stroked his hair, started to push herself rhythmically against him and tried to find his lips.

'Sarah, this is a vet's surgery,'

'Mmm, could be fun, eh?'

Dan tried to free himself. 'Look, I'm sorry, it's nothing against you, but I'm not exactly feeling my best at the moment.'

She gave him an alluring pout. 'You sure?'

'Very.'

Sarah ruffled his hair. 'It was worth a try. OK then, tell me what happened?'

Dan got himself another drink of water, then told her about the run in the park and the steaks.

'He was poisoned?' she said, appalled. 'How horrible. Do

you think whoever did it was trying to get Rutherford, or just any dog? Whoever would do something like that?'

Dan recoiled at the merciless impact of realisation. The possibility had simply not occurred to him. In the shock of what happened all he had thought about was Rutherford, how to try to save him and whether he would live or die.

Now a new understanding took hold, spreading fast through his mind. And with it, a firing flame of anger.

'Are you OK?' Sarah was saying. 'You've gone white.'

'Yeah. Listen, there's something I need to do. I'm sorry, I don't want you to think I'm not grateful for you coming out here, I really am, but there's just something I need to do. I need to do it now and I need to do it alone. Would you mind?'

She got up from the chair. 'Dan, what the hell's going on?'

'I – I can't tell you at the moment. I will explain, but it'll have to wait a day or two.' He led her firmly towards the doors, opened them, and with a careless afterthought planted a kiss on her cheek. 'I'll give you a ring.'

She got into her car and drove quickly off, didn't wave. Dan hardly noticed. He walked back to the operating table. Rutherford was still prone, unmoving. Another blade of anger stabbed at him.

Dan picked up his mobile and called El.

'Mate, you OK?' came the sleepy reply.

'Yeah, kind of. Listen, tonight, were you doing as we arranged?'

'Yeah.'

'The whole night?'

'No, not all of it. I was there until you left the flat with your dog. You had your gym kit on. I figured you were out running and that you'd be fine in a public place.'

'Did you get anyone?'

'There were a few people coming and going. I did get the feeling this one guy was checking the flat when he walked past, but that was about it.'

'Did you snap him?'

'Yeah, of course. Hang on, I'll get me camera.'

Dan could hear a scrabbling at the end of the phone. Finally

El said, 'Right, hang on, just spooling through. Alright, got him.'

'Describe him to me.'

El did. Dan leaned back on his chair, then tilted his head and screamed wild abuse at the ceiling. He stood perfectly still for a few seconds, and then let it vent once more. The seething, boiling, septic, venomous and bubbling rage.

Dan strode around the surgery, shouting and yelling. He pounded his fists on the wall, kicked out at a bin. It went spinning and clattering across the floor. He followed it with another kick, then another, pitting its shiny surface with dents. He fell to his knees and pummelled his knuckles into it, drugged and demented with dizzying fury.

He grabbed for the taps, ran the water ice cold and plunged his head under it, opened his eyes and watched the droplets cascade from his face. He gripped the sides of the sink until his hands turned white.

Finally, Dan stood back up and forced himself to breathe, great shuddering gasps of air.

Rutherford had been deliberately poisoned. And the description of who did it could match only one man.

Chapter Nineteen

THE SWIRLING RUSH OF red-hot rage propelled Dan towards the door of the surgery. He groped for the keys and fumbled them in the lock. He was about to open the door when a noise stopped him.

Rutherford. And he was spluttering.

Dan spun around and lurched back into the operating room. The dog's chest was heaving, more saliva foaming from his mouth.

Dan heard himself moan. He grabbed his mobile and called Cara.

One ring, two, three.

More coughing from Rutherford. More jerking. Dan ran a hand over the dog's head and let it slide down to his chest. He was fearful to do it, but felt for the heartbeat. Sometimes, short seconds can feel so very long.

There was a pulse. It was faint, but steady.

He groaned in relief.

Another ring from the phone, and another.

'Come on, come on,' Dan urged.

Rutherford twitched. The coughing stopped. Dan pressed his hand harder to the dog's body. The heartbeat was still there, still regular.

Another ring from the phone, then, 'Hello? Dan! Is he OK?'

'I don't know. He's coughing, spluttering, twitching.'

'How much?'

'A couple of coughs. Then a bit of a shudder.'

'What's he doing now?'

Dan studied his dog. He was lying still and breathing evenly. 'Nothing. He's just sleeping.'

'Let me hear. Hold the phone to his mouth.'

Dan did. 'What do you think?' he asked, after a few seconds. 'Is he OK? What does it mean? Had you better come back? Give him some more drugs? See if there's anything else you can do for him? I'll pay, I don't mind what it costs, if you need to come back, the call-out, anything you need …'

'Dan!' she interrupted. 'He's doing fine. A bit of movement and some coughing is perfectly natural. We're doing all we can for him. He just needs to rest.'

'OK, but …'

'He just needs to rest. As I'd suggest you do.'

'I'm staying here.'

'OK then. Look, he's doing all right. There's nothing more we can do at the moment.'

'Cara – just one more thing.'

'Yes?'

'I'm sorry I bothered you, but I got so frightened.'

'That's OK. I understand.'

'How did he sound?'

'What?'

'When you listened to his breathing – did he sound like he was getting any better?'

Her voice grew softer. 'Dan, it's too early to tell.'

'But – I mean – it must be a good sign that he's survived the first few hours, mustn't it? That he's still going?'

'Yes. That is a good sign. Every hour that passes, the chances of him recovering get better.'

'So the odds have improved?'

'A little.'

'How much?'

'Dan!'

'No, please, I need to know. How much?'

A sigh, then, 'It's probably about 55-45 now that he's going to be OK.'

Dan could have pulled the numbers from the air and danced with them. A fifty-five per cent chance of survival felt so much better than evens. The gods had smiled and tilted the odds in his favour. He found some tissues and gently wiped the spittle from around Rutherford's mouth, stroking the dog's head all the while.

He was comfortable and cared for.

Now it was time for revenge.

The clock on the wall said it was a quarter past one. The

temptation was to leave the surgery, go home, get in the car and hunt down the person who had poisoned Rutherford. But he would need Adam's help, and it was the middle of the night. His friend had sounded tired enough earlier and could do with being allowed to rest.

He could go alone. But to where exactly, and what would he do when he got there?

Another twitch from Rutherford. Dan was back beside the dog, holding his paw. What if Rutherford had another fit? He could easily relapse and there would be no one here to help him, no one to call Cara. The dog couldn't be left alone overnight.

Facing the poisoner could wait until the morning. Coolly, logically, the confrontation didn't have to happen right now, no matter how much Dan wanted it. He forced himself to sit back down again and ran a hand over his face. It was flushed with anger.

He would stay with Rutherford. At first light he would call Adam, explain what had happened and who had done it. And, more importantly, why.

And then they would act.

Dan was woken by a hammering at the door. He jerked awake, got up, ignored the persistent noise and instead checked Rutherford. The dog's breathing was still even, his heartbeat regular.

More banging from the front of the surgery. It was Cara. Dan had left the keys in the lock and she couldn't get in. He opened the door.

'How is he?' she asked.

'Doing OK, I think.'

She tested Rutherford's heartbeat, changed the drip, took some blood and fussed over him. Dan watched in silence. His neck was aching from where he'd fallen asleep on the chair and he noticed he felt cold, but none of that mattered. Only the prone dog was important.

Eventually Cara pronounced, 'Yep, he's doing OK.'

'And?'

'And what?'

'You know what.'

'Well, he's still not out of the woods. There's a long way to go.'

'But he's got though the first night.'

'Yes.'

'Which has to be good.'

'Yes.'

'So his chances must have improved.'

'Dan!'

'No, look, it's just that – well, the numbers seem to help. Give me sixty percent that he'll be OK?'

She shook her head. 'I don't want you to go away thinking everything's all right. He could still suffer complications.'

'Sure, I understand that. But it was fifty-five percent earlier. And he's got through the night. So it must be up to sixty now.'

She frowned. 'Any advance on sixty?'

'Please, Cara.'

'OK then, if it makes you happier, a sixty per cent chance of survival it is.'

Dan reached out and hugged her, held her tight. Only a pointed cough from behind made him disengage. It was a middle-aged man, dressed in a suit. He was carrying a poodle, but doing so at arm's length, as if the dog were crawling with the most foul of infectious diseases.

'He's been sick all night,' the man said, with sharp distaste. 'The wife wanted him rushed in here. She couldn't do it herself, naturally.' He handed the dog to Cara. The creature was a masterpiece of topiary, all spheres, discs and patterns of white fur. 'His name's Whiteball, by the way.'

A phone began ringing in the man's jacket. He took it out and answered. A few seconds later another rang in a different pocket. He answered that too and asked the caller to wait.

Cara placed Whiteball down on a table. The dog turned, teeth bared and tried to bite, but she was too quick.

'Occupational hazard,' she told Dan. 'You get to know which animals are going to be the awkward ones. Oddly enough, they usually take after their owners.'

She cast a glance at the man, who was entirely oblivious. He had a phone clamped to each ear and was trying to talk into both at the same time. And now yet another mobile rang. The man wedged one of the pair currently in use under his chin and fumbled in his trousers to find the latest call on his precious attention.

Dan stared in disbelief. Three phones. He was kept plenty busy enough by one.

And then came the beautiful instant, like a beam of sunlight through the clouds. Where before all was blurred and indistinct, suddenly the picture was clear.

Dan sat down heavily on a chair.

'Are you OK?' Cara said. 'Maybe I should see if I've got something to treat you. How about a nice big horse suppository?'

'No, yeah, um, right, err – I'm fine,' Dan managed. 'Just a little tired. After the stress of the night.'

She nodded understandingly and returned to her patient. The poodle began an unpleasant yapping, but Dan hardly heard. All he could see was John Tanton, detonating his bomb in Wessex Minster, and the phone call the young man had made just minutes beforehand.

The call that was the key to the case, which would give them the radicaliser. And now he knew who that was, and what the person had done with the phone, the one piece of evidence which would lead to a conviction.

It was almost half past seven. They would have to move fast.

'Cara, is Rutherford going to be OK today?' Dan asked quickly. 'If I go off to work?'

'Yep. I'll be here to keep an eye on him.'

'Right, great. I'll ring you later.'

Dan made for the door and started walking home, striding quickly. Everyone he passed stared at the strange man wearing trainers, shorts, and a white lab coat. A group of schoolchildren pointed and laughed. Some even shouted abuse.

He noticed none of this. Dan walked fast, heading automatically for the flat, took out his mobile and called Adam.

Chapter Twenty

SOME DAYS, LIFE FEELS different. All around is exactly the same, but something has changed within.

It was how Dan had come to think of the turning points of the investigations he'd worked on. The time after that dizzying epiphany moment of sheer realisation, when in a single second the inquiry had shifted from the slog of a search for a faceless criminal to a beatific understanding.

Once, at the end of a long Dartmoor walk, perhaps tired and light-headed, he'd confided to Claire the only analogy he could imagine. And she'd laughed so hard the tears had poured from her eyes.

It was, Dan said, a feeling like the hours after the first time he'd had sex. Aged sixteen, walking around his home town taller and stronger than ever before, empowered with having made a great leap of experience. A man who had just undergone an initiation into an esoteric club.

All around remained just as it had been. But something had changed in his own world.

Thus it was with the great possession of the solution to a case. Around Dan, the world progressed as it always had. Men and women commuted to work. Children walked to school. Radios played. Cars drove. The world turned.

But something felt different.

They met at the Minster. Adam wanted to go straight to the shopping arcade, but Dan found he couldn't.

'I'm not sure why,' he explained on the phone earlier. 'I just need to see the smashed window again.'

'It's still smashed,' the detective objected, with emotionless practicality. 'We've got to get on with the case. We don't have time to mess about.'

'It's only a minute from the Minster to the arcade. And I kind of – well, I need to get a sense of the crime again before we actually solve it.'

A groan on the end of the line. 'Your bloody melodrama

just gets worse. This isn't a book, you know. It's a criminal investigation. And a big one. Dead people. Terrorists. In case you'd forgotten.'

'It'll only take a minute. See you at the Minster in an hour, then.'

'If you must.'

It was another fine September day. The drive to Exeter was quiet and easy. Dan had inadvertently timed the trip well, just a little too late for the rush hour, a little too early for the shoppers. There were plenty of parking spaces in South Street. Automatically, he bought a ticket and walked through to Minster Green.

A couple of tramps sat outside the Homeless Mission, drinking cans of cider. The time was a quarter past nine. Pigeons and crows wandered across the freedom of the grass, undisturbed yet by the inevitable assaults of human visitors. A man washed the windows of the row of shops, whistling a tune to himself. The odd bubble floated free in the sunshine. Office workers carried take-away teas and coffees, or talked on mobiles as they walked.

Adam was already waiting when Dan arrived, pacing back and forth. He'd obviously left his house in a hurry. His usually impeccable tie was just a little off-centre, and – horror amongst horrors – there might even have been the slightest of a suggestion its narrow green stripes clashed with the blue of his shirt.

'Right, there it is, the smashed window. You've seen it again, now let's get on with the case.'

'Just indulge me a moment.'

'I indulge you too much.'

'Just a minute, that's all.'

Dan stood staring at the ruined window, while Adam pointedly and petulantly tapped a foot on the pavement.

He could see John Tanton, walking along the cobbles outside the Minster, a mobile phone at his ear and a rucksack on his back. Now he could hear the deafening explosion, the hissing of shrapnel, the shattering of glass, the silence, and then the moans and the screams. And he could smell the blood, just as he had when they filmed inside.

'Right,' he said. 'Let's go.'

They crossed the shopping precinct. Dan felt his mind slipping to Claire and that phone call earlier. He allowed the memory to linger for a second as they walked.

When she turned her mobile on that morning, it had registered a missed call from his number. She rang to see what he wanted and Dan explained what happened to Rutherford.

'No! Oh, Dan, no. How's he doing? How are you? Is there anything I can do?'

Dan reassured her he was coping OK, or some very rough approximation, and that Rutherford was making progress. They chatted for a couple more minutes, solely on the safe ground of the dog, then Claire said, 'Can I see him?'

'What?'

'I'd like to see him. It might help him to know I'm thinking about him too.'

'You really want to see Rutherford?'

A pause on the line, then Claire said quietly, 'This might come as a surprise to you, but I loved that stupid dog. I came to think of myself as – I don't know, mother to him I suppose, to your dad.'

'Really?'

'Yes. Very much really.'

'Well, OK then, yes, of course you can see him. When?'

'Tonight.'

It was a statement, not a question.

'Sure.'

'Give me a call later, when you're back in Plymouth and I'll come up to the vet's.'

'OK.'

'And Dan …'

'Yes?'

'Maybe we could have a drink and a chat afterwards?'

This time it was a question, and a tentative one, soft with vulnerability. But he didn't hesitate. 'I'd like that.'

'So would I.'

And then came a vision of Rutherford, choking after eating

the poison pellets, the dreadful dull thud as he collapsed. Dan had told Adam about that earlier too, who he thought had done it, and why. It took his friend several minutes of hard persuasion to stop Dan going after the poisoner first.

'See the bigger picture,' Adam said firmly. 'He'll still be around later. But time's running out if we're going to get Ahmed. His solicitor's coming to Heavitree Road this morning and is expecting us to release him.'

Ahmed. In his cell, counting off the minutes until he was released. Anticipating a swaggering walk from the police station, a middle finger up to the forces of law and decency. Back on the streets of the society he detested, spreading his toxic propaganda and doubtless keeping a predator's eye out for someone else like John Tanton.

Adam was right. They had to go after Ahmed first.

The penetrating warble of his mobile brought Dan back to the shopping arcade. It was a withheld number. That meant the newsroom. In the whirl of the morning he hadn't even bothered to check in with the early producer, let alone tell them he was going to Exeter.

Dan switched the call to his answer machine. Later, he would have a great exclusive for Lizzie. The charging of Ahmed, with plotting a terrorist attack and conspiracy to murder.

Or so he hoped. It all depended on the next few minutes.

Adam waited for a delivery lorry to pass, then crossed the road. He stopped outside the arcade. 'Right. Now get on with it.'

Dan blinked hard, tried to free his mind of the vision of confronting the man who had poisoned Rutherford, and of Claire, and the thought of seeing her later.

'OK,' he said slowly. 'Ahmed comes running into the arcade. If we're assuming he is the radicaliser, as we've suspected all along, he knows he's only got seconds before you arrest him. And he knows that in his pocket is the one piece of evidence which will see him convicted. But he knows too that he can't just dump it, because either someone will see, or, even if they don't, that you're probably going to carry out a search and find it.'

'Yeah, OK,' Adam replied impatiently. 'But we've been through all that. Just get to the point will you?'

Dan started walking into the arcade. 'I don't think Ahmed's panicking. He hasn't in any of the interviews we've done with him. He didn't when you arrested him. He's calm and deliberate. He knows he has to get rid of that phone which Tanton has called just a few minutes ago.'

Adam rolled his eyes. 'Will you please just get to the point? I hate all this teasing.'

Dan wondered whether to mention the irony of Adam accusing someone else of enjoying the irritating vice of delayed gratification, but decided against it. He walked further into the arcade, his footsteps echoing on the tiles.

'So, Ahmed's looking around for a hiding place – somewhere he can't be seen. He spots the CCTV cameras, but ahead he can see an area where there aren't any. There are cops behind and he knows there are going to be cops coming from the other entrances too. He's got to find somewhere to hide the phone here and he's got to do it fast.'

Dan stopped, said suddenly, 'So what does he do?'

They were standing at the intersection of malls where Dan had timed Adam hiding his mobile. Around them were the greengrocer's, supermarket, optician's, and the second-hand shop. Ahead were the couple of stalls, selling winter-wear accessories. The floor had been polished and was alive with reflections of people passing by, the sweet smell of wax lingering in the air.

'He hides the phone,' Adam said tetchily. 'We've been through all this. He sticks it in the drain and we come along and find it later. But that just brings us back to the same problem. We can't link that phone to the call Tanton made, and we can't break the code in the names and numbers to find out what Ahmed was trying to hide.'

Dan nodded, but then said quietly, 'There is no code.'

Adam stared at him. 'What?'

'There is no code. No hidden message, no riddle, no magic solution to the case all bound up in that mysterious list of names and numbers. There's nothing in there at all.'

'But – there has to be ... surely? What's the point of it otherwise? And if there isn't anything in it, what the hell are we doing here?'

'That phone was a decoy. It was a beautiful way of throwing us off the track and giving us something to work on for days, just wasting our time while the clock ticked towards Ahmed being released. He's smart. Just on the tiny little chance that the cops do catch up with him, he's all ready. He's got the everyday phone he uses, the one you found on him when he was arrested, and he knows there's nothing incriminating on that. He's got the mobile he used to talk to Tanton, the one we need to find, but he's also got a decoy phone. It's full of random names and numbers he's invented, to give us a lovely puzzle to play with. And we're never going to find anything in it – because there's nothing to find. That's why only a few of the numbers were real and none corresponded to the names. Ahmed just made them up and typed them in. A huge red herring.'

Adam sat down on a bench. 'So, if that's the case – why bother taking all that trouble to hide it?'

'To throw us off the real scent. Because he knew we'd do a search and that we'd find it. And that would be it. We'd be happy with our clever little discovery. We could work away at the hidden clue contained in it, like good investigators, and we'd never think that ...'

Adam let out a loud groan. 'That there was something else hidden here. The missing thirty seconds.'

'Exactly. We only lose Ahmed for forty seconds. By our own experiment, he took about ten of those to hide the decoy phone, just doing it well enough to make it look realistic. So, what was he doing with the other thirty seconds?'

They waited while a couple of kids rode their bikes through the arcade, sending shoppers dodging from their path. One old man waved a walking stick at them. Adam must have been distracted. The paragon of the law didn't look remotely like intervening.

Finally the detective said, 'He was hiding the real evidence.

Getting rid of the actual phone that Tanton had called. He used those thirty seconds to hide it.'

'Exactly. And where do you think he did that?'

Adam looked up and down the arcade, an expression of puzzlement growing on his face. It was a cheap emotion, admittedly, but Dan couldn't help enjoying it.

'It has to be here?' the detective said.

'Yep. Ahmed only had those few seconds. He couldn't have gone anywhere else.'

'But we searched everywhere.'

'Almost everywhere.'

'Where did we miss then? Come on, stop this bloody teasing, will you?!'

Dan sat down beside his friend, stretched out his legs and rolled his neck. It was still stiff after the night in the vet's surgery. He knew he should feel tired, but didn't.

Finally, he said, 'Ahmed put the phone right in your face. Directly under your nose. The one place he might guess you wouldn't see it.'

'What? What are you talking about?'

'Do you know what one of the wisest teachers at my school used to say? It was very clever. I'll never forget it.'

'What? Dan, what the hell are you talking about? Look, Ahmed's going to be released at any minute and if this phone's here, we need to find it. I don't have time to mess about with your bloody teasing and ...'

Dan stood up. 'Come on then. Let's go get it.'

'Get what? The phone? Ahmed's mobile?'

'Yep. Follow me.' Dan pointed along the mall. 'It's just up there, waiting for us. Shall I tell you what my old teacher said, while we walk?'

'What?'

Dan smiled, couldn't help himself. 'It's this. He used to say – where better to hide a pebble than on a beach?'

Adam's mobile rang. He glared at it, but answered and held a brief, almost monosyllabic conversation as they walked along the arcade. Ahmed's solicitor had been in some heated discussions with Greater Wessex Police's legal department. There were threats of a writ and High Court action. Now, unless any new evidence could be found, the solicitor would be calling at Heavitree Road police station at half past ten to have his client freed.

Dan glanced down at his watch. They had an hour. It should be enough.

If all went smoothly.

He checked the message on his own mobile. It was indeed Lizzie, and she was on fizzing form. The non-good morning greeting lasted almost a minute, of which approximately ninety-five per cent was a list of demands for another story on the bombing. The ratings apparently had the temerity to sag a little overnight and needed immediate boosting with an exclusive. The weight of the very future of broadcasting was set squarely upon Dan's shoulders.

He sighed. It was ever thus with his manic editor. He would call in later when he had the ritual sacrifice of a story to offer. He hoped.

Adam hung up and passed a couple of choice comments about the legal profession. Shameless parasites hanging onto the blistered backside of humanity was the gist of it. He was so wrapped up in his tirade he didn't notice that Dan had stopped walking.

'Come on!' he barked, looking round. 'Ahmed's going to be free in an hour. Quit the bloody pantomime and tell me where you reckon his phone is.'

Dan just waited. 'See anything here that might help us?' he asked.

He was standing outside the second-hand shop. Adam swore again and came striding back over. 'Look, I've had enough games …'

Dan raised a finger to his lips, took a pace backwards and leaned against the shop window.

'What the hell are you doing?' Adam snapped. 'We're trying to catch a terrorist, we've got just minutes to do it, and you're behaving like a …'

'Look!' Dan interrupted, angling his head to the window.

218

Adam growled, but did so. Dan watched his friend's gaze range over the display. Video games, binoculars, cameras, satellite navigation systems, computer accessories, mobile phones.

The detective's eyes stopped and his expression changed.

'Shit,' Adam groaned. 'A pebble on a beach. It was right in our faces. That's what he was doing in those missing seconds.'

'Yep,' Dan replied. 'That's what I reckon. So, let's go get it.'

'Let's just hope it's still here, after all this messing around,' the detective replied sulkily.

A thin man with a smattering of acne was standing behind the counter. He greeted them with the kind of uncertain smile that suggested his young life had already equipped him with the ability to recognise a plain-clothes police officer.

Adam explained what they wanted. The smile vanished.

'I'll have to ask the manager,' the lad said. 'He's in town, doing some banking. He'll only be an hour or so.'

'There's no time for that. I want a list of when all these phones were brought in.'

'I can't do that without …'

Adam propelled his warrant card forwards so it was almost touching the assistant's nose. He recoiled and blinked hard.

'List of phones now, or you under arrest for obstructing the police, team of cops in here to pull place apart, shop closes down and you out of a job.'

The two men stared at each other, then Adam allowed a detective's smile to form on his face. It was the product of years of practice of intimidation, as warm and welcoming as the glint of a guillotine in the first morning sun.

'I'll get the list,' the young man said.

He brought them a couple of tatty sheets of paper. The shop only bothered to buy the most modern phones. Older models didn't sell, were rendered obsolete too fast by the typhoon of technological advancement. The entirety of their stock was in the window, around forty models.

Adam walked back to the doorway. The assistant went to

follow, but was waved away.

'If Ahmed walks in here, can he just lean into the window and place the phone in?' the detective asked.

Dan tried it with his own mobile. The display wasn't sealed and it was simple to do, just a case of shifting a panel and reaching over.

'Yep,' he said. 'It'd only take a second or two.' He looked across the counter. 'And whoever was on duty wouldn't see it.'

'Then let's get looking at these phones. Whichever one doesn't match the list, that's the one we want.'

Adam lifted the display from the window and set it down on the floor. He began working through each mobile, while Dan ticked them off from the list. A clock on the wall said it was almost a quarter to ten. They had forty-five minutes.

The phones were described by colour, condition, manufacturer and model number. They checked off ten with no luck, then twenty. Adam let out a low sigh and pulled his tie a little from his neck.

It was surprisingly warm in the shop, the air still, close and stale. Dan noticed an earwig crawling out from under a display. He scratched at his back. It was odd how the sight of an insect often prompted an itch.

A cleaner walked past and brushed around the doorway with a broom. The man's efforts succeeded more in rearranging the dirt than removing it. An announcement boomed out from the mall. A special offer on beauty products was underway. Eternal youth was yours, and for a remarkably reasonable price.

Marketing people never understood the meaning of moderation.

Thirty phones checked now. Still no success.

Dan shifted his weight and noticed a hole in his sock. He'd have to do some clothes shopping soon. The prospect of the oncoming winter was bad enough, without his socks offering extra opportunities for the cold to spread its insurgent chill.

They kept working through the phones. Adam's own mobile rang again, but he ignored it. 'We're almost there,' he said. 'Keep going.'

At the top of the window, a spider scuttled to the corner of its web. The light caught in the gossamer pattern of spun strands. A couple of shoppers stopped to watch the two middle-aged men in their suits, squatting in the shop doorway, going through a pile of mobile phones. The assistant walked over to ask how they were doing.

'Fine,' Adam replied without looking up, conveying in one sharp word another unmistakable dismissal.

The clock on the wall chimed ten. There were just half a dozen phones left.

'I'm getting a bad feeling about this,' Dan muttered.

'It has to be here. It has to.'

Adam hesitated, looked up and then said more slowly, 'Are we sure about this? What if Ahmed hid the phone somewhere else?'

'Well, if we're thinking like that, what if he's not even the radicaliser?' Dan replied. 'What if we're on the wrong track entirely and it's someone else? What if …'

'We can't go into that at the moment,' Adam interrupted. 'This is our best shot for now.'

They continued working. Now they were down to the last three phones. Dan shifted his position again and stretched his legs. His knees had started to throb. Adam held up the first of the remaining mobiles. It was a silver Nokia.

Dan found it on his sheet of paper. 'Check.'

Next, a black Siemens phone. Dan knew it was there on the list, but he looked twice, just to be sure. 'Check.'

The final phone. Another Nokia, red and silver, a little battered at the edges. Dan heard himself muttering a prayer.

Their last chance.

Another blast of advertising from the tannoy. This time, more eggs than an army could breakfast on in a week was the current special offer at the supermarket. Autumn, apparently, was the perfect time for an omelette.

Dan found himself fancying one. He was feeling peckish.

One of the strip lights flickered and began an annoying buzz. It was dusty in the store, the attack of the fine imperceptible haze drying mouths and teasing noses.

Adam held up the last mobile. 'This is the one. It has to be. Come on, tell me it's not on the sheet.'

Dan traced his way down the piece of paper. The movement was forlorn with miserable expectation. There was just one line left he hadn't put a tick by. A red and silver Nokia, in average condition, a few scrapes and scratches.

'It's here,' he said quietly. 'The bloody thing's here.'

Adam leaned back on his haunches, then sat down heavily on the carpet. 'Shit,' he hissed. 'We're stuffed. And I thought we had him. Now he's going to walk free and there's nothing we can do. So much for your brilliant idea and all the bloody melodrama too.'

Dan didn't have the spirit to retaliate. 'I'm sorry. I just thought it made sense. It all seemed to fit. And I was so damned sure.'

He sat down too. Suddenly, he felt very tired. A young woman walked into the shop and gave them a curious look, picked her way past and towards the counter.

'Unless,' Adam said, 'Unless, someone's come in and bought it. Maybe that's why it's not here.'

'Is this the kind of place where they'd sell a phone if they didn't have any record of buying it in the first place?'

Adam gave him a scornful look. 'What do you think?'

'OK, but how does that help us? They don't keep notes of the people who buy things.'

Adam got up, span around and pointed to the counter. Above it was a small CCTV camera.

'No, but they do have security. And maybe we can identify who bought the phone. If we can get a picture and show it around all the local cops, someone might recognise him, or her.'

'Maybe I can do better than that,' Dan said. 'Lizzie wants another story. What if I put out a TV appeal for whoever it was to come forward. It won't stop Ahmed being released, but …'

'If we put a tail on him, and if we can find the phone, we can arrest him again later,' Adam interjected. 'We can still get him. Come on.'

The young assistant looked even more worried as Adam bore down upon him for a second time.

'CCTV,' the detective said, pointing to the camera. 'How long do you keep the recordings for?'

'A week.'

Dan breathed out a sigh of relief. One hurdle overcome.

'I want to see the recordings. Right now.'

Evolution had not passed the man by. This time he didn't even bother arguing. He led them to a small office at the back of the shop. The walls were covered with pictures of naked women and the room smelt strongly of cigarettes. A DVD recorder was attached to a television set and a couple of black boxes, coloured lights blinking on their front.

The assistant pointed to a rack of silver discs and begrudgingly handed Adam a remote control. 'We use one a day. They've got the days written on them.'

He walked back out to the shop. Adam picked up the disc marked *Monday*, loaded it into the machine and pressed play.

The image was black and white, but impressively clear. Dan ticked off another of his mental list of potential pitfalls. Much of the CCTV footage he'd seen in his career was so indistinct that attempting to make sense of what was going on was like trying to pick out a golf ball in a snowstorm.

The camera was static and fixed on the counter and till.

'We won't see Ahmed coming in then,' Dan observed. 'So we won't get confirmation he did hide the phone in the window.'

'No, but that's not the most important thing. We'll have to assume he did. What we need is to spot anyone who buys a mobile.'

There was a digital clock in the corner of the picture. Adam found the time of the bombing and began fast forwarding, then pausing whenever someone came to the counter. It was fortunate the shop was not busy or the task would have been a long one.

A woman bought a computer game, a young lad an ipod. The focus of the camera was sufficiently sharp to make out even small details, like the money they were handing over. It was interesting that everyone who came to the counter glanced up at the camera, as if instinctively aware they were being monitored.

Dan noticed Adam looking at his watch. It was ten past ten.

'Try not to think about it,' he told his friend. 'We're going to have to accept that Ahmed will be freed – for now. But we can still get him later.' He patted Adam's shoulder. 'And we will.'

'Yeah, I know. It just – well, sticks in my throat. We're so close. I can sense it.'

Dan nodded. 'There's no point going back to the station and trying to bluff him, is there? Now that we think we know how he hid the mobile. We could try to scare him that we've found it – you know, something along the lines of "Guess what I've just bought from the window of a second hand shop in that arcade where you were arrested?"'

Adam ran a hand over his chin. 'It might be worth a try. But I don't reckon we stand much chance. He's too smart. He'd just sit there, nice and quiet, and wait to see what it is we've got. He'd soon realise we haven't actually got anything. I think we work at it this way, try to find who bought the phone and see if we can trace them. It's our only chance of getting some evidence that'll stick.'

Adam spooled on a few minutes. The recording showed an elderly couple talking to the young assistant about a camera. He was demonstrating how it worked.

Another twenty minutes forwards. Some kids at the counter, looking at watches, but not buying. Now an older man who seemed to be trying to sell a video recorder. He left again quickly with it under his arm.

The only place he was likely to secure a sale was in an antiques shop.

Video recorders. When Dan was young, he had marvelled at the magnificent new technology; its revolutionary boast that you no longer had to be sitting in front of a television at a defined time to see the programme you wanted. And now –

Sometimes, the pace of life's progress could leave you feeling more than a little old.

It was a quarter past ten. Ahmed would be free in fifteen minutes, strolling out into a gentle autumn day. Perhaps he would walk past the Minster, sit on a bench and enjoy the sight of the atrocity he had been so instrumental in inflicting.

A bald man, his head flaring in the image, was talking to the young assistant about a radio. It was placed in a bag, the till opened and closed and the man left.

Another few minutes on. Another man appeared in the shot. He put a mobile phone on the counter.

Adam lurched forwards and hit the pause button.

It was a mobile they were waiting to see. And one sat on the counter, the man and the assistant frozen in their discussion.

But it wasn't the phone at which Dan and Adam stared. It was the man who was buying it. Who was holding a brief conversation, handing over a spray of bank notes, refusing a bag, quickly putting the phone into his pocket, turning and walking out of the shop.

A man who kept the collar of his jacket turned up the whole time. Who had clearly wanted to make the purchase as fast as he could and escape. Who hadn't looked at the CCTV camera once, unlike all the other customers. But it was a man who, nonetheless, was very familiar and instantly recognisable.

Adam and Dan both leaned back on their chairs. For several seconds, neither could speak. All they did was to stare at the dusty old screen.

It was one of the pleasant quirks of Adam's character that he rarely swore, and when he did the words tended to be only mild.

But on this occasion, Dan couldn't quibble with the way the detective expressed his feelings.

'Fucking shite,' Adam gasped, pointing a shaking finger at the TV. 'What the bloody hell is he doing in here, just a few hours after Ahmed came in? And just after we finished searching the arcade and reopened it? He must be after Ahmed's phone, he must be. What the fuck is going on?'

He rewound the DVD and played the sequence one more time. Just to be entirely, utterly, a hundred per cent and more sure.

And however extraordinary, what they were watching was incontrovertible.

The man on the screen, buying the phone, was Oscar.

Chapter Twenty-one

TWENTY PAST TEN.

'How long to Heavitree Road?' Adam snapped.

'Ten minutes. A bit less if we run.'

'Then run.'

Adam ejected the disc and stuffed it into a pocket. 'Evidence,' he said.

They jogged through the shop. A tall, well-built man in a dark suit tried to stop them.

'I'm the manager here and I want to know ...'

'Later,' Adam barked. 'This is an emergency. Out of the way or you're under arrest.'

The man backed off, muttering some abuse about paying his taxes and the growth of a police state.

Adam ran along the arcade, Dan following. The tiredness had fled. The city centre was still quiet, only a few early shoppers and business people disturbing the morning's reverie.

'What are we going to do?'

'First, stop Ahmed being freed. We need to give ourselves some time.'

'For what?'

'To go through the phone. To check it is the one Tanton called. And to link it to Ahmed. Test the flakes of skin on it, fingerprints, that kind of thing. It'll be full of them. Then we've got him.'

'But ...'

'But what?'

They emerged into the sunlight of the day, ran on and turned left, past the Minster. A crocodile of schoolchildren was being escorted through the grounds, each one clutching paper and pens. They watched as Adam and Dan ran past.

'But,' Dan continued, 'we don't have the phone. The spooks have got it.'

'Then they'll have to hand it over. I've had enough of them and their damned plotting. I want to know what the hell's going on.'

'Yeah, right. Look, Adam, something's badly wrong. If Oscar came in the shop to get that phone he must have known it was Ahmed's. He can only have wanted it to stop us from getting it.'

'OK.'

'So he's protecting Ahmed.'

'Yeah.'

'So he's hardly going to hand over the phone on demand, is he?'

They turned into Southernhay. The greens were deserted. The only movement was a slight rustling of the trees in the gentle breeze, the furtive run of a grey squirrel, and the slow stroll of a parking attendant, awaiting the day's victims. But at this hour, he was the definition of underemployed.

Twenty-five past ten. They should just make it to the police station for half past.

'What do you think is going on?' Adam panted.

'I don't know. But they're spooks. You said it yourself. Nothing's straightforward with them. Perhaps Ahmed's one of them. All I know is they must be protecting him. They must have realised how he hid that phone and went into the shop to stop us getting it.'

'Let's go tell them that, then. I've had a guts full of their bloody deviousness.'

Adam sprinted across a road, ignored the blare of horns from a couple of cars. They were almost at the police station.

'Just stop a min,' Dan gasped. 'I can't run and think. I've got enough blood for either my brain or my muscles, but not both.'

Adam glanced at his watch. 'We don't have time. Ahmed's going to be free in three minutes.'

He lurched towards the police station. Dan stretched out, grabbed Adam's shoulder and span him round.

'Get off me!' the detective yelled.

'No! You start bloody listening!'

Adam tried to slap away Dan's hand, but he dodged the blow, instead grabbed the collar of his friend's jacket and pushed him into a bus shelter. Together they thudded into the hard plastic of its walls.

'What the hell are you doing?' Adam yelled. 'I'll arrest you too if you like.'

They wrestled together, each trying to get a grip on the other, pushing and shoving. A stagger, a feint, a battle to hold their balance. The walls bumped and bowed with the struggle. Discarded wrappings from take-away food flew around their feet. Dan caught his knee on the hard metal angle of a seat, making him gasp. An old woman who was sitting in the shelter opposite looked on, open-mouthed.

'Adam!' Dan shouted. 'I'd love to go in there and confront the bastards. After what they've done with the phone, and ...' He swallowed hard, 'that – other thing ... but it won't do any good! We've got to be smarter than that.'

Adam was breathing hard, his face dark, sweaty and tight with a scowl. 'Take your hands off me,' he hissed, his voice low and threatening, 'Or you're under arrest, you're off the case and we never work together again.'

'Adam! I'm trying to make you see sense. No one wants revenge more than I do, but we won't get it this way.'

'Hands off. Now.'

'You're an idiot! A fucking fool. Go on then, march in there and screw it all up!'

The two men glared at each other in the cramped, smelly space. Then, a woman's voice interrupted, sharp and reproachful.

'You should be ashamed of yourselves.'

They both looked round. It was the old lady who had been sitting in the bus shelter opposite. She was pointing an umbrella at them.

'What kind of an example do you call this? Don't we have enough trouble with young people today, without you behaving so badly?'

The umbrella shifted to under Dan's nose. 'You. You're that chap off the television, aren't you?'

Before he could reply, the silver tip had shifted to between Adam's eyes. 'And you. I've seen you on the TV too, haven't

I? You're a detective. You're investigating that dreadful Minster bombing. I'm disappointed in you both. You're letting yourselves and the rest of us down. You've both got important jobs to do and you should be getting on with them, not larking around.'

Dan felt the grip on his collar loosening. He too released his hold on Adam.

'That's better,' came the chiding voice again. 'Now, apologise to each other.'

Adam began mumbling some words. Dan reciprocated them. The umbrella fell from eye level.

'That's better. Now, off you go, and don't do it again.'

They each nodded, straightened their jackets and walked off, escorted by the woman's glare. In just a few cutting words, she had ushered them back through the years into childhood.

They took a series of paces in an embarrassed silence, then Dan said, 'Bet she used to be a teacher.'

Adam snorted. 'I reckon you're right. Look, I'm sorry about that. It's just the case, getting to me.'

'I'm sorry too. I guess I was feeling ragged, what with Rutherford and not sleeping last night.'

'OK, forget it.'

They shook hands. 'Right, back to the real business.' Adam checked his watch. It was a minute away from half past. 'Ahmed's about to be released. How do we stop it?'

'We need to buy some time. Is Claire in the station?'

'Yep.'

'Call her. Tell her to find a delay. Just fifteen minutes or so. That'll be enough.'

Adam took out his mobile. 'How?'

Dan found his brain was racing. A flush of anger was a wonderful stimulant. 'Throw tea over the paperwork so it has to be re-done, something like that. We can't go in there without a plan. We've got to be much more cunning. That's the game we're playing now.'

Adam made the call, rushing out the words. Dan doubled over and tried to gather his breath. Stars spun in the globes of his eyes. Distorted images assailed his flying thoughts, a hall of mirrors of the mind. Rutherford, unconscious on that metal slab of a table. Fighting Adam in the street. Tonight and seeing Claire.

Dan screwed his eyes shut, as tight as he possibly could and explored the darkness. And then, sweet and simple, came the idea.

Once more, Dan had to force Adam to wait. They were both dishevelled, out of breath and sweating, their faces flushed after the little altercation. They needed to look calm for the plan to work. But it wasn't easy. The detective was still as angry as Dan could remember having seen him.

'I just want to go in there and confront the bastards,' he kept saying. 'What the hell are they up to?'

'I know and I understand. I feel the same. But that won't work. We've got to be cool and clever.'

He led Adam to a bench in the benevolent shade of a tree, made him sit down and explained the idea. Some of the colour drained from the detective's face.

'You sure about this?' Adam asked. 'If it doesn't work, I'm going to have more than a little explaining to do.'

'Have you got any better ideas?'

'No.'

'Then that settles it. Was Claire OK about delaying Ahmed's release?'

'She said it would be a pleasure. I told her about the throwing tea on the paperwork idea and she liked it. In fact, she asked if it came from you.'

'What did you tell her?'

'I said yes.'

'And what did she say to that?'

'She said, "I thought so".'

Dan and Adam held a look. 'What was her – err – tone?' Dan asked finally.

'More than a little fond.'

They sat in a canyon of silence. Then Adam said, 'It's hardly the time and place, and hell, I don't want to set myself up as your dad, but – she's a great woman, you're a good

231

bloke, and I always thought you made a fine couple. Maybe you should think about sorting it out.'

Dan nodded slowly. 'Maybe you're right.'

A bus rumbled past, its side covered with a colourful advertisement for a local stately home and what a wonderful backdrop it provided for the perfect wedding.

'Right,' Adam said, standing up. 'Let's get to it then.'

They walked into the police station. A smartly suited man was sitting in the Waiting Room, tapping a hand impatiently on his black leather briefcase.

'You're a solicitor, sir?' Adam asked politely.

'That is correct. And I am being kept waiting.'

Adam pulled a face which looked as full of genuine sympathy and concern as an undertaker at a hospice.

'I'm sorry to hear that. I'll see what I can do to help. Who do you represent?'

'Mr Ahmed Nazri.'

'I'll make some inquiries and get you a cup of tea.'

'Thank you.'

They walked along a corridor towards the Bomb Room. Adam stopped a young detective and told him to take some tea to the Waiting Room.

'It's for a solicitor,' he said. 'So use the special milk.'

'Special milk?' Dan queried.

'We always keep some that's well out of date. For our most valued guests.'

A couple of police officers walked past. Adam lowered his voice and said, 'Right, I'm off to the Bomb Room. Stand by for my call. It might take a few minutes for the positions to be right.'

'OK. Where should I go?'

The detective pointed back up the corridor. 'The kitchen's up there. When you've done what we discussed, wait for it all to go quiet, then come and find me. And if you have a cup of tea, make sure you get the right milk.'

Dan sat himself on a small stool and tried to read a copy of a lifestyle magazine, but wasn't surprised to find he couldn't concentrate on the words.

A notice on the fridge warned people not to steal others' food. Dan was tempted to add – "It's the law". He kept his eye on the small red square of metal and thin glass on the wall.

A couple of people came and went. One asked if he was OK. 'Fine thanks. I've just been asked by Chief Inspector Breen to wait here.'

The shield of a senior officer's name did its familiar work. Dan was left in peace.

His mobile rang. Dan got up, ready to do the deed. He realised he was shaking. He checked the phone's display. It was a withheld number.

'Hello?'

'Stories! I want stories! Where are you, what are you up to, and what have you got for me? I want a story, I want it exclusive, I want it good and I want it now.'

Lizzie never bothered with introductions. It would be as pointless as a bomb politely inquiring if anyone minded whether it detonated. 'I'm just working on one,' Dan lied. 'It should be OK for tonight.'

'What about the lunchtime news?'

'It's at a delicate stage. I don't think it'll make lunch.'

'Is it about the bombing?'

'Yep.'

'Is it good?'

'Yep.'

'Exclusive?'

'Yep.'

'Then that may just be almost barely approaching adequate.'

She hung up before Dan could get another word in.

The square of red metal on the wall was calling. Dan stood up and ran a finger around it. He hoped the glass wouldn't cut his hand. He hated the sight of blood, particularly his own.

Dan grabbed a kitchen cloth and wrapped it round his fingers. He found himself thinking of Rutherford and wondered whether he had time for a quick call to Cara. No, she would

233

ring if anything happened. All was well. Silence was golden, or at least hopeful. He had to be waiting for Adam.

Tonight, Dan would see his dog. And Rutherford would be better, well enough to open an eye and recognise his master. Claire would be there too. It would do the dog good to see them both. It might even do his master good to see Claire.

And he wondered; what would it mean for Claire to see Dan?

The phone rang again. And this time it was the call he was waiting for.

Dan gulped hard and drew back his hand.

The spooks were standing in the corner of the Bomb Room, whispering to each other. The briefcase was at their feet. No good.

Adam walked over to the whiteboards, ran a finger over his chin and pretended to study them. Claire joined him.

'How long have we got?' Adam asked quietly.

'That tea made a terrible mess of the paperwork. No use at all for a legal document. I'm having it all redone, but it'll probably take at least another twenty minutes.'

'Good. In a moment I want you to distract Sierra. I need her somewhere away from that corner.'

Claire raised an eyebrow. 'OK. How?'

'Ask for a word in private. Take her outside. Tell her you're worried I'm not doing my job properly. Or ask for some advice about getting into FX5. Anything. But, Claire …'

'Yes?'

'Between us, I heard there might be some kind of fire drill this morning. If the alarm does go off I want you to make for the exit, like a good cop, but then disappear and double back here. OK?'

Claire nodded slowly. 'Yes, sir.'

She walked back to her desk and busied herself with some papers. Adam felt the phone in his pocket. He reached out and ran a finger down the list of names and numbers on the board. At the fringe of his vision, he could see Claire walking up to Sierra. They chatted briefly, then disappeared out of the door.

Halfway there.

Adam turned and caught Oscar staring at him. The scar on the man's neck was prominent in the fluorescent brightness of the room. He beckoned and the spy hesitated, but paced over to the boards.

Adam's hand slipped to the mobile.

'I was just wondering if I could see some kind of pattern in there,' Adam said, pointing to the list. 'I was reading this book the other day and there was something in it about substitution codes.'

Oscar folded his arms. He looked entirely unimpressed. 'Oh yeah? This may come as a surprise, but the way we work isn't quite like in the books.'

Adam did his best to smile. 'No, I appreciate that, but just give me a moment. I did wonder if there might be something in it.'

The spy was still too close to the briefcase. Adam turned, walked over to a desk and picked up a piece of paper. Oscar watched him all the way. When he returned, Adam positioned himself on the other side of the man.

'By the way, I hope you don't mind me asking this,' Adam said lightly, 'but I have been wondering and now seems as good a time as any to ask. How did you get that scar?'

The spy scowled. His fingers rose to his neck. He looked about to speak when a deafening bell began ringing, filling the room with its shrill clamour.

'Fire alarm!' Adam shouted. 'Come on, everyone out, quick.'

He spread his arms and began ushering people through the door. Oscar tried to dodge around him and get to the briefcase, but Adam barred the way.

'Come on, you know better than that. No returning for any belongings. Get going!'

He shoved the spy towards the exit. Oscar glared at him and pushed back, but Adam was ready.

'I'm a fire warden,' he yelled. 'Responsible for your safety. So get out! Now!'

Oscar turned for the door, but it was a feint. He spun back

around and lunged towards the briefcase. He almost made it, but Adam caught him around the middle in a rugby tackle and dragged him back.

'Get out of my fucking way, you twat!' the spy shouted. His breath was stale, made Adam grimace.

Oscar stretched forwards, as far as he could, fingers grasping for the case. He was fit and strong and Adam only just managed to hold him. The two men stood, locked together, pushing hard at each other, panting and sweating.

The exodus to the door slowed. Other detectives were stopping, watching the wrestling match, unsure what to do.

The bells rang on, clanging and clattering, deafening in the confines of the room.

Adam planted his foot against a desk and used the leverage to give Oscar a shove. He stumbled backwards and looked about to try to lunge again for the briefcase when a sizeable detective grabbed his shoulder.

'That's the fire alarm, if you hadn't noticed,' he grunted. 'Door's that way – sir.'

Oscar squared up to the man, but another joined him, then another, until he was facing a human wall.

'You fucking amateurs!' he shouted.

'That way,' the big detective retorted, giving the spy a push towards the door.

Oscar stumbled and loosed off a few more insults, but headed for the exit, his uninvited escort just behind.

The room was empty. Adam checked the corridor. A line of people was heading for the building's main entrance. Sierra was amongst them, Oscar just behind.

Claire emerged from a side door and nipped in to the Bomb Room. Another door opened and Dan strode out to join them.

Adam grabbed the briefcase. 'Right,' he said. 'I reckon we've got maybe ten minutes before they realise what we're up to.'

Chapter Twenty-two

IN THE BOTTOM DRAWER of the cabinet beside Dan's bed, well hidden beneath a pile of yellowing warranties, receipts, bills and bank statements, as well as the deeds to the flat, is a black, A4-sized diary. No one else has seen it, nor even knows of its existence, not even Claire. Rutherford has been allowed the occasional peek, particularly when Dan is completing an entry, but, in that idiosyncratic way of his, the master has sworn the dog to silence.

The diary is too personal for other eyes; filled not just with facts, but authentic and vulnerable feelings. Not of a day to day kind, the mainstay of most such chronicles, but case by case. It is fattening considerably faster than Dan ever expected when first he began writing. Some of the cases are mundane, his involvement transitory, advisory or fleeting; crimes which inconvenienced the world with only minor flurries of interest and which were solved within days.

Others are amongst the most notorious the South-west has seen, and, in some cases, even the country.

The sensitivity of many of the details is such that Dan once, sitting on the great blue sofa, writing up a successful investigation after a couple of whiskies, had one of those little moments of melodrama to which he is more than prone. He mused that the diary should perhaps only be released to a doubtless fascinated public after his death, and quite possibly, as is the case with the national archives, after a period of another fifty, or maybe more, years.

As to the mechanics of the entries, Dan followed a maxim of his profession – or his official profession, at least – and kept them short and sharp; one page per case, no matter how extraordinary, devious, shocking or complex.

But with this current investigation, Dan broke the personal rule and gave the next few minutes a whole page to themselves. They formed a brief but bizarre interlude, worthy of the finest of Hollywood thrillers, and so felt deserving of the accolade.

He even gave them a subtitle – *The Pressure Puzzles* – and thought, albeit a little pompously, that summed up the episode rather well.

Adam laid the briefcase gently down on a table. Dan and Claire gathered around and together they studied it.

It was obvious it was no high street model. It was unusually heavy, probably reinforced with metal, or more likely some kind of secret high tech spy material. Dan ran a hand over it. The leather felt particularly tough and oddly cold, making him suspect it wasn't leather at all.

'Be careful,' he muttered. 'If you press the wrong thing, it probably self destructs.'

'Seriously, we had better take it gently,' Adam replied. 'If we don't manage to get into it, we don't want the spooks knowing we've been trying. If we hear people coming back into the building we've got to get out of here.'

On the front of the case, in the centre, was a sturdy, shiny handle, and on each side a lock. Both required three digits, chosen from the wheels of numbers.

The fire bells stopped their clamour. The clock on the wall said 10.50. 'I reckon we're OK until eleven,' Adam added.

Dan poked at the left hand lock and tried pulling the briefcase gently open. He was expecting firm resistance, no give at all, but was surprised by a slight movement.

'Naughty naughty,' he said quietly. 'I think the master spy Oscar has succumbed to our familiar friend laziness.'

He tried the catch. It sprung open. Dan let out a whistle. 'That's a bit of luck. He only kept the one side locked.'

'Which still leaves us with the other side,' Claire replied.

'Yep,' Adam said. He tried the other catch. It was firmly locked. 'Bugger,' he grunted. 'I thought it was too much to hope for. Right, what number do we try?'

A pause. Only the soft ticking of the clock sounded in the quiet of the room.

10.51.

Claire said, 'Do we have any records on Oscar? Like – when's his birthday? What house number he lives at?'

'No,' Adam replied. 'None.'

238

'Do we know anything about him? Has he talked about a single thing which might help us?'

Another hesitation. They all stared at the briefcase.

'No,' said Adam finally. 'The spies just don't talk about anything, apart from work. They're like robots.'

Dan nodded and said, 'True, but we've got to try something. What about putting in numbers at random?'

'It'll take too long. We don't have the time.'

More silence. The clock turned.

10.52

'I know,' Dan ventured. 'We used to do this trick on bike locks when I was a kid. Because the three different cogs work in a line, if you got the first one and wiggled the lock, it gave a bit. That told you that you'd got the number right, so you could move on to the next one.'

'I doubt a spook's briefcase would work like that,' Adam said.

'It's worth a try, surely,' Claire replied. 'Go for it.'

Dan bent down and tried turning the first tumbler to different digits, testing the case for any give each time.

One. No movement.

Two. No movement.

Three. No movement.

He kept going. Six, then seven. Still nothing.

'It's not working,' Adam groaned.

'Give it a chance. I haven't done all the numbers yet.'

Eight. No movement.

'Last shot,' Claire whispered.

Dan turned the tiny wheel to nine and tried the case. There was no hint of the lock easing.

'Shit,' Adam hissed. 'What now?'

A lorry grumbled by outside. The second hand of the clock kept moving.

10.53

Claire asked, 'Are we even sure the mobile's in there?'

'No.' Adam snapped. 'We're bloody not. There might just be his damned lunchbox and some extra small condoms.'

Dan noticed his hearing had grown attuned to the sound of

the clock. He could sense each ticking second, the soft clunk of the hands as they measured off another precious minute.

10.54

He picked up the case, put his ear to it and moved it gently from side to side. Something within slid back and forth.

'I reckon the phone's in there,' he said. 'That sounded like a mobile moving around.'

'It could be anything,' Adam grunted. 'Your bloody imagination runs away with you. It's always been your trouble.'

Dan glared at his friend. 'It's my bloody imagination that's got us this far, in case you hadn't noticed.'

'I would have got here without you. Don't start thinking you're Sherlock Holmes again.'

'Whose idea was it, about where the phone was hidden?'

'Who thought of checking the CCTV in the second-hand shop?'

The two men stared at each other, their faces set hard. Claire's pointed voice interjected, 'Do you think we might just concentrate on more important things than your investigators' beauty contest?'

10.55

They turned back to the case, impervious and aloof, dominating the desk.

'We've only got five minutes left,' Adam snapped. 'Dan, start trying some numbers at random, like you suggested. It's our best hope.'

Dan bent down and began spinning the little wheels, clicking up random numbers, trying the case each time.

416   No movement.
946   No movement.
221   No movement.
602   No movement.

Dan groaned. 'This is not happening. There are far too many numbers to work through.'

10.56

'We're running out of time,' Adam moaned.

'I've got an idea,' Claire said suddenly. 'What about lazy

numbers?'

'What?'

'You know, like 123, or 999, or 111. Oscar left the first lock open. Maybe he's been lazy enough to set the other one to a number that's easy to enter.'

Dan nodded eagerly and quickly started clicking up the numbers.

111 No movement.

123 No movement.

222 No movement.

Adam let out another loud groan.

'Hang on, there are a few more to try,' Dan said.

He span the wheels as fast as his fumbling hands would allow. 333, 444, 555, 666, 777, 888. All produced nothing.

Dan paused. Next came 999.

Of course. It had to be.

Claire and Adam saw it too. They exchanged a look of hope.

The emergency number. They should have seen it before.

It must be the one which opened the case.

The digits clicked into place.

999

The briefcase remained firmly locked.

10.57.

Dan stood up, stretched his aching back, swore loudly and suffered a reproachful look from Claire.

Adam kicked out at a chair, sending it rocking back and forth. 'Bollocks!' he yelled. 'And we were so damned close.'

'What do we do now?' Claire asked.

'We'll have to confront the spooks anyway. But without the phone as evidence they'll probably just bluster it out.'

He swore again. Dan stared at the briefcase, willing it to give up its secret. What did he know about Oscar that could help?

Very little was the answer. The man was arrogant, supercilious and annoyingly full of himself. He'd given nothing away in the brief conversations they'd had.

Dan could almost imagine Oscar practicing his patter in the

mirror. A gun in one hand, a finger pressed to his lips, he would whisper the warning to his reflection. *Careless talk costs lives you know.*

The man thought of himself as a real life James Bond.

A firework lit up the darkness.

Dan lurched forwards, shoving Adam out of the way.

'Hey, what're you doing?' he complained.

Dan didn't answer, instead bent down and entered the three numbers. A zero, then another zero.

His hand was sweating so much he could hardly move the wheel to push the last digit into place. Finally he managed a grip and rotated it around.

007.

Dan took a shaky breath. He tried the briefcase.

It clicked open.

Adam emitted a noise the like of which Dan had never before heard from him. It was an unlikely sound from an experienced and hardened Detective Chief Inspector well into his forties in measure of years on earth. The sound was difficult to describe, but might best be compared to that made by a young girl, who'd spent Christmas morning unwrapping a series of pleasing, but distinctly modest presents, only to come to the end of the pile with a sense of bafflement.

Where was the headline gift?

Then comes the smiling parental leading to the window of the house, to see a pony contentedly grazing in the back garden.

10.58.

'Well don't just stand there gawping at it,' Adam yelped, with Olympian chutzpah. 'Turn the bloody thing on. We've got to find out if it's the one Tanton called. And if it is – if it is …'

The briefcase contained a few papers about a new car, a diary, a hairbrush, some pens, a copy of George Orwell's *1984*, and a mobile phone, tightly sealed in a plastic evidence bag.

They clustered around. Dan reached out and switched on the phone. He could feel Claire next to him, her shoulder rubbing against his.

The mobile's display flickered and blinked into life.

Enter PIN code

But it wasn't those familiar words which drew their attention. It was the numbers, pulsing by their side.

100, 99, 98 …

'What the hell's that?' Adam yelped.

'It looks like a countdown,' Dan replied.

'No shit. Thanks Einstein. A countdown to what?'

An unwelcome memory nudged at Dan's mind. It was something the Geeks were very proud of, had installed on their own phones and computers and gleefully demonstrated. They were so proud, in fact, that the technological feat entailed a host of spins on their chairs, multiple high-fives and much squealing.

90, 89, 88 …

'It's a memory wipe thing,' Dan said quickly. 'Paranoid people use it. Not content with setting a PIN code, they program the phone to wipe its entire memory if the PIN isn't entered in a specified time. Everything goes, the SIM card, the memory card, the whole lot. It's popular with bankers, politicians, business people, anyone with sensitive information.'

'So if we don't get this PIN right,' Adam groaned, 'and in the next few seconds, all my evidence disappears.'

'Yep. You'll have nothing concrete against Ahmed, or the spooks either. And that's not all. If I remember rightly, we only get three tries at the code or the phone wipes itself anyway. So, no chance for random guesses. We've got to be cleverer than that – and fast.'

59, 58, 57 …

Adam filled the air with some creative obscenities. 'This is

243

worse than a bloody film,' he moaned.

'Shall we just get on with trying to crack it then?' came the voice of reason which was Claire. 'As we don't have a lot of time.'

48, 47, 46 …

'Right, what do most people use for a PIN?' Adam snapped.

'Their birthday. The year, or the day and month,' Claire replied.

'What's Ahmed's?'

'Don't know.'

'Where are his records?'

'In the custody suite. At the other end of the station.'

38, 37, 36 …

Adam swore again. 'How old is he?'

'About 35.'

'So he'd have been born in …?'

Dan said, '1975 – ish. Shall I try that?'

'But it's only a bloody guess.'

'Any other ideas?'

28, 27, 26 …

'Try it,' Adam gasped.

Dan did. The display blinked, then changed.

Incorrect PIN. Enter PIN code. 2 attempts remaining

Adam let out a low wail. Dan thought he even heard Claire swear, but that could have been the tension getting to him.

23, 22, 21 …

'Shall we try another year close to 1975?' Dan asked.

'Any other ideas?'

The ticking of the clock on the wall was the only reply. It was slightly out of time with the changes on the phone's display.

18, 17, 16 …

'Try it,' Adam barked. 'What else have we got? Try 1974. Go!'

Dan typed in the number. His hand was trembling badly.

Incorrect PIN. Enter PIN code. 1 attempt remaining

Outside, in the corridor, a door banged. They could hear a rumble of voices.

'They're coming back in,' Claire said calmly. 'The spooks will be here in seconds.'

13, 12, 11 …

Adam wrenched at his tie. 'Come on, come on, come on,' he urged. 'Come up with something. Please! It's our last chance.'

No one spoke. The voices outside were moving closer. The room felt very warm.

8, 7, 6 …

'It's our last chance,' Adam prompted. 'Try anything. What the hell have we got left to lose?'

Dan spun through his memories of Ahmed. They needed something, anything that might provide a clue about the number he would use to protect the phone. He glanced at Claire and could see she was doing the same. She was standing perfectly still, her eyes closed.

And she looked beautiful.

4, 3, 2 …

Adam let out another moan. 'We're screwed. So near and yet so far.'

Claire reached past him and typed in a number.

0911

The phone's display froze, then went blank.

'What's it doing?' Adam whispered. 'What the fuck's happening?'

'It's either wiping itself or letting us in,' Dan replied. 'But, whatever, that was a hell of a good shout, Claire.'

'It was the best I could think of,' she said softly. 'The most notorious terrorist outrage in history. Just the sort of thing a bastard like Ahmed might use for his PIN.'

The phone's display was still blank.

'The trouble is,' she added, with all the incongruous cool of an iceberg in the desert, 'the way it's referred to isn't universal. 9/11 comes from how Americans talk about the attacks. But in our calendar it's 11/09. So I could be on the right track, but still wrong.'

The display flickered. A couple of lines played along the screen, but it remained empty.

'It could just as easily be 2001, from the year of the attack,' Claire added. 'If we're even on the right track at all, which is by no means guaranteed, of course.'

Still nothing from the phone.

'It's wiping its memory, isn't it?' Adam said quietly. 'We're stuffed.'

'Well, I reckon it was a damn good idea and well worth a try,' Dan said. 'We had nothing else.'

He patted Claire's shoulder and she smiled.

Footfall in the corridor. Voices, loud, outside the door. Oscar and Sierra.

The door of the Bomb Room swung open.

Now the phone's display was changing. In motion so slow as to be agonising, it illuminated. And formed a word.

One simple word, so very common, but at this moment, in

this place and this context, so very beautiful.

Welcome

Chapter Twenty-three

IF EVER IT'S POSSIBLE to condense the menace of a coming storm into one small room, then that time was now.

It felt as though the air was drying to aridity. The pressure rising, squeezing eyes and eardrums alike. The cloying tightness of the claustrophobia closed in around. The light dimmed, the blackness colouring each shade of grey, the smell of electricity, slowly building, ready to split the air. And all a preparation for the twilight unleashing of the rage.

And if a storm has a nexus, the driver of the beating winds and whirling clouds, and the furnace of the lighting bolts, then that was Adam. He stood, perfectly still, eyes unnaturally bright and unblinking, staring at the door. Only the ruddy colour of the detective's complexion betrayed the wrath.

Oscar strode into the room, calm and cool, swaggering and cocky. But he stopped in a second when he saw the briefcase, open on the desk. 'What the fuck are you doing?'

Adam took a couple of steps towards him and held up the plastic bag containing the phone. Its display was still glowing. His voice was low and full of menace.

'We're solving a dreadful crime. We're bringing justice to the families of the people who were killed and injured. And we're uncovering a conspiracy amongst the very people who are supposed to be protecting the public.'

A finger jabbed out, right in Oscar's face. 'That's you, in case you were wondering. Would you like me to charge you with being an accessory to murder now, or later?'

A voice from the doorway. Sierra. 'I think we all need to calm down. This isn't quite as simple as you might think.'

Adam snorted unpleasantly. 'Well, what a surprise. Do you know, I thought you might say that?'

She turned to the group of detectives who had gathered in the corridor, ushered them away from the Bomb Room, closed the door and walked over to stand beside Oscar.

'There's a bigger picture here,' she said.

'Really?' Adam replied scornfully. 'Funnily enough, I suspected that might be the case too. One that's far too complicated for a mere country cop like me to understand, by any chance?'

'Look, you ...' Oscar began, but Sierra laid a hand on his shoulder, quietening him.

'I think the time's come to share some information with our colleagues,' she said.

'Well, that'd be nice,' Adam replied. 'Only if it's not too much trouble, of course.'

Oscar was shaking his head angrily, but the firm pressure on his shoulder kept him silent. Sierra sat on the edge of a desk, her voice soft and reasonable. 'You have to appreciate, Adam, that in our job, we can't always tell you everything we might like to. But now, given what you've found, I don't think we have any choice.'

Adam folded his arms. 'Let's hear what you've got to say then. We can discuss the charges you'll face later.'

'For fuck's sake,' Oscar yelled, pulling away from Sierra and striding to within feet of Adam. The detective didn't react, just held his ground, the contempt ingrained in every line on his face.

'Who the hell do you think you are?' the spy ranted. 'One click of my fingers and you're squashed mate. You disappear. You're history. You're nothing and nobody. You'd better remember that.'

'That'll do,' Sierra snapped. 'Now, let's talk.'

And so they did.

The story they told was extraordinary. Dan could feel himself wanting to interrupt at points and could see it in the faces of Claire and Adam too. But with every new and provocative revelation, Adam flashed them a warning look. He wanted to hear what the spooks had to say before he let fly with all that he thought.

Dan could sense it coming. His friend's neck was red, throbbing, and his tie was low on his collar. Even the usually diplomatic and restrained Claire had let out a couple of hisses of breath at what Sierra told them.

Only part one of the confrontation had been played out. Part two was coming, and quickly.

The spooks knew all about John Tanton and Ahmed. The source inside the Islamic Centre had tipped them off. Ahmed had been expounding his extreme views and Tanton was absorbing them, filling with venom and longing to unleash it. He was growing ever more radical. The danger signs were clear.

They were put under surveillance. Sierra didn't go into details, but it was apparent their mobile phones and computers had been tapped and that teams were watching their homes and movements. This had been going on for a period of several weeks. Then came the first disclosure that made Adam recoil.

The spooks knew about the plan to attack the Minster.

They had bugged a park bench in Plymouth, one where Tanton and Ahmed often sat to talk. It was the final meeting before the bombing, and held on the Friday afternoon. For those who knew what was truly going on, the watchers, it must have been a surreal sight. Two men, sitting, in the midst of a park, quietly and calmly chatting about a plan for mass murder, while families walked past, their kids riding bicycles, flying kites and kicking footballs.

Tanton had been nervy, but also excited, continually talking about becoming a martyr. Ahmed was calm and reassuring, first telling him of the righteousness of his choice, then once more filling him full of the fires of zealotry with another ranting attack on Britain, its immorality and its persecution of Muslims. They had gone through the checklist of the ingredients needed for the bomb and how to detonate it in order to cause maximum casualties. It was as orderly as a business meeting.

A low growl from Adam, another hiss from Claire. As for Dan, he found he could hardly believe what he was hearing. An amazing story was unfolding in front of him and he wondered how much of it he would ever be able to report. He'd thought about trying to record some of the conversation on his phone, had fumbled in his pocket for the mobile, but Oscar's look was an effective deterrent.

Dan managed to give the spy a tight smile. He had an issue of his own to raise with the man, if such limp words could ever describe it that way. And whatever Adam said or did, however much he tried to intervene, Dan was going to do it.

Tanton and Ahmed had got up from the bench, embraced, and gone their separate ways. The attack was set for Monday. The irrevocable countdown was running.

'For God's sake!' Claire interjected. 'Not only did you know, but you had three days warning. You could have stopped it, you could have arrested them, you could have closed the Minster, you could have ...'

'Please just let me finish,' Sierra interrupted coolly. 'Then I hope you might understand.'

All weekend, Tanton was kept under surveillance as he bought the final materials for the bomb. On Monday morning, he assembled them, placed them carefully in his rucksack and caught a train to Exeter. He was watched the whole way.

Adam lowered his head into his hands.

'Look, I know how you're feeling,' Sierra told him.

'I can guarantee you don't,' Adam snapped. 'A train – a bloody train. Filled with families, and kids – and you just let him get on it. And sit there, with a bomb at his feet.'

She was growing impatient now and shot back, 'Remember, I don't have to tell you any of this. Please, let me finish before you judge us.'

Tanton walked for ten minutes from Exeter Central station to the Minster. He stopped at a newsagent's to buy a bottle of lemonade and sat on a wall in the city centre to drink it. Then he began the final walk, to Minster Green.

Dan could see it, as surely as if he was following. Each step taken was one closer to murder and suicide, an outrage in one of the holiest buildings in the country, at the heart of an ancient and peaceful city. A bombing from a clear, sunshine sky.

But now Tanton was showing signs of agitation. The surveillance teams reported he was becoming more difficult to trail, was sweating heavily, kept looking back over his shoulders. He stopped a couple of times, stared up at the sky and even lay the rucksack down.

'We thought he was going to bottle it,' Sierra said. 'That was one of the worst parts of the operation. If he'd run off and left the rucksack behind, we'd have had to evacuate the city centre.'

'Rather than just letting him blow up the Minster,' Adam muttered.

She gave him a cold stare, but ignored the jibe and carried on with the story.

Tanton had been seen talking to himself, probably saying some prayers, according to a surveillance officer who walked past. He was hunched over and mumbling. The prayers seemed to rally him. Tanton picked up the rucksack again and headed to the Minster.

He'd walked along a narrow alley between some shops and pubs and emerged into the great green space, the iconic heart of Exeter. The sight had unsettled him. He stopped again, then walked over to a secluded part of the green, beneath an oak tree and made a phone call.

The phone call.

'To Ahmed?' Adam prompted.

'Yes,' Sierra replied.

'And you've got all this on tape, no doubt.'

'Yes.'

'Then why the hell didn't you tell us?'

Sierra held up her hands. 'Let me finish and then you'll understand.'

'I've heard enough of this "I'll understand" business. I'm betting you I won't.'

'Just let her finish,' Oscar grunted.

The call had been made. As Adam suspected, Tanton was acutely nervous and in need of reassurance. Ahmed had given it, re-stoked the furnace of the young man's anger. And so Tanton had said one final prayer, walked into the Minster and detonated his bomb.

The aftermath was observed too, including the moment when the plan almost went wrong. Ahmed was chased into the arcade and had hidden his phone in the shop window, forcing

Oscar to retrieve it later.

There was a silence in the room. Claire was staring at the floor. Adam ran a hand through his hair. Oscar had folded his arms and was looking at them defiantly. All Dan could manage was to tap a hand on the desk.

The spooks knew about the plan to explode a bomb in the Minster. And they let it happen.

Adam broke the silence. He said heavily, 'I don't know about the rest of you, but I feel sick.'

Sierra walked across the room to the window and stared out. They watched her, wondered what she was going to do. She just stood, occasionally with the slight movement of a shoe on the carpet tiles, or perhaps a barely perceptible shift of the shoulder.

The clock ticked loudly. Oscar cracked his knuckles and yawned, then picked a morsel of food from his teeth. Adam's breathing was hard and heavy.

The best part of a minute passed before Sierra turned to them once more.

And there was a surprise in her eyes. She was crying, faint tears glistening traces over her flushed cheeks.

'It was the hardest call I've had to make in almost twenty-five years,' she said softly. 'But I still think it was right.'

No one spoke. Dan glanced at Claire. He could see his own thoughts in her expression. Surprise at Sierra's tears, and suspicion, so much doubt and dubiousness, an unavoidable question as to whether the emotion could be genuine. A relentless torrent of lies makes it difficult to believe in the hope of a whisper of truth.

'Go on,' Adam replied, warily.

She half smiled. 'I sense you're feeling distrustful.'

'Well, there's a surprise. As you've been lying to us all along.'

Oscar emitted a growl, but Sierra held up her hand. 'Our colleague has a point,' she said. 'For what it's worth, I regret having to do so. But what I've told you is the truth. And let me give you some more of it.'

Another silence in the room. Sierra rubbed at her eyes, then, in a more brisk tone she said, 'Right then, this is the reason we've had to deceive you.'

They had tampered with the bombs.

'I can't give you the details of what we did,' Sierra said. 'Simply because I don't entirely understand it myself. But one of our technical people made a few amendments which meant only one of the bombs could go off.'

The spooks kept surveillance on Tanton's home over the weekend. On Sunday morning, Alison went out to see some friends and John left to play football. The spies had broken in and a technician examined the bombs.

There were four, in large glass bottles, filled with an explosive mixture of chemicals and nails. They were hidden under Tanton's bed, just the way young men had concealed their secrets for countless generations. But seldom quite like this.

The bombs were crude, but entirely viable, quite sufficient to cause carnage. The confined space of the Minster, and its great stone walls would serve to amplify the blast. The shattering glass and flying nails would create dreadful shrapnel. The technician's assessment was that scores of people could be killed.

'That was another difficult call,' Sierra said, in a measured tone. 'We had to make sure casualties were kept to an acceptable level.'

Adam spluttered. 'An *acceptable* level? *Casualties*? I think what you mean is – innocent men, women and children being murdered and mutilated.'

'If you like,' she replied wearily. 'Anyway, I had another decision to make. To stop it all and lose ... well, I'll explain what in a minute. Or to let it go ahead and risk so many ...' She glanced at Adam, '... deaths of innocent people.'

A rapid discussion had taken place. Sierra asked if the technician could interfere with the bombs, to make them less lethal. The reply was negative. In layman's terms, a bomb was a very straightforward beast. It either detonated with its full explosive power, or it didn't go off at all. There was no middle ground.

So, the decision was made. It was possible to add a little chemical to the devices without Tanton being able to notice, some form of reaction neutraliser, to stop them detonating. Sierra gave the order to do so with three of the four.

'I was warned that one bomb could still kill many people,' she said. 'So it was a very difficult call indeed. But I felt I had no choice.'

Adam looked about to speak, but Claire beat him to it. 'Why?' she said simply. 'Why not just disable all the bombs? Why not arrest him? Why not stop the attack?'

Sierra looked at her and managed another thin smile.

'That,' she replied, 'is where we come to the crux of the matter.'

Many justifications they may have expected, but not one which looked back almost seventy years in history. They were taken to the time of the man who is, by common consent, Britain's greatest modern leader.

'How much do you know about Churchill?' Sierra asked.

Adam's bubbling temper was approaching the boil. He flung out an arm. 'What the hell are you talking about now?'

'Let her finish,' Oscar grunted. 'You might learn something.'

Adam took a pace towards the man, then another. They were now just a foot or two apart.

'Like how to be an accessory to murder?'

Oscar reached out a dismissive hand and pushed hard at Adam's chest. He slapped the arm away. The two men stood glaring at each other.

'That'll do,' Sierra admonished sharply. 'I'm going to finish my story, then you can make up your minds what you think. But for now – cool it.'

Oscar held up his hands. 'I'm OK. Nothing wrong with me.'

Adam stared at him, then backed off. 'Get on with it then,' he grunted.

Sierra nodded and said, 'There's a lot of claim and counter-claim about this, even now. For what it's worth, I don't think

Churchill was guilty. But be that as it may, it does sum up the dilemma.'

Whatever he might think of her, her job, and the world of lies in which she lived, Sierra had a hypnotic voice and a mesmeric storytelling style. Dan felt his eyes closing as he imagined his way through the passing years.

The story went back to the night of the 14th November, 1940, and the apocalyptic bombing of Coventry. Dan could see the hordes of bombers, blackening the moonlit sky, and the firestorms growing on the ground, rising from blast after blast of the countless bombs. A relentless night of raining death. The razing of a proud city and the taking of so many lives.

But it was the days and months before the raid on which Sierra concentrated.

The allies had cracked the German Enigma codes, the so-called *Ultra* secret. Most historians believe the breakthrough shortened the war by several years. It was probably the most precious source of intelligence against the Germans and guarded as a priceless secret. An invaluable insight into what the enemy was planning. Churchill himself referred to Bletchley Park, where the codes were deciphered, as "the goose that laid the golden egg, but didn't cackle".

Sierra paused before coming to the key moment of the story. 'My family comes from Coventry,' she told them quietly. 'We didn't escape.'

There was clear emotion in her voice. Dan was going to ask what had happened, but she was already carrying on, as if needing to cover up the weakness, the moment of humanity.

In the run up to the raid, the codebreakers deciphered German messages about plans for the biggest bombing raid so far seen on England. Codenamed *Moonlight Sonata*, there were suggestions in the exchanges it could have been targeted at Coventry, but no definite proof. Many believed London would again be the victim. To this day, historians debate what Churchill knew.

What no one disputes is that the *Ultra* intelligence was vital to the war effort and could not be compromised. The theory went that Churchill was aware of the impending attacks on

Coventry, but to ensure no suspicions were aroused amongst the Germans that their Enigma code might have been broken, he allowed the raid to go ahead without warning the city and emptying it of people.

The bombing lasted the whole night. Almost six hundred people were killed, nearly a thousand more seriously injured. Come the morning, the city was in ruins, even the great medieval cathedral almost destroyed, just a skeleton of its walls remaining.

Sierra finished her story and looked up.

'Fascinating,' Adam said sarcastically. 'And forgive me if I'm being dense, but what the hell has this got to do with the modern day terrorist bombing of Wessex Minster and you not actually bothering to stop it?'

Sierra sighed. 'They come down to the same basic dilemma. Whether to allow one outrage in order to prevent a bigger one.'

'Go on,' Adam prompted.

'Before I do, I must emphasise this – what you're about to hear is extremely sensitive, and must not be repeated.'

Adam nodded. 'Carry on.'

She sat down on the edge of a desk. 'We believe Ahmed is on the fringes of a very radical and embittered group who are planning mass murder. By that I mean on the scale of the July 7th bombings in London but possibly even worse, and we fear the attack may be only weeks away. We've tried, but can't penetrate them. They're too tightly knit, too well organised, but we know Ahmed has links with them. We also believe they need someone with computer skills to help them send encrypted messages to their terrorist contacts in Pakistan. Ahmed would be ideal. We believe they were watching his efforts down here, to see how committed and valuable he could be, and so whether he might be deemed worthy of joining them.'

She paused and took a long breath. 'There's no easy way to say this.'

'Try me,' Adam replied tersely.

'We decided to allow Tanton to detonate his bomb in order that this group would let Ahmed join them. We hoped they would take him on board, giving us a way to monitor them and stop an attack which we fear could kill hundreds of people.'

The room was silent. No one even moved. Adam was staring into space, Claire studying the window and the passing world. Dan could feel his heart beating hard.

Finally Adam spoke. 'Forgive me for putting it this way, but that's one fuck of a lot of airy hopes to justify letting an attack you definitely knew about go ahead.'

'Yes,' Sierra replied. 'But that's our job. Rarely, if ever, are things simple, straightforward and certain. We felt it was our best guess to save the most lives.'

'Right. Shall I tell you what I think of that?'

'If you must,' she replied heavily.

'Oh, I must.'

'I think it's utter bollocks. If you know about a crime being planned, you stop it. We're talking about murder – that's *murder*. It's not shoplifting, or scrumping apples, or dropping litter. If you have any hint it's coming, you stop it. It's as simple as that.'

'Maybe in your little black and white world,' Oscar sneered.

'Fuck you.'

'No, fuck you.'

Sierra raised her arms. 'OK, that's enough. I don't plan to get into a debate here. I don't need your understanding and I certainly don't need your judgement. So, Adam, I've told you what happened and why. Now what are you going to do?'

It was almost an appeal, the first time Dan could remember her using the detective's Christian name in a personable manner. And if it was an attempt at ingratiation and camaraderie, it failed with all the elegance of a hippopotamus attempting to fly.

Adam studied her, then replied with false calm, 'I'm tempted to tell you what I think of you, but I hope you already know. I'm well aware you can bring all sorts of powerful people jumping down on my back, and I have no doubt you will. But this is what I'm going to do anyway.'

He paused, to make absolutely sure he had their attention. 'I'm going to talk to my Deputy Chief Constable. I'm going to tell him I plan to charge Ahmed with his part in murder and you two as well.'

'You can try, mate,' Oscar sneered. 'If you want to land yourself in more shit than you've ever known.'

Adam began walking towards the door. Oscar made a gesture and mouthed 'wanker' at him, but the detective ignored it.

Dan was about to follow his friend, but stopped. After this moment, it was more than likely he would never see the two spies again. And he had something to say.

Dan swallowed hard and found his voice. 'There's just one more thing.'

'Oh, Sherlock speaks,' Oscar replied sarcastically. 'What does our great reporter detective want? If it's an exclusive on his mate being kicked out of the police, we might just be able to help. He could make himself useful – for once.'

And for Dan, if there was any doubt about what he was going to do, that decided it.

He took a step towards Oscar. 'Why did you poison my dog?'

'Who says ...'

'Don't bother denying it. I've got a friend who'd make a better spy than you ever will. I've got photos of you outside my flat, watching me and following me.'

Oscar shrugged. 'So? Who gives a shit about a dog? Maybe you should be a bit more careful. Routines are dangerous you know.'

Dan noticed his legs were striding across the room. He felt his fist drawing back, his muscles tensing, his knuckles strong and steely, ready to plant the blow in the middle of Oscar's sneering face.

The spy was just staring at him. 'Try it then,' he said coldly.

And Dan knew he would. His arm felt stronger than he had ever experienced, filled with the energy of the universe, his fist as hard as granite. And he was about to propel it forwards. He could feel the spy's nose breaking under the impact, the cracking of fragile bone, the ripping of cartilage, the spurting of blood and the man's scream of pain.

And it would be beautiful.

A pressure. A tight hand clamping around his arm. Dan turned and saw Adam standing beside him.

'No,' the detective ordered. 'Stop. Leave him.'

Dan stopped. Oscar was smirking.

'Let me guess,' he chuckled. 'You're going to say – *He's not worth it*. How inspiring. How very original.'

Adam gave the man a look that Dan couldn't read. 'No,' he said and sounded surprised. 'No, I wasn't going to say that at all.'

With remarkable speed, the detective drew back his fist and smashed it into Oscar's mouth. Blood sprayed from the spy's lip and he folded, dropped from the end of the desk and lay moaning on the floor.

Adam looked down at the crumpled figure, nodded with satisfaction and then turned for the door.

'I was going to say I wanted to do it myself.'

Chapter Twenty-four

IT WAS A STRANGE place for such a discussion, but some things just feel right.

Claire and Dan sat side by side on the hard plastic chairs in the half light of the vet's surgery, gazing at Rutherford and talking. First about the dog, then into progressively more dangerous territory. The investigation, terrorists and spies, rights and wrongs, and to the most perilous destination of all.

The *we* word. You and me, the relationship between us, if even such a thing exists.

It was just after eight o'clock in the evening. Cara had finally been allowed to go home, after suffering another exhaustive interrogation from Dan. Yes, the treatment appeared to be working. Yes, Rutherford was doing well. No, he wasn't completely safe yet, there was always the possibility of a relapse, but yes, the chances of survival and complete recovery had risen.

No, she still didn't want to put a figure on it. But if she must …

She must.

… then it was about eighty per cent.

Dan felt a constricting tension leave him. Eighty per cent. Seldom in his unpredictable and often ridiculous life did he encounter such favourable odds. He felt like the favourite in a race where all the other runners had pulled out, he'd just crossed the last fence and could see the finishing line ahead.

And as if Rutherford could sense the discussion going on over his prone body, he opened an eye. Dan stroked his head and the dog's mouth shifted and twitched. The expression was almost his smiling face.

Dan had to turn away to hide the nascent tears.

He felt Claire's hand slip into his and squeezed it, let the grip linger, but then released it again. It would be a long journey to make such symbolic contact comfortable again.

Cara told Dan he could do no good there, that he looked

tired and needed to go home and rest. She was right, of course, he'd hardly had any sleep of late and well he knew it. The leaden cloak of fatigue swaddled his body. She reassured him Rutherford was doing fine, would happily sleep through the night, and tomorrow might well be strong enough to get up from the table. But Dan wanted to stay and sit with the dog anyway, even if only for an hour or two, so the young vet again left him a set of keys and said goodnight.

And Claire and Dan were alone.

'He's looking OK,' she said.

'Yes.'

'He's breathing well.'

'Yes.'

'He looks peaceful.'

'Yes.'

'He's strong and fit.'

'Yes.'

'He's going to be OK.'

'Yes.'

'He is, you know.'

'Yes.'

A long hesitation and then Claire said softly, 'Can we talk about us now?'

'Yes. No. I mean – in a minute. Probably. Maybe.'

It was scarcely the finest sentence he had ever constructed, but it made the point. She looked at him and smiled ruefully. 'Are you still as screwed up as ever?'

'Yep.'

'Because of me.'

It was more fact than theory. And there was no point in lying. Claire knew. She always knew.

'Yes.'

'I'm sorry. For everything.'

'It was as much my fault.'

'No, it was …'

'Look,' Dan interrupted. 'I'm not sure I'm up to this at the moment. It's been a hell of a few days. My brain feels addled. Can we just sit and chat a while, be with Rutherford and see

262

how it all goes?'

She nodded. 'Sure. But we will have to talk sometime.'

'I know. Just – not quite yet. And not quite here, either. It'd have to be – I don't know, Dartmoor, or somewhere like that. Some big, wide-open space. Let's just take it easy for now.'

'OK.'

And they sat, in silence, on the hard plastic chairs and watched the sleeping dog.

Dan found his thoughts wandering back over the day. Something was wrong, he was sure of it. His tired mind knew it was there, some small inconsistency which betrayed a greater secret, but he couldn't quite bring home what it was. He worked through all that had happened and tried again to find the knot in the morass of emotions and revelations he had experienced of late.

Ahmed had been charged with conspiracy to murder and terrorism offences. The phone they found in Oscar's briefcase was indeed the one Tanton rang, just before he detonated the bomb. It could be conclusively linked to Ahmed with DNA and fingerprints. The evidence against him was compelling. Faced with it, on the advice of his solicitor, he had confessed, hoping to receive a lighter sentence for his cooperation.

Stephens's analysis was right. The man, so untouchable on the surface, would do whatever he needed to improve his lot.

Dan had not been privy to it, but in Adam's words there had been a "robust exchange of views", between Greater Wessex Police and FX5, which had escalated to the Home Office for a decision. The whole episode reeked of the emperor of all rows.

The spies wanted to free Ahmed and keep the evidence to hold over him. They hoped he would become a member of the radical group which Sierra had spoken about, allowing them to gain vital intelligence. The police argued that there had to be a trial after an outrage like the bombing and, with Tanton dead, such an integral figure as Ahmed could not be allowed to evade justice. It was in the public interest that he had to be charged.

The Home Secretary had taken the police's side. There was too much uncertainty about whether FX5's plan would work. The public must see Ahmed in court to lift their confidence in the forces of law and security. It would be a high-profile and popular conviction.

And a General Election was due next year.

Adam spat out those words, but followed them with his own little summary of the situation.

'At least they're doing the right thing, even if it is for the wrong reason.'

'Which, as I recall, TS Eliot called the greatest treason,' Dan mused, a little surprised by the surfacing of an old memory from his schooldays.

'Whatever. If it means Ahmed rots in jail for the rest of his life, I'll happily take it,' came the reply from his pragmatic friend.

Dan nodded and then broached the subject of whether there had been any retaliation from the spooks for Adam's delightfully effective right hook.

'No. I think they've just taken it as a scar of battle. They're still around, but keeping out of the way. I reckon they'll be here a day or two longer, then scuttle off back to London.'

'Good.'

'Yep. But you know, I should have realised something was going on sooner. There was a giveaway clue – how quickly they got here after the explosion. That supposed meeting near Bristol, it was nothing of the sort. They were waiting for the bombing, ready to come in and make sure the investigation went the way they wanted.'

'I wouldn't hold that against you,' Dan said. 'You hardly expect someone who's supposed to be on your side to be working against you.'

Adam agreed, and added a couple of forthright opinions on the warped world of espionage. Partly to distract him, Dan said, 'Do you have any idea who their source was? The one in the Islamic Centre?'

'I've got no evidence, but I've got a suspicion.'

'Which is?'

'Abdul.'

'Any particular reason?'

'Circumstantially, just that he was well placed to see

everything that was going on. More specifically, that he told us Ahmed didn't have the guts to do anything violent. I wonder if that was him trying to help the spooks by putting us off the track.'

They chatted a little longer, then Dan asked the question which had been needling him.

'Why did they target me, do you think? They knew so much about me – and that attack on my car, and when it didn't warn me off, what they did to poor Rutherford.'

Adam shrugged. 'They did their homework. If they've got an operation to run, they'll be sure to look at some of the characters in that area. They'd have known you tended to get involved in the big inquiries down here and you're a hack and a maverick. You'd have been marked down as a possible complication. By the way, it was a neat trick to spy on the spies with that weird little snapper mate of yours.'

'Yeah. I don't know why I did that. I think I sensed something odd was going on too and I needed someone to watch over me. They don't come any better than El.'

The photographer had been happy to help, for no more payment than a night out, funded by Dan. El was a delightfully cheap date. No fancy meal of small portions but sizeable prices was required, no extortionate wine list, no upmarket venues, just a procession of pints in a series of increasingly dodgy pubs and a lamentable nightclub to end the evening.

One more issue was bothering Dan: Oscar's reaction when Adam hit him. The spy had picked himself up from the floor, dabbed at his bloodied lip, refused Sierra's offer of help and said, 'Don't worry. I'll get it patched up by our medics. They can work miracles.'

It was the tone of the man's voice which had imprinted on Dan's mind. Despite his injury, it was still sneering and arrogant, filled with the hint of arcane knowledge in no way accessible to lesser mortals.

'What do you think he meant by that medics and miracles stuff?' Dan asked Adam.

'I don't know,' the detective replied wearily. 'And you know what? I don't think I care. Just more of his crap, probably. Ahmed's been charged. The spooks will soon be gone. Case solved. I wouldn't say I'm happy with how things have gone, but we've come through it and I'm as content as I can be.'

Then had come the prickly question of what Dan could report. He knew enough to write a scoop of a stature which would win a host of awards and bring considerable acclaim. It was an incredible story, and for a man who would occasionally be honest enough to admit he did have more than the average ego, tempting indeed.

But Dan knew too that he had no chance of getting it on air.

The government could wade in, using an intimidating battery of legal powers to stop the reporting of anything which might harm national security, the so called Defence Advisory, or DA notice system. And he was under pressure from the police too.

'I'd be delighted for you to report the lot,' Adam told him. 'The more dung you fling at the spooks the better, in my view. But as the Deputy Chief points out, it would hardly look good for the force.'

'Which, though I hate to say it, is no concern of mine. It's my job to tell the truth.'

'Which I told him. But then there's the issue of whether you'd ever be allowed to join me on an investigation again.'

The line hummed as both men considered that.

'Which I'd hope you would see as rather more important,' Adam added finally.

'Yes.'

'And anyway, there is another possibility, which might work out better.'

'Go on.'

'Just between us.'

'As ever and always.'

'I won't be happy until the spooks are gone and Ahmed's been sentenced. Up until that point they could still try something to get him freed, or have the case abandoned for some murky reason. But knowing all you do, and using the threat of exposing it, that gives us a powerful weapon if they do try anything.'

'Yes, it does,' Dan replied thoughtfully. 'But there remains a hell of a story to be told, one which it must be in the public interest to air. And however much I get drawn in to working with you, there's still a journalist's instinct inside me.'

'Yes, I'm well aware of that,' Adam said meaningfully. 'But, when the court case is done, I'm thinking there could be a way of getting some of what happened into your reporting. As an exclusive, naturally.'

To a simple hack it was the golden word. To Dan, it was even better. Awards, acclaim and the continuation of the new life as an occasional investigator that he had come to love.

'I think that may well be acceptable,' was his euphemistic verdict.

Adam started coughing. Dan used the opportunity to check his notes and said, 'There is one other thing I've been meaning to ask. Why do you think the spies gave us Tariq, Ahmed's cousin? They must have known he wasn't involved in the bomb plot.'

'For just that reason, I'd say. To give us a distraction, to muddy the waters and to make it look like they were keen to crack the case.'

'When that was the opposite of what they were up to.'

'Exactly.'

So, there remained just a single problem to resolve, and it was a familiar one. The unavoidable demand from the ever-insatiable Lizzie for a story.

'Do you think you can hold off from releasing the news about the charging of Ahmed for a while?' Dan ventured.

They had worked together long enough now for Adam to have seen it coming. 'Let me guess. Until just after half past six?'

'Yep. That way, I get it as an exclusive for tonight. I can illustrate the story with the mobile phone video I took of you arresting him. Call it a double scoop, just like the best ice creams.'

The dirty deal was done. But as Dan got into his car to drive back to Plymouth, another story parachuted upon him. Ali Tanton rang, and she was in tears again.

'I'm going to have John's funeral tomorrow,' she said, in a choked voice. 'They've finally released his body. I went to see him a little earlier. It was the first time since the bombing. But Dan … Dan …'

He waited to let her gather some composure. 'Just take it easy Ali.'

'I – I could hardly recognise him. He was so badly injured by the bomb going off. And his face – his poor face.'

Her voice was lost in another wave of sobbing. Dan checked his watch. It was lunchtime. He could pop in to see her on his way back to the studios and still have plenty of time to get a report together for tonight. This type of conversation was never best over a phone line.

He called Lizzie, told her about tonight's story, received a verdict of "acceptable to reasonable", on the proviso it was an exclusive, naturally, and drove to Stonehouse to see Ali.

Dan was walking up the path when the door of the house flew open and she ran out, flung her arms around him and gave him a squeezing hug. She looked wretched, tired and drawn.

'Thank you, thank you so much for coming. I just needed someone to talk to.'

He sat her down, made a cup of tea, as the English rule book of coping with emotion dictates, and did his best to calm her.

Ali had been to Tamarside Hospital, where John's body was being kept. Her description of what she found made Dan flinch. The young man's face had been so badly injured there was little left of the son she had known. Ali said she had collapsed in tears and been led away by a man who was dressed in a suit, but who she suspected was a police officer.

A spy, more like, Dan thought. No doubt John's body had been released because of their showdown with the spooks and the subsequent decision to charge Ahmed. The news of the funeral would be nicely submerged in the reporting of the charges, any criticism of how long it had taken effectively muted.

He sat with Ali for almost an hour before she asked the question she was obviously preparing.

'Do you think you could come to the funeral? It'll only be a very small do and it won't take long. It's just that I don't know how I'll cope, and having you there – well, you've been very kind to me. No cameras, it's a private event, I don't want it on the television, just you.'

Dan felt touched. Apparently years of the emotional erosion of being a hack, not to mention a fair portion of the similar experience of a detective's life hadn't entirely eroded his soul after all.

'Of course I'll come,' he said. 'It's the least I can do.'

He would have the argument with Lizzie tomorrow. She'd never got the hang of sentiment and wouldn't see the point of him disappearing if a story did not duly materialise afterwards. He was owed some time back after all the hours he'd put in on the bombing and would take some of them tomorrow, no matter what his manic editor said. It was the right thing to do.

Dan drove back to the studios and broadcast the story about Ahmed being charged. He added that John Tanton's funeral would be held tomorrow and then headed straight for the vet's.

There was still something bothering him, but he couldn't quite grasp what. It was somewhere in all that Ali had said, but trying to turn the drifting, insubstantial notion into a solid realisation was like grasping for bubbles in the air.

Claire shivered and breathed hard into her hands, the sudden movement bringing Dan back to the surgery. She wrapped her arms around her body. 'It's getting cold in here. Perhaps it's time to call it a night? How about that drink we talked about?'

Dan realised his eyelids were sagging. The insanity of the past few days was coming home. 'Yes, maybe you're right.'

He got up and ran a gentle hand over Rutherford's head. The dog was sleeping easily. It was fine to leave him, really it was. But still, with each step he took towards the door, Dan couldn't help looking back.

They walked outside. It was another pleasant, but chilly,

September night, stars shining in the clear sky. Cars rushed past, the flying headlights chasing shadows.

'You look shattered,' Claire said.

'Yes. I am.'

'We don't have to do the drink thing. Why don't you just get home and have some rest?'

'Look, I don't want you to think I'm running away from talking to you. I want to, I do. It's just that at the moment, it doesn't ... I don't know, it just doesn't feel right. Not yet, anyway. Not in this state, at least.'

She put a hand on his shoulder and looked into his eyes. 'I understand. But there is one thing I do want to ask before you go. It's something I need to know.'

Her voice was thinner now, hesitant and filled with trepidation. 'Sure,' was all Dan could find to say.

Claire turned away. When she looked back, she avoided eye contact and instead stared down at her shoes.

'What you said on that last night we talked. About – about hating me, and loathing me, and wishing you'd never met me. The stuff about longing to erase me from your life, so I'd never existed. About detesting me for disturbing your emotional hibernation, and daring to give you hope you wouldn't always be on your own and you'd finally escape that vicious depression of yours. About longing for me to leave you alone, and letting you be free from feelings so it could just be you, on your own, with your damned dog, and your walks and your beer, with nothing to challenge you, no one to hurt you ...'

She choked and took a shallow breath, a respite from the rush of words.

'Just tell me that wasn't true, was it? Please say it wasn't.'

And now, for the first time, Dan understood that it wasn't just him who had been so very badly hurt by what happened between them.

A wall of brick and concrete, steel and stone, was breached in an instant.

Dan reached out and held Claire to him. He didn't hesitate, didn't think twice, just did it. And there was no resistance, none at all.

'No,' he said softly. 'No, I didn't mean it. God, how I didn't.'

Chapter Twenty-five

IT IS ONE OF life's simplest, but most savoured, surprises; to sleep well when you have no expectation of doing so.

Dan had gone to bed with a mind full of everything that had happened that day and an increasing frustration at being unable to identify exactly what it was that was bothering him. Claire edged in to the maelstrom too, the pain in her voice from that conversation outside the vet's, and the image of Rutherford lying on the metal table was inescapable, a continual backdrop to the meanderings of the imagination.

Despite all that, he slept long and was only awoken by the morning sun, edging its call around the curtains.

Dan's first thought was to get up quickly, so he could take Rutherford for a brief run before work. Then came the memory. The flat felt empty without the padding of the dog's feet and the way he would follow his master around, watching as he brushed his teeth, salvaged some unidentifiable breakfast from the back of the fridge and rummaged in the wardrobe for a shirt in a sufficiently passable state of repair to be worn in front of a television camera.

The sombre black jacket and tie hanging on the back of the door reminded Dan of what the day would bring. The funeral was scheduled for eleven. He'd have time to go and see Rutherford, then get down to the church for about half past ten. Ali had asked him to arrive early. She couldn't bear the thought of being there without someone beside her.

It was just a question of whether to pop into the newsroom to tell Lizzie about the funeral in person, or to do it on the phone. The honourable route would be to go in, the remote means easier.

Well, he didn't have to decide on that now. First, a visit to Rutherford. The rest of the day could follow.

Dan turned on his mobile. There was a text, from Sarah Jones, sent at just after two o'clock in the morning. The woman didn't sleep.

Hello stud. Am off to bed and wishing you were here to play with. Come see your favourite tiger again soon. Grrr ... xxx

Dan shook his head. It was usually a personal maxim that it was better to be in demand than not, but he wasn't sure he could cope with quite this level of expectation. Sarah's demands would require a Viagra factory to fulfil. He would answer the message later. With Rutherford still poorly and a funeral to endure, Dan suspected he would hardly fit the billing of stud at the moment.

A wonderful sight awaited at the vet's. Rutherford was sitting up. He looked a little groggy, his tongue hanging out and his eyes unusually dull, but he was alive and awake and all in the world was suddenly well. He was going to be OK.

Dan knelt down and wrapped his arms around the dog. Rutherford nuzzled into his neck and let out a small whine.

'Go steady,' came Cara's kindly voice. 'He's still weak. But I don't think it'll be long before he's back to normal. I'm going to keep him in for another night, maybe two, then he can come home.'

Dan knew his face had adopted a stupid, vacuous smile, but he couldn't quite shift it. Later, he would stop in at the supermarket, buy the dog some turkey, ready for his homecoming, and get himself a few cans of beer to join the celebration. If the store had one, he would even buy a *Welcome Home* banner. The dog deserved it after all he had been through.

Over the turkey, he would tell Rutherford of Adam's fine punch for the man who had poisoned him. Together they would have a good chuckle about it.

The impressively long list of numbers on the vet's bill didn't even dim Dan's mood. He handed over a credit card without a murmur of protest.

Rutherford was coming home.

He gave the dog a last pat, said goodbye to Cara and

reminded himself to also get her a bottle of some fine wine when he went shopping. She had been magnificent and should know it. Without her prompt action, Rutherford might not have survived. A letter of commendation was in order too. Were it in his power, she would even have a peerage.

He leant back on the side of the car, enjoying the sunshine. It was half past nine. Now Dan had to decide whether to go in to the newsroom to face the editor beast in her lair, or ring. It was too pleasant a morning for a face-to-face row. He fumbled the mobile from his jacket pocket and was about to make the call, when the thought arrived.

That, in fact, was a wonderfully grand understatement. To say it arrived is like describing a tsunami, or an earthquake, as merely arriving. The repercussions tend to be immeasurably greater than the neutral word conveys.

Dan knew what it was that had been bothering him about what Ali Tanton said yesterday. He realised what it meant and what would have to happen now. He understood there would be another confrontation and a great scandal. And he saw that Lizzie would have her story, and it would be one of the biggest *Wessex Tonight* had ever known.

But it was dangerous. It would have to be played out so very carefully. They needed all the evidence they could get. And securing it was going to be particularly unpleasant.

Dan closed his eyes, spun fast through a mental check-list and counted off everything he had to do. First, ring El.

Next, he needed Nigel's help. And what he wanted was a great deal to ask.

He rang his friend and got the cheery greeting he expected. Nigel was very much a morning person.

'Are you assigned to any jobs yet?' Dan interrupted.

'No. I'm just sitting in the canteen, enjoying a nice cup of tea.'

'Then make some excuse about having to go out. I can't tell you why at the moment, just believe me that it's very important. And make it fast. Then come meet me at Ali Tanton's house.'

'What's going on?'

'I can't tell you over the phone. Just meet me there as soon as you can and I'll explain everything. Trust me. Please.'

Dan was tempted to call Adam, but stopped himself. He would need his help too, but it was more than likely that both the detective's phone and his own were being bugged and he couldn't afford to give away what he knew. Not yet.

For now, it was down to him. Dan jogged to the car and drove to Ali's house. He had to stop her before she reached the church.

Finally, Dan thought he understood just how ruthless was their enemy.

It took a couple of rings before she answered the door. Ali was dressed in a black trouser suit. It was obvious she had spent much of the morning crying. Even through the heavy layers of mascara, her eyes were sore and red.

'What are you doing here?' she asked. 'I thought you were coming to the church.'

'I am. Well, I was. I thought I'd pop in on you first, as I was early. Can I come in?'

She led the way through to the lounge and stood watching him.

'Dan, you look really out of it. What's happened? Are you OK? What is it?'

For once, Dan was lost for words. He'd never had to say anything remotely like this before. And the effect it would have on the woman standing in front of him, when she had already been through so much … he didn't want to think about it.

Dan wondered briefly if there was any other way. Perhaps he could explain what he knew to Adam and leave it to him to sort out. Maybe he should just forget the whole thing. How strong sometimes is the temptation to walk away.

No. It was impossible. The consequences of not revealing what he suspected were far worse than doing so. He would never be able to live with the knowledge. It would nag and gnaw until one day it would undoubtedly emerge. He had to tell her, and now.

She must have seen the agonising in his face. 'Dan – what is it? You're frightening me. What's the matter?'

One deep breath and he would tell her. A few more seconds before he let it out.

Dan hesitated. Nigel's reaction had been bad enough.

'You want me – to do … what?' the cameraman had asked. 'Do – *what*?'

He sounded more appalled than Dan had ever heard. He put a hand on his friend's shoulder.

'You're joking me,' Nigel managed finally.

'No.'

'You must be.'

'I'm not.'

'Seriously?'

'Yes.'

'What, film all of it?'

'Yes.'

'Even – close-up shots?'

'Yes.'

'In the coffin?'

'Yes.'

'In the church?'

'Yes.'

'Shit.'

Dan explained why. Nigel had gone quiet, thought it over, but finally accepted it. He too could see no other way. The cameraman was waiting outside, ready to do what he must.

Now it was just a question of telling Ali.

'Dan!' she moaned. 'What's going on? Please, just tell me.'

She was staring at him, her face taut, lips quivering.

'Ali,' he said, but his voice dried. The photos of John kept catching the edge of his vision.

Dan swallowed hard and tried again. 'Ali, there's no easy way to say this, so I'm just going to give it to you straight. You've got to stop the funeral.'

She looked stunned. 'What? But we're burying my son. My John. We're going to lay him to rest at last. I don't care what he's done. I don't care what people say about him. He's my son and …'

276

'Look, you've got to trust me,' Dan interrupted. 'It's going to be horrible, but you've got to believe what I'm about to tell you. First, you've got to cancel the funeral.'

She sat down heavily on the sofa, didn't speak, just stared up at him. Her cheeks were ashen.

'Then, you've got to come with me to the church,' Dan continued. 'We've got to take Nigel too. Then we've got to go to Charles Cross Police Station. Please, just trust me. It's the only way we're going to get to the bottom of this.'

Chapter Twenty-six

THE GIFT OF A philanthropist, St Matthias's Church was built in the 1850s on a grassy, greenfield site on the northern outskirts of the Victorian city centre. But the sprawl of the passing years prompted Plymouth to grow, cluster and cuddle around it. Where once its shining limestone tower would have dominated the area known as North Hill, now, like a shy suitor, it competes forlornly for attention amongst the blocks of flats, shops and stores, and glass towers of the university.

Today, it is a true city centre church, its once sizeable yard eaten away by endless development and limited to a small and defiant periphery. Its fine stone is continually under attack from the corrosive fumes of the relentless traffic and in need of regular cleansing to keep the old lady looking her best. The church has also become host to a modern-day tradition; gangs of smokers, barred from the environs of the surrounding offices and bars gather under its portico to share the shame of the social outcast.

St Matthias's is rare amongst the churches in the city in surviving the Plymouth Blitz almost undamaged. Some believe that was deliberate, endowing the church with an unfortunate legend. Its distinctive tower was reputed to have provided a useful landmark for the German bombers as they rained down their destruction.

After a brief discussion, it was here they decided to come first. Dan was working on the principle it was better to get the most unpleasant task out of the way. Nigel took his camera out of the boot and checked it over, shaking his head the whole time.

'I've only ever filmed one dead person,' he kept saying. 'And that was by accident. It was a car crash. I was doing a close-up when I realised the body of the driver was still in the front. I had nightmares for months.'

'I'm not exactly filled with delight at this either,' Dan replied. 'But we've got to do it.'

He'd sent Ali off to talk to the vicar, to apologise in person. He very much didn't want either of them around during the filming. She'd calmed down a little now, but was still intensely fragile and kept whispering to herself, "My John, my poor John, what have they done to my John?"

Dan did his best to comfort her, but with what she had been through it was hopeless.

And there was worse yet to come.

He made a quick call to Adam, giving nothing away, but checking all was as he suspected.

'How're you doing?' Dan asked his friend, hoping his tone was light and chatty enough to put anyone who might be eavesdropping off guard.

'I'm doing some paperwork. It mounts up when you're out on a big case.'

'You at Charles Cross?'

'Yeah.'

Now Dan tried to sound as nonchalant as he ever could. On a day like this it wasn't easy.

'And how're our dear friends, the spooks?'

'Who cares?' Adam grunted.

'But they're still around, I take it?'

'Yeah. They're downstairs in some office they've taken over. They're working on tidying up a few loose ends in the case, or so they say. I'm trying to avoid them, to be frank.'

The question was answered. The pieces of the puzzle were in place.

'Are you around all morning?' Dan said.

'Given this pile of paperwork I'll probably be around all month. Why?'

'It's just that I could do with popping in for a chat. Nothing important, only a discussion about a few ongoing cases.'

'Sure. I'll be glad of the distraction.'

So, all was set for later. But first, there was another ordeal to face.

The church's walls were panelled with dark oak, amplifying the sound of their careful footsteps. It reminded Dan of Wessex Minster, where this whole story had begun. It was only days, but it felt a long time ago now, with all that had come to pass.

One corner was given over to a memorial for lost children, an entire section devoted to those who had died in the Blitz. There were so many tiny stone panels, wooden crosses and words redolent with grief. The inscribed ages were all poignant, from days and months to only a handful of years.

Together, Dan and Nigel walked softly past the rows of pews, candlesticks and tapestries, and towards the altar. It was dominated by the whorls and eddies of an intricately carved wooden screen. They reached the plain dark mass of the coffin, its brass handles shining in the gentle church light. The lid was closed.

And here they stopped. And looked. First at the casket and then each other.

'You open it,' Nigel said. 'I can't.'

'Down to me, is it?'

'All this is your idea.'

'Get your camera ready then. I don't want to spend any longer here than I have to.'

Dan braced himself and opened the lid. It was surprisingly light, moved easily. He groaned at the sight. The jeans, T-shirt and hoodie that John Tanton wore on his bombing mission were clearly recognisable and mostly intact, except for a few rips and holes, edged with bloodstains. But the corpse's face was mutilated.

One eye was gone, the dark socket gaping open. Part of an ear was missing, sliced away, a couple of teeth broken, their edges jagged and yellowing. Skeins of muscle, like dark, woven cords stood out in the ochre pastiche of dried blood, flecked a dirty white with exposed ridges of bone.

Dan turned away and concentrated on counting off the seconds as Nigel took his shots. The cameraman was whimpering as he worked.

'Just get it done,' Dan urged. 'As quick as you can.'

'Damn right I will. Do I have to do close-ups?'

'Yep. Close-ups, wide shots, the lot. Everything.'

A heavy smell of chemicals was rising from the body, slowly drifting in the still air. The embalmers had been at work. Dan gritted his teeth and had to force himself not to be sick. He made his mind picture Rutherford, collecting him from the vet's later, taking him back to the flat and settling the dog in the warmth of the bay window. In a day or two, they would try their first walk since the poisoning. The sun would shine and this dreadful case would finally be left behind.

'That's it,' Nigel gasped. 'Enough.'

'One last task,' Dan replied. 'Look away.'

'What?'

'Just look away!'

Dan took out the scissors he'd borrowed from Ali, braced himself and did what he had to do. He went to close the coffin lid, but it slipped from his sweating fingers and fell. Wood crashed onto wood, the noise booming thunderously loud in the quiet hollowness of the church.

'Come on, let's get Ali and get out of here,' he said, his voice shaky and thin.

Nigel was already heading for the door.

In moments of tension and suspense, a pressured mind can often find a little release in a whim or musing. Just one such came to Dan now.

They were effectively creating their own version of the infamous grassy knoll in Dallas, he thought, albeit hardly on the same scale as that which shook the world back in 1963.

By the side of Charles Cross Police Station, amidst the bars, church and library of North Hill, is a small harbour of green, sloping gently between the main road and the Art College. It's topped by a couple of bushes and a compact gang of trees, only mere saplings on the botanical scale, but sufficient enough to provide cover for a small group of people who might want to hide themselves.

The plan was in place. Nigel would wait here, camera set up and microphone ready. Ali had decided to stand with him. Dan would join them later.

'Look, you can stay in the car you know,' he told her. 'You don't have to come for this bit.'

'I want to,' she said forcefully. 'For what those bastards

have done, believe me I want to.'

'You might be waiting a while. Stake-outs are like that.'

'I'll wait all day if I have to.'

She nodded hard to emphasise the words. The tears had dried, the shock and grief of earlier turning fast to anger. She was ready to be interviewed later, when Dan had confirmation of what he thought he already knew, and Ali promised that what she had to say would be powerful.

He gave her a hug and shook Nigel's hand. 'Be careful in there,' his friend said, in his pastoral way. 'You know what kind of people you're up against.'

'All too well,' Dan replied and headed for the police station doors.

Adam was waiting in his office. He put a finger to his lips, got up and beckoned Dan out of the door. They walked in silence, up a couple of flights of stairs to the top of the station. By the lift was a door marked *Plant Room*. Adam looked around to check there was no one else about, took out a key and opened it.

The cramped, dark space was full of heavy pulleys and shining metal cables, rumbling, grinding and groaning as they worked the lift. It smelt of oil. Dan pushed some dusty cobwebs away from his face. Adam closed the door, magnifying the relentless noise.

He leaned over and said, 'I reckon this is the one place they've got no chance of bugging. They've made me paranoid, I can tell you that.'

'Wait till you hear what else I've got to say,' Dan replied. 'How did you know I needed to talk to you in private?'

'You've got that look on your face which says you're up to something. And I heard it in your voice earlier. I've never known you want to have an innocent little chat about anything.'

Dan smiled, but without humour. 'Yep. Let me tell you what I reckon they've done, and why.'

He related the story to Adam. The detective leaned back against the door and blew out a long breath.

'Bloody hell,' he said finally. 'You really think that's what happened?'

'I'm sure of it. Why else would the spooks still be here? And why in Plymouth today, instead of Exeter?'

'Yeah.'

'And look at what Oscar came out with when you whacked him. That thing about having medics who can work miracles. Now it makes sense.'

A couple of levers clunked loudly and an electric motor ticked, then whirred. A spray of sparks crackled in the gloom.

'OK,' Adam said. 'I wouldn't put it past them, not at all. So what do you want to do now?'

'Confront them.'

'I thought you might. But before that – you do realise you could be walking into a whole world of trouble? They're powerful people and they're not exactly keen on you, as it is.'

'Yep. But the same goes for you.'

'Yes, it does. So let's go do it.'

They slipped out of the Plant Room. Adam brushed off his jacket and they started down the stairs.

The spies had taken over an office which was used by the Child Protection Team. The room was small, just half a dozen desks arranged in an irregular rectangle. On the walls were posters warning of the dangers of childhood, one modern, one timeworn; the internet, and the shadowy outline of the foreboding stranger. The office was three floors up, a long window looking out to the north of the city, all houses and streets. A couple of cactuses drooped at either end of the sill.

Through the glass in the door they could see Sierra sitting at a desk, Oscar standing beside her, the briefcase at his feet. They were involved in a whispered conversation.

She leant back on her chair, nodded and began writing a note on her pad. His face warmed into a smirk.

Adam pushed open the door and was about to walk in, when Dan shouldered his way past. The two spies looked round.

'What the fuck are you doing here, dickweed?' Oscar snapped.

Many words Dan had been rehearsing, ready for this

283

moment. He was tempted to shout abuse at them, blurt it all out, even try to find some dramatic Hollywood-style line about justice and truth.

But instead, all he could say was , 'I know.'

There was just a second's pause, if even that. But how revealing can be a hesitation. It was long enough. The two simple words had hit the invisible target.

There was a secret hidden in the silence.

Adam saw it too. Even people so very well trained and experienced in the art of deception can give themselves away.

Oscar slipped a fast glance at Sierra.

And Dan knew. It was all true. Speculation had turned to certainty in an instant.

He knew, too, what was coming next. The last desperate refuge of the liar. A final bluff.

'What do you know?' Oscar took a step towards him, fists knotting. 'What the fuck do you think you know?'

And now Dan found himself laughing. It was stupid, ridiculous, but he couldn't help it. First a chuckle, then building momentum to great, wracking guffaws. Of all the reactions he had expected from himself, it wasn't this. But the spies were at last naked before him, and it was bizarrely comical.

'What the fuck do you think you know?' Oscar repeated. He was almost in Dan's face now, his expression hot and dangerous. 'And who the fuck do you think you are?'

Adam was at Dan's shoulder, a calm, menacing presence.

'And if you don't want a bottom lip as fat as the top one, you'd better back off,' he said quietly.

Oscar glared at him. 'You were lucky last time. You caught me by surprise.'

'I'd be very happy to do it again with you fully prepared.'

The spy held his look for a second, then took a step backwards, his hand raised to the swollen lip.

'Come on then,' he grunted. 'Entertain us – wanker. What do you think you know?'

Dan waited, let the moment run. The story was so extraordinary he scarcely knew where to begin. Sierra stood up from her desk. 'Yes, please Dan,' she said, in a friendly voice. 'Do tell us. Particularly if it might help with the case.'

She gave him a warm smile. In reply, Dan snorted. 'Trying it on to the last, eh?'

'Just get on with it will you?' she retorted. 'We don't have time to waste with amateurs.'

Dan nodded. 'So – the nice spy act didn't last long then, did it? You know Sierra, or whatever your name is, I was almost convinced by your little show of tears yesterday. In fairness, I think it was a tough call, letting Tanton explode his bomb. But knowing what I do now, I don't think you had any hesitation whatsoever.'

He sat down on the edge of a desk. 'I can't help you with the case, as well you're aware, because you've been in control of it all along.'

'We've been through all this,' she replied. 'Is that it, this revelation of yours? Because if that's all …'

'I never said I had any revelation,' Dan interrupted. 'So what could it possibly be that you're worried about me knowing? It's an interesting choice of word that. *Revelation*. It's biblical stuff, isn't it, all about an astonishing disclosure? And that, I would say, just about sums it up. Your last little secret. The one you're so obviously scared of us knowing.'

'What the fuck are you talking about man?' Oscar sneered. 'What planet are you on?'

'One you've clearly never visited. It's called – Planet Truth.'

'Fuck off, you arsehole.'

'Shut your foul mouth,' Adam growled at him. 'Come on, Dan, get on with it. I don't want to be spending any more time with these two than I have to.'

Dan closed his eyes and swung a leg back and forth. At last, he said simply, 'John Tanton is alive, isn't he?'

Sierra leaned forwards and peered at him. 'What?'

'There's no need to carry on with the act. It's wearing thin. Tanton's alive and being held by you, in London I suspect, well away from his home and his mother.'

'What the fuck are you talking about now?' Oscar jeered. 'I

285

don't know if you missed this, but Tanton was a suicide bomber. It's in the job description that they don't tend to get out alive.'

'Yes,' Dan nodded. 'He was supposed to be a suicide bomber. And a state-sponsored one at that, courtesy of you two. But he lost his nerve at the last minute, didn't he? That was where your precious plan nearly went wrong. He dumped the rucksack and ran. And he was injured in the explosion.'

'And then died later in hospital,' Sierra said softly.

'Yes, of course he did. And his funeral was to be today. A funny coincidence, that you two should be here in Plymouth as it's happening?'

Sierra replied, 'We're just sorting out some loose ends in the investigation.'

'And not keeping an eye on the funeral? Checking that the last bit of evidence which could reveal your secret is safely buried.'

'Whatever might make you think that?'

'Just the obvious reason. The simple one.'

Dan let his gaze run over the watching faces, waited and then said, 'That it's not John Tanton's body in the coffin.'

The room stopped. No one moved. A bird flew past the window, a black, flitting shadow. In the distance, a horn sounded, a long, angry blare.

Adam folded his arms, stared at the spies and said quietly, 'So, what have you got to say to that?'

'What do you expect?' Oscar spat. 'It's bollocks. Tanton died from his injuries.'

Dan shook his head. 'In which case, it was quite a bomb, wasn't it? Half of Tanton's face was injured in the explosion, when he couldn't resist looking back. But it's strange how that grew. To mutilation beyond recognition. It gave you a bit of a problem. You had to obliterate the body's face, so his mum wouldn't know it wasn't him. You could put Tanton's clothes on it – and you did – but there was still that little issue. So you – well, shall we say, "enhanced" the injuries. What truly lovely people you are. You'll stop at nothing, will you?'

Sierra said dangerously, 'You're suggesting we got ourselves a corpse and put it in the coffin to back up our story that Tanton was dead? And where are we supposed to get a body from?'

Dan grimaced. 'That I don't want to think about. But I don't doubt you have your ways. There are lots of down and outs who die and have no family, no one to claim their bodies. And that's being generous to you. I'm sure you've got all sorts of creative ways to get hold of a corpse. Not to mention creating one.'

She ignored the jibe. 'And why would we do this extraordinary thing?'

'For the reasons you told us about yesterday. You needed this terrorist ring you're hunting to conclude Ahmed was safe to recruit. When he walks free, as you'd originally planned, having made the bombing happen, that should do nicely for his credentials. He's proved himself. But what about Tanton? He's a problem, isn't he? If he's still alive, in prison somewhere, your jihadists will always be worried about him talking. Telling the authorities about Ahmed's role and so leading the police to them. The only way to be certain Tanton can't talk is if he's dead. You thought he would be after the attack, but it didn't work out that way. And so you had to arrange it. You spirited him away and announced his death, expecting Ahmed to be released a few days later. Everything was working beautifully – until we screwed it all up by finding Ahmed's phone, of course.'

'Yeah, so sorry about that,' Adam muttered.

'And what evidence do you have of this bizarre plot?' Sierra asked.

'You know, I thought you might ask that. So we filmed the body in the coffin, and then – well, you'll hardly believe this, what I had to do, but it seemed the only option. I can still scarcely believe it myself.'

'What? What did you do?'

Dan's mouth felt dry at the memory. 'I took some nail and hair clippings from the corpse. Ali Tanton is perfectly prepared to give us a sample of her hair. We'll DNA-test both sets and compare the results. It should be interesting, don't you think?'

Silence. Sierra was staring at Dan, her face set. The scar on Oscar's neck was throbbing.

'I notice you haven't denied any of this,' Dan observed.

The spies didn't reply. Adam adjusted his tie and then folded his arms again.

'So,' Sierra said quietly. 'What are you planning to do now?'

'Now?' Dan managed to sound surprised. 'Now I'm going to do what journalists do of course, and I'm going to delight in it. I'm going to blow the story. I'm going to expose you for what you are.'

'Are you?'

'Yes.'

'You really think you'll be allowed to?'

'Well, I'm going to have a damn good try. I think the moment I get it broadcast it should be picked up by all the national and then international media. TV, radio, newspapers, websites, the works. I suspect by tomorrow there won't be many people on the planet who haven't heard it.'

Dan waited, but there was still no reaction. 'There is one thing I need to ask you first though, before I splash it,' he added.

'Which is?'

'I'd like an interview please. I need to formally put all those points to you, to get your response.'

For the first time, Sierra looked surprised. 'An interview?'

'Yes.'

'An interview?'

'Still yes.'

'The intelligence services aren't known for giving them.'

'I'm aware of that. But nonetheless, I have to ask. For fairness and balance and all that.'

'And you really need me to answer?'

The trap was set. Dan took out his notebook and a pen.

'Yes, please. I'd like to formally request an interview about the security services claiming John Tanton was dead when he was very much alive and putting an unknown body into a coffin to pretend it was his. Oh, and the rest of the scandal too – you knowing about the bombing, not stopping it and all that.'

'No one will be interviewed and no comment will be made,' she replied emphatically.

Dan smiled. 'Fine, thanks then.' He turned for the door. 'Right, I have to be off to write the story. You know, I'm rather looking forward to it.'

'It's not the end of this,' Sierra called after him.

'I don't doubt that in the slightest,' Dan replied.

Chapter Twenty-seven

AND SO THE ARMIES readied for battle; in the modern way, not with massed ranks of warriors and the incessant beat of a drum, but more subtly, albeit just as certainly.

Of the spies' preparations they could know nothing except that they were surely afoot. Behind the inscrutable walls of Charles Cross, in that small office once dedicated to child welfare, even before Dan had left the great concrete block of a building, he knew they would be set in discussion and then on to the phones. Calling powerful people in secret places, rushing through briefings, working over scenarios and marshalling their plans. Oscar, loud and with sentences laced with profanities and abuse, Sierra calm but redoubtable.

The faceless forces of the unseen state were being arrayed. It felt like a mighty boot slowly materialising in the sky, ready to stamp down and crush the irritant of a tiny, insignificant insect which had the temerity to crawl out from cover, the very action an intolerable challenge to the unquestionable hegemony.

And standing in the way? Dan noticed he didn't want to think too hard about that.

He sat on the grassy knoll, leant back against one of the trees and began the work of his own. First, he borrowed Nigel's phone – just in case his was being bugged – and rang El and the Geeks. Nigel and Ali watched, listened, and nodded approvingly as the skeleton of the plan formed.

Then it was a more difficult prospect. A call to Lizzie, to outline the story. She listened in silence – a rare enough phenomenon – before saying simply, 'Shit.'

Despite her messianic pursuit of news and continual hectoring of her staff, Lizzie Riley was of the Adam school of attitude when it came to swearing. She was quite able to communicate urgency, intensity and insanity without obscenity.

Dan waited, then prompted, 'Good story, eh?'

'Stratospheric,' she sighed. 'And you're absolutely sure of all this? Not just copper-bottomed, but copper-entombed?'

'Yep.'

'And you've got the evidence?'

'Yep.'

'So we can back it all up, one hundred per cent?'

'Yes.'

'And it's an exclusive?'

'Naturally.'

'It's going to cause all sorts of problems with the government.'

'Yep.'

'But it's all true?'

'Yep.'

She didn't sound at all daunted. 'Then let's do it. I've always wanted to say this – publish and be damned!'

Dan thanked her and was about to hang up, when she added, 'Oh, and one more thing.'

'Yes?' he said warily.

'Very good work.'

She cut the call before he could react. Dan stared at the phone in amazement. His editor had issued warm praise, for once free of all clauses, provisos and caveats.

It was truly a seminal day.

Dan turned his mind to the Editorial Guidelines and the section on *Doorstepping*. It was summarised as a rarely used, but powerful technique, only to be employed when a journalist has evidence of serious wrongdoing and the person responsible refuses to be interviewed. In such a situation, the surprise appearance of a television crew and reporter to put the important questions is deemed justified.

In layman's terms, it is an ambush.

But there was a problem.

'There are two exits from Charles Cross,' Dan had said to Adam, as he walked out of the police station. 'And we can only cover one.'

'Well, we have had problems with the electronic locking system on the back door,' the detective replied. 'Anyway, I've got to get back to my paperwork. And as it's a fine day, I think I'll have a walk around and go in the back way.'

Dan left the building, but made a point of standing on the steps, pretending to take a phone call. A few minutes later, a couple of uniformed police officers walked out to begin a patrol, moaning loudly about the back door jamming again.

Ali was sitting on the grass, her arms wrapped around her knees. 'I still can't believe what they've done,' she said. 'I feel like going in there and demanding to see John.'

'You will see him,' Dan reassured her. 'But he's not in there. They wouldn't be that daft. Play it my way and I think it'll work out.'

'I want to get them. I want to go in there and tell them what I think of them.'

'And you will,' Dan soothed. 'But trust me. If it doesn't work my way, you can go charging in there and we'll film it all.'

She nodded. 'OK. But can we do my interview now? There's so much I want to say.'

It was coming up for half past twelve. All was set. The only nagging problem was that they had no idea when the spooks would emerge from the police station. And time was against them. With a story of such sensitivity, Lizzie would have to sit in on much of the edit and the programme lawyers would need to be consulted. It all took time.

If the spies didn't emerge until later in the day, maybe even five o'clock, or worse, Dan would stand little chance of getting the report on air.

But such was the way with an ambush. Timings were out of their control. All they could do was be ready. They would only get one chance. If they recorded Ali's contribution and Sierra and Oscar emerged, it would simply be a question of stopping and running after them, a matter of a couple of seconds.

Nigel adjusted the tripod, slotted the camera onto the top and checked the focus and exposure. 'Ready,' he said. 'I'm going for quite a tight shot, to emphasise the power of Ali's words.'

The sunshine through the trees made for a moody, dappled

light. Ali brushed away a lock of hair, the determination strong in her face.

'There are really only a couple of questions for you,' Dan began. 'Firstly, what do you think of what the spies have done?'

As he had expected the words came fast; the full force of a flood unleashed.

'I think it's despicable. John may have done a dreadful thing, but the point of our society is that he's dealt with fairly and decently. I accept he'll have to be punished and sent to prison. But to go through this charade of pretending he's dead, it's worse than some evil old Soviet state. People don't just disappear, not in Britain in the 21st century. And as for putting someone else's body in the coffin and pretending it's John, being prepared to see me bury it as my son – well, words could never communicate my anger and contempt.'

She shook her head hard, the shimmer of loathing in her eyes. 'What else can I call it but utterly sick, depraved and despicable? In my view, what they've done makes our security services as bad as the people they're fighting, if not worse.'

Dan paused to frame his next question. 'And what effect has all this had on you?'

'It's a damned torment. Can you imagine it? I was preparing to bury what I thought was my son. It was the morning of his funeral. I'd been up all night crying. I hadn't slept. And then I find out it isn't John's body and I have to call the funeral off – it's twisted and tortured my emotions. I thought he was dead, but now I hear that he's alive. What the hell are they doing? Who do they think they are? I was so upset I thought I would never stop crying. But now – I'm so angry I want to fight. And I won't stop fighting, until I get the truth revealed.'

Nigel stopped recording. Ali stared up at the sky, then reached out and gave Dan a hug. She was breathing hard.

'Was that OK?'

'A bit more than that. It was one of the strongest interviews I've ever heard.'

'They deserve it. All that I've said. And more.'

They sat back down on the grass, Nigel with the camera

between his legs, Dan holding the microphone.

'So, what are you going to do?' Ali asked.

'Confront them. Get the lens right in their faces. See if I can rile them into saying something. Then put it all together, along with your interview, into a great big exposé.'

'Can I come with you when you film them?'

Dan put a hand on her shoulder and said gently. 'I'd rather you didn't. These things can get nasty. Nigel and I have done them before. It's better if you sit here and leave it to us.'

Ali held his look, then turned away, but said nothing.

The traffic queues around the roundabout were growing. Lunchtime, people going about errands in their break time, or just picking up some food. Most of the car windows were open. It was still remarkably warm for September.

Nigel leaned forward and peered through the sunshine. A man and woman were walking out of the police station. Dan gripped the microphone and started to get up.

'False alarm,' Nigel said. 'Too young.'

Dan eased back against a tree. 'It should be an easy job, getting paid for just sitting around. But stake-outs always make me tense.'

'Me too,' Nigel agreed.

'You get tense before any decent story.'

'No, just keyed up. And that's only professional,' came the huffy reply.

Across the city, a distant clock rang out a single chime.

'If they're coming out it'll be soon,' Nigel said.

Dan's mobile rang. Dirty El. He held a brief, hushed conversation and hung up.

A couple of cops emerged from the police station, both carrying notepads. A young man swaggered in, a baseball cap low over his eyes. Above them, a plane droned across the blue sky.

'I hate waiting,' Nigel whispered. 'Action I can do. Waiting I can't.'

'Ditto,' Dan replied.

'You two are making me even more edgy,' Ali said. 'Shall I get us some coffees?'

She got up, slipped through the trees and across the road. As she reached the café Ali must have dropped something. She knelt down, fumbled around and placed some objects in her bag.

'She's been through a hell of a time,' Nigel observed. 'And she's handled it with such dignity. A very decent, not to mention attractive woman. Is she – err ...'

'Is she what?'

'You know. Is she ...'

Dan grinned at his friend's discomfort. 'Is she single? Is that what you're trying to say? Do you fancy her?'

Nigel was blushing. 'Maybe.'

'Do you want me to put in a good word for you?'

'Don't you dare. Is she single?'

'I think so. But can you leave it until we're done here to apply your charm?'

Ali was walking back, balancing three plastic cups. 'Don't you say anything,' Nigel hissed.

'Any news?' she asked, as she sat back down.

'Nothing. Well, not about the stake-out, anyway,' Dan replied knowingly.

'Meaning?'

Nigel was blushing harder now. 'Nothing,' Dan said. 'Just a call from a friend of mine about a project we're working on.'

They slipped back into silence and sipped at their coffees. Dan managed to spill some on his hand, making him yelp.

'Serves you right,' Nigel said quietly.

They waited. A pigeon landed in the tree above them, puffed out its chest and began a rhythmic cooing. A line of ants crawled across a patch of baked mud. They were amongst that sizeable set of creatures who are permanently in a hurry.

The police station wasn't busy, just an intermittent passage of people, coming and going. Nigel's eyes didn't shift from the door.

'Young man, no go. Older man, no go. Middle-aged woman, no. Hang on, couple of people coming out.'

Dan rose, then crouched and peered at the door. 'No. Too old.'

Ali let out a groan. 'This is really tense.'

'You should try doing it for a living,' Dan replied.

'And without this doorstep thing, you can't run the story?'

'Well, we could. I'd just say the spies refused to comment. But this is the fun part. Doorsteps always make great TV. The audience love them. It's the thrill of the hunt for the villain.'

Dan began picking at a thread on his jacket. Ali kept flicking her hair. Only Nigel was still, intent on the doors.

Half past one. An ice cream van pulled up over the road, its familiar tune jingling out.

'I thought they didn't exist any more,' Dan mused.

'There are still a few,' Nigel replied. 'And they make the best ice cream going. Much better than anything you'll get in a supermarket.'

Ali nodded her agreement. 'John always loved them. Have you got kids?' she asked Nigel.

'Two, in theory. But they're more like young men now.'

She smiled. 'You mean – full of adolescent troubles?'

'To say the least. And precocious with it.'

'It's always been the way. And always will.'

'Yep, you're right. It's just not easy to remember it. I reckon ...'

'Hey, hey,' Dan interrupted. 'Man and woman coming out the doors.'

He was on his feet again, squinting through the trees. The sun glared hard from the glass of the police station's frontage. Dan could see two silhouettes walking out of the station. They looked familiar, he was sure of it.

'I reckon this is it,' he whispered. 'Stand by.'

Nigel was next to him. 'Ready to rock.'

'Just hold it a sec. Let's make sure it is them before we break cover.'

Dan gripped the microphone. Ali was standing too, blinking in the sunlight. 'I want to see them,' she whispered. 'I want to know who the bastards are.'

A woman walked past, pushing a pram, briefly blocked their view. Nigel hoisted the camera onto his shoulder. He took a step forwards. Dan reached out and grabbed his arm.

'Hold your nerve. Just wait a sec. We need to be sure. We'll only get one chance.'

A motorbike roared past, the engine gunning loud.

'Come on, come on, come on,' Dan mouthed to himself.

The two figures emerged onto the steps. It was Sierra and Oscar.

'Let's go,' Dan said.

Nigel was already away, striding towards the spies. Dan broke into a jog to catch up. They were approaching from behind, their feet silent on the soft grass.

Perfect tactics.

The two spooks were walking side by side, whispering to each other. Oscar was holding the briefcase under his arm. The scar on his neck shone in the sunlight.

Nigel was covering the ground fast, Dan right beside him. They were twenty yards away.

Sierra and Oscar were heading for the subway under the roundabout, still whispering, oblivious to the onrushing ambush.

Fifteen yards now.

Dan kept rehearsing what he would say. The questions he had to ask. What he would do if Oscar attacked them. How to react.

He dodged around a rubbish bin, overflowing with flaps of food wrappings.

Ten yards.

Nigel was breathing hard, starting to pant. A pair of young women walked past and gave them a curious look.

Five yards.

They were on the concrete, their feet pounding. Now Oscar was starting to turn, his head moving quickly. The spy's eyes widened. He reached out and nudged Sierra. She turned too.

They stopped suddenly. Dan and Nigel stopped. The world stopped.

Dan thrust the microphone forward.

'John Tanton's alive, isn't he? You said he was dead when he was alive.'

No response. The spooks just stared at him.

'You put someone else's body in a coffin and pretended it was him, didn't you?'

Sierra's mouth was falling open, Oscar's face creasing into a scowl.

The camera's motor whirred as Nigel zoomed in the shot.

'You would have let Tanton's mother bury that body, thinking it was her son, wouldn't you?'

Oscar's hand was tightening into a fist. There was probably time for just one more question before the blow came. And it would be captured for all the world to see.

It would make compelling television. But a corner of Dan's mind was hoping it didn't hurt too much.

He'd always known he wasn't the bravest of men. He didn't handle pain well.

One final question then, and probably the most important. That fist was bunching fast. It looked alarmingly large.

'You knew about the bombing of Wessex Minster, didn't you?' he blurted out. 'But you let it go ahead. Why did you do that when you could have stopped it?'

Oscar's fist was rising, moving quickly, heading straight for Dan's face. The knuckles were white with the gripping pressure of the looming impact. Dan wondered where they would hit him.

Not his nose, he hoped. It had always been a little too large as it was. It didn't need any expanding.

He closed his eyes and steadied himself, ready for the shock.

It didn't come. Something else was happening.

Dan could hear footsteps, fast, to his side. An object was swinging. He could feel the motion as it cut through the air. He dared to open his eyes again.

It was something dark, squat and square. Arcing, blurring. Moving very fast.

Smashing into the side of Oscar's face.

He let out a low groan and crumpled to the floor.

Ali Tanton was standing next to Dan, panting hard, her bag grasped in one hand. It was bulging and made an odd clicking noise as she lowered it. A large stone fell out, then another.

On the ground Oscar was moaning, blood dripping from a deep gash above his eye. Sierra knelt beside him.

'You bastard,' Ali yelled at him. 'I hope you bleed to death. That one's for John and all the others you let suffer.'

Chapter Twenty-eight

FOR A WORD WHICH is defined by an absence, quiet can have many forms. There is the delicious, like the rare peace of a countryside evening, or the reflective, as with a church congregation asked to take a moment to meditate on life. There is the surprise or the shock, and there is another form, oft commented upon, and one which can be equally revealing.

On the very few occasions Dan had ever been pressed into helping to care for children – just the odd wedding, as far as he could recall – he had learned one very important lesson about quiet. When applied to youngsters, it inevitably meant trouble.

Keep an eye on what they're doing, the parents would say, but most importantly keep an ear. Shouts and screams are perfectly normal. If it goes quiet, that's when they're up to something.

Of that insight, Dan was reminded now.

All was quiet. Very much too quiet.

The time was coming up to five o'clock and they had heard nothing from the authorities. Lizzie was expecting a barrage of calls from government lawyers and ministers; threats, pleas, injunctions, gagging orders, any of the arsenal of weapons at their disposal. But nothing had come. From officialdom there had been only silence.

A highly suspicious silence.

But, if it stayed that way for another hour and a half, it would be too late. The story would be out there, repeated endlessly in newspapers, on radio and TV stations and all over the web. That was the wonder of the internet age. Instant and extensive communication. A planet shrunk to no more than a neighbourhood.

Just another 90 minutes and the story would blow. Like a geyser exploding from a mudflat, or a volcano erupting from beneath the sea. With fire, smoke and flames.

Only another hour and a half. The duration of a football match. An infinitesimal interlude in an average lifetime.

For a man who spent much of his life trying to beat deadlines, who often wished he could create more minutes in an unforgiving hour, Dan found himself wanting the time to slip by as fast as ever it could.

Something was going on, that they did know. Adam rang, from a public telephone, just up the street from Charles Cross. The spies had come striding back inside after Dan's doorstepping. They locked themselves in the room they'd commandeered and within half an hour, two cars had arrived, six people piling out and jogging up the stairs to join them.

Several were carrying those distinctive black briefcases. Adam thought he recognised one as a senior government lawyer who had handled the media strategy after some nuclear submarine plans were stolen from Devonport Dockyard three years ago.

'What do you mean, handled?' Dan queried. 'I don't remember the story. And I would. It's huge.'

'Quite,' Adam replied.

'Ah.'

Another half hour passed. They had rung the Home Office from one of the studios. Lizzie insisted on the call being recorded so they could prove the government had every chance to respond to the story. A high-ranking official came on the line, told them in a clipped tone that they were aware of the report *Wessex Tonight* was planning to run and were considering their response.

And that had been it. There was no response. No court orders, no denials, no rebuttals, no retaliation, no reprisals, no nothing.

Just a dense and ominous silence.

Dan sat in an edit suite with Jenny and cut the report. If he did say so himself – and he did – it was spectacular.

The only dilemma was how to begin. Dan could have told the story chronologically, starting with the pictures of the Minster in the aftermath of the bombing. But the viewers had seen them several times before and it would mean a lot of recapping before he got to the real revelations.

It was a mistake commonly made by amateur reporters.

They learned in training college that telling a story as it had happened was a safe technique, and so that was what they did for the whole of their inevitably undistinguished careers. There was always another way.

The most dramatic material was the doorstepping of the spooks and Ali's subsequent assault. If Dan wrote the newsreader's cue for the story cleverly, to explain what the viewers were about to see, he could begin with that.

He started typing. "We can reveal the British security services knew about the bombing of Wessex Minster and could have stopped it, but didn't. We have also learnt the man who carried out the attack is not dead, as the authorities had claimed, and they were prepared to allow his funeral to go ahead today with an unidentified person's body in the coffin. We broke that news to his mother earlier and confronted two FX5 agents with it. What follows in this report by our Crime Correspondent, Dan Groves, is the extraordinary result."

Jenny laid down the shot of Dan and Nigel approaching the spooks, through the trees and across the grass, the jerking of the camera adding to the drama. Dan wrote just one line to set up the confrontation. The images alone told the story beautifully.

'These are the secret service agents responsible for allowing the attack on Wessex Minster to go ahead.'

They let the sequence run, Dan's shouted questions, the spies' refusal to answer and then Oscar raising his fist.

Now time for one more line to explain what was about to happen.

'John Tanton's mother Ali had been watching this, and then joined in – forcefully.'

They added the sequence of her attacking Oscar. The thudding noise of the impact of her bag against his skull made Jenny recoil.

Then it was a couple of shots of the spy lying on the ground, dazed and bleeding. Dan tried not to enjoy them, but utterly failed. *Wessex Tonight* wouldn't normally show such violence, but in this case it was justified. It was the honest reaction of a woman who had suffered a grievous wrong. To alert anyone who might be upset, or to give them time to stop any children watching, Dan added a final line to the newsreader's cue.

"The report contains violent scenes which some viewers might find distressing."

Far from putting people off, it was generally accepted in the news trade that such warnings only served to make the audience watch more closely.

After the attack on Oscar came Ali's interview. Then Dan recapped on the story, using the pictures of the damaged Minster to talk about how much the spies knew of the plot and how easily they could have stopped it. He signed off by saying that despite repeated requests, there had been no comment from the government.

The edit suite door opened and Lizzie strode in. She had been pacing the corridor the whole time. 'Still no word from the Home Office,' she said. 'They're up to something, But the lawyers are on standby, ready for them.'

Jenny played the report. Lizzie watched in silence, her eyebrow rising into an arch.

'Not bad,' she concluded.

Dan sighed. The era of unqualified praise had clearly passed. It was briefer than an electron's orbit of an atom and was anyway probably just a moment of weakness, never to be repeated. Normality had returned.

'So, what now?'

A stiletto heel ground into the carpet. 'Now, we wait.'

The clock on the wall said it was half past five.

One hour to go.

A newsroom has a distinctive atmosphere when a big story is unfolding. Normally sedentary creatures, hacks abandon their chairs, instead stand, watching the bank of TV monitors, or the news wires flashing up on their computers. The usual hum of conversation quietens, even the shouted requests and instructions abate. All watch and all wait.

In this case though, they had no idea what they were expecting. It was a unique and unnerving situation, like being under siege from an enemy they knew was out there somewhere, but couldn't see.

The newsroom clock ticked around to a quarter to six.

Lizzie was staring out of the window. 'What the hell are they up to?' she barked. 'I was sure we'd have heard by now.'

'They're planning something,' Dan replied. 'I reckon we'll hear any minute.'

'How do you know?'

'Sources.'

'What sources?'

'Just sources.'

She flicked her hair and turned back to the window. Dan debated whether to tell Lizzie about the call from Claire, just a couple of minutes ago. She was whispering, and Dan had to retreat to a corner of the newsroom and clamp the phone to his ear to hear.

'Why are you speaking so quietly?' he asked.

'I'm in the loos.'

'What is it?'

'Something's happening. The spies have commandeered a load of cops. They're waiting in the car park.'

'What for?'

'They won't say. Just that they're going on some kind of operation.' She hesitated, then added, 'They're after you, aren't they?'

'I think you might be right.'

'Dan.'

'Yes?'

'Just be careful, will you? You're dealing with some really nasty people. They're not like anyone you've ever gone up against before.'

Dan gulped. 'Don't worry. I'll be fine.'

He wondered if the words had ever sounded more hollow.

'I've got to go, someone's coming,' she whispered urgently. 'Just call me later, to let me know you're OK?'

'I will.'

'And if you need me to come round I'd love to see you. Take care of yourself. I still need you.'

Dan got himself a cup of water from the dispenser. It

bubbled and churned. His throat felt very dry. He sat down by Lizzie's desk, then got up again. He tried looking through a couple of newspapers, but the words made no sense. Instead, he paced over to the map of Devon and Cornwall on the wall and tried to imagine a new Dartmoor walk to take Rutherford on. Nothing stuck in his mind.

Ten to six.

'What the hell are they up to?' Lizzie said again.

'Leaving it to the last minute,' Dan replied. 'Standard tactics. If they've got some kind of injunction, we won't have a chance to get it lifted in time for the programme.'

His mobile warbled with a text. Dan was expecting a message from Claire, or Adam, but it was Sarah.

The tiger is growing RAVENOUS. Come feed her soon, big boy. xxx

Her timing wasn't the greatest. First an attempted tryst at a vet's surgery, now this. Dan deleted the message. With all that was happening, his libido had gone missing, presumed lost.

He walked over to Lizzie at the window. 'What are you expecting?' he asked. 'Storm troops?'

'Something like that.'

He sat on the edge of a desk, got up again, itched tetchily at his back and had another cup of water. Half of it was discarded into the pot plants which lined one side of the newsroom. A growing stain of dampness seeped across the carpet tiles.

A door banged. They all turned. It was just one of the cleaners, carrying a couple of rubbish sacks.

Five to six.

A phone rang. One of the newsroom assistants answered.

It was a report of the London to Plymouth train running twelve minutes late. A signalling fault.

Dan swung a leg back and forth. He could do with some new shoes. These were getting scuffed and the colder days were coming on.

He wondered if Claire would be around to help warm them. It was strange how the winters they spent together had never

305

felt cold.

A fax whined and began disgorging a sheet of paper. A couple of journalists paced over, bent down and studied the lines of print.

It was a long range weather report.

Almost six o'clock. The sun was dipping in the western sky.

Lizzie's voice. 'Dan. Dan!'

'What?'

'Come here.'

He joined her at the window once more. She was pointing along the road outside the studios. The trees were lit with flashes of blue.

Through a break in the foliage they could see a police car, then another. Now a police van, a motorcycle, and a large, black jeep.

The convoy was moving fast, cutting easily through the traffic.

It was heading for the *Wessex Tonight* building.

Chapter Twenty-nine

LIZZIE HAD MANY FAULTS, in Dan's humble view, but in fairness she had quite a few assets too. She wasn't one of the all too many editors who were mere wage disciples, would only ever play it safe, uncontroversial and bland. She hadn't become institutionalised, knew a story, and she would fight to get it.

And she was never, ever, one to shy away from a confrontation.

Within seconds, she was standing in the arch of the studios' front entrance, watching the police cars, vans and motorbikes park. Her arms were folded, her thin lips set and a stiletto was already grinding hard at the paving stones.

Dan almost felt sorry for the spies. Oscar had already suffered a couple of nasty wounds and now was about to experience the tempest of his editor's wrath.

He should at least return to London disabused of the notion that Devon was strictly a quiet and placid place.

On the way downstairs, Lizzie grabbed the lawyer, a reedy, middle-aged man called Tipper, who always smelt faintly of pipe smoke. She said nothing to Dan, just beckoned, which he assumed was his invitation to join the battle. And she had also pulled a masterstroke, using one of the very few weapons they had.

Alongside them in the archway stood Nigel, camera upon his shoulder. He was filming the convoy's arrival and under instructions to record everything that came to pass.

As they stood awaiting the full vengeance of the state, Dan had a brief thought that they must be one of the most unlikely posses of outlaws the history of crime had ever seen. A dishevelled-looking TV reporter, his bristling and defiant editor, a crusty, bespectacled lawyer wearing a suit that fashion had long forgotten, and a kindly cameraman in a faded pullover.

Dan forced himself to stand still and copied Lizzie's lead in folding his arms. It looked good, and besides, it disguised the shaking of his hands.

It was clear the police officers didn't quite know how to go about this raid. It could hardly have been like any they'd joined before. There was no leaping from cars, running headlong into a building, no doors to smash down, no drug dens to uncover, no thugs to wrestle. They just milled around, looking towards the final vehicle in the convoy, the black jeep with the tinted windows.

The doors opened and Sierra and Oscar got out. Dan was gratified to see a large plaster above his left eye.

Nigel panned the camera as the pair walked towards the entrance, then slowly up the steps. The police officers spread out behind them. Dan recognised a couple from a previous case and nodded. One shrugged in response.

Sierra walked up to Lizzie. She angled her head, but otherwise didn't move.

Nigel shifted a little to get a close-up. The women stared at each other, two generals heading their own armies, each strong with the righteousness of their cause, finally meeting in the long anticipated showdown.

Philosophers might just have been getting an answer to the old question of what happens when an irresistible force meets an immovable object.

'I have a warrant here for your arrest,' Sierra said at last. She produced a piece of paper. 'We will also be arresting a member of your staff, a reporter called Groves. Him, I believe.'

She pointed to Dan. He felt a lurch in his stomach, but managed not to react, just kept still with his arms folded.

'Finally,' she added, 'we have authorisation to search your building and to seize materials which may endanger national security.'

'On whose authority?' Lizzie asked.

'The Home Secretary and a High Court judge.'

Tipper held out his hand. 'If I may see the warrant?'

Sierra passed it over and he studied the sheets of paper.

'I will be applying urgently to a judge to have this overturned,' he said.

'That is your right,' she replied calmly. 'But you accept it is in order?'

'It appears so.'

'Then step aside and let us in.'

'A word first with my clients.'

'Make it quick. No stalling.'

Tipper ignored her and retreated into the lobby with Lizzie. Dan followed. He noticed all the windows of the building were filled with the faces of staff. Most looked genuinely alarmed.

What was unfolding in the car park of a small regional television station in the liberal democracy of a free society felt akin to the stories of the worst repressions of Soviet times.

'You have little choice,' Tipper was saying. 'That warrant is as draconian as I have ever seen. If you try to resist, they can arrest everyone, take the programme off air and even have you closed down.'

'Can you fight it?' Lizzie asked. 'On public interest grounds? You must be able to, given what we know.'

'We can try. But I doubt it. Sad as it may be, the law no longer takes a great deal of notice of a public interest defence. And anyway, it will take time. For now, my professional advice has to be to pull the broadcast of your story and cooperate. Hand over all that they ask for. If you don't, they will simply rip the place apart and take anything they want.'

Lizzie swore, then said, 'Will we ever get to broadcast this story?'

Tipper took off his glasses and polished them on his tie. 'In my considered opinion – unlikely at best.'

Lizzie stared down at the ground for a moment. When she looked back up, Dan could have sworn her eyes were shining. 'Let the bastards in then,' she said, in a strangled voice.

She walked over to reception and took the tannoy.

'All staff, this is an urgent message. We are being raided by the police. I instruct you to cooperate and hand over any materials that they request.'

Police officers were marching past her, up the stairs towards the newsroom, their heavy feet pounding in the old Victorian hallway. Portraits of present and past newsreaders and editors looked down upon them.

'I'm proud of what we have tried to do,' Lizzie added. 'And I never thought I would see this day. But know this, all of you. I believe we were right in what we attempted to reveal. We will try to find a way to fight this. But for now, the fight is over.'

Sierra walked in, followed by Oscar. He was clapping sarcastically.

'Beautiful,' he sneered. 'I'm so moved.'

'Proud of your police state, are you?' she snapped.

'Without people like me, you wouldn't have any of the freedoms you're so happy to spout on about,' he retorted.

Oscar stopped next to Dan and leaned forward, right into his face.

'I'm going to arrest you myself,' he said quietly. 'But not just yet. You can watch us carry away your precious little scoop first. You'll never see it again. It'll all be safely buried, like so many things we've done.'

Dan desperately searched his wits for some killing put-down, the hero's brilliant rejoinder so beloved of the scriptwriters, but nothing came to mind. Suddenly he felt very tired, and not in the least heroic. All his efforts, all he had tried to do to expose the truth was going to be futile.

He could taste the seeping rancour of defeat.

'Yeah? We'll see,' was all Dan could manage.

Oscar's smirk grew. 'We don't have to wait to see. I'll tell you how this finishes. We always win in the end. Now you stand there, like a good little boy, watch us tear the place apart and then I'll take you away too.'

He raised his hand and gave Dan's cheek a couple of lazy slaps.

It was only a gesture, a symbol of victory. It hardly stung, barely even smarted.

But it was enough.

Dan bowed his head and let out a low whimper.

Oscar bent forwards to maximise the enjoyment of his gloating, just as Dan suspected he would.

'What's the matter?' the spy cooed. 'Going to have a little cry are we? You poor, poor …'

He got no further. The knee Dan propelled into his stomach made sure of that.

He was away, running, down the corridor towards the canteen. Behind came a volley of shouts and drumming feet. They were close, they were younger and they were fit. He didn't have long.

Dan tried to calm his racing mind and think clearly. What the hell was he doing? He'd just assaulted a spy. That was resisting arrest. Now he was trying to get away, from two spooks and a whole load of cops.

He was a fugitive.

For the first time in his mostly law-abiding life, Dan was on the run.

And wow, it felt strangely good.

Or that might have been the memory of the force of his flying knee in the softness of Oscar's stomach. The spy crumpling to the floor. Again.

It was only fair. Adam had laid him out, as had Ali Tanton. Dan was just taking his turn.

As the old saying goes, all good things come in threes.

He almost grinned. But he was too busy running.

What was he thinking about? It must be the adrenaline, the tiredness, the sudden rush of the chase making him light-headed. He had to have a plan.

The pounding feet were growing close. He risked a glance behind. Ten yards grace, no more. They would soon be upon him. The gang of cops was tumbling up the narrow corridor. Past the door to engineering. Past a management office.

The tannoy crackled. Lizzie's voice. 'Dan, what the hell are you doing? I told you to help them, not hit them. Give yourself up!'

She didn't sound in the least sincere. He'd always wondered what Lizzie really thought of him. Now Dan imagined how her opinion would change, given what they had gone through in the last few minutes.

The reporter who assaulted a spy.

It sounded good.

If he still was a reporter. If he still was anything. If he ever escaped a prison cell and saw the sky again.

Still, it would be something to tell El over a beer or two.

El!

That was what he had to do. They would be expecting him to head upstairs, to the newsroom. To try to grab the tapes on which the whole story was recorded. But all he needed was a few seconds to call Dirty El.

Voices behind, shouting, "Stop! Police! Stop!"

No chance. Dan was enjoying himself.

He risked another glance back. The cops were only five yards behind. And he was tiring, panting hard, his chest hollow with the effort of the chase. They were almost upon him. He had to find more time.

Ahead were the stairs up to the newsroom. No go, it would be swarming with cops, searching for the material on the bombing. There was the door to the studio. No use, a dead end. And there was the door leading to the garden.

It had a security lock. Needed a pass card.

Which he had. And which the cops didn't.

Dan forced his weary legs into one last lunging sprint. He fumbled the card from his jacket pocket and waved it at the reader. It bleeped. The little green light blinked on.

He fell through the door and slammed it shut behind him.

Just in time. The squad of police officers piled into it, but the door didn't move.

Angry faces were staring at him through the glass, palms slapping, hands gesturing, mouths shouting.

But the door was good. It was strong. It held. What a beautiful door.

From now on, every time Dan used it, he would give it an appreciative pat.

He gulped in a couple of breaths of air. He felt the sunshine on his back. He was outside.

The fugitive was leading the law a merry dance. And he needed only a few more seconds.

It was just a shame he would be spending the evening in the cells. He could have taken Rutherford for a short walk, to start his recuperation. Another kind autumn evening was in prospect.

Dan wondered who would look after the dog while he was in prison. Claire, it had to be. There was no one else. She would take care of Rutherford and come and visit his master. He would need something to look forward to, to get him through his sentence.

Dan wondered how long he would be locked up for. No more than a couple of years, surely. Some killers got less.

But it still felt an awfully long time. Two warm summers, two rejuvenating springs, two golden autumns, two crisp winters.

And no beer at all. And no walking his beloved dog.

Dan blinked hard. The battle was lost, but the war was yet his to win. And he had just one chance to do it.

He had to shake off this bizarre sense of unreality and concentrate. Get moving and get working.

Dan turned from the door.

Straight into Oscar.

'Evening again,' he said, spinning Dan around, slamming him into the wall, grabbing his arm and locking it behind his back. 'Not quite as smart as you think you are, eh? I reckoned you might double around on yourself. Now, let's have a little walk back to reception so we can do the formal arresting you bit. I'm looking forward to it no end.'

Chapter Thirty

BLOOD WAS SEEPING ONTO Dan's tongue, its acrid taste making him grimace. There was quite a gash on the inside of his mouth and he wondered if the impact with the wall might have chipped a tooth as well. He let Oscar push him back towards the front of the building, his arm still held in a painfully enthusiastic lock.

'Don't try anything,' the spy said. 'It'd be the work of a second to break your arm.'

Dan didn't bother replying. He knew Oscar meant it. And he didn't have the strength.

The spy shoved him up the steps and into reception. Nigel and Lizzie stood up from their chairs. The expressions on their faces said he wasn't looking his best.

'Dan, are you OK?' Lizzie asked.

'Just about.'

'What were you doing, trying to run off? You idiot.'

She sounded oddly proud. It was all he could do not to cuddle into her and ask for a hug.

Oscar pushed him down onto a chair. 'Sit,' he commanded, as though to a dog. 'There's a good boy.'

Dan felt more drops of warm blood dripping onto his tongue. 'Can I get some water for my mouth?'

'No. We'll be taking you away in a minute. They'll check you over back at Charles Cross.'

'But it hurts.'

'It hurts, it hurts,' the spy mocked. 'You don't know what pain is.' He tapped the ribbon of the scar on his neck. 'That's real suffering. So don't bleat to me about your poorly little mouth.'

He started to recite the words of the caution. Dan hardly heard. He sat back on the chair and closed his eyes. He felt like curling up into a ball and drifting off to sleep. Only the stabbing, stinging pain from his mouth was keeping him awake. He worried at a tooth with his tongue. It felt loose.

314

'Do you understand?' Oscar was shouting at him. 'I said, do you understand that you have been arrested and are now under caution? Acknowledge me!'

'Yes. I understand.'

Dan massaged his temples, rubbed at his mouth and winced with the pain. His cheek was grazed too. He could feel the grit of the building's stonework in the gash. He considered standing up to look in a mirror, but thought better of it. Some sights are better not seen.

In the corner of reception, Oscar and Sierra were talking quietly. Dan wondered whether he could make another run for it, but dismissed the idea as it formed. A couple of police officers were standing by the doors. They looked sharp and alert. And he didn't have the energy to do anything except sit and submit.

They had lost. It was as simple as that. The time had come to accept it.

A line of cops walked carefully down the stairs. They were carrying boxes, filled with video tapes, scripts and running orders for the programme.

Lizzie watched, her face taut. 'Who ever thought we would see the day? A raid on a news programme because it was about to expose a scandal.'

Outside, police officers were loading the boxes into a van. A couple lit up cigarettes and stood blowing smoke into the air. Nigel reached out a hand and patted Dan's shoulder. He nodded his appreciation, but couldn't find any words to say.

It was half past six. Usually the building would be buzzing as journalists ran around, checking the details of late stories for the programme. But not tonight. There was only a silence.

On the television in the corner of reception, a test card read,

Wessex Tonight would like to apologise for the loss of this evening's news. This is due to technical problems.

If only the public knew.

But they never would. All the evidence was about to disappear in a police van, doubtless never to be seen again.

They were bound up tight in the unyielding fetters of the law, unable to reveal all that they had discovered.

More blood seeped around Dan's mouth. He gulped hard, swallowed it and almost retched. A shock of nausea jarred his body.

And the memory returned.

'Right,' Sierra said, walking over to Dan and Lizzie. 'I think that concludes our business here. Now it's time to get you two to the station.'

Lizzie got up, but Dan remained sitting.

'Come on then,' Oscar grunted. 'On your feet. Unless you want to try resisting arrest again?'

Dan quickly rose too, but didn't make towards the door. The spy beckoned. 'Come on. You can walk. I'm not helping you down the steps like some little old retard.'

Still, Dan didn't move. 'Come on,' Oscar repeated impatiently. 'Get moving. Or shall I give you some more of my special help?'

Dan took a deep breath and found what little was left of his courage. He rubbed at his cheek, then squeezed the gash inside his mouth.

Fresh blood spurted onto his tongue. It was sticky, hot and sickening. Dan gagged, then retched. He felt the vomit eject from his body in a series of shocking spasms.

And some he managed to spray onto Oscar.

'Jesus,' the man yelled. 'For fuck's sake!'

Dan turned and lurched towards the toilets by the side of reception. Oscar kicked out, but missed him. He followed, hurling abuse. A pot plant went spinning across the carpet tiles, shedding dry soil.

Dan felt his stomach heave again. He flung the door open. It slammed against the wall and juddered back and forth. He tried to stem the flow of sickness with a hand, bent over the toilet and threw up once more.

The spy was behind, standing over him. 'You're pathetic,' he grunted. 'You make me want to puke myself. See what you've done. These trousers cost me hundreds.'

Dan looked up. Oscar's shoes and knees were spattered with sick. The smell was giddying, vile. But he was still standing there, glaring down.

It was wretched, but he had to do it. Dan closed his eyes, looked as pitiful as he knew how, and forced some of the sickness from his mouth, letting it dribble slowly down his chin.

'Urch,' Oscar groaned. 'You disgusting piece of shit. Finish your foul puking and let's go.'

At last, the spy turned away. Dan quickly fumbled the mobile from his jacket pocket, shielded it from Oscar in case he looked back and found El's name.

He retched again, coughed and gasped to cover any noise from the phone, rang the number and hid the mobile away once more.

Dan gave it a few seconds, then slapped theatrically at the wall and wailed loudly, 'Why did you spies have to come here to our studios? Why raid us? Why bring all these cops? Why arrest me? Why seize all the material on the Minster bombing? Why did FX5 have to let Tanton do it, when you could have stopped him? And do you really think you'll get away with trying to cover it all up?'

Oscar turned back and swore again. 'Going to cry are you, wanker?'

'No. Never. Even though you're going to take me to the cells right now and interrogate me.'

Oscar grabbed for him again. 'Come on you shitty little creature,' he said. 'Let's get going.'

Ten minutes, Dan estimated. He had to find ten minutes. More if possible, but ten at least.

He rested his head against the toilet. It was smooth and cool, felt good and calming.

Oscar was prodding at Dan's body with a foot. 'Come on. I've had enough of your arsing about. I want to get you in the cells and get back to my hotel so I can have a good dinner.'

A hand reached for the scruff of Dan's jacket and pulled at it.

He tried to summon up more vomit to force Oscar away.

Dan bit again at the gash in his mouth, felt the blood flow and his stomach turn, but there was no sickness left to come. All he could taste was bile.

He leaned over the toilet, retched hard, then began gasping, panting for the air.

The cubicle smelt noxious, the cramped space filled with a revolting mix of Dan's own vomit and the hint of bleach. He saw a memory of teenage years, a sixth form disco, his first overdose on drink and the wretched consequences in the cold darkness of the school toilet.

Oscar was pulling hard, forcing Dan onto his knees. He staggered, then flopped down again.

'I said, come on you stinking little shit,' Oscar threatened.

'I can't. My legs won't move.'

'I said – come on!'

The spy gave a mighty yank on Dan's jacket. There was a ripping sound as a seam split.

'Even your bloody clothes are cheap,' Oscar grunted. 'Now – come on.'

Dan tried to slap away the man's hand, but he was too weak. He was rewarded with a kick in the ribs. It wasn't hard, but it was enough to play upon.

A hollow groan faltered from his mouth and he slumped back onto the floor. Dan vaguely noticed how dirty it was. If he ever came back here, worked as a journalist again, he would mention it to Lizzie. It created a bad impression for visitors.

The mental countdown kept running.

That hand again, pulling hard at his jacket.

'If you don't get up, I'm going to have you carried out. In front of all your little friends. So they can see you for what you are. A despicable piece of shit.'

Dan staggered to his knees, but stayed there, bent over, panting hard.

'Just give me a minute. My head's spinning.'

'You think this is bad? You wait until I've finished questioning you.'

'I'm almost ready. Nearly OK.'

'Not trying to stall, are you? No one's coming to help, you

318

know. It's all over.'

Dan managed not to react, kept his eyes set low on the wall. There was another sharp tug at his jacket. 'Come on!'

Seven minutes, or so. But Oscar was growing ever more impatient. He couldn't eke it out much longer.

Dan creased up his face and began to cry. First a snivel, growing to gulps, then tears, tickling the dry sweat on his face.

'For fuck's sake,' Oscar barked. 'You pathetic, useless piece of shit. Stop your bleating and move!'

A voice in the doorway. Nigel's, loud and protesting. 'What the hell do you think you're doing? Look at the state of the poor man.'

'Get out of here.'

'Where the hell's your humanity?'

'I had it surgically removed when I joined FX5. Now fuck off, or you get arrested too.'

Dan looked up and wiped at his eyes. He could see Nigel being led away by Sierra, his face full of concern.

But his friend's intervention was more precious than he could know. He had used up a little extra time.

'Last chance,' Oscar was saying. 'Up now, or you get carried. And not gently.'

Dan nodded, gripped the side of the toilet and levered himself up. He reached for the wash basin and placed a hand on the tap.

'Just let me get some of this sick off my face.'

'No. We're going. Now. Start moving.'

'But it's disgusting.'

'I don't care. It's your own puke. Live with it. Get shifting.'

Oscar took a step forwards and reached for Dan's shoulder.

'OK, OK,' he said, holding up his hands in submission.

Five minutes. He had to find just five little minutes. It was nothing, the time it took to make a cup of tea, to brush his teeth, to idle away some passing thoughts while watching the world from a window.

Five tiny, insignificant minutes.

But there was nowhere else to go. No other games to play. All the possible procrastinations had been spun out.

Four large policemen were waiting in reception. Oscar was beckoning to them.

'I've had enough fucking around. Haul him out.'

The officers began moving forwards. Oscar stood back to let them pass.

Dan steadied himself. He thought about Rutherford, the dog comatose on that cold slab of a table after being poisoned. Ali Tanton and her son, the other people killed and injured in the Minster bombing.

And the spies complicit in it all.

The cops were almost upon him. Reaching out their burly arms.

Dan could see the toilet on the edge of his vision.

He took a step, felt his knees buckle and his body collapse. He was falling through the air, closing his eyes, ready for the impact.

The hard, white rim caught the side of his head and all the world blinked into blackness.

Chapter Thirty-one

DREAMS ARE GREAT. DAN had always thought so. Some wonderful things happened to him in the travels of the night, and, unlike many people, come the morning he usually remembered what they were.

Some could keep him grinning for much of the day.

He only tended to have one nightmare, a recurring theme of being in an exam hall, turning over the paper and finding he couldn't answer any of the questions. There was a variation too, in that sometimes he would be *sans* trousers. Dan occasionally wondered if it was a metaphor for his life, but was reassured after reading in a weekend paper that it was a common spectre. Apparently it was to do with unpreparedness and the traumatic effect of exams and often stayed with many people for the whole of their days.

So, in at least one aspect of life he was relatively normal. Dan found that oddly comforting.

His enjoyable visions were far more ranging, from the standard sunshine days of simplicity on Dartmoor with Rutherford, to being the superhero captain of a spaceship. He would defeat the hordes of evil aliens and save the human race on a daily basis, and with such audacious panache that it could have been part of the job description.

He tended to gloss over the interpretation of that one. Dan knew from unpleasant experience that some of the avenues of his mind were best left unexplored.

But of these particular dreams, whether it was because they were enforced by unconsciousness, or just that his brain needed a break after the shocks and stresses of the last few days, Dan had no memory. There was only blankness, a void, a time when he was unaware even of being alive.

And when he did finally come around, Dan had to wonder whether he was still in that happy land of fantasies. Because he was being applauded.

And in Dan's experience of the real world, that never

happened.

He blinked hard, was aware of some surprised sighing and muttered conversation, a couple of whispered voices, growing louder, filling with excitement. There were colours too. They were dancing, shifting, like a kaleidoscope in his eyes. Now shapes were forming. An oblong, filled with streaming light.

A window. Dan thought he remembered that was the correct technical term.

Now a square, a screen with black surrounding it. A television. Some brown wood, tall and patterned. A wardrobe. A cylinder, with protruding flowers – a vase. A green and grey twisted thing which might have been art.

And two ovals. Pale coloured. One topped with darkness, the other more straw. Looming closer.

Faces! That's what they were. Familiar faces. And they were smiling.

Both were moving very close now. They were still clapping. And they were pushing parts of their faces onto his.

Kissing. It was called kissing. This seemed pleasant.

Perhaps he was still dreaming. Kissing and applause from two women at once.

It did feel like a familiar fantasy.

Now sound. Soft, and rhythmic. Coaxing. Speech! The faces were talking to him.

'Dan! You're awake! You're back with us!'

Apparently this wasn't a dream.

He raised a hand. He had to concentrate and it felt heavy and shaky, but it moved mostly fine under his control. He waved it and found another hand reaching out to take it, squeezing his palm.

The two faces were talking to each other. The older one was saying, 'Do you want me to leave you alone for a while?'

'No,' the other replied. 'Not at all. You've stayed by him the whole time. Don't leave now. Besides, I think he's going to need both of us to tell him everything that's happened.'

Dan wondered what they were talking about. But the younger face was still smiling and holding his hand, so it couldn't be all bad.

The focus was coming back to his eyes. The younger face was very pretty. Lovely dark hair too, just what he suspected he remembered was his type.

He thought he might try a little charm when the power of speech decided to grace him with its return. She probably had a boyfriend, but he'd give it a go anyway.

Perhaps he'd tell her a story. He had plenty of good tales. Dan vaguely recalled that telling stories had always been a part of his life. He might even have been paid for it once. Something called a job.

And what a ridiculous job it would be. Being paid for telling stories!

The older of the two faces was talking to him. She was pretty too, although she looked tired and sad. She was asking how he was.

It was a cue for some of that famous charm. Dan wanted to wink and say "How do you think I am with a beautiful woman either side of me?", but the words were reluctant to form. So he favoured her with his best smile instead.

Now something less good was happening. The smile brought with it a pain. He ran his tongue around his mouth. It was swollen and it stung. How did that happen?

Come to that, another pain had arrived. It must have decided to join its friend. Sociable creatures, pains. They seldom called alone, annoyingly. But this one was in his head. It was coming from the side, a dull, drumming thud.

Dan raised his hand to its source and was surprised to find some thick padding. He poked at it and was rewarded with an enthusiastic stab of discomfort.

It was clear this particular pain wanted to be left alone.

He decided to concentrate on other matters. He could come back to the pain later. It didn't feel like it was going anywhere fast.

The room was interesting. It was very white. And it smelt funny. Not just clean, in a way his flat rarely did, but more than that.

Antiseptic. That was it.

A hospital! He was in a hospital. Ah, now he understood.

He must have had an accident. Probably a car crash. Nigel was always telling him to drive more carefully. Well, at least he had survived, albeit with a couple of injuries. He hoped no one else had been hurt.

And then it came back. All and everything. In the rush of a second's realisation.

Dan gasped and sat up in the bed. Gentle hands immediately started easing him back down.

'I've remembered,' he stammered. 'The bombing. The cover up. Trying to expose it. What happened? How did it all end?'

The two faces were still smiling, but more broadly now.

'Just take it easy,' the dark-haired one said. 'It all worked out.'

They exchanged a look and the other face added, 'I suppose we'd better tell you what happened.'

Dan had been unconscious for two days. And what a time he'd missed.

He hadn't judged the crack on his skull quite right. In fact, he had come close to getting it terminally wrong. Instead of a glancing blow, one which would leave him incapacitated for perhaps twenty minutes or so, he'd managed to deliver a full and stunning impact to a particularly sensitive area of his skull.

A white-coated and ridiculously young doctor breezed into the room, fussed around, checked his bandage and made no attempt whatsoever to welcome Dan back to the world. Instead, she delivered a scolding when he admitted to inflicting the injury deliberately.

'You were very lucky,' she said, wagging a finger. 'You could have fractured your skull, if not worse. It's a good job you've got a thick head and a less than sensitive brain.'

She was out of the door again before Dan could thank her for the pastoral care and kind words.

The spies had been forced to call an ambulance, just as Dan had hoped. But instead of a few minutes delay it had been more like half an hour as the paramedics checked and stabilised him. Dan was taken to hospital, and there remained oblivious to the extraordinary events unfolding outside of his little white room. Claire and Ali had taken turns to sit by his bedside.

El had plenty of time to go about his work. He would have heard Dan's blubbing in the toilets via the phone, realised what was happening and scrambled to the studios. There, he hid himself, but took snaps aplenty of the police in the car park, the van full of tapes, papers and running orders, and most importantly, the two spies.

Most of this Dan was imagining. But he knew El well enough to guess that was precisely what he did. And he had some good evidence for the assumption. Because on his bed was a spread of national newspapers, and the headlines were breathtaking.

THE GOVERNMENT'S BOMBING
FX5 IN STATE-SPONSORED BOMBING COVER-UP
THE SPIES WHO BOMB THEIR OWN
HOME SECRETARY TO MAKE STATEMENT ON TERRORIST BOMB COVER-UP

The pages were accompanied by photographs of the police raid on *Wessex Tonight*, and close-ups of Oscar and Sierra.

'Ooh,' was all Dan could find to say. 'Was that me?'

Claire folded her arms. 'We assume so. Would you care to explain how you made all this happen, despite being unconscious?'

Dan noticed his face was forming into a smile. 'I've no idea. But perhaps I could hazard a guess – hypothetically, of course. First though, tell me a little more about what's been happening while I've been on my holiday from the world.'

If Dan had one complaint, it was that he hadn't been there to see it all.

He imagined it as a great party which he had organised, one of the finest the country had ever seen. Everyone was invited, the entertainments were wonderful, the twists and turns of the event thrilling. It would go down in history and be something the population talked about for years to come.

And he was the only one not to make it along.

El had all the pictures he needed and the information too. From his guardian angel's work, shadowing Dan to see who was following his friend, to the detailed briefings he'd been given on how the case was progressing. Just in case Dan disappeared, or was somehow silenced, as he suspected might happen, to that final call from the toilets, Dan had kept the photographer up to date with every development.

El knew about the raid on *Wessex Tonight*, the arrests, the using of John Tanton and the attempted cover-up. He knew everything about what the spies had done. He had the pictures to prove it. The only problem was bringing it all to public attention.

And it was a big one.

None of the mainstream media would have a chance of airing the scandal. Like *Wessex Tonight*, they too would be silenced in an instant by the crushing boot of the government and the legal system. So, there was only one way.

It had long been a maxim of Dan's that if you couldn't win by the rules, that left only one option – to change them. And that required two unlikely saviours for the cause of truth.

Dan had taken a very deep breath, drunk a couple of fortifying beers, steeled himself and let the Geeks in on the secret of what was happening. For once, there was no squealing, not even any spinning on chairs or high-fives, only a nonplussed silence.

Inevitably, it didn't last long. Not only did they embrace the idea of exposing the scandal and getting one over on the establishment, they delighted in it. And they improvised a far better plan than Dan could ever have managed alone.

His original idea was to set up a website detailing what the spies had done.

'Can you do that in a way which'll make it impossible to trace back to you?' Dan asked. 'And difficult for them to close down?'

He was rewarded with two sets of excited emanations, noises like fireworks ascending into the sky.

'I take it that means yes?' Dan asked, when he had lost patience with the show.

'Easy peasy, chilli and cream,' came the delighted, if puzzling response. 'We'll just get our cyberpals to help and have it hosted somewhere miles out of their clutches. Russia's a good one. Or some commie nation somewhere. That always annoys the Brit cops. It's a cinch to do.'

Dan briefed them on what he needed for the content of the site. He also introduced them to El, who would be providing the pictures and more material if something should happen to Dan. He expected the photographer to find the Geeks unsettling, but El wasn't at all bothered by them, even showing some interest in a new website they were designing to make internet gaming easier.

Forget opposites, it was more a fact that oddballs attract. And here, in this dark and musty room, they had three of the finest specimens on the planet.

Dan didn't stop to wonder where he would rank in that particular chart.

He was about to leave, when the creature known as Flash squealed, 'Hey, hey, hang on Dan, Dan, the TV man.'

He grimaced, but waited.

'A website's cool for starters, but it won't do what you want alone, will it Gordon?'

'No way, Jose,' shrieked Geek Two. 'There's too many of the little fellas out there. It's like fish in the ocean. There's tonnes of them swimming around. You've gotta make your little tiddler a big whale.'

Dan sighed. 'In English? Meaning?'

'Meaning, your plan is to make your naughty little scandal so well known they can't cover it up no more?'

'Yep.'

'Then we gotta work at it. We gotta make it jive. But don't worry. I think we have a little ideary-poo.'

'A what?'

'Don't worry, Dan, Dan the TV man. Just leave it to us. We're going surfing in cyberspace.'

A spin on the stools and a high-five sealed their plan. And

more they would not say.

But the Geeks had been as good as their word, if not very much better.

El must have taken his photos from the raid straight to the Geeks, along with the latest information on what happened. They had added it all to the website they'd set up, and published it.

But, as Flash and Gordon had so very eloquently squealed, that alone was nowhere near enough. So they had gone about turning their tiny twinkle in cyberspace into a shining star.

First, they had set up a large number of duplicate sites, with similar names, to attract more attention. But even that wasn't sufficient for a real flare of interest. So the Geeks had gone viral.

El explained their plan in one of the final briefings Dan gave him. It wasn't exactly clear how it would work, probably because neither El, nor Dan, truly understood. But, in essence, it took advantage of the prevalence of mobile phones, email and the internet to spread word of the scandal.

First, the Geeks had set up a program to send out many millions of emails. They had a way to make sure they avoided spam filters, and, anyway, the title tended to demand attention. These emails got read.

"Security services cover up their role in British terror bombing. Revealed – the story they didn't want you to see."

Dan nodded his approval. He wasn't sure he could have written a better headline himself.

The emails were admirably brief, containing a short account of what the spies had done. The problem was, a reader could easily dismiss the allegations as lacking proof, the work of cranks and conspiracy addicts. And so came the Geeks masterstroke.

They had tackled the issue head on, by including a link to the website. *Click here for the pictures and evidence*, the email said. *And then forward this to everyone you know to help us expose the crimes being committed by the very people who are supposed to be protecting us.*

And the masses did. In their millions.

But the Geeks hadn't finished yet.

They set up a messaging program, to send texts to millions of mobile phones, each with a couple of lines about the scandal and also containing a link to the website.

And millions went to look. And more websites picked it up and even more people got to hear about it.

The authorities inevitably tried to shut down the sites. But there were too many, too widespread, and they were far too late. It was like trying to beat out the flames of a wildfire.

And so the story gained momentum. Until it reached the very ears Dan had hoped it would. Those of some inquisitive and troublesome MPs.

He thought he could see what happened. They had made inquiries of their contacts in the media and found that all the national papers, radio and TV stations knew about the story. All were intensely interested, but prohibited by law from reporting it.

Then came the inevitable question. Was it true?

Out went more feelers to other contacts, in the Home Office, the Security Services and the police. And the response came – off the record, naturally – that indeed it was true.

And so followed the diamond moment that the story became official, detailed in the newspapers strewn across Dan's bed. Questions are asked in the House of Commons. And because of the ancient protection of parliamentary privilege, which shields MPs and those who report on their debates from any legal action, no matter what may be discussed, the media are free to begin their coverage.

A feeding frenzy begins. Which forces the Home Office to respond. Which eventually, and very reluctantly, they do.

And the scandal fires anew.

At Dan's request, Claire turned on the television and found one of the news channels. And there the story was, the lead, covered extensively and building momentum all the time.

A political correspondent was giving details of the latest developments. The Home Office was blaming "rogue" elements within FX5. A full investigation was underway. The government would make a statement later. Two security service officers had been suspended.

The report did not name them. But Dan settled back happily on his pillows, content that he at least knew exactly who they were.

TOMORROW, LIFE WOULD START again, and, with luck, with some degree of normality, although Dan accepted that was a concept which always had, and probably always would, do its best to evade him.

He was going to be kept in hospital for another night, but come the morning Claire was picking him up. They would drive to the vet's to collect Rutherford, then back to the flat. And if both canine and human convalescents were strong enough, they would go for a little walk around the park.

To Dan, it felt like his own personal holy grail at the end of a long and arduous quest.

He lay back on the pillows and let his mind wander through the day. It was coming up to seven o'clock, the sun setting in an autumnal blaze, lighting the room with its softening fire. He had finally managed to persuade Ali and Claire that he would be fine if left alone. If anyone really wanted to harm him they would surely have done so by now, he pleaded. Dan was tired and wanted to sleep, ready to go home tomorrow.

Not that he would be allowed to recuperate in peace. Amongst a succession of visitors in the day had come Lizzie. She didn't stay long – had the programme to look after, naturally – but said she wanted to make sure he was "doing OK".

Dan noted that part of the conversation lasted for about twenty seconds. The next five minutes were taken up with demands about what story she wanted from him tomorrow. It had taken the intervention of first Claire, then Ali, and lastly the doctor before she accepted he wouldn't be going out on the road reporting for a few days. Finally, and reluctantly, she had said she would settle for his appearance live in the studio to talk about the raid on *Wessex Tonight*.

Yes, Dan thought he was up to that. She was about to leave, when he prompted, 'I thought you were brave, trying to get the story out and standing up to them in that raid.'

The hint didn't register. 'Well, it was a disgrace, what they were up to. Damned Stalinist, if you ask me.'

Dan gently, but pointedly, prodded the bandage on his head. 'Oh, and you did quite well too,' she added, letting the door shut behind her.

A loud yawn crept from Dan's mouth. He fumbled in the drawers by the bed and found the diary. Claire had brought it from the flat. She'd finally been allowed to know of its existence, but had sworn not to look inside. Dan was about to start work on this latest entry when he felt the soft pull of sleep, relaxing his body. Maybe he would leave it until tomorrow to write up the case.

Adam hadn't come to visit, but sent his apologies via Claire.

'There's a big investigation going on into all that happened,' she explained. 'It's very high level. He's tucked up in that. You'll both need to be questioned independently about what the spooks did. It can't look like you're colluding.'

Claire leaned further forwards, then added, 'But between us, he says he thinks he knows and very good work.'

'Knows what?'

'How you managed to get the story out. And he thinks it was a stroke of genius that there can't be any comeback because you were unconscious when it all happened. That's some alibi.'

Dan smiled in a way he suspected would look smug. 'What a suspicious detective's mind he has.'

They'd gone on to talk about tomorrow and picking up Rutherford.

'Why didn't you just get him and look after him yourself, rather than leaving him at the vet's?' Dan asked. 'I'm sure he'd have preferred that.'

'I wasn't sure whether you'd want me to. It felt a bit …'

'A bit what?'

'A bit presumptuous. A bit coupley.' She hesitated. 'And we're not a couple, are we?'

Dan found himself staring down at the sheets. Suddenly their blue edging was the most fascinating sight in the world.

'We'll talk about all that when I'm feeling better,' he

mumbled.

Claire went off to get herself a coffee and make a few phone calls. It was just as well she did. Only a matter of seconds after she'd left there was a knock at the door and in teetered Sarah Jones.

She rushed over to the bed, flung her arms around Dan and deluged him with kisses.

'Hello,' he managed, through a brief hiatus in the attack.

'I read about you in the papers. My poor soldier. Fighting those nasty spies. What a hero you are.'

More kisses. Lots more kisses. And a few additional ones as well. It was quite a barrage. Dan felt the lipstick adhering to his skin. Please, great God of Luck, give me a break and keep Claire busy with her calls for a few minutes. This wouldn't be a straightforward sight to explain away.

She stood back to look at him and ruffled Dan's hair. She was dressed in jeans so tight they could have been a second skin. The green top didn't allow much more leeway.

Dan let his eyelids droop. 'Thank you so much for coming in, you've made me feel a lot better,' he said, not stopping to wonder how smoothly the lies were slipping out. 'I'm sorry if I'm not up to talking much, but I had a nasty bang on the head. I feel really tired and the doctors have ordered me to rest.'

'That's all right, my little trooper. I just wanted to let you know I'm thinking about you. And that I'm looking forward to when you're feeling stronger,' she added meaningfully, running a hand over the sheets covering Dan's groin.

He put on a weak smile. 'Great. I just hope they let me out soon, then.'

'Any idea when?'

'They're not sure. Perhaps a few days.'

Sarah pouted and flicked at her flaming hair. 'Shame. The tiger's ravenous.' She took a quick look around and slid her hand over Dan's body once more. 'Are you sure you can't find a little energy now? I've never done it in a hospital.'

'I wish I could. But all I want to do is sleep.'

There was some understanding clucking, another assault of kisses and she left. Dan waited a handful of seconds, then got up and washed away the lipstick residue before Claire returned. With an afterthought he also opened a window to usher out the lingering scent of perfume.

The rest of the afternoon had passed easily. Ali Tanton visited, to tell them she had finally been allowed to see John. He was still very poorly from his injuries, but was expected to make a full recovery, apart from some scarring.

'When the story was coming out about what the spies had done, they were still trying to hush it up,' she said. 'You wouldn't believe it. They tried to bribe me by offering us both a new life in some other country. They're just incredible, these people.'

John would stand trial for murder and terrorism offences and Ali accepted that. But she was hopeful that a judge, hearing all the circumstances, would not impose too severe a sentence, leaving the young man with a hope of release and some life to look forward to.

She had also taken Dan into her confidence. 'Can you do something for me?'

'Of course.'

'Nigel asked me out for a drink. I said no – not because I don't like him, but because there's so much going on at the moment I can hardly think. Would you tell him that is the real reason and it's not just some brush-off?'

Dan promised he would, but noticed a sense of sadness at her decision. In his mind Ali and Nigel would have made an excellent couple. They both deserved happiness.

The time was coming around to half past seven. Dan checked the TV guide, but there was nothing worth seeing, as was usually the case. Besides, he didn't much care for television and rarely watched it. It was penance quite enough, working in the industry.

He took out a pen and debated what to write about the last few days. A title would be a good start. He jotted down a couple of possibilities and crossed them out again. None seemed to sum up the soul of the story.

He yawned. Maybe it was time for sleep. He could write up the case tomorrow.

The door clicked open and a man in a white coat backed in. Dan sighed and rolled his eyes. Yet another doctor, come to poke and prod him. He'd be more than glad to be out of here.

The man turned around. It was Oscar.

Dan sat up straight in the bed. He suddenly felt very much awake.

The spy held up his hands. 'I can see what you're thinking. Don't panic, I haven't come to kill you – even if I might like to.'

It wasn't the most relaxing of reassurances. 'Err, good,' Dan said. 'I'm pleased about that.' He let his hand slip through the covers and felt for the panic button beside the bed.

Oscar stood by the door. He showed no sign of wanting to move any closer.

'You can press that if you like, but then you won't hear what I've got to tell you.'

A few seconds passed. They stared at each other. Dan placed his hand back on the bed.

'OK. So – what is it that you want?'

'Can I sit down?'

'Err, sure.'

Oscar pulled up a chair and rubbed at the scar on his neck. He kept doing it, more and more agitatedly, turning the skin raw. When he finally spoke, all he said was, 'I'm not sure you deserve it, but I've come to tell you why.'

The spy sat beside Dan's bed, hunched forwards on the chair and told his story. It was clear from the look on his face and the emotion in his words that for the first time everything he said was true.

'I was in Israel, working with their security services when we got word of an imminent terrorist attack. The target was a school. We rushed out there, but it was too late. As we got to the place, there was an explosion. A suicide bomber had blown himself up amongst the kids, all milling about at the front. It was carnage.'

Oscar's voice grew softer as he spoke. Dan had to lean forward to hear the last couple of sentences.

'Have you ever seen the aftermath of a bombing?' the spy asked suddenly.

'No. Only in the Minster. And that was well after it actually happened.'

'Yeah. When it's all cleaned up. Sanitised. Well, I can tell you this – you don't forget what a bomb does in a hurry. Especially not to kids.'

Dan kept quiet and let the spy continue. He still wasn't convinced he was safe, but Oscar had made no move to threaten. There was something strange about the man. He was talking with a sense of detachment, as if he wasn't fully comprehending the words, just letting them flow. He was relating something he had witnessed, been a part of, but had somehow divorced himself from, perhaps as a way of coping.

'I'm not out of FX5 you know,' he said.

'Sorry, what?'

'Officially I've been suspended. I'll get a disciplinary. There'll be comments on my record, all that shit. I'll be found a backroom job until all this blows over. But I'm a damn good operator. I don't mind getting my hands dirty. And we've done worse before and we'll do even worse again, if it's right.'

He paused and looked Dan in the eye. 'And it was. Sometimes it's not about fighting fire with fire, but fighting dirt with filth.'

Dan didn't want to get involved in a debate. Winding up the spy struck him as an eminently bad idea.

'You were talking about Israel,' he prompted.

'Yeah.'

Oscar went quiet and rubbed at the scar again. 'Do you know how bombs kill?'

'No.'

'In a variety of ways is the answer. Sometimes the shock waves destroy your internal organs. The funny thing about that is it can look like there's not even a scratch on your body. Or they can do it in the nasty way and blow you to pieces.'

A small trickle of spittle was forming at the corner of the man's mouth and his voice was growing louder. Dan felt his hand moving back towards the panic button. He wondered just how stable Oscar was.

'This bomb did it the nasty way. It blew the kids apart. Can you imagine it? There were severed heads, rolling around on the road. Some had their eyes open, some were still smiling from the games they'd been playing. There were limbs everywhere, just ripped from their little bodies. And all this was mixed in with the satchels and packed lunches and footballs and games they'd been carrying. School books and pencil cases in the middle of the corpses of young kids. And the smell – of charred and dismembered bodies.'

Oscar stared up at the ceiling. His face was flushed, red, the worm of the scar pronounced on his neck. Dan kept his fingers by the panic button. He reckoned he could hold the man off for maybe a minute or two if he tried anything, probably just enough time for help to arrive. The spy looked manic.

'Then comes the silence,' Oscar went on finally. 'Did you know that? After a bombing there's a silence. It's one of the quirks of carnage. Just for a few seconds. People can't believe what's happened. They look around at the devastation and they can't take it in. And they're checking themselves too. To see if they've lost arms, or if they've been wounded by the shrapnel. If there's blood pouring out of them. It takes a while, you know, to register the pain. And sometimes it takes a while to die as well. A few of the kids around me were finding that out.'

He slipped back into silence. Dan said nothing, just kept his eyes on the man, ready if he should attack. Footsteps passed by the door. Dan wondered briefly about trying to call out, but decided against it.

Despite the fear, he wanted to hear what Oscar had to say.

Damn his curiosity. How many times had it lured him into trouble.

'Then came the gunfire,' the spy continued. 'As if it wasn't bad enough, the bomber's got an accomplice. He's going to finish off anyone he can find. Bullets are spraying around me. And so the screaming starts. My partner's one of the first to fall. He takes a round right in the side of the head. And he drops. There's none of this screaming and flailing around you see on the TV. No whispered last words. There's just a spurt of

337

blood and a dead man.'

Oscar rubbed hard at his scar. Dan realised he was about to find out how the spy had got it. He knew he was in danger, but he was fascinated, nonetheless.

'I must have acted instinctively. I dropped too. I was behind this car. It was pitted with shrapnel and I could see the terrorist walking towards us. He was only young, just a kid really, not much older than John Tanton. He's got an AK47 in his hand and he's spraying bullets at anyone who moves. There are badly wounded kids and their parents, lying on the pavement, trying to get away, and he's raking them with gunfire. More people are dying every minute. So I go for my gun.'

He let out a long breath, then said, 'And here's the problem. The bloody thing's jammed. Maybe it's where I've hit the ground, maybe it's the dust and smoke. And this guy's walking towards me, shooting people dead all around, and I've got no gun. And then it gets even better. I see he's got a suicide belt on too. He's going to take himself out and as many people as he can as well. And you know what? I bet you think I'm going to tell you I wasn't scared, I just did my duty. Well, that's bollocks. I was shitting myself. I was shaking and I was crying and I was saying goodbye to my wife and kids and all my family. Even spies have them, you know. I was more frightened than I'd ever been in my fucking life.'

The spy's voice was trembling now. He swallowed hard, twitched and dabbed at the sweat on his forehead.

'He was still walking towards me. I was crouched down by the car. And when he came up alongside, I leapt out. I managed to knock the gun away. And then I grabbed for his hands, to stop him detonating the belt. But the bastard was strong. They work out before they go on these missions, you know. They get trained. It's a bloody profession to them. I had hold of his hands, but I couldn't keep my grip. I just wanted the police or army to get there, to shoot the bastard. But his hand was almost on the cord. It was getting closer and closer. I couldn't stop him. I knew I was going to die. And then he pulled it and that was all I remember.'

Oscar was panting hard and scratched once more at the scar.

It was inflamed a vivid red now. He got up from the chair and pushed it away with a jarring scrape. Dan felt his body tense, but the spy didn't approach, just paced over to the sink, ran some water and splashed it onto his face.

He walked back to the door and reached for the handle.

'I was lucky,' he said. 'Only part of the bomb went off. The detonator. Hence the scar. The army arrived, shot him and got me to hospital. A few months later and I was OK. Back to work. Back to Britain. As if nothing had happened. As if ...'

Oscar opened the door, went to walk out, but hesitated. Half of his face was in shadow, half in the light.

'The ring of terrorists we were trying to break, the ones we hoped Ahmed might lead us to – before you got in the way. They're some of the worst we've ever gone up against. They want to carry out the vilest attack Britain's ever seen. A glorious atrocity to shock the world and teach the west a lesson it'll never forget.'

The spy's hand was tight on the door handle. There was one final pause and he added, 'Our intelligence says they're planning to attack a primary school.'

He stared for a second, then walked out. The door clicked closed. Dan lay back on his pillows and let out a very long breath. He noticed he was trembling. He shut his eyes and tried to stop himself thinking about what Oscar had said, but couldn't. The sterile hospital room had filled with the screams of dying children.

He got up, poured himself a glass of water, then another and gazed out of the window at the last light of the day. The sun was sinking fast now, just a red segment left lingering over the distant hills.

Dan walked back to the bed, thinking of Ahmed, John Tanton, Sierra and Oscar, the spy's story of the attack on the Israeli school, and his own role in the extraordinary events of the last few days.

He picked up the diary. He had the title now.

In an unsteady hand, Dan slowly wrote, *The Balance of Guilt.*

Also by Simon Hall

The TV Detective

Television reporter Dan Groves needs a crash-course in police work; the solution is to shadow Detective Chief Inspector Adam Breen on a high-profile murder inquiry, which doesn't go down well with some members of the police force.

The victim is a notorious local businessman, Edward Bray, a man with so many enemies that one of the problems the inquiry faces is having a surplus of suspects. Tensions abound between Dan and the police, and he comes close to being thrown off the case - until the detectives come to realise he might actually be helpful, in using the power of television to tempt the murderer into a trap…

ISBN 9781907016059
Price £6.99

The Death Pictures

A dying artist creates a series of ten paintings "The Death Pictures" which contain a mysterious riddle, leading the way to a unique and highly valuable prize. Thousands attempt to solve it. But before the answer can be revealed, the painter is murdered.

A serial rapist is plotting six attacks. He taunts the police, leaving a calling card counting off each victim.

Dan Groves covers the stories and is drawn in by the baffling questions. Why kill the artist when he would soon die naturally? Could it be connected with the rapes? He crosses the line from journalist to investigator, forced to break the law to try to solve the crimes.

ISBN 9781906125981
Price £ 6.99

Evil Valley

A psychopath is out to teach the world a shocking lesson and the clock is ticking. Can the police crack his cruel riddles and stop him from committing the ultimate crime? Chief Inspector Adam Breen and crime-fighting TV reporter Dan Groves are reunited in the hunt for a masked man who boasts of plans to commit a crime so evil it will shock the nation.

ISBN 9781906373436
Price £ 7.99

The Judgement Book

We all have our shameful secrets and one of our greatest fears is seeing them revealed.
The Judgement Book – just a pocket diary, but festering with so much sin.
A faceless criminal, seeking not money, but revenge.
Secret after secret of the prominent and powerful is revealed… sordid sex, corruption and murder… and suicide, scandal and humiliation follow.
And then crime fighting TV reporter Dan Groves and his detective friend Adam Breen discover they too are in The Judgement Book…

ISBN 9781906373733
Price £7.99